FIREWALL

FIREWALL

An Emma Streat Mystery

EUGENIA LOVETT WEST

SparkPress, a BookSparks imprint
A Division of SparkPoint Studio, LLC

Published by SparkPress, a BookSparks imprint,
A division of SparkPoint Studio, LLC
Phoenix, Arizona, USA, 85007
www.gosparkpress.com

Published 2019
Printed in the United States of America

ISBN: 978-1-68463-010-3(pbk)
ISBN: 978-1-68463-011-0(e-bk)
Library of Congress Control Number: 2019910064

Formatting by Katherine Lloyd, The DESK

PART ONE

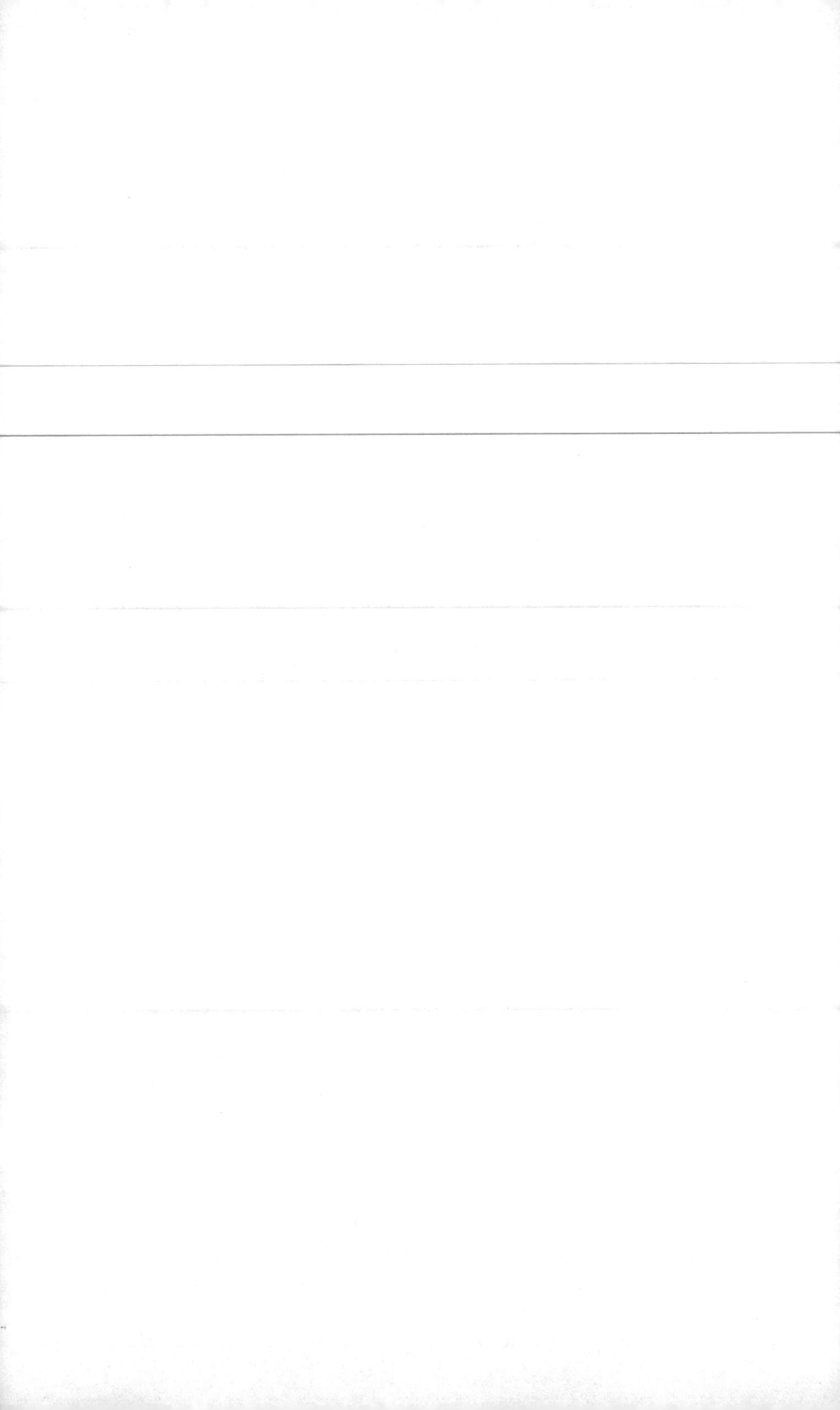

CHAPTER ONE

March 25

A spring blizzard was cascading snow over Boston's Public Garden. I poured my first cup of coffee and went to the living room window of my temporary apartment. People going to work struggled along the paths, heads bent, feet slipping. I watched, glad that in a few days I'd be on an island in the Caribbean. Lying in the sun with a man. Finding out if a dynamic former relationship could be renewed.

My phone on the counter sounded its little chime. I picked it up and saw that the call was from my godmother, Caroline Vogt. She never called before noon, but today the gravelly tuba voice reverberated in my ear.

"Emma, I need you, and I need you *now*."

This was demanding, even for Caroline. I took a deep breath. "*Why* do you need me? Are you still down in the Keys?"

"I'm back in New York and something has happened."

"What?"

"Oh God, I can't believe it, but someone's trying to blackmail me."

"*Blackmail?* You? When?"

"Just now. I was simply sitting in my bed, eating my breakfast, and the doorbell rang. Minnie went to open it. No one was there, just a note shoved under the door telling me to pay a million dollars to an account in a Miami bank. Pay it today. If I don't, my dirty little secret will go to the media tomorrow. All the media." The tuba voice wobbled.

I shifted the phone. Caroline's usual reaction to trouble was assault mode. Strike back. Never show weakness. This call for help was totally out of character—and the timing couldn't be worse.

"Look. I can see why you're upset," I said, trying to apply calm. "Blackmail is nasty, but it happens. The dirty little secret bit—everyone has secrets and that person is just trying to scare you. If you're really worried, I think you should call the police or a detective. Someone who has real expertise."

"No. Absolutely not. I won't have strangers prying into my business. You're the person we all trust in a crisis. You found Lewis's killer. You exposed those virus terrorists and saved your niece Vanessa. You have credentials. You have to find this bastard before he comes back and wants more."

"Wait. Let me think." I pushed back my hair. No way did I want to be the family detective, involved in another crisis, but Caroline was now in her eighties, a mega heiress from Chicago, a fixture in New York society. Divorced four times, no children. I was the closest thing she had to family and she was frightened. I must go, but with any luck I could still get to that island. Spend three days sorting her out, then fly there from New York.

"Emma?"

"I'm here. Listen. It's snowing hard in Boston, a freak storm, but I'll try for a flight today. Failing that, I'll take the train. I'll let you know. Relax, no need to be paranoid. Love you," I said and clicked off.

A siren went shrieking down Arlington Street, the sound that signaled trouble. I sat down on the stool at the counter and reminded myself that I owed Caroline. She had been my unfailing support from the day I was born. She had taken the place of my dead mother. Fourteen months ago she had given me a stern lecture:

"You're still young. You survived losing your rising opera career. You've done a superb job bringing up those two hunks of boys, but now they're off to college. Cut the cord and let them go. You've got the money and the energy to do something important. Different."

Good advice, but three days later, my husband was murdered and my world had gone up in flames along with my beautiful old house on the Connecticut River. I still had Jake and Steve, but creating a new life wasn't easy. It was time, past time, to move forward.

I took a deep breath and picked up a pad of paper. First, call the airlines, then cancel this morning's appointment for a haircut. Start packing.

By now experience should have taught me that one small incident can spiral into a tsunami of trouble. But no siren sounded, warning me that by helping Caroline I would be targeted by a network of cybercriminals. No way of knowing that her call would take me to many countries, lead to heartbreak, and nearly cost me my life.

CHAPTER TWO

Planes from Logan airport were flying, but a lot of white-knuckle types had canceled. Once we were above the clouds, the flight was smooth, and by seven o'clock my taxi was heading into the city.

Caroline's Fifth Avenue apartment occupied the entire floor of an exclusive old building. A bastion of wealth and prestige. The view of Central Park was extensive and sweeping. Caroline once told me that she had bought the apartment from the estate of her third husband's mother, a notable grande dame.

"Everyone thought I was crazy, the jumped-up heiress from Chicago just getting her kicks, but the high ceilings give me room for my grandfather's old masters. Turns out most of them are fakes painted by an apprentice. That's the grandfather who invented hairpins. Knew nothing about art."

I seldom visited, but the uniformed doorman greeted me with a smile. "Good to see you again, Mrs. Streat. I'll have your bags sent right up."

Caroline's elderly Irish maids had been with her for years. As I came out of the elevator, white-haired Minnie, wearing her black dress and starched white apron, met me at the door.

"Ah, Mrs. Streat, 'tis a pleasure to see you. I hope you've been keeping well."

"Thanks, Minnie. I have."

"At last. You're late." Caroline came sweeping down the hall. She was wearing a silk caftan and her signature armful of charm bracelets. The bleached blonde hair was too long for her aging face. Heavy makeup acted as camouflage for irreversibly sun-damaged skin. She gave me a double air kiss. "Do you want a drink or will wine with dinner do you? Don't bother to change, we'll go right in. Minnie, don't just stand there. Take Mrs. Streat's bag to the peach room. That's where she always stays."

I winced. Caroline could be cutting with friends, she was a master at puncturing pretensions, but she was never sharp with people who worked for her.

"Thanks, but don't unpack for me, Minnie," I said, not wanting her to see that the duffel was filled with cotton shirts, sandals, and a bikini.

Like most of the rooms, the dining room could have graced a stately English home. Minnie's cousin Kathleen served us with plates of steaming tomato bisque. Another relative, known as Cookie, had come from the bogs of Ireland and been taught to make pleasurable—if not memorable—meals.

Caroline picked up her spoon, tasted, and put the spoon down. "So, tell me your news. How are the boys?"

I hesitated. Childless Caroline could never understand why I had spent so many years as a hands-on mother, driving in carpools and watching soccer games.

"They're fine," I said. "In case you've forgotten, Steve is in his first year at Harvard. Jake is a sophomore at Brown."

"Drugs? Women?"

"They'd never tell. I try to keep in touch, but not too much."

"High time. When are you going to get out of that apartment and find a new house?"

"Didn't I tell you? My brother Ned is going to sell me land in Manchester, that's less than an hour from Boston. My architect wants traditional shingled seaside, but I'm after an Asian look, serene, with lots of glass."

"What's he like, this architect?"

"Intelligent. Creative."

"Good in bed?"

"He may be interested, but I'm not." According to Caroline, sex was rejuvenating, like going to a spa. Lewis had been dead for less than two years, but already she was fixated on finding me a man.

"Why wait? It's against your nature to be celibate." She gave me an assessing look. "Not bad. Tomorrow I'll treat you to a facial and massage. What about a Botox?"

"No Botox. I don't mind a few lines." I pushed back my hair, a thick auburn mane, cut a little above my shoulders. My eyes were still a bright blue, blue as a Kerry lake, my Irish nurse used to say. Not a classic beauty, but I had what my old press clippings called *brio* that could mesmerize up to the third balcony. My opera career had ended when I lost my voice, but men still paid attention when I came into a room.

"Are you sure?"

"I'm sure," I said and concentrated on finishing my soup.

Kathleen removed the plates and brought chicken croquettes, followed by a strawberry mousse. Caroline picked at her food and nattered in a tense way about problems with her Spanish palazzo in the Florida Keys. True, we couldn't discuss blackmail in front of Kathleen, but as soon as we left the table, I would have to speak out and not waste time.

As we left the dining room, Caroline turned. "Darling girl, you must be exhausted after all that rushing to get here. I think an early night is in order—"

"No way." I took her arm. "This morning you called and ordered me to drop whatever I was doing and get down here today. It wasn't in the least convenient, but I came. Now you're avoiding the subject. Why? Have you changed your mind about needing my help?"

"Tomorrow—"

"No, now. I want to see that note and I want to see it *now*."

CHAPTER THREE

The library was the vast apartment's most comfortable room. The chairs were large and soft. One wall held bookshelves to the ceiling. Other walls were covered with red damask. There was a fully stocked bar in one corner.

A little fire was burning behind the polished brass fender. Caroline and I faced each other on either side. "All right," I said. "Let's get down to business. That note. Where is it?"

"In my address book. Top drawer of my bedside table."

"I'll get it."

The blue leather address book was embossed with gold initials. I pulled out a piece of paper and hurried back. Opened the paper and scanned it quickly. It was handwritten in block letters on plain white paper.

> *Wire one million dollars to account #396276 Bank of the Constitution Miami. If deposit not confirmed by end of this working day, full disclosure of your dirty little secret will be sent to all media.*

I read it twice. "Ugly, but not very convincing. After all, everyone has secrets."

"It says full disclosure to all media."

"But no specifics. Maybe whoever sent it was hoping a threat would open the money spigot. Of course you didn't pay."

The bracelets rattled. She looked away.

"What? You paid? Once you give in to blackmailers, they're always back for more." I put the note down. "It's not like you to give in without a fight. How did you do it?"

"I called my money manager in New York. I told him to send it straight off."

"Didn't he ask questions?"

"I told him to follow my orders. He did."

"Well, that's that, then. End of story."

"But it's not. That person was *here*. He came to my door. I know who's behind this. He's going to want more."

I stared. "You knew all along who was doing this? Why on earth didn't you tell me?"

"There were reasons. I can see what you're thinking, but . . ." She shook her head.

"But *what*?"

"Oh God, Emma, I was afraid if you knew the truth about me, you'd end up sitting in judgment. Despising me. I couldn't bear for that to happen." She clutched my hand. A diamond ring cut into my finger.

"If that's all . . ." I reached out with my other hand and touched her shoulder. "Nothing, absolutely nothing can change the way I feel about you. The way I've felt ever since I was a little girl."

"It might." She was close to tears. I had never seen Caroline cry. My throat tightened.

"Try me. At least try me."

A long silence. She dropped my hand. "All right. I will. Get me a vodka and tonic. Make it strong. Get one for yourself. It's a long story."

I went to the bar, poured two drinks, and handed one to her. She took a large gulp. "Sit down," she said. "Sit down and don't interrupt."

"I won't."

"Is that a promise?"

"I promise."

She took another swallow. I waited while she struggled to regain control. Finally, she raised her head.

"It's the dark ages to you, but your mother and I had just graduated from Wellesley, an odd couple to be roommates and best friends, the proper Bostonian and the rich girl from Chicago. She wanted a nice teaching job, but I was aiming higher. There were parties up and down the East Coast that summer. The biggest was the annual charity ball in Newport. A very well-known VIP was there. A household name. I was a wild girl, at least by the standards of those days. He was addicted to women. We slept together twice in one night. I was extremely proud of myself for getting his attention. I went off to New York to work for a fashion magazine and in October I realized I was pregnant."

She paused and put down the glass. "Remember, this was before the pill. Abortions were totally illegal. At first, I couldn't believe it. It couldn't be happening. Not to me. I was furious, he was to blame, but I wasn't in any position to make accusations. I got the name of a backstreet doctor, a horrible place, but even that doctor wouldn't do it. Too far along."

"Oh Caroline—"

"No interruptions." Her voice was detached, as if this was someone else's story. "I finally had to tell my editor, a marvelous woman. She could have fired me. Instead, she sent me to Switzerland on an extended assignment. I had the baby in a Lausanne clinic. The baby, a boy, was given up for adoption over there. I never saw him or gave the father's name. I came home with a portfolio, pictures of beautiful people skiing in Gstaad and Davos. Went on with my job, became a fixture at El Morocco, the Stork Club. Tried to pretend it never happened. Hoped it would never be picked up by the press."

I leaned forward and took her hand. "Terrible for you, terrible. There's one thing, though."

"What?"

"After all this time—it's over fifty years—where's the threat from a blackmailer? The media won't pay attention, no matter who the father was."

"Wrong. I promise you, the tabloids would salivate. Headlines, that this man—he's dead—once had an illegitimate son and that son is out there walking around somewhere. There might even be a search. A lot of people could be affected. It must never, never come out, no matter how much I have to pay."

"All right. Back to basics. How many people knew about this baby?"

"Three people. The editor. Your mother. I had to tell someone, and I could trust her."

"My mother's in the grave. What about the editor?"

"Dead. Which leaves my first husband. Pierre Hallam. It's the kind of thing he would do—that is, send someone to blackmail me."

"When did you last see Pierre Hallam?"

"Not for years. I last heard he was in France, but he's a bastard. Always was. I know what's going on. He's run out of money and he's figured out a way to get it. This is just the beginning."

I stared at the fire, trying to work out the facts. "Pierre Hallam," I said. "Tell me about him. When did you meet?"

"A year after I came back to New York. I was drinking, using drugs, trying to block out the past. Along comes this charmer and my God, he was a charmer. Half French. Tall and dark, great in bed. Divorced with a son and an ex-wife. He was paying big alimony and child support, so not much money, but he had a job in a big bank. Anyhow, he set his sights on me and I was vulnerable."

"Why did you tell him about the baby?"

"I told you. I was drinking, using. That's when you do stupid things. He said he loved me, that the baby didn't make any difference, he wanted to marry me. So we did marry. Big wedding, ten bridesmaids, your mother was maid of honor. Classic case of out of the frying pan into the fire."

"How long did it last?"

"Three years. We were quite the dashing young couple around town. Very dashing, until I discovered he was forging checks. He had a mistress in Palm Beach, ex–chorus girl, ex-mistress of a Broadway entrepreneur. Last straw, he took my mother's diamond bracelet and other jewelry out of the safe and sold it all. When I confronted him, he was violent."

"He hit you?"

"I could have had him put in jail, but I was afraid he would get lawyers and use the baby story against me. In those days the scandal would have been even worse."

"What did you do?"

"I pulled strings at his bank. He lost his job. No more alimony or child support for his son. In the end, he had to leave the country and go to France where his mother lived. As far as I know, he's been there ever since. Never a word until now, but nothing's too low for Pierre. He used to be mixed up with crooks and swindlers like himself. Now he needs money, and he'll do anything to get it. Anything." She closed her eyes.

I sat still, sorting out this sad tale. A rotten husband. A furious Caroline who had exacted a full pound of flesh—and then some. Not surprising that Pierre Hallam might take belated revenge, especially if he had run out of funds. And—it wasn't hard to imagine the young Caroline. Headstrong, too much money, a bad judge of men. Four marriages—and she never had another child.

"Thank you for telling me the story," I said. "I'm beginning to understand why you're so upset. The thing is, what happens now? Is the man still in France? Is he working with someone else? To find out, you're going to need to bring in experts, but even if he's responsible, he just got a big chunk of change. Why stick his neck out and take another risk?"

“Because he’s twisted and so were his friends. He may have paid one of them to deliver that note. He’s going to use that baby against me. I know it.” Her hands were shaking. For the first time she was showing her age.

I put my arm around her thin shoulders. “You’re getting your panties in a bunch. There’s nothing to be done tonight, but I can’t believe, I really can’t believe that you thought I’d be shocked or sit in judgment. You’ve always been there for me. Now I’m here for you. Relax. Tomorrow we’ll make a plan.”

CHAPTER FOUR

March 26

I slept fitfully and woke with the feeling of weights pressing down on my head. The clock was running. If I had any hope of leaving the day after tomorrow, I'd have to find a way to reassure Caroline. I'd see her, then a run in the park might trigger inspiration.

Minnie was coming out of her room. "Morning, Minnie," I said. "Is Mrs. Vogt awake?"

"Not yet, so I'll not be taking her tray. About yer breakfast. I'll bring it to the library. Will ye have eggs and bacon with yer coffee and toast?"

"Just eggs. Scrambled. Minnie, you're a treasure."

Outside, the weather was blustery, with the look of possible snow. The trees in Central Park stood straight, their bare branches extended as if reaching for spring.

I was finishing my coffee when Minnie spoke to someone in the hall. "Good morning, Mrs. Whitten. Nasty weather."

I put down the porcelain cup. Delsey Whitten was Caroline's trusted personal assistant—it seemed that the ultrarich needed at least one Delsey in their lives.

On my rare trips to New York, I had seen very little of Delsey. She was always in the background, ensconced in her cubbyhole of an office. As I went into the hall, she was hanging up her coat, a calm, stolid woman whose plain black dresses reached her ankles.

Her gray hair was pulled severely into a ponytail. Her makeup was heavy and white.

Caroline had given me her history. "First she was a temp, now she's a fixture. Pays bills, runs my houses, makes reservations, handles the paperwork for my foundations. She wanted to be a dancer, hard to imagine, then she got pregnant. The daughter is grown and has a good job, but Delsey looks after a mother with Alzheimer's and the poor old trout gets spacier every day. Always trying to escape and swim across the Hudson River."

"Good morning, Delsey," I said. Enlisting Delsey's help might be key to my getting away.

"Mrs. Streat. I didn't know you were coming."

"Neither did I, but yesterday Mrs. Vogt sent for me. I'd better tell you that someone's trying to blackmail her. She's upset, and she's convinced that something else is going to happen." I stopped. The rest of the story had better come from Caroline.

"Blackmail? There's a lot of that these days. Has she called the police?"

"She doesn't want police. She says she doesn't want anyone meddling in her business. She called me, but I have to leave the day after tomorrow. I think she should get in professionals. Right now she's still asleep, so I'm off for a run in the park."

The park was nearly empty; there were only a few people walking dogs. I ran past the zoo—I never liked seeing caged animals—and struck out on a long straight path. As I ran, I forced myself to think ahead. If Caroline was in no condition to be left alone, I would have to let Rodale know.

I ran faster, remembering my first impression of Lord Andrew Rodale. Dark hair, tall, gray eyes. A strong face with two vertical lines. Impressive looks that masked a brilliant mind. Rodale was a British peer who sat in the House of Lords. Rich, age fifty-two, divorced with two grown daughters. He juggled addictive skills in bed with the ability to lead a double life as an undercover crisis solver for the Secret Intelligence Service. A number of high-flying English women would kill to be the next Lady Rodale.

We first slept together in Venice, much-needed therapy after I was nearly burned alive by my husband's killer. Then again at his Palladian house in England. It seemed as if we might have a future together until he rushed off to London as if I didn't exist. I had ended the affair with a memorable burst of anger—and was taken aback when he called three weeks ago inviting me to an island.

Running faster, I passed a dog handler with six assorted dogs on leashes. As Caroline said, I wasn't cut out for celibacy, but I needed a man who would always be there for me and get on well with my boys. After a serious mental struggle, I decided to see Rodale again with eyes wide open. Indulge the senses in the hands of a master, then decide whether or not we had a future together.

Back in the apartment, I took a hot shower, changed clothes, and went to see Caroline.

She was lying between Porthault sheets, finishing her breakfast. The room was filled with pictures, needlepoint pillows, and English chintzes—the signature style of Sister Parrish, her long-gone friend and decorator.

I leaned over and gave her a quick kiss. "How did you sleep?"

"Well enough." She motioned me to sit down. "Darling girl, I apologize for putting you through the wringer, but never in this world did I expect to hear from Pierre Hallam. It was a shock, but I've made some decisions. That man will never threaten me again."

"Never?" I sat down on the edge of the bed.

"I've summoned my money manager. He'll be here at five o'clock to get instructions. I want you to meet him. For several reasons." She smiled. I knew that little smile. She was hatching a plot and it involved me.

"What reasons?"

"They can wait." She pushed back her tray and looked me up and down. "Your clothes. They should go to a church rummage sale."

"They're not *that* bad. Face it, I'm no fashionista and I never will be."

"Don't argue. Steps must be taken. I'll be busy all morning with Delsey, but you know my driver Clancy, Kathleen's uncle. He'll wheel you around the shops and you can use my credit card. Why are you looking shell-shocked?"

"I—that is, no reason. No reason at all," I said and stood up. No wobbly voice, no shaky hands. Caroline was back in assault mode. Shopping was a small price to pay for this unexpected release—and I could use a new bikini.

On my way out, I stopped at Delsey's cubbyhole. She was sitting at her computer. "Sorry to interrupt," I said. "I've just been in to see Mrs. Vogt and she seems to be herself again, barking out orders. I'm to go shopping and then meet the man who manages her money. Who is he?"

"His name is Breck Langer, of Nickerson and Haversat, an old firm. Very conservative. They take care of clients like Mrs. Vogt and her friends."

"How long has she been with him?"

"Over a year, ever since her former manager retired. Most of the partners are getting on, but Mr. Langer is quite young. Sometimes she asks him to take her to functions."

"Well, I hope he's good with her money."

"She seems to think so." Delsey's lips tightened. Was this man more than just an escort? I wouldn't ask any more questions. Best to go with the flow and be on that plane tomorrow.

CHAPTER FIVE

I was never much of a shopper, but I braved the crowd at Bloomingdale's, bought an expensive suede jacket, then had Clancy take me to the Frick Museum for a soothing look at my favorite Fragonard paintings.

At three o'clock, Caroline showed every sign of being back to her usual routine. I pulled out my phone and punched in Rodale's London number. Five beeps, then a request to leave a brief message.

"It's Emma," I said. "Slight change of plans. Please call me back."

A moment later the phone rang. "Sorry about that," he said. "My calls are being screened. No problem, I hope."

"I had to go to New York and help my godmother. That's done, but the flight change means I'll be at least two hours later getting to Tortola."

"Not a problem. Nothing will bother me once I'm out of London and away from work."

"Away from work? I never thought I'd hear you say that. What's going on?"

"How much do you know about cybercrime?"

"Just the usual. Hackers and bad guys taking down grids. I'm not a techie, never will be."

"Then get your head out of the sand. Cybercrime is our greatest threat and we're dealing with an epidemic of APTs—Advanced Persistent Threats. These people have sophisticated networks. It's not like the old days of collecting evidence, then putting the villain in handcuffs. They've made a lethal weapon out of cyberspace and when the attack comes—enough of that. I'll meet you at the airport, then a boat will take us to the island."

"Is it far? Have you ever been there before?"

"Once. I know the owners. It used to be a sugar plantation, but now the house is just for themselves and friends. No one else will be there. Snorkeling and swimming in a private cove, and the generator goes off at ten every night. Simple living."

"How simple? Will I have to cook?"

"There's a staff but they don't live in." A pause. "I've missed you, Emma. I want to be with you again. For God's sake don't get caught in a storm and have to cancel. Safe trip."

I sat there, holding the phone. I'd never heard him sound so stressed, but a week in the sun should relax that overworked mind.

At half past five, wearing the new suede jacket and wondering why she insisted on having me here, I was sitting in the library with Caroline.

A fire burned brightly. I watched as Kathleen brought in the heavy silver tea service. Small plates and lacy napkins. A muffin stand with sponge cake, macaroons, and cucumber sandwiches. The well-oiled wheels were running smoothly; Caroline's mother-in-law would have approved.

Caroline had enthroned herself in a high-backed chair behind the tray. She was wearing a long, black velvet dress and black shoes with silver buckles, but the grande dame effect was spoiled by the bleached blonde hair and clanking charm bracelets.

"Before he comes, you'd better fill me in," I said. "What age?"

"Middle. I'll be interested to see what you think of him."

"I have a feeling you're trying to fix me up. Or maybe warning me to keep off your property."

"Don't be vulgar, he only handles my money—" She stopped as Minnie appeared at the door.

"Mr. Langer, madam."

As he came in, Caroline gave him an imperial nod. "You're late. What kept you?"

"There's a VIP in town. Traffic jams from here to the airport."

"Well, no matter. This is my goddaughter, Emma Streat."

We nodded and shook hands. As he took a seat opposite Caroline, I made a quick assessment. Good build, hair graying slightly at the sides. Well-tailored dark suit, discreet tie, but there was something a little too correct about him. I'd seen it before. A carefulness in men and women who had worked their way up the ladder and now had to compete with peers who were born to the best boarding schools, the best clubs.

"Emma, you like your tea strong with lemon. Mr. Langer?"

"The same, please."

She poured and handed him the cup. "Help yourself to cake and sandwiches. I asked you to come to talk about the million you sent to that bank."

"You refused to give me a reason."

"Well, I'm telling you now. It was blackmail. A note was left at the door yesterday morning. Threatening me if I didn't pay."

Breck Langer put his cup down on the nearest table. "Blackmail. You shouldn't have paid. Did you notify the police?"

"No, and there were reasons. I happen to know who's responsible."

"You know?"

"It's my first husband, Pierre Hallam. I divorced him when I found out he was stealing from me. He went to live in France many years ago. Since then, we've never been in touch, but now the crook has run out of money and he thinks he can get it out of me. I'm telling you this so you can watch for anything out of the ordinary."

"We'll take every precaution."

"See that you do." She took a sip of tea, bracelets jangling, and gave him a sharp look. "There's something else you should know."

"Yes?"

"I'm going to call in the private security agency I've used before. Expensive, but worth it. They'll be able to trace that money and expose him, the first step in stopping him from getting more. They'll want to talk to you, and I want you to work with them."

I glanced at Langer. Did he mind being treated like a lackey? Or did he just figure that was the price one paid when dealing with rich clients?

He picked up his cup and put it down again. "Mrs. Vogt, you're right to be concerned. This blackmail must stop, but using our firm would be the logical first step. I need to trace that money, and tracing money requires a particular kind of expertise. Our people are specialists in this field. They've had extremely good results."

"That may be, but this agency has multiple resources and they can act quickly. I've made up my mind. Please be ready to give this agency any help they may need."

"Of course, if that's what you prefer."

"It is." She looked at her watch, gave the skirt of the velvet tea gown a tweak, and rose to her feet. "That's settled, then. I must leave you, but Emma will give you more tea. By the way, she has my power of attorney. She can act for me, so I want her to know the people who handle my affairs."

Neither of us spoke.

"Thank you for coming, Mr. Langer," she said, and swept out of the room.

I watched her go, wanting to follow and give her a good shake. The nerve, to ask a busy man to come here, snap out orders, and leave. If this was her way of pushing us together, she should have known that it wouldn't work.

Breck Langer was on his feet. I felt sorry for him and forced a smile. "All I can say is, this blackmail thing has upset her. Quite a lot. I think we both could use more tea."

He straightened his tie and sat down. "Well, blackmail is no joke. I'm surprised she didn't call the police."

"She has her own way of dealing with trouble," I said. "Give me your cup. Lemon and no sugar?"

"That's right."

I poured, thinking fast. Now that Caroline had introduced me to him as the person who could act for her, I might as well push the charm button and find out more about him.

"Caroline and I have always been close," I began. "She's a wonderful godmother, but we never talk business. Have you been with her long?"

"One year. When Mrs. Vogt's manager retired, they asked me to take over her accounts, see if they could be made more profitable."

"I shouldn't ask, but are they?"

He smiled. "As a matter of fact, they are. It helps that we both like opera and support the Met."

"Opera," I said, grasping at the conversational straw. "You wouldn't know, but I used to be a singer. Mostly in Europe until l lost my voice."

"You lost your voice? That must have been a blow."

"It was, but I survived. Got married and had two boys. We lived in Connecticut until my husband died." I paused. "How about you? Are you in the city or do you commute?"

"We lived in New Canaan, but after my wife and I divorced, I moved to the city. My twin boys spend weekends with me."

"Twins. How old?"

"Seventeen. We're starting to look at colleges for one of them. It's a complicated business."

"I know. I can't tell you how relieved I felt when mine finally got accepted."

"Where?"

"One at Brown, one at Harvard."

"I'm impressed. You must have done something right. I do my best to listen and not push."

"Do they have a sport? It helps if a coach wants to recruit them."

"One is pretty good at squash. The other has medical problems. Good kids, both of them." An affectionate voice.

"I'm sure they are." My efforts to make up for Caroline's appalling rudeness were paying off.

As he reached for a sandwich, he glanced at my legs. "Where do you live now, Mrs. Streat?"

"Emma, please. In Boston, at the moment."

"Will you be staying in New York long?"

"Not this time. More tea?"

"Thanks, but I have a meeting downtown and taxis are scarce this time of night."

"Especially when it's raining. I'll walk you to the door."

As we went down the hall, I made another assessment. From the age of fifteen I had always divided men into two groups: those I could sleep with, and those who would never in a million years lay a finger on me. On a scale of one to ten, Breck Langer rated somewhere in the middle. Attractive in a conventional way. He had showed empathy toward his boys and was interested in opera. Even more to his credit, he had handled a demanding client with restraint and patience she didn't deserve.

As we got to the elevator, he turned. "Look. She really ought to let our people trace the money. They're experts, they have the tools. Detective agencies can run up a big bill with no results. Put in a word, if you have a chance. It might save a lot of disappointment."

"I can try."

"Good." He took my hand, held it for a second, and let it go. "Will you let me know when you're here again? You seem to have done well with your boys. I could use advice about mine."

"Not sure when I'll be back, but I'll be in touch." It was the least I could do. The elevator arrived. Seconds later he was gone.

I took a deep breath and went to find Caroline. She was in her room, changing into one of her exotic kimonos.

"You had a bloody nerve," I began. "Summoning him up here, acting like royalty, then leaving me to hold the can. As for that crap about my needing to meet your people—what was that about?"

"Never mind. What did you think of him?"

"Nice enough, but don't get your hopes up. By the way, why aren't you using the specialists at his firm?"

"Because this way I keep control. I know the detective agency, they're good, and it's easier to give them orders. I want them to make mincemeat out of Pierre Hallam. Leave him in tatters."

I nodded, relieved that the job of punishing Pierre Hallam was being delegated to an agency, not to me.

"Madam." Minnie was at the door. "Will ye be wanting dinner in the dining room?"

"No, we'll have trays in the library."

Outside, gusts of heavy rain sounded behind closed curtains. As we ate, we watched the evening news, the usual potpourri of disasters. Rioting in Chicago. Congress in gridlock. Candidates for the next presidential election hurling insults at each other.

One was a newcomer named Calvin Fullerton with the clean-cut looks of a Charles Lindbergh. He talked confidently about his middle-class background in Ohio, his service in the Marines, his schoolteacher wife, and his three promising children.

But as he laid out his goals, we learned that his independent party was called America Wins. As its head, he would bring the country back to its former glory. Keep out immigrants. Repeal laws allowing abortion and gay marriage. Stop funding foreign countries. Instill a new work ethic with no handouts to the ungrateful poor.

"I don't believe this," I said as he finished. "He sounds more extreme than the extreme."

"He'll go far. This country is going down the drain. There'll be a crash. That's one reason I wanted you to meet Langer. It's time I start dispersing my money."

"Not a bad idea."

"No, and I'm giving most of it to you."

I took a deep breath. So this was why I was left alone with Langer. With Caroline, it was important to pick the right battles, and this was one I had to win.

"Don't even think about it," I said. "I don't need your money. I don't want it."

"Nonsense. Why not?"

"Because that kind of money would change my life and that of my boys—and not in a good way. I know too many men whose lives have been ruined by never having to work."

"Well, we'll talk about it later."

"Talk all you want, but I won't change my mind." Knowing Caroline, this was a strategic retreat, but the threat was there, and I must stand firm.

She shook her head. "Remove that mulish look from your face. Tomorrow I'm taking you to lunch and then to my hairdresser. He has a great way with thick hair like yours."

I hesitated. This might be the right moment to tell her I was seeing Rodale again. Months ago, when she learned I had given him the shove, she was scathing. "Foolish girl. What were you thinking? I was looking forward to calling you Lady Rodale and staying at your stately home."

Kathleen removed the dinner plates and gave us little pots of chocolate soufflé. I picked up the spoon. Best not to raise Caroline's hopes, not when a future with Rodale was so uncertain. Far safer to concoct a sudden emergency. Something that required me to hurry back to Boston, but tomorrow I'd go to this hairdresser and be a model of compliance.

"Sounds like a plan. Let the hairdresser loose on me. Whatever makes you happy," I said, and dug into the soufflé.

CHAPTER SIX

March 27

I went to bed, slept hard, and woke to the sound of a muffled crash. It seemed to come from Caroline's room. I sat up and reached to turn on my bedside lamp. No light came on. There was no faint glow from the electric clock. A massive power failure. The room was totally dark—and there was no way to know if it was midnight or early dawn. That crash. Had Caroline tried to get up, fallen, and broken one of those fragile bones?

Blackness covered me like a blanket as I groped my way to the door. I opened it and started down the hall, keeping my feet on the oriental runner, wincing as my knee hit a corner of the Boulle chest.

A slight sound came from the bedroom. "If you're awake, I'm coming," I called. "Don't move until I find a flashlight."

Footsteps thudded from Caroline's room. A blow on my shoulder knocked me to the floor and a blinding light from a torch shone in my face. A man—a tall dark shape—stood over me. I raised my arm to ward off another blow, but it never came. He disappeared down the hall.

I lay there dazed, my cheek pressed against the carpet runner. A man in the apartment—in Caroline's room. What had he done to her?

After a moment, I got to my knees and crawled forward.

Struck my head on a door frame. Scrabbled to the bed. Ran my hands under the coverlet until I felt her arms.

"It's me, it's Emma. Did he hurt you?"

She didn't move. I pulled myself higher and laid my head on her chest. Her breathing was so slight I could barely feel her ribs move. She could be bleeding to death in the dark.

"Caroline," I shouted in her ear. "*Caroline.*"

No answer. The blood was rushing from my head. I felt faint, but I must get help. Call 911 on the white landline telephone on the bedside table—no use. I couldn't see the numbers.

I turned and began to crawl back toward the hall. "Minnie," I shrieked at the top of my damaged voice. "Minnie, come quick. Bring a light." Shrieked again, then flattened myself against the wall. The man could still be here.

"Minnie, Minnie, *Minnie.*" At last a wavering beam shone at the end of the hall.

"Mrs. Streat, where are ye?"

"Here. On the floor. A man got into the apartment. He was in Mrs. Vogt's room. He may have hurt her." The constriction in my throat was making it hard to breathe.

"Holy Mother of Jaysus." She hurried down the hall and handed me the light. We ran into the room. Being able to see helped to neutralize the panic. I shone the flashlight on Caroline's face, then pulled down the sheet. She was unconscious, but there was no pool of blood.

Minnie stood behind me, wringing her hands. "Sweet Jaysus, has she passed?"

"No." I reached for the telephone, then stopped, my hand in midair. Calling 911 meant going by ambulance to a crowded emergency room. Waiting for hours with drug addicts and victims of knifings and gunshots.

"Listen, Minnie, does she have a doctor? Someone who would come here?"

"There's Dr. Jermyn two floors down. He came when Cookie sliced her hand with the vegetable knife. Mrs. Vogt always said if she had a heart attack in the night, we were to call Dr. Jermyn."

"Where's his number?"

"In her book."

I picked up the blue leather book. "Jermyn, Jermyn—I'll call him first, then security. There must be security in the building. A night watchman."

"Ah, there's only the doorman at night and the superintendent. He lives in the basement."

The clock by the bed showed a quarter past three. Dr. Jermyn's telephone rang and rang. Finally, a woman answered.

"Yes?"

"I'm sorry, I'm sorry to wake you, but it's an emergency in Caroline Vogt's apartment. A man broke in and attacked her. Attacked her in her *bed*. She's unconscious, she's hurt, I don't know how badly. I know it's a terrible imposition, but could Dr. Jermyn come?"

"Mrs. Vogt—attacked in her apartment? I'll wake the doctor. He'll be up shortly."

"Thank you." I handed the phone to Minnie. "Now the superintendent. He knows you."

As Minnie talked, I went to a window and pulled the curtains open. The streetlights were working, providing some light. No massive blackout. Somehow the man had managed to turn out the lights in the apartment. It must have been the sound of the bedside lamp crashing to the floor that woke me. Had Caroline heard him and thrashed out?

She moaned, a tiny sound. I went over and lay down beside her. "You're safe," I said in her ear. "The doctor's coming. It's all right." A few feet away, Minnie was praying loudly, calling on the Holy Mother and all the saints.

Suddenly the bedside clock began to glow. The chandelier in

the hall lit up. I got off the bed and looked at Minnie. She was wearing a plaid flannel bathrobe, her white hair in a braid. "You'd better go and let the doctor in," I said.

"I will, so." But as she reached the door, she turned. "The super is here," she said in a low voice. "I hear him shouting. He's not a nice fella. Will ye speak to him?"

"I most certainly will." Panic was giving way to anger. I reached for Caroline's kimono, pulled it around me, and followed her down the hall. Two men were standing outside the library. The young one had on a doorman's gray uniform. He was holding his head in his hands. The other was middle-aged, unshaven, and he was wearing a long brown overcoat. He turned and pointed a finger at me.

"Who are you? What's going on up here?" An accusing voice.

Adrenaline surged. I walked forward. "I'm Mrs. Vogt's goddaughter. A man just broke into this apartment and hurt Mrs. Vogt. Dr. Jermyn is on his way. What I want to know is, how could this have happened? Don't you have any kind of security?"

He shuffled his feet. "Tell her, Charlie."

The chubby doorman raised his head. "I was sitting in the lobby, miss. This man, he comes in like he's a doctor, carrying a bag. He says he's been called to see Mrs. Vogt. I start to take him to the elevator. He turns and gives me a whack with the bag. Jeez, before I know it, I'm in the closet where we keep the shovels for when it snows."

I looked at the super. "That man knew exactly where to go. How did he get into this apartment? What happened to the lights?"

"Nothing to do with me, miss." He was almost stuttering with the attempt to remove himself from blame. "I keep telling management we need another man at night besides Charlie, but they won't listen—here's Dr. Jermyn now. Evening, Doctor," he said as a big man with a bag appeared.

"Evening, Ernie." He looked at me.

"I'm Emma Streat, the one who called. I'll take you to her."

As we went into the room, Caroline's eyes opened. She seemed to be trying to orient herself.

He sat down on the edge of the bed. "Dr. Jermyn from the third floor. You know my wife. If you don't mind, I'll just have a look at you."

I stood still and watched. Dr. Jermyn seemed to be in his late sixties or early seventies. White hair, early morning stubble on his chin. He took her wrist and held it for a moment. Reached into his bag, pulled out a stethoscope, and listened to her chest. Slowly, I let out my breath. Dr. Jermyn was successful enough to live in this building, but he had the bedside manner of a country doctor. The calm authority that produces confidence.

Caroline lay quietly, eyes closed. Finally, he nodded, then patted her hand. "You'll do." He looked at me. "Where can we talk?"

"In the library."

The super was waiting in the hall. "How is she, Doctor?" A voice between a whine and aggression.

"In a moment, Ernie."

I led the doctor to the library and shut the door. Dr. Jermyn motioned me to a chair. "Sit down, young lady. This has been distressing for you. Are you a relative?"

"A goddaughter, but we're close."

He sat down at the desk and put his bag on the floor. "When my wife said Mrs. Vogt had been attacked in her room, I didn't think it was possible. What happened?"

I took a deep breath and tried to concentrate. "I woke up when a lamp crashed and there weren't any lights. I thought it was a blackout all over the city. I was afraid Caroline had fallen, so I started down the hall. I called out and said I was coming. That man must have heard me. He ran out and knocked me down. I didn't see his face. I thought of calling 911, but then Minnie told me about you. I can't thank you enough for coming."

"Glad to, but this is the situation. Mrs. Vogt has marks on her throat. I think the shock may have triggered a vagal nerve reaction. The heart may slow down, causing a temporary blackout. She's conscious now, but there's a cardiac arrhythmia, an uneven heartbeat. Do you know of any previous heart trouble?"

"No. I don't. Is it serious?"

"Not necessarily, but I'm not a cardiologist. Mrs. Vogt is not my patient and I don't know her medical history. There's no need for alarm, but I think she should go to a hospital and be evaluated."

"A hospital? Now?"

"Here's what will happen. I'm on the staff of the East Side Medical Center. I'll contact the physician on duty in the emergency room and ask him to do tests. The results will go to a cardiologist. He will contact Mrs. Vogt's primary physician."

"But that would take all night. Maybe days."

"I'll arrange for a room. The bruises are superficial, the arrhythmia may take care of itself, but when an older person has had a severe shock, it's best to take precautions. With your permission, I'll call an ambulance." He pulled out a mobile.

I sat straight. "I want to be with her."

"Better call a taxi. I'll have a word with Ernie, then check her again."

Ernie was standing close to the door. As it opened, he moved back. Dr. Jermyn frowned.

"In case you didn't hear, Mrs. Vogt is going to a hospital. I expect her to recover, but an intruder was able to get into this building and into her apartment. The police must be notified."

Ernie shifted his feet. "Doctor, that man tricked Charlie. If the board lets me get more security, it won't happen again."

"We need to know how a man got into Mrs. Vogt's apartment. Why there were no lights. I'll make the call."

"But Doctor—"

"Bring them up and answer their questions." A firm voice. Ernie disappeared.

We went back to Caroline. She hadn't moved, but her eyes were open. Dr. Jermyn took her hand. "Mrs. Vogt, you've had a bad shock. I'm sending you to the Medical Center for a few tests. Just a precaution, nothing to worry about."

Her eyes closed. Dr. Jermyn took her pulse, nodded, and motioned me to follow him out of the room. "I won't bother her again with the stethoscope. Now for the police. I'll call the nearest precinct and report the incident. I know a lieutenant there. Is there someone besides the maid who can be here when they come?"

"I'll get hold of her secretary. You—you've been so kind. So very kind."

"You managed very well under the circumstances. I'll wait until the ambulance comes."

I ran back to my room and pulled out my phone. Delsey answered on the second ring, her voice groggy with sleep.

"It's Emma," I said. "I hate to wake you, but it's an emergency. A man—this man broke into the apartment. He went into Mrs. Vogt's room, he had his hands around her throat. Thank God Dr. Jermyn came. He says she has an arrhythmia, a heart thing. He wants her to go to East Side Medical Center for tests."

A smothered gasp. "She's going to a hospital?"

"I'll meet her there, but he's calling the police, and someone needs to be here when they come. There's only Minnie saying Hail Marys and the superintendent dancing around, making a fuss."

"That man. I'll come. I'll ask my neighbor to stay with my mother. I'll be there in less than an hour."

"You're a saint. There's something else. There were no lights in the apartment. I woke up and it was pitch black. Oh God, Delsey, if I'd slept, if he hadn't heard me coming, right now she'd be lying dead in her bed."

CHAPTER SEVEN

When I arrived at the East Side Medical Center, Caroline was being wheeled into a bay in the emergency room. Her eyes were closed. Without makeup, her face looked wrinkled and old. Without the signature bracelets, her wrist was pitifully thin, the bones as fragile as a bird's.

I turned to the nurse who was covering her with a heated blanket. In a crisis, dropping names never hurt. "Dr. Jermyn on the staff wants the ER doctor to see her right away," I said.

"He'll come when he can. Do you mind waiting outside while we hook her up to the monitors?"

I nodded and stepped out. Last year I had taken my niece Vanessa to the emergency room at Boston General. Different city, different place, but there was the same feeling of organized chaos. Lifesaving intensity.

A gurney went by, pushed by attendants, shoes thumping on the floor as they ran. A Dr. Rubin was being called on the intercom. At Boston General, I had known that Vanessa was deathly sick. Caroline's situation seemed less threatening, but she was much older.

Beside me, in the bay, a stream of technicians went back and forth. The EKG machine. The X-ray machine. A lab technician with a tray of bottles. A nurse paused to speak to me. "The waiting room is down that hall, if you want to sit down."

"Thanks, but I want to speak to the doctor when he comes."

It was now after five in the morning. A group of young men and women wearing green and blue scrubs went by. Outside other bays, people were talking in low voices. A large woman dressed in purple sweats was wiping her eyes. Strangers, all of us, doing our best to cope with fear and pain.

At last a young man in a short white coat pushed the curtain aside and went in. I followed.

"Mrs. Vogt?" he asked, leaning over the bed. "I'm Dr. Binder, come to have a look at you."

No answer. Her eyes stayed closed. He pulled up a chair and took Caroline's pulse. Looked at the swelling bruises on her throat. Glanced at the monitors. He seemed much too young to be fully qualified. A resident, on duty for endless hours? There were dark circles under his eyes.

"Mrs. Vogt?" he said in a louder voice. Again, no answer. He got up and motioned me into the hall. "Are you a relative?"

"Her goddaughter. How is she?"

"Her blood pressure is low and there's arrhythmia. That may right itself or it may become an issue. Blood was drawn. I'm waiting for a report from the lab."

"What will that show?"

"Enzymes indicate whether or not the heart has been affected. She seems unresponsive, but that may be from shock. I'd like to keep her on a monitor for the next twenty-four hours. We're short of beds, but Dr. Jermyn was able to make arrangements. She'll be moved as soon as I can do the paperwork."

"How soon will that be?"

"I can't say. It's a busy night."

I went back, sat down on the blue metal chair, and took Caroline's hand. Her eyes opened. "Emma," she croaked. "My throat—I heard something—"

"It's over. You're in a hospital. You're safe, absolutely safe. No one can hurt you here."

"Hospital. Safe." Her eyes closed.

The monitors ticked steadily; there was a surge of sound when the blood pressure monitor kicked in. I leaned back and rested my head against the wall. The bruises on my shoulder where I hit the hall floor were beginning to ache. Until now I had been in crisis mode, trying to think one step ahead. Exhaustion was setting in, but the horror kept coming back. The blackness. The blow. The tall shape towering over me. It would be almost impossible to identify his face.

Time passed. At last a nurse and two aides came in. They transferred Caroline to a gurney. She was asleep or pretending to be asleep as they left. There was nothing more I could do.

It was daylight when I arrived back at Caroline's building. Another doorman was on duty in the lobby. Delsey met me at the door.

"I was getting worried. How is she?"

"I should have called you. She's not critical, but they're keeping her to check on this arrhythmia thing."

"What a night. Chamomile tea is very soothing. I'll bring it to your room."

A few moments later, Delsey appeared with a china pot and a large cup. She was wearing the same black dress, the same heavy white makeup. I picked up the cup and tried to warm my cold hands. "Did the police come?" I asked.

"Around five. They brought a Mobile Crime Unit and looked for fingerprints. There weren't any. He must have come up in the back elevator, broke the lock to the kitchen, found the panel in the back hall, and turned off the lights and the alarm. They said he must have had inside help."

"That miserable little super didn't want to call the police."

"He wouldn't. Last year Mrs. Vogt had a fight with him about the fuses. She made him install her own panel. Later she found out he was shaking down the workmen, twisting their arms for money."

"Why is he still here?"

"He has friends on the board, at least until now."

"Some crook could have paid him well. After all, it was three in the morning—and no one was supposed to wake up. What about the doorman?"

"Charlie's not the brightest. He's not sure if he'd be able to recognize the man again. Just that he was tall, wearing a brimmed hat, carrying a doctor's bag. They—the police—want to talk to you. Find out what you saw and if you could identify him."

"Not sure. He was shining his flashlight in my eyes. I've never been so scared in my life. Being in the dark made it worse. I suppose he was after her jewelry and heard me call out. But why hurt her? That's what I don't understand."

"The police may have some answers, though they weren't very hopeful."

"We'll have to keep after them." I handed her the cup. "Delsey, you need to get back to your mother, but first would you leave a note for Minnie? Ask her not to wake me unless it's a call from the hospital."

"I'll do that. Try to sleep."

"No fear, I will. Like the dead. No, no, no, not like the dead."

CHAPTER EIGHT

March 28

The gnarled roots of a mangrove swamp were twisting themselves around my ankles, pulling me into the sinister black water. A man wearing a black mask was laughing and raising his hand to hit me. I screamed and flung out an arm to protect myself.

"Madam, madam." I opened my eyes. Minnie was standing by the bed. "I'm that sorry to wake you, but Mrs. Vogt's doctor is on the telephone. He's wanting a word."

I put a hand to my head. "What? Who?"

"Dr. Prosser. Mrs. Vogt's doctor. He wants a word."

Slowly, my brain clicked into gear. Caroline. The attack. The hospital. He was calling to say that Caroline had died. I reached for the landline phone, bracing myself for the blow.

"Yes?"

"Mrs. Streat, it's Dr. Prosser, Mrs. Vogt's primary care doctor."

"What happened? Is she worse?"

"No. The hospitalist has been in to see her. The arrhythmia is stabilizing. The blood pressure is still low, but that's not a concern. She should be released today, but she refuses to leave the hospital. She says she feels safe there and she's not going to leave her room. The hospital wants her bed, there's a shortage, but she's a very determined woman."

I shook my head to clear it. My eyes felt full of sand. "Yes, she is, but a man got into the apartment and tried to strangle her. She's frightened. Can't she stay a little longer?"

"There are patients lined up in ER, needing beds, and if Mrs. Vogt continues to be obstructive, the hospital will be forced to act. Maybe put her out in the hall. I believe you're close to her. Do you have any suggestions?"

"Like moving her against her will? I have her power of attorney, but where would she go? Certainly not back here after her scare."

"I think the best solution would be a nursing facility where she'd be well cared for until she recovers."

"A nursing home?" I pushed back my hair. "We both know how she'd react to *that*. Even drugged to the eyeballs, she'd make the most terrible fuss. She'd never speak to me again. Or you."

"Possibly, but action is required. There's a place called Woods House in Connecticut. Several of my patients have gone there for rehab. It's expensive, but the care is excellent. In fact, they pride themselves in looking more like a good hotel. As I say, it's expensive."

"That's not an issue, but would they take her on such short notice?"

"I'll talk to the manager myself. My secretary will be in touch with you."

I put down the receiver and groaned. Decisions loomed—difficult decisions—and I was the only one who could make them.

Less than an hour later, his secretary called. Woods House could receive Mrs. Vogt as soon as tomorrow. I wasn't surprised. No doubt Woods House had checked Mrs. Vogt's financial status and was happy to reel in this big fish.

Now for Caroline. It was noon when I walked through the lobby of the East Side Medical Center and joined the fishbowl of assorted people, all swimming in different directions. After a wrong turn, I found the elevator to Caroline's wing.

The atmosphere on this floor was quiet. No curtained bays or aides running with gurneys. Caroline had been taken to a semi-private room. When I came in, she was lying in the fetal position, eyes closed. The woman in the other bed was hooked up to a profusion of tubes.

I went over to Caroline's bed. Someone had combed her hair, but it lay flat and limp on the pillow. I leaned down and kissed her cheek.

"It's Emma," I said. "How are you feeling?"

She opened her eyes. "I'm not leaving this room."

"I see." I sat down and took her hand. "Listen. I know how you feel, but you aren't sick enough to stay here. The hospital needs the bed."

"I don't give a damn what they need. That man got in, God knows how. He knew where I was, and if you hadn't been there, I'd be dead. I'm staying where it's safe. Tell them I'll pay whatever they ask."

"It's not a question of money. You have to go, but don't worry, it won't be back to the apartment. I've talked to Dr. Prosser. He knows a place where you'll be well looked after—"

"Not one of those places. Poor old trouts tied to their wheelchairs, wetting themselves—I'm not leaving this bed." Her eyes closed, shutting me out.

I folded my hands and summoned patience. Reminded myself that Caroline was the closest thing I had to a mother—and I knew, all too well, the fear that comes with being a target. The sense of waiting for the next blow.

A food cart came rattling down the hall and stopped at the door. A large aide, her bottom jiggling under her flowered smock, came in with a tray. She pulled the bedside table around, set the tray down, and left. I leaned over and lifted the covers. Meatloaf. Stewed tomato. A container of milk. Caroline hated milk.

"Your lunch is here," I said. "Shall I raise you up?"

"No."

I sat still, struggling for a solution. I could talk with a hospital administrator, present a best-case scenario. If that didn't work, I would have to use my power of attorney. Give permission for Caroline to be drugged and transported to Connecticut. Face the fact that I would never, ever be forgiven.

"Caroline," I said at last. "Open your eyes and listen. I know how you feel about being in control, but it won't work here. The hospital has the authority. They could move you out into the hall and ignore you. The alternative is to go to Dr. Prosser's place of your own free will. He says it's run like a good hotel. I'll take you there myself. Make sure you're comfortable."

A nurse came and adjusted the other woman's tubes. Caroline opened her eyes. She began to pluck at the sheet.

"Never mind the comfort. Will I be safe there?"

"I'll take it up with their management. No visitor will come near you unless they have permission from you. Calls can be screened."

Silence. She seemed to be thinking. After a moment she looked at me. "You're treating me like an imbecile child, but I'll go. On one condition."

"What condition?"

"I was going to call that detective agency today. Have them find out whether Pierre Hallam is in France or over here, but you've been involved from the start. You have experience when it comes to sleuthing. You know how to ask questions—"

"Hold it." I got to my feet, knocking over the carton of milk. "You want *me* to find this man and confront him? Maybe go to France?"

"That way it stays private. No outsiders. If you agree, I'll leave without any fuss. If not, I'm calling my lawyers. I'll make a complaint about the rights of patients. Sue the hospital, God knows on what grounds. Those officials won't like it."

I stood up and went to the window, clamping down on dismay. I knew from the past what Caroline could do when crossed. There would be lawsuits, a long drawn-out battle. A waste of everyone's time.

After a moment, I turned and went back to the bed. "This is pure blackmail and you know it. It's outrageous, it's unfair, but I'll do it on one condition."

"What?"

"If I find him, if he can prove he's done nothing, then you have to accept it. No more carrying on about Pierre Hallam. Is that understood?"

"You won't get me into that place and change your mind?"

"No. I'll go. I promise."

CHAPTER NINE

By the time I got back to the apartment, second thoughts were striking with full force. Madness, to even think of going to France and confronting Pierre Hallam. Caroline had rolled over me like a tank. Now I had to pull myself together and face the consequences.

Delsey was in her little office, working on the computer. "It's done," I said. "It wasn't easy, but I'll be taking her to Woods House tomorrow. She's still very frightened. I'll get her settled and go on to Boston. Will you arrange for a car?"

"Of course." She swiveled around. "Mr. Langer called about investments. I didn't tell him about the attack, just that she was in the hospital having a few tests. Other people will be calling. What should I tell them?"

"I think until the police have some answers, we should be as vague as possible. Not say where she is."

"That's probably best."

I went down the hall to my room feeling drained. This was the moment I'd been dreading. It took every ounce of willpower to take my phone out of my handbag and make the call.

Rodale answered on the first ring. I cleared my throat and plunged. "Bad news. Really bad. I thought I could leave New York but I can't. Something terrible has happened."

"What?"

"This." I gave him the facts about the attack.

He listened without comment. Then: "What do the police say?"

"That it's a professional job with help from inside."

"I gather the bloke didn't leave any fleece in the hedges."

"Meaning?"

"Just a way of saying he didn't leave any evidence, which indicates a certain amount of expertise. Where is your godmother now?"

"In a hospital. Terrified. She refused to leave and her bed was needed. In the end, I had to make a deal."

"What kind of deal?"

"She's still blaming her ex-husband. The deal is, if *she* goes to a rehab place, *I* have to find him and confront him, even if he's in France. Don't say it, I know it's mad, but I was desperate and she's my surrogate mother."

"Mad, indeed. Let me get this straight. You told her you'd go to France if necessary, and confront this man?"

"To try to wring the truth out of him."

"I see." A long pause. I waited. I had expected more emotion.

"Emma, tell me this. How much do you know about this ex?"

"Not much. He was divorced with a son when he met my godmother. They lived the high life in New York until he stole her jewelry for his mistress. Forged checks. Being Caroline, she gave him a hard time. Very hard. He lost his job and moved to France. He's half French and his mother had property there."

"What's his name?"

"Hallam. Pierre Hallam. Caroline swears there's been no communication until the blackmail note, but she was sure something else would happen. It did. Someone tried to kill her. In her *bed*."

"Steady on. When would you go?"

"The sooner the better."

"Hallam is an unusual name." A pause. "Look. Before you go any further, let me check with a colleague in Paris. Find out if the the man lives there and has committed any crimes."

"Will that take long?"

"Not long. I'll ring you," he said and then he was gone.

At three o'clock, a plainclothes detective from the precinct came to get a statement. I told him what little I knew. He made notes and went away.

At a little after five, Rodale called back. "I've talked to my colleague in Paris. Where are you now?"

"In my godmother's apartment."

"Does she have a landline telephone?"

"That's all she has."

"Ring back on one of those phones. Less likely to be contaminated." Rodale was always paranoid about secure lines.

"One minute," I said and switched to the white phone on my bedside table. "Okay. I'm back."

"Emma, this is serious. I know how you feel about my work, but hear me out. My French colleagues and I have been working on locating and bringing down a certain cybercrime network. A week ago, one of them was arrested and interrogated. I can't give you details, they're too sensitive, but it turns out that Pierre Hallam is a person of interest. It's possible that his place is being used as one of their safe houses. In fact, he's about to be put under surveillance."

"Wait. Let me get this straight. Are you saying Hallam is more than just a blackmailer?"

"It's possible. You could be stepping into trouble."

I shifted the phone. A red flag went up. Rodale didn't want me to do this—and he was far too used to getting his own way.

"Look," I said evenly. "I have to go, but I won't be alone. My godmother was about to bring in a detective agency but then she decided to use me. I'll ask someone from the agency to go with me. That way, I'd have help in case Hallam gets nasty."

"Will that detective understand the French legal system? Will he have contacts with French intelligence? My colleagues and I consulted, and we've come up with a plan."

"What?"

"I can hear you starting to dig in your heels, but try to keep an open mind. Again, no details, but here's the outline. Hallam lives an hour south of Paris. He owns an old mill that he's converted into a small upscale hotel. I would go as a guest, bringing my American girlfriend as cover."

"Please. Don't tell me French intelligence would let a Brit and his girlfriend loose on their turf."

"Wrong. They realize a Brit touring around the countryside with his girl is far less suspicious than a French couple. We could have two nights and a day together in Paris, then drive down to the mill. You'd have your agenda plus backup. I'd have mine. The French get two experienced operatives. It could end with good results for both of us."

My mind raced to find the flaws. Twice Rodale had used me as a means to an end. Twice I had been summoned to England on short notice. I had jumped when he said jump.

"Hold it," I said. "I need to know more. Are we using different names? What do we do about passports?"

"False passports."

"Very James Bond. When would I go?"

"You'd fly over Friday night. There's a little hotel on the Left Bank. It used to belong to the Fleurie family. Very discreet. It won't be the island in the sun, but better than nothing. One other thing. You'd have to leave your phone behind."

"What if there's an emergency at home?"

"Not an option. It's one of the ways criminals can track and follow you. I can't take that risk—and I should warn you, there could be risks." A pause. "That's all I can tell you. Are you in or out?"

I closed my eyes and tried to concentrate. Hallam was in serious trouble, about to be put under surveillance. Rodale would be there to cover my back. When it was over, we might have a better sense of whether we could make a life together.

"Emma. Yes or no?"

"Don't push me. Yes. All right. I'm in."

CHAPTER TEN

March 29

At three the following afternoon, my hired limousine drew up in front of the Towers Apartments on Boston's Arlington Street. The doorman, known as Jolly George, hurried to meet me. "Good to see you back, Mrs. Streat. Any more bags?"

"Just the duffel," I said, resisting the urge to ask what kind of security the Towers laid on at night.

Settling Caroline at Woods House had gone better than expected. A pretty young aide had helped me unpack the special pillows, her kimonos, her pale blue cashmere throw. I made sure that the administrator understood that there must be no visitors. No calls put through to Mrs. Vogt except from her secretary or from me. No need to tell the administrator that a potential killer was still at large and dangerous.

During the drive from New York up congested I-95, I did my best to extract information from a heavily sedated Caroline.

"I'm keeping my promise, I'm going to France to meet Pierre Hallam, but I need to know more about him. Everything you can tell me."

Caroline had roused herself enough to pour out a stream of vitriol. I mustn't believe a word he said. A crook to the core, and a stupid crook at that. He should know he couldn't blackmail Caroline Vogt and walk away with a whole skin.

My apartment seemed tiny compared to Caroline's. I picked up a pile of mail and looked around. Like most people, my life had been a series of transitions: the heady world of opera crashed when I lost my voice. Then came years of corporate wife and hands-on mother. But after Lewis was murdered, and my beautiful house on the river was bombed, I was left without husband, pot, or pan. Gone, my collection of early American antique furniture. Gone, the Andrew Wyeth painting and the Willard clock. Last fall, after deciding to embark on a serene Asian look, I went out and bought two white sofas, added pillows in Thai silks. Placed Chinese scrolls on the walls.

I walked to the kitchen, put the electric kettle on, and went to the window. The remnants of last week's snow had shrunk to a few gritty piles against the fence in the Public Garden. I stared out and thought about my boys, always my top priority. What was my duty as their mother? Should I let them know that I was involved in another rescue mission? One that involved even greater risks?

I stood there, struggling for an answer. Jake was twenty, his face morphing into his father's craggy features. Steve, at eighteen, had my dark red hair and blue eyes—and he deeply resented my detecting. I had tried to explain to him that when people close to me needed help, no way was I going to slam the door. I wasn't a trained professional, but I could see unlikely connections that helped me solve problems.

He hadn't accepted the explanation. Shouted that when I was mixed up with the police, I seemed to belong to them. I wasn't a mother anymore. Jake had tried to make peace. His theory was that Steve was still getting over the loss of his father and he was afraid of losing me.

An ambulance came racing down Arlington Street, siren screaming, that sound I hated. Was there something about me that attracted trouble? Was I obsessed with the idea of playing detective? The idea had never entered my mind until Lewis died.

For years my life had been filled with soccer matches, car pools, cooking huge meals for the hordes of boys that were in and out of the house by the river. The big round kitchen table was always covered with crumbs and homework.

I had married Lewis on the rebound when I lost my voice, but the marriage had worked. He was a brilliant man with great vision, a man who hated show and pretension. Like heads of separate but equal departments, I had been the caregiver while he worked his way up to becoming the CEO of a huge international company. We were good friends in bed and out, and I missed his calm control. His good judgment. The boys still needed him—and they must never know that I had slept with a man a few months after his death. With any luck, Steve would never find out that I had gone off on another detecting venture.

Had I reached a new chapter in my life? I twisted the thin gold wedding ring on my ring finger and thought about Rodale. The relationship had started as a rescue mission when I was nearly killed in the stately home of the woman who had engineered Lewis's murder. It had turned into high-octane sex, plus the adrenaline rush that came when we were together in a crisis. We had no experience of the myriad daily events that build a solid foundation.

As the water came to a boil, the kettle clicked off. I walked away from the window and picked up a mug. It was time to face facts. I was committed to this risky operation. Rodale had a one-track mind, and I could end up being used to further his agenda, not mine. It would be hard to confront Hallam with nothing more than the blackmail note, but there was no turning back. All I could do now was to summon up resilience and go forward. One step at a time.

CHAPTER ELEVEN

April 3

Paris. Beautiful, seductive Paris. It was twenty-five years since my performances on the stage of the Opera Garnier. I walked through the soaring geometric angles of de Gaulle Airport with a mounting sense of anticipation. Never mind that I was here on a precarious mission. This was a special place, a city of the senses where, like Violetta in *Traviata*, one could live for the moment.

Yesterday Rodale had called to say that he was held up in London and a driver would meet me. There was always a twinge of worry that arrangements had misfired, but a uniformed man in Arrivals was holding up a sign for Mrs. Streat.

Getting through the suburbs took time, but at last we were in the heart of the city. I looked out, remembering the clear light, the wide boulevards, the ancient plane trees now showing green buds. Remembering small cafés and brasseries where appreciation of good food and drink was a cult.

Near the Pont des Arts pedestrian bridge, we crossed over the Seine River and entered the Left Bank. After going down several narrow streets, the driver slowed, turned through a pair of high gates, and came to a stop in a cobbled courtyard.

"Hotel de Fleurie, madame," he announced.

Leaving him to bring the duffel, I walked into the foyer. It was small but conveyed the feeling that here an exacting clientele would receive the ultimate in privacy and comfort. A woman came forward. She was wearing an elegant black dress. In excellent English, she assured me that it would be a pleasure to serve me in any way, I had only to ask.

Our room was on the third floor. I walked around, taking stock. In the old days, this might have been a privileged daughter's bedroom. Large casement windows, swathed in heavy blue damask curtains, looked over the courtyard. There was a carved armoire, a chaise longue, a huge bed with square pillows covered in starched white linen. An arrangement of fresh mimosa stood on an antique desk. Bathrooms could disappoint, but this one contained a bidet and a large well-appointed shower. No need to use the deep tub, a death trap for the elderly or arthritic.

It was now eleven in the morning—and I had no idea when Rodale would arrive. My stomach had the hollow feeling that comes after a long night in the air, and the traumas of the past few days had left me frazzled to the bone. I drank a bottle of mineral water, took a long shower, and began to pull clothes out of the duffel.

Back in my apartment, I had agitated over what to bring. Early April weather meant warm things for the country. As for Paris, I was all too aware that my all-purpose black dress and old Prada shoes were barely suitable for a good restaurant. No way could I compete with the seemingly effortless elegance of French women.

Last Christmas, Caroline had given me one of her authentic kimonos, along with a lecture on the alluring effect of wisps of black lace. A wasted effort. I still wore cotton tees at night, even if they proved to be token coverings. I put the kimono on, then curled up under the duvet for a short nap.

I must have slept. Hours later, the sound of footsteps woke me.

"Emma." Before I could speak, Rodale was beside me under

the duvet. "Don't say a word." He put his arms around me. "It's been too long. I want you. Now."

Any uncertainty about this meeting wafted up into the mimosa-scented air. The magic was back. Full force.

CHAPTER TWELVE

April 4

The first act of Verdi's *Traviata* was always a challenge for me. I took a deep breath and opened my mouth: "*Ah, fors'è lui che l'anima, solinga ne' tumulti, solinga ne' tumulti . . .*"

"Emma." Rodale was leaning on his elbow, looking down at me.

I reached up and touched his face. At some point, lying in the big bed, I had cast off all personas of conventional wife, mother, caregiver.

"Who the hell is Alfredo?" he asked. "You were muttering about him."

"A tenor. Opera. *Traviata.*"

"*That* Alfred. I was beginning to wonder." He lay back and put his arms around me. "I once told you that you had the most amazing eyes. You're an amazing woman all over. Inside and out."

"You're not too bad yourself. What time is it?" I said, stretching.

"Nine thirty." He kissed my neck, then swung himself out of bed. "Let's go and find some food."

With half-closed eyes, I watched as he unpacked, fitting himself into a small space with military precision. I was more apt to leave clothes on chairs or fling them into a heap on the floor.

"After we eat, what then?" he asked.

"No museums. No shopping. Maybe just wander. For once I don't have a list."

"A walkabout. Better bring a coat—it may be cold, even in the sun."

"We can always come back and warm up in bed."

"Have mercy, woman. Give me a few hours to mend."

There were a number of antique shops along the street. At the corner, we stopped at a booth and ate cheese-and-onion crepes. "The aria I was trying to sing," I said, wiping my mouth. "That *Traviata* was a nightmare. Alfredo was a pervert. I couldn't wait to leave for London and *The Marriage of Figaro*." No need to tell Rodale about an intense pre-marriage affair in London with conductor Maestro Anthony Battia.

"Where to now, madam diva?"

"Quai Voltaire? My guidebook says that Voltaire, Richard Wagner, Sibelius, and Oscar Wilde all lived there, though not at the same time."

We walked, but after a while I realized that Rodale had gone silent, as if his mind was in another place.

At noon we stopped at a café near the Boulevard Saint-Germain, a period setting of red velvet banquettes and mirrors. "Maybe Jean-Paul Sartre and the intellectuals used to hang out here," I said, trying for a light note.

"What?"

"It doesn't matter." I pushed away my omelet. If this was a test of how we would deal together in ordinary life, it was not going well.

He glanced at me and put down his napkin. "Sorry. It's time we went back to the room and talked about the operation. When we're close to the hotel, go ahead in without me. The less we're seen together the better."

"You actually think we're being followed?"

"It's possible."

I didn't answer. My try for easy companionship was over. We were back in work mode.

The maid had been in with flesh flowers. "Cobblestones are murder on the feet," I said, kicking off my shoes.

"All right. Down to business. You take the chaise. I'll sit here." He turned the Louis XIV chair around to face me. "I take it the New York police haven't produced any evidence. Nothing that could connect your godmother's attacker with Hallam."

"Not yet, and now that we're safe from eavesdroppers, I'd like to know why we're here. Why Pierre Hallam is under surveillance."

"Do you want me to spell out the basics?"

"Yes, I do."

"Then understand that the greatest threat to the civilized world is cyberwarfare. Nations fighting asymmetrical wars in cyberspace. No rules or Geneva Conventions. Every intelligence agency—yours, mine, the French—is working flat out to get their fingers in the dike before there's a monumental disaster, possibly involving terrorists."

"It's that bad?"

"The perpetrators, whether they're countries or bad actors, are getting harder to trace. They're going dark, using encrypted messages or avoiding them altogether. Even with false passports, they're avoiding PWLs—the passenger watch lists. They build thick firewalls and move undercover. Some of them travel by car using safe houses. My job is to find out if Hallam is part of a criminal network."

"What if you think he is?"

"I'm not working alone. There are rapid response teams that go in quickly and take out specific targets. The DGSI is available for backup if needed."

"What's that?"

"In English, it's French security. It's involved in terrorism and counterterrorism."

"If you needed them, how long would it take them to get to this mill?"

"Not long. Here." He went to the armoire, took out a case, unlocked it, and pulled out a passport embossed in gold. "Your fake passport to show when we get to the mill. Made from our files on you."

I reached out and took it. "Do I really need this? Hallam's not likely to connect the name Streat to my godmother."

"Never assume anything. I want to keep your name out of the operation. Starting tomorrow, you are Ellen Strong, age forty-eight, born in Philadelphia, now living in Dedham, Massachusetts. I picked the name Ellen because it sounds a bit like Emma."

"Ellen Strong from Dedham. Who are you?"

"Andrew Reed. Born in Harrowgate. Residence, London. We've come because I'm interested in the lesser known chateaux, and there are several nearby. That gives us an excuse to go driving about. Take notes and pictures."

"Where did we meet?"

"At a friend's house in Cadogan Square." He gave me an assessing look. "Try to come across as a silly American chatterbox. Always talking. All excited about your first visit to France."

"And I suppose you'll be a silent laid-back Brit. Am I allowed to embarrass you with stupid questions?"

"By all means, but keep your eyes open for any little detail that doesn't seem right. It's a given that any undercover activity will be well hidden from guests."

"Do my best."

"And your best is very good." He leaned over and ran his hand down my back. "Bed, and then we'll eat. There's a restaurant just down the street."

It was a little after seven when, after satisfying the senses, we dressed again and went out. The nearby restaurant had green trees in tubs at the entrance and at this hour it was almost empty. One other couple sat on a dark red banquette, feeding a small Yorkshire terrier bits from their plates.

I studied the menu and settled for the escargot starter, then the plat du jour, followed by Camembert cheese. Rodale ordered duck.

"Champagne?" he asked.

"Why not?"

The waiter did not announce that he was our server tonight. We ate slowly, saying very little. Rodale never talked about his two grown daughters. I avoided discussions about my sons. There were no mutual old friends or extended family, so no small talk about a cousin's latest promotion or an uncle going senile.

I stared at his hands carving the duck. Later, engaged once again in the ultimate intimacy, would he be thinking about cybercrime? Was he too driven to lead a normal life?

The man had an uncanny way of reading my mind. He put down his knife. "What is it?"

"Nothing. Well, if you must know, I just can't wrap my head around cyber stuff. I absolutely hate the idea that hackers and criminals are beavering away out of sight. The idea that they can find out everything about us. It's as if the whole world is changing."

"Get used to it. We just have to keep holding their feet to the fire. The new lot is clever, but luckily they leave footprints and make mistakes." He turned his head and looked at me. "Are you having second thoughts about tomorrow? It's not too late to change your mind. You can stay here and fly home tomorrow."

"That's insulting. In case you've forgotten, I was involved in an arms race, then in the transport of lethal viruses. I didn't do too badly."

"True. I apologize. Would you like pudding?"

"Couldn't."

"Coffee, then." He raised his wine glass and smiled. "Here's to the remarkable Ellen Strong. May she find her first trip to France rewarding."

I took a sip and nodded. "Here's to the crafty Andrew Reed. May he be successful and may justice be served."

CHAPTER THIRTEEN

April 5

By nine thirty the next morning, we were ready to leave the blue room. Rodale was wearing a Barbour jacket, a checked shirt, and brown suede shoes known to the English as brothel creepers. I had on my useful black trousers, a sweater, and the short, quilted coat.

"You look very county squire," I said, making a last-minute check of the armoire.

"County squire is good camouflage."

At the desk in the foyer, Rodale paid the bill, then reached into a pocket and pulled out a ticket. "For my package in your safe."

"Ah yes, monsieur." In a moment the elegant concierge was back with a small canvas bag. Expressions of mutual esteem were exchanged.

A taxi took us to a branch of Auto Europe where Rodale hired an inconspicuous gray Mercedes sedan. Soon we were speeding along the Peripherique, the highway that circles Paris.

"Thank God for GPS," I said, as we passed signs leading southeast to Lyon. "My map reading is a family joke. If Ma says go right, go left. By the way, that bag you took out of the safe looks heavy. What are you smuggling?"

"Equipment for a night operation. Special night-vision goggles. Stun gun. Camera. If there's a hiding place for illegals outside the mill itself, it's bound to be camouflaged. Maybe guarded." A pause. "By the way, no talking in the bedroom, not even in the car tomorrow. Someone could get in and tamper with it overnight."

"We can only talk in the open?"

"Or pass notes."

"Shades of school." I shifted on the seat. It was second nature for him to trust no one, but I must think twice before I opened my mouth. Be wide-eyed, talkative, and *careful.*

The congestion of the city gave way to suburbs. The traffic lessened. Suburbs became open fields, still in their drab winter colors. Rows of poplars, so loved by painters, stood straight and tall. I could almost hear Angelus bells ringing, see peasants with pitchforks trudging home.

"We must be close," Rodale said as we passed a run-down equestrian center; a number of thin horses were huddled against a fence. Another field, the road widened, and all at once we were on a village street. A row of stone houses stood close to the pavement. There was a boulangerie, a café, a notaire. Two sturdy women with shopping bags stood talking outside the épicerie.

"Exactly my idea of how a small French village should look," I said.

"You've never been in the country?"

"Only in Paris to sing. Don't forget, this is Ellen Strong's first trip to France."

"Right you are. Shows how easy it is to slip."

"God, yes." From now on my brain must be hardwired to think Andrew and Ellen. Disaster if I should make a mistake and endanger the operation.

At the end of the street, the road narrowed again. We passed more fields, lined with the ever-present poplars. The GPS began to squawk: "Five hundred yards to destination. Five hundred yards to destination."

He looked at me. "Start of opera. Conductor on his way to the pit. Ready?"

I nodded. I had once been a Violetta, an Elisabeth, a Tosca with great success. I was more than qualified to play the part of a gushy American.

A gate led to an open space where several cars were parked. In the field beyond, sheep were grazing. We passed through a high arch in an ivied wall and into a cobbled courtyard. A weeping willow tree stood in the center; hens pecked busily in the small circle of grass. A cat walked across the cobbles, hissed at a hen, and ran up the tree.

I got out and looked around. The mill itself was a long, low stone structure. Two smaller buildings were attached, forming three sides of a square. The trim around the small casement windows was painted bright blue.

"Postcard picturesque," I said.

Andrew went to a heavy wood door and knocked. No one came. He knocked again. We waited. At last, farther down the wall, the top of a Dutch door opened. A black lady wearing a brightly printed turban leaned out.

"'Allo?"

"It's Mr. Reed and Miss Strong. We're expected."

She disappeared. Another head took her place, a younger version of the first. "No one here. You early. I come."

The heavy door opened with a creak as if it was rarely used. The younger woman was bony thin, wearing a long print dress. Andrew picked up the bags and we walked into a small tiled hall cluttered with coats and walking sticks, then followed her up a twisting flight of stairs with narrow, uneven treads. I went carefully; it would be all too easy to slip and crash down onto the tiled floor.

She led us down a short hall and opened a door. "For you," she said.

I stopped at the threshold and stared. The space was vast, with no ceiling. Soaring beams crisscrossed under the high roof. A huge bed was hung with yards of faded chintz.

Andrew spoke to the woman. "Do you understand English?"

"Small."

"We go out now. We come back later. You understand?"

"Yes, m'sieur."

She left. I walked around, needing to take possession of this amazing room. The beams looked original, as if it had once been a loft, maybe a storage area for grain. On one side, two windows, set in thick stone, looked out on the courtyard. On the other, three equally small windows showed a rough lawn, then a stone wall with open fields beyond.

"I'm off to find the bathroom. I hope it's not miles away," I said loudly in case of implanted listeners, and opened another door. "Oh, Lordy, no shower, just one of those awful tubs like horse troughs. Honey, you'll have to pull me out."

Andrew was running a small debugging device over the walls, but the beams were too high to reach. He shook his head. "No shower? Well, never mind. I'm hungry. I saw a restaurant in that village. I say we eat, then take a long walk."

"Not too long, honey bun. You walk fast and you never stop."

"Put on your running shoes. Better bring your camera." He picked up the bag taken from the safe and looked around, frowning. I could see why. The bag was far too large to carry around. It had to be hidden in a safe place.

"Wait while I change my shoes." I took the bag, wrapped it in one of my T-shirts, then put it, with the Save the Dolphins logo facing out, in the back of a drawer. "I just hope this Mr. Hallam speaks good English," I said, glancing up at the rafters.

"Why?"

"I don't have any French and you have about ten words."

"We'll manage. Move, woman." He pushed me toward the door.

We felt our way down the stairs, through the hall, and out into the courtyard. The hens were still scratching in the dirt, the sheep had moved to another part of the field. Peaceful enough, but I was reminded of a well-known painting. The foliage was thick. All was calm and serene until you looked closely—and saw a tiger with bared teeth peering through the big green leaves.

CHAPTER FOURTEEN

We ate well at the little village restaurant, simple food washed down with local wine, and walked in the fields. When we returned, the younger woman met us in the hall.

"M'sieur, he send message. You please to come to the salon for aperitif. At seven by the clock."

At a few minutes after seven, we walked into the long salon. Two men were playing backgammon at a table near an open fire. One got to his feet.

"Miss Strong? Mr. Reed? I am Pierre Hallam," he said in good but stilted English. "I apologize for not being here when you arrived, but I was told it would be six at the earliest."

"The travel agent must have made a mistake," Andrew said. "It happens."

"No matter. Welcome to the mill, Miss Strong." Pierre Hallam bowed over my hand.

"Oh, goodness me, I'm not used to being called Miss Strong. Just call me Ellen," I simpered.

Pierre Hallam was a handsome man, with a shock of white hair and slanting dark eyes. A silk cravat was knotted around his neck. I could see why his European sophistication had turned a young Caroline's midwestern head.

"Allow me to make introductions," he went on. "Mr. Wade and his niece, Miss Culmhoff. What will you drink, er, Ellen?"

"A kir. I'm just crazy about kirs."

"And you, Mr. Reed?"

"Scotch and soda for me."

"One moment." He went to a table that held glasses and bottles.

I sat down in a chair next to Mr. Wade. He was elderly, maybe in his seventies, wore thick glasses, and was extremely thin. The woman was much younger and was built like a decathlon champion.

Hallam handed me the kir. "Thank you, kind sir," I gushed. Sipped, and glanced around. The massive antique furniture needed a good polish. Worn quilted chintz curtains hung from the tall French doors. They matched the slip covers and must have cost a fortune when new. Paid for by Hallam's mother?

Pierre Hallam gave Andrew his drink and went to stand in front of the fire. He looked at me and raised his glass. "To your very good health. May I ask what brings you to the mill so early in the season?"

"My boyfriend, he's mad about old chateaux and he heard there were several nearby. He had to drag me by my fingernails away from Paris, but I forgive him because I'm just crazy about this place. It's so quaint. I want to know everything about it."

"That is, how shall I say, a tall order, but I will do my best. I trust your agent explained that life here is informal. Meals are served in the kitchen. I am the chef, assisted by Dede and Nita. They came recently from the Cote d'Ivoire, sponsored by relatives in Lyon."

"I love their turbans," I said.

"They add color." He touched his cravat. "Mr. Reed, be good enough to give me your passports. A nuisance, but necessary if one runs a hotel, even a small one."

"Right." Andrew reached into a pocket and produced the two fake passports.

"They will be returned shortly. Now, if you will excuse me, there is a special sauce that requires my attention."

He left. I took another sip of kir. The first step had been taken. I must keep establishing myself as a bubbly, somewhat childish American—and at the same time be alert to any little abnormality. Could Mr. Wade be a brilliant expert in some area of cybercrime? Escorted between safe houses? It wouldn't hurt to ask questions, but I mustn't overdo my part.

"When did you arrive, Mr. Wade?" I began.

The heavyset niece answered for him. "We come yesterday. My uncle, he wished to see the Chateau de Dampierre." She had a thick accent, not German and certainly not French.

Andrew cleared his throat and turned to Mr. Wade. "What was your impression, sir? We're thinking of going there tomorrow."

"Ah." Mr. Wade pointed to a brochure on the table next to me. I picked it up and began to skim:

> *. . . built in 1675 for the Duc de Chevreuse with gardens designed by Andre Le Notre. The interior is considered to be one of the finest in France. Three kings have stayed in the royal apartment . . .*

"Lordy," I said. "It sounds like Versailles. Are you a professor? Or an architect?"

The niece gave me a sharp look. "My uncle, he takes an interest in old buildings. Why do you ask?"

"No reason." I managed a high-pitched laugh. "Everyone at home in Massacusetts says I have a nosy nature and I talk too much."

No answer. She picked up a piece of knitting. Tan greasy wool. A suspicious, unpleasant woman. Were we all random players in this game, watching the opponent's every move?

There was a long silence, broken only by the crackling of the fire. At last Hallam appeared in the doorway. "Ladies and gentlemen, dinner is served."

The kitchen was large, with the same aura of former wealth. A stove at the far end had a surround of blue tiles and copper pots hanging from hooks. The long dining table looked out on the courtyard, now illuminated by concealed lighting in the weeping willow tree.

As we sat down, the exotic helpers brought majolica dishes containing smoked salmon served with lemon quarters, brown bread, olive oil, and capers. This was followed by roast lamb, potato *frites*, and a casserole of winter vegetables cooked to perfection.

"*Vin du pays*," Hallam said, filling glasses. "Rather good, I think. The lamb is from my farm."

I tilted my head. "My goodness, you have a farm *and* a hotel? Oh, that's right. I did see sheep in the field. Do clever sheepdogs herd them back and forth?"

"No sheepdogs."

"No dogs at all? I love dogs," I said, wanting to rule out watchdogs.

"No dogs, I regret to say. Just an abundance of cats."

"One was in the courtyard, chasing a hen. Do you live at the mill or do you have another house?"

"I live in one of the connecting buildings. My workers come from the village."

"I saw a man on a bicycle wearing the sweetest little beret. He was leaving when we came back from our walk."

"That would be Jacques, my caretaker. He lives with his sister in the village. A good worker, but lacking in wits. In my mother's time there was more land and a far larger staff." He smiled and leaned toward me. "May I tempt you with more lamb? More vegetables?" I had the feeling he hadn't lost his taste for women.

I tilted my head and smiled back. "Absolutely scrumptious, but I can't eat another bite."

"Ah, but you must try my special *tarte*, made from our cherries."

"You're spoiling us, you really are. By the way, what time is breakfast? It takes wild horses to drag me out of bed, but my friend likes to be up and running at the crack of—" I stopped. Someone was pounding at the kitchen door. Pounding hard.

"My apologies," Hallam murmured. Opened it and went out. I twisted around so I could see through the window.

Jacques was standing there. Hallam took his arm and moved him out into the courtyard. The man began to talk, waving his arms, making frantic gestures. This went on for several minutes. Finally, Hallam nodded. Jacques turned and took off on his bicycle, pedaling as if his life depended on speed.

Hallam came back. "Again, my apologies." He picked up a bottle. "More wine?"

Andrew coughed. "That fellow looked upset. Nothing serious, I hope."

"He thinks a boy from the village has stolen one of our sheep. I told him to go home, that we would deal with it tomorrow. Jacques is very protective about the place, not a bad thing except when he becomes agitated over small matters, a sign of the mental deficiencies." He shrugged his shoulders. "Now for my *tarte*."

The *tarte* was followed by cheese. "Dede will bring coffee to the salon," Hallam announced, and we returned to the salon.

The niece went back to the fire and picked up her knitting. Andrew switched on the small television set. There were three black-and-white channels and the talk was in rapid-fire French. Hallam and Mr. Wade sat down at the backgammon board again and began to shake the dice. With glazed eyes, I watched a French movie and thought about the caretaker's wildly agitated appearance. Still, Hallam had given us a reasonable explanation.

At last it was nine o'clock. "You have outplayed me quite unmercifully, Mr. Wade," Hallam said, pushing back his chair. "I owe you one hundred and fifty euros." He looked around. "Will anyone have a liqueur?"

"I'm for bed," Andrew said, and stood up.

"So am I," I said.

Hallam made a little bow. "Then I wish you a good night. Here are your passports." He handed them to Andrew. "Breakfast is served in the kitchen at any time after eight. By then I will be back from the boulangerie with fresh croissants."

"Fresh croissants," I burbled. "What a treat. You'll never be rid of us."

"A delightful prospect, Mademoiselle Ellen."

Back in the room, I sat down on the bed. "Wow, what a meal," I said, directing my voice up to the rafters. "That Pierre is one fantastic cook and I love his lord of the manor look. What do you call that silk thing he was wearing around his neck?"

"A cravat. Do you want the bathroom first?"

"Lordy Lou, it's cold in here. Must be all this stone. Where did I put my robe?"

"Wherever you left it." He reached into the drawer with the recce bag. After studying the T-shirt, he took out a pad of paper and a pen and began to write:

> *There was no special sauce. My sponge bag was moved, but not your tee. Jacques incident suspicious. We'll talk in bed. Don't undress.*

I swallowed and tore up the note. "Here's my robe," I said. "Honey, you sure weren't a ball of fire down there."

"Not much to say. That man and his niece bored for Germany or wherever they're from."

"What do you mean, bored for Germany?"

"Just an expression. Means they were dull bores."

"That awful television—I kept thinking what a waste of time when we could have been up here."

"Get yourself ready. Soon warm you up."

Moments later we were under the duvet, fully clothed. "I'm going to do a recce around the property," he said in my ear. "Jacques may not be all that retarded. He could have had a message about that couple or about us."

"He acted pretty frazzled over a missing sheep. Do you really have to go tonight? What happens now?"

"Put on your acting hat. We create an X-rated diversion and hope Hallam's listening."

"Are you serious?"

"Get out from under the covers. Lay it on thick."

We emerged from under the duvet. I pounded the pillows for a moment, then let out a loud groan. "Oh, God, that's good."

"Turns you on, does it?"

"You know it does. Why do people say Brits are reserved? Not in bed—oh God, do that again, sweetie . . . don't stop . . . again . . . harder."

More groans. A scream. Silence. I stuffed my hands in my mouth to keep from laughing.

"Roll over, babe, I'm knackered," Andrew muttered. "Need to sleep." He pulled me back under the covers. "Well done," he said under his breath. "It's after ten. We allow three hours for everyone to settle, then I go out through the window and start looking."

"The window? They're so small."

"On a rope. I'll be gone for at least several hours. Your job is to keep holding that rope until I get back."

My brain did a seismic shift. "Wait a minute. You want me to hold that rope for hours, maybe all night?"

"I can climb down, but not up. When you feel a tug, go down and unlock the big front door. I'll give you a torch."

"What if someone's awake and hears me?"

"Mind the creaky old floors. If you're in the hall and someone comes, get behind the row of coats hanging on the wall."

"What if *you're* seen?"

"There's a number written on the bottom of my sponge bag.

If it gets light and I'm not back, call that number. Paris will send a rapid response team."

I clutched my throat. It was hard to breathe under the duvet. "How long will it take them to get here? What do I do while I'm waiting?"

"Go downstairs for breakfast. Say you never heard me go out, but I often take long walks in the early morning. Draw it out as long as you can."

"What if Hallam doesn't believe me?"

"He won't do anything violent without getting orders. Just keep up the bouncy American act until reinforcements arrive. I'll wake you when it's time." He rolled over onto his side.

I lay still, my nails pressed into my palms, fighting a surge of anger. This was asking too much. In Paris, he had spoken of risks, given me a chance to back out, but he'd said nothing to indicate that his life might depend on me—or that I could be in danger of losing mine.

CHAPTER FIFTEEN

April 6

The light tap on my shoulder woke me. A hand clamped down on my mouth. In seconds I was fully awake.

Andrew was standing by the bed. He was dressed in black and looked like a nocturnal creature, one that might have crawled out of a Florida mangrove swamp.

In silence I followed him as he went to a window that faced the back terrace. He handed me a small torch, then fastened a thin rope to the hinges and edged himself through the small opening. I leaned out and stared at his gloved hands as he went hand over hand down the rope, a test of muscular strength over gravity. There was a slight thump as his feet touched the ground. He disappeared into the night.

For a moment, I stood there and shivered. The air coming in through the open window was cold, but there was no wind, only a slight stirring of bare branches in the trees beyond the terrace. The sound of water rushing over the old milldam was muted and distant.

Walking carefully on the old boards, I went to the other window and looked into the courtyard. There were no lights in any of the adjacent buildings, a good sign.

No way was I going to stand at that window for endless hours. I picked up a small chair, lifted the duvet from the bed, and carried them to the window. Untied the rope, breaking two fingernails, then wrapped one end around my wrist. If I fell asleep, the slightest movement at the other end would wake me.

There was nothing to do but wait. I tried deep breathing, but as time passed, a list of possible disasters began to fill my mind. *If* a camera was hidden in the beams, every move we made had been transmitted to watchers. Andrew had been followed and was being tortured. The athletic niece had unlocked my door and was dragging me down to face Hallam. "We know how to deal with spies," he said, pulling out a pistol. My son Jake could work through the angst, but Steve would be in trouble.

My right hand and wrist were hurting. I let the rope slacken and imagined that I was lying on a white beach, looking up at an azure sky. The door of my new house would be a bright Chinese red. Caroline was back in her apartment.

I was drifting off when a loud creak propelled me into full alert. Someone in the house was awake and moving. I twisted around until I could see the bedside clock. It was four o'clock. I held my breath and listened. If the sky lightened and there was no sign of Andrew, I'd have to get up and find the number on the bottom of the sponge bag—such a stupid name. Call for help. Eventually, I'd have to go down and face the consequences.

I dozed again. The tug, when it finally came, bit into my wrist and galvanized me into motion. He was back—and I must swallow my fear. Go down to the front hall and let him in. My fingers were all thumbs as I untangled myself from the duvet and reeled in the rope.

It was still dark in the room. I snapped on the tiny light Andrew had given me and pulled a robe over my clothes. If anyone appeared, I would say I was looking for a book or a glass of milk.

No Amazon warrior woman stood at the door, ready to pounce. Darkness enveloped me, thick as a shroud, thick as the darkness in the apartment when Caroline was attacked. I tiptoed to the stairs, gripped the iron railing, and felt my way down step by step, but as I reached the tiled hall, something warm touched my foot. My knees buckled. I dropped the light and lunged toward the coats on the wall. There was a loud hiss as the cat from the courtyard ran past me.

The light still shone. I stooped to pick it up and crept to the front door. It was fastened by two heavy bolts. I tugged with all my strength until they gave way. Andrew slid in through the narrow space.

"Up. Quick," he muttered. I followed with the light as he pulled himself up the stairs, dragging his leg.

Once in the room he peeled off the black tracksuit and stuffed it into the armoire. Took a packet of pills from his sponge bag, swallowed three, and crawled into the big bed.

I dragged the duvet back from the chair. Lay down beside him and touched his hand. It was icy cold. I rubbed it to give warmth and spoke into his ear.

"You're hurt."

"Twisted my bad leg running."

"You were out there forever. What did you find?"

"Underground room with a vent. In the back field under a pile of compost. Someone had been there—I may have been seen."

"Oh God. What happens now?"

"Paris . . . sending people . . . may have trouble before they get here." His voice trailed off. He turned on his side, curled himself into a fetal ball, and passed out.

I lay there, holding his hand. Paris . . . sending people . . . trouble before they get here . . . what kind of trouble? Better not to think what could happen if they didn't get here in time.

CHAPTER SIXTEEN

I woke to the sound of rain beating down on the tiles above my head. I was still wearing trousers and a sweater and there was a painful red welt around my wrist. As I lay there, a replay of the endless night came surging back. The rope. The cat running over my feet. The sheer terror that Andrew might never return. I reached out to touch him. He wasn't there.

I sat up. "*Andrew*," I called out, forgetting about listeners, but he was limping through the bathroom door, a towel wrapped around his waist. He shook his head and pointed to the rafters.

"Get your skates on, woman. I want my breakfast," he said loudly, then picked up the pad of paper. *Keep acting. Drag out breakfast. Be ready to bolt to the car.*

It took all my willpower not to crawl back under the duvet. If Andrew *had* been seen in the field, Hallam would have notified higher-ups. Right now, they could be on their way to dispose of us—and I was being told to go on with this ghastly charade.

"Move it, woman. I want to get to that chateau."

I took a deep breath and told myself to get a grip. "Don't rush me," I whimpered. "You're a tiger between the sheets, honey. What a night—I need a decent shower, not that awful tub. Using a hose is like washing a dog."

Minutes later we walked into the kitchen. Andrew was wearing his county squire clothes. He was making an effort not to limp on the leg shattered by terrorists in Ireland. I'd done my best to hide the circles under my eyes. Applied blusher with a heavy hand.

The kitchen was warm and smelled of bacon cooking. The two African ladies, wearing their colorful turbans, motioned us to sit down at the table.

"Coffee, madame?" one asked.

"Yes, please." I wrapped my hands around the mug and gulped down the reviving drink.

"Good morning. I hope you both slept well." Pierre Hallam appeared from the hall. He was wearing gray linen trousers and a striped cotton shirt, the very model of a well-dressed host with nothing but daily chores on his mind.

"We did," Andrew said.

"Like logs," I added.

"*Bien*. For breakfast, there are new-laid eggs. Dry cereal, which Americans seem to prefer. Croissants fresh from the boulangerie." He went to the counter and brought over a basket.

I looked around. "Where are the others?"

"Mr. Wade and his niece decided to make an early start. I understand that you wish to visit the Chateau Dampierre."

"Not me," I said, pouting.

"Ah, but the chateau is charming and there are several auberges—inns—on the main street where you can lunch well. Let me give you more coffee."

His hand was steady as he poured. If he was feeling strain, it didn't show. I shook cornflakes into a faience bowl and began to eat slowly, a few pieces at a time.

He went to the other end of the kitchen and busied himself with pots and pans. I leaned closer to Andrew. "This may be my only chance to ask him about blackmailing Caroline," I whispered.

"Not until we get reinforcements."

Outside in the court, the cobblestones were slick with rain. No hens clucked about, pecking for grain. I picked at the cereal, ignoring the ladies who stood nearby, waiting to collect our dishes and get on with their chores.

Hallam's phone chimed. He wiped his hands and pulled it from a pocket. I tried to follow the rapid French.

"*Entendu, mon vieux*," he was saying. "Understood, my friend." Not the tone of a man who was planning violence, but I had learned, the hard way, that deception had no limits. This could be the order to carry out a fatal accident. Bury the bodies somewhere in the field. A Mr. Reed and a Miss Strong had never arrived at the mill.

It was after ten. I finished the cereal and put down the napkin. "What do we do now?"

"Look," Andrew said under his breath.

I followed his eyes to the courtyard. Two men in shiny waterproof capes were hurrying toward the building. They were dragging Jacques the caretaker between them.

"Are they—"

"Yes."

The knocking on the kitchen door was loud and authoritative. It opened and the men erupted into the room, holding a struggling Jacques. His sparse reddish hair was wet. He began to shout, showing bad teeth.

"*Assez*," Hallam said to him sharply and turned to the men. An exchange of bullet-speed French followed.

"Jacques was seen burying something in a field," Andrew muttered. "He ran when he saw them. Hallam's asking the men to identify themselves. Playing it cool, but it won't work. Here comes my colleague, a *commissaire*."

I stared at the man who walked through the door and took off his hat. He was balding, with a neat little mustache. He reached under his dripping cape and handed a card to Hallam. Whatever was on the card impacted Hallam like a physical blow. His head jerked back. He began to talk again, but in a different tone of voice.

"What's he saying?" I whispered.

"Change of tactics. He's telling the *commissaire* that if anything illegal has happened on his property, he knows nothing about it. Blaming it on the caretaker."

Jacques was fighting to get free. He spat on the floor and burst into another tirade.

Andrew translated for me. "He's saying that Hallam is lying, that he knows very well how his property is being used, that he, Jacques, was only following orders."

The *commissaire* nodded at Andrew, establishing rapport. Then he turned back to Hallam. "Monsieur, I repeat," he said, switching to English. "We have evidence that criminals are being hidden on your property."

Hallam drew himself up. He was several inches taller than the *commissaire*. "And I repeat that I know nothing of this matter. My caretaker is mentally deficient, as you can see. He may have been used by others for their purposes. This hiding place you speak of—I demand to see your evidence."

The *commissaire* looked at his watch. "No demands, Monsieur. I am required to take you to Paris where you will be questioned. My car is waiting. If you wish to collect a few personal effects, one of my men will accompany you."

For the first time Hallam's face showed concern. He raised his hand. "Go to Paris? For what reason? I must point out to you that I own a small hotel. I have guests who arrived yesterday." He motioned to the table where we were sitting. "These people must not be inconvenienced."

"You have seen their passports?"

"Yes. All is in order. They are here to visit the Chateau Dampierre."

"That is not so. I can now tell you that Monsieur Reed collaborates with our intelligence. Last night he discovered an underground room beneath a compost heap in your field. It was recently occupied."

Hallam stiffened. "I tell you, I know nothing about criminal activities on my property but I know the law. You have no reason to remove me. I do nothing without the advice of my lawyer."

The *commissaire* frowned. He hesitated, then came over to the table where we were sitting. "This presents difficulties. I want him out of here, but unfortunately, he has rights. We must produce more evidence—ah. What is this?"

The door opened. Two gendarmes pushed Dede and Nita into the kitchen. They were wailing, wringing their hands. Suddenly the kitchen was filled with agitated people, pushing and shouting.

One of the gendarmes spoke to the *commissaire*. He listened, then turned to Hallam.

"My men observed these two running across the fields as if escaping. When questioned, they said they work for you. I wish to see their *cartes de séjour*."

Hallam raised his shoulders. He looked annoyed. "Why they should wish to leave—no matter. I regret, but the *cartes* are in the hands of the relatives who brought them. Relatives who live in Lyon."

"The *cartes* should have remained in your hands, monsieur. You are now charged with harboring illegals, a punishable offense." He motioned to two of the gendarmes. "Escort him to the car."

I looked at Andrew. This was happening too fast. Once Hallam was taken off to Paris, I might never see him again. "Tell them to wait a moment," I said urgently. "I *have* to speak to him."

"No time for that now—"

I dug my fingers into Andrew's arm. "Listen to me. I could have done this a few minutes ago but you wouldn't let me. Damn it, after how I helped you last night I'm owed. I'm owed, and you know it." My voice was rising.

"I hear you. No need to shout." Andrew shook loose and walked over to the *commissaire*. "Before you leave, Mrs. Streat wants to speak to this man about a private matter. It's important to her and she was indispensable to the operation last night."

"Then let her be quick."

Hallam was standing a few feet away, flanked by the two young gendarmes. I went forward and faced him. "I'm not a spy," I began. "I'm here because my godmother Caroline Vogt sent me to talk to you—no, Vogt was her fourth husband's name. I'm talking about Caroline, your second wife. She's being blackmailed. A few days ago, she received a note asking for a million dollars. She thinks it came from you."

"Blackmail? A million dollars?" He ran a hand through his white hair. "That woman ruined me. I want nothing to do with her. Nothing."

"But"—I struggled to find a foothold—"you have connections in New York. You have a son—"

"After that woman took everything, I never saw my son again. This is madness. That woman is mad. She wishes to hurt me again." A vein in his forehead was throbbing.

The *commissaire* drew Andrew aside, said a few words to him in French, then turned to me. "You have your answer, Madame. We go." He motioned to the gendarmes. They took Hallam's arms and marched him through the door. Jacques and the sobbing ladies were herded into the courtyard. Cars were waiting, engines running. The cavalcade disappeared through the archway.

After the noise and the shouting, the silence in the house was startling. I leaned against a wall and looked at Andrew. "I don't think he was lying. Do you?"

"Hard to say. We have to pack."

Once in the room, he began to open drawers. Pulled out the recce bag and handed me my duffel.

"My God, I can't believe it's over," I said. "What happens now?"

"The *commissaire* wants a full account of what happened last night. I'm to go straight to DGSI's head office."

"Then what? Back to the Hotel Fleurie? Do I meet you there?"

"No." A long pause. He turned. "You've been involved enough in this operation. More than enough, and it's over. The *commissaire* is getting you a seat on the next flight from de Gaulle to Logan. A gendarme will drive you to the airport. Here." He reached into his wallet. "You'll need your valid passport and some euros."

I dropped the shirt I was holding. "What?"

"The *commissaire* has made arrangements to fly you home. The sooner you're out of here, the safer for you."

"You *bastard*." Sheer fury rose to the surface. I took the euros and threw them on the floor. "You utter bastard. You used me, I served a purpose, and now I'm excess baggage."

"Emma—"

"Sure, you went through the motions of making love to me in Paris, but I could have been anyone. Then the Andrew and Ellen pony show. Last night I sat by that window holding on to a rope, *paralyzed* for fear you might never come back. I did everything you asked and has there been one word of thanks? One pat on the back? Nothing."

"Emma, be fair. You got to confront Hallam—"

"Only after I put your feet to the fire. Your work has always come first, but this time you've gone too far. Don't think you can snap your fingers and jump into bed with me between jobs. That's over, never again, but don't worry. There are plenty of women who would leap at the chance. Dozens. Use them for your dirty work and get out of my life."

At last I had his attention. He put a hand on my shoulder. "You're wrong about when we're in bed. You mean a lot to me." A pause. "You're upset, it was a bad night. Go home and rest. I'll be in touch and we'll sort this out."

"Save that crap for the next sucker. I never want to lay eyes on you again." I knocked his hand away and began to yank clothes from the armoire.

"Emma." Another pause. "You've made your point. Now get a grip on your feelings and listen. We still don't know who was handling Hallam, but you may have been identified. You could be followed."

"More crap." I picked up the Prada shoes and threw them into the duffel.

"Not crap. I mean it. When you get back, keep your head down. Don't ask questions about the attack on your godmother. Let the police handle it. They have the training and the resources for that kind of investigation."

To be patronized was the last straw. I turned my back and wrestled with the zipper on my overloaded duffel.

"You'll break that." He applied muscle and picked it up. "One last word. If you take the bit in your teeth and get yourself into trouble, here's a name. Agent Howard is in your Secret Service and good at what he does." He wrote on a piece of paper and put it in my handbag. "Be careful, Emma. Be very careful." He picked up the luggage and led the way from the room.

A man in plain clothes was standing at the bottom of the narrow stairs. "A gendarme is coming with the rental car, m'sieur. He will drive madame to the airport and return the car to the agency."

Andrew nodded. He put the duffel on the floor, went through the door, and got into the waiting car. No parting word, no backward look. The engine started. Seconds later he was gone.

I stood there, staring out at the weeping willow in the courtyard. The tree was dripping with rain. The cat came slinking from the deserted kitchen and began to rub against my ankles. I kicked it away. This mission had been a mistake from beginning to end. I had nothing to take back to Caroline. As for Rodale, history repeated itself. Once again, I had let my heart rule my head. I should have known that coming here with him would end in tears. My tears.

The gray Mercedes rental came through the archway and pulled up in front of the door. The young gendarme picked up my duffel. "Is that all, madame?"

"That's all."

CHAPTER SEVENTEEN

April 7

A baggage handler's strike in France delayed the flight. Severe ground conditions had kept us circling in the skies over Logan Airport. Endless hours later, I walked into my apartment and crashed.

Jet lag sets its own clock. I slept until nine in the morning, then crawled out of bed, washed my hair, and went into the kitchen to make coffee. There had been time, as the plane droned over the Atlantic, to go over those last moments at the mill. I might have overreacted with Rodale, but his comments about no training, and being told to stop asking questions were unforgivable.

I poured coffee into a mug and gulped it down. Resilience was key. As for a future with Rodale, to expect anything but good sex from that man was delusional. My only regret was that I had lost my temper and screamed at him like a fishwife. What I needed in my life was someone who would treat me as an equal. Someone who would think I was wonderful, a sheer joy, the best thing that ever happened to him. Rest in peace, Lord Rodale.

Jogging was a no-fail way to clear the mind. I threw on my running sweats, and moments later I was on the Esplanade, the long promenade beside the Charles River. Last winter, when I lived on Beacon Hill, this run had saved my sanity. I knew every crack in the pavement.

The day was warm; an eight-man shell was out rowing, training for upcoming races. There were other joggers and dog walkers on the Esplanade, all of us leading different lives, all of us faced with choices. Mine was to ignore Rodale's warning about being followed. Not likely, and I was committed to finding who had blackmailed and attacked Caroline. It wouldn't be easy. I had no agency resources behind me, only my gift of seeing the odd discrepancy. After Lewis had been killed, a Sergeant Johnson gave me valuable advice: "Out of the blue, one little lead can get the case rolling." If not Pierre Hallam, who? One time-honored solution was to follow the money—and in this case the money had started with a note asking for a million dollars.

Back in the apartment, I sat down, picked up the phone, and got to work. First, a call to Woods House. The news was not reassuring. Mrs. Vogt was still agitated and it was necessary to keep her sedated.

Next, Delsey. She was in her office. "I'm back," I said, "and I got zero zilch from Pierre Hallam. Have the police found anything?"

"They say they're working on the case, but they're up to their ears with that pop singer murder."

"What about the superintendent?"

"He was fired by the board, but he hasn't been arrested."

"Too bad. Anything else?"

"Mr. Langer keeps calling. I put him off, but I can't do that much longer."

"No, you can't. You know, maybe I should talk to that detective agency Caroline uses. They're supposed to be good. Could you try and get me an appointment the day after tomorrow? I could stop on the way and see Caroline."

"I hope she's improving. Whenever I call, she's always sleeping. It's a nasty drive, all those trucks. Why don't I get you a car and driver?"

"You're an angel. You know the address. Tell him to be here at nine—and don't bother to wait for me. It may be late afternoon when I get to the apartment." I put down the phone and sat back. It might be a shot in the dark, but the first step had been taken.

CHAPTER EIGHTEEN

April 8

Woods House had maintained the look of a nineteenth-century country mansion. The front hall was paneled in dark wood. There were fresh flowers on a center table and the cost per day was staggering.

The young woman at the Queen Anne desk looked up as I came in. "Good afternoon," I said. "I'm Mrs. Streat. I'm here to see Mrs. Vogt, but first I'd like to talk to the administrator."

"Yes, Mrs. Streat. I'll let Mrs. Stone know you're here." A moment later I was being led into the administrator's office, decorated in the style of a Downton Abbey library.

"It's nice to see you again, Mrs. Streat." Sheila Stone was a youngish woman making the most of a plain face and a good figure. Today she wore a black tunic over black tights, and a silver necklace. "May I offer you coffee? Tea?"

"Nothing, thanks. I'm on my way to New York."

"Please sit down. Frankly, I was thinking of calling you. We're quite concerned about Mrs. Vogt's lack of progress."

"That's not good news. Is it the arrhythmia?"

"No, that righted itself, but she doesn't seem to be recovering from the trauma of being attacked in her apartment. We brought in a psychiatric social worker. A highly qualified professional who's helped a number of residents confront their fears.

Mrs. Vogt refused to talk to her. Told her to get out in very strong words."

"Actually, I'd say that was a good sign."

"I'm afraid not. She often becomes agitated, says she has an ex-husband who is trying to rob her. Our resident doctor is keeping her well-sedated, which is why you will find her . . . lethargic."

"I see." I shifted in my chair. "One question. I left instructions that no one was to see her or talk to her on the phone without checking first with me or her secretary."

"We've kept a careful record." Mrs. Stone went to a computer on her desk and brought up a screen. "Here it is. Calls from her secretary and one from her brother."

"Her . . . brother? Do you have a recording of the call?"

"Just the time, date, and a note. He said he was in New York for a few days and wanted to know when she was leaving. He was told that we do not give out information about our residents without authorization."

"Did he give a name?"

"No, but the note says he was persistent."

I took a deep breath. It was important not to show dismay. "Mrs. Stone, for your information, Mrs. Vogt has no brother."

"Oh?" Mrs. Stone closed the computer with a snap. "Mrs. Streat, we've never asked for details about the attack on Mrs. Vogt, but this raises concerns."

I leaned forward. God forbid that Mrs. Stone would decide that Caroline was a risk that had to be removed. "Nothing will happen. It's only a matter of monitoring calls. As you already have."

"In any case, I'll alert the staff. Frankly, we're not set up to guard individuals. Do you want to be contacted directly if he calls again?" Her voice was cool.

"Yes. I do. And I very much appreciate your care for her."

"We do our best for our residents." She pressed a button. "Tiffany, please take Mrs. Streat to Mrs. Vogt's room."

Tiffany was a pretty twentysomething. She led me to the second floor where gracious country house style was mixed with the equipment for medical care. As we walked down the long hall hung with cheerful paintings, I could see patients lying in hospital beds covered with white blankets. A cart with medications, pushed by an attendant in a bright flowered smock, stopped at a door.

"Time for your pill, Mrs. Chandler," she called brightly.

In another room, a woman in a wheelchair was being helped to her feet. She was dressed neatly, her white hair curled, but there was a blank look on her face. Tiffany spoke to her. "You're looking lovely today, Mrs. Giles." And to me: "We keep our residents moving as much as possible."

At the end of the hall, she stopped at a door. "Have a nice visit. When you're ready to leave, just go to the nurse's station down the hall. I'll meet you there."

I nodded, relieved that guests were not allowed to wander freely.

The room was furnished like a good hotel, with repro furniture and floor-length curtains. Caroline was propped up with pillows, wearing her cashmere shawl over a cotton nightgown. She was staring at a television with no sound that showed cowboys around a campfire, but at least she was awake. I went over and kissed her cheek. She didn't move her head. After a long moment her eyes shifted toward me. "Emma?"

"I've been in France—why I didn't come sooner."

"France?"

"I went to France to see Pierre Hallam. You asked me to go there and talk to him," I said, and sat down on the edge of the bed.

She stared at me for a moment. "I know that name. He stole my mother's diamond bracelets. Gave them to that floozy in Palm Beach. I never saw him again." She pulled the shawl tightly around her shoulders. "You can go now. It's time for my show." Her eyes went back to the soundless television.

I stood up, wanting to put my head down on the bed and cry. There would be no grilling about Pierre Hallam and what I had found. Where had she gone, the feisty woman I had known all my life? A poor picker of husbands, but always ready to give advice or take the starch out of people with pretensions. Instead of lying here drugged to the eyeballs, she should be attending opening nights. Giving parties. Throwing her weight around on museum boards, not vulnerable to another attack. Who was still trying to harm her? Why? Any doubts I had about going on with my search were dissolving. Gone.

"Bastard," I said aloud. "I don't know who the hell you are or what you want, but if it's the last thing I do, you're going to pay. In full."

CHAPTER NINETEEN

It was after six when I walked into the Fifth Avenue apartment. No Delsey. No Minnie, Kathleen, or Cookie. Delsey had left a note:

I'll be here at nine tomorrow. Food in the refrigerator. We now have a concierge and a security guard at night.

The apartment was eerily empty and quiet. I made myself a sandwich and watched the evening news—nothing but more shootings and Calvin Fullerton exhorting the country to keep out immigrants. I went to bed early, tired, expecting to sleep well, but disturbing fragments kept rotating through my mind. Caroline's drugged eyes . . . the nonexistent brother who knew where she was.

Toward morning I dreamed I was back in my old house on the Connecticut River. The boys were sitting at the big round table in the kitchen doing homework. I was making lasagna, listening for the sound of the helicopter bringing Lewis home from the New York office.

As I woke, the illusion faded. The house was gone. Lewis was dead, and once more I was caught in a tangled web of responsibilities that I had never anticipated or wished for.

Delsey appeared at nine o'clock. "Sorry I wasn't here to let you in," she said. "How did you find Mrs. Vogt?"

"Drugged, not making sense, but that's not the worst. A man called saying he was her brother, wanting to know when she was leaving. That means someone is still after her. I had to tell the administrator. She began to talk about security. God help us if she decides Caroline must leave."

"This is not good news."

"No. Who knew she was going there?"

"Only the doctor. You. Me. The hired driver."

"Well, not much we can do. Were you able to get me an appointment at the detective agency? All the more reason to use them."

"Mr. Hanson is the top person. He'll see you at eleven. And I think you should call Mr. Langer. He says there are papers that have to be signed."

"I'll do it right now. I have Caroline's power of attorney, so that should give me some rights."

In Central Park, the bare trees were showing their first pale green, my favorite color in the seasonal palette. I sat down in the library, called Nickerson and Haversat, and was connected to Mr. Langer.

"It's Emma Streat," I said. "I'm back in New York. I hear you've been trying to reach Mrs. Vogt."

"I have, but her secretary isn't helpful and I'm worried. How is she?"

"Improving, but these neuralgia things take time," I said with a twinge of guilt. As her money manager, he had a right to know more. "Has anything come up?"

"Papers that need her signature. I've had her accounts scanned for hackers. Nothing so far, but cybercriminals are a problem and Mrs. Vogt is a major client." He paused. "About that blackmail. She might like to know I've made the million back with several good investments."

"I'll tell her, but losing that million is turning into a crusade with her, a matter of principle. She thinks it's important to fight blackmail, that people shouldn't be allowed to get away with it.

She's still hoping that the detective agency can find the culprit. Otherwise he may try again."

"Not likely. In fact, I'd say she's just wasting her money." A pause. "We could talk about it over lunch. Besides the papers, there are several other concerns."

"I can't do it today, I have to carry out her orders, but maybe tomorrow. I'll let you know." I clicked off and sat looking at a Sargent portrait. Something didn't seem right—but a gut feeling was no substitute for evidence.

Delsey was in the kitchen making coffee. "I just talked to Breck Langer," I said. "Tell me if I'm wrong, but I get the impression that you don't exactly like him."

She frowned and lifted the pot. "It's not for me to judge, but I know he's mean to people under him. Old Mr. Dexter was a real gentleman. Why do you ask?"

"No reason, but we're always hearing about money managers who figure they can help themselves to their rich clients' money and get away with it. Never mind. Right now, I'd better figure out what to tell this Mr. Hanson."

An hour later, I stood under the green entrance awning, glad to be out in the fresh warm air. Traffic streamed by. Two babies in strollers passed, pushed by mothers in leggings. Across the street in the park, forsythia was starting to bud into small yellow furls.

Charlie the doorman was helping an old lady out of an ancient Lincoln. This was going to take time. I'd better try to catch a passing taxi.

I stepped forward to the curb and raised my hand. A woman walked by, talking to a little boy with a backpack. A jogger was running behind her. He was wearing gray sweats and a red baseball cap with the visor pulled down. He dodged around the boy and careened into me, knocking me off balance. I teetered on the curb.

"*Watch* it," I snapped, and tried to turn. He grabbed my arm, twisted it, and threw me past the line of parked cars and out into the street. As I went down, I could see the round lights of a car coming at me. The monster wheels were inches from my face. Brakes screeched. There was a smell of asphalt and burning rubber.

I lay on my side, too dazed to move. A man leaned down and shoved his big face close to mine. "You crazy?" he yelled. "I coulda killed ya, I came *that* close." Horns began to blow.

"Mrs. Streat, what happened?" It was Charlie. "You hurt bad? Shall I call an ambulance?"

It took a few seconds to speak, but I was able to move my arms and legs. There was no pool of blood. "No ambulance," I whispered. "Apartment."

"Never touched her," the other man shouted over the noise. "Fell down in front of the van, coulda been a big accident, cars hitting each other. You know her?"

"Yeah, she lives in that building."

"Then take her away before the cops come. I'm outta here." Seconds later the van roared off.

The cars were still honking. Charlie put his hands under my shoulders, lifted me to my feet, and half carried me to the curb. A small crowd had gathered on the sidewalk, but there was no sign of the man with a red cap.

"That jogger pushed me," I croaked to Charlie as he helped me into the lobby. "Did you see it?"

He shook his head. "I was getting Mrs. Gould out of her car." He turned to the concierge. "Mrs. Streat had an accident, Harry. She fell in the street and she's real shocked, maybe hurt. I can't leave the door. You take her up and don't let her fall."

Elderly Harry put a tentative arm around me. As we got out on the fifth floor, he rang the bell. After a moment, Delsey appeared.

"Back so soon?" she began, then saw my scraped hands and knees. "Good heavens, what happened to you?"

"Charlie says she had an accident, fell down in the street, she may be hurt bad," Harry said.

"I'll see to her." Delsey closed the door. Taking my arm, she propelled me to my bed and took off my shoes. "Does anything hurt? Should I get help?"

"No. I was waiting for a cab . . . this big jogger came by . . . he threw me into the street . . . the wheels were so close . . ."

Delsey gasped. "He threw you—are you saying that jogger did it on purpose?"

"Yes." I couldn't go on.

"I'll get hot tea." She disappeared. In a moment she was back. "Chamomile," she said, handing me a mug. "First Mrs. Vogt, now you. Were you able to get a look at him?"

"A glimpse. He was tall, he wore a red baseball cap. He must have been waiting. He knew I was going out. He . . . he . . ."

"Well, it could have been worse. I'll call Mr. Hanson and say you'll be in touch later. Try to rest."

She left. I lay still under the down comforter, trying to control the shivers. A street accident—the classic way to kill without leaving a trace. It had happened so quickly, the sudden blow, the horror of being crushed under those wheels. The attempt had failed, but who wanted me dead? Would he try again?

I lay there, eyes closed, but after a while my mind began to function. Twice in the past, I had almost been killed. I had survived, not by cowering in bed, but by summoning up my wits. No use calling the police, and locking myself up in the apartment for weeks on end was not an option.

In the past I might have turned to Rodale for help, but I had burned my bridges that day at the mill, telling him to use other women for his dirty work. He hadn't lashed out. Instead, he had warned me that I might be followed, to throw away my phone, and to stop asking questions. I'd done none of those things, but I had the name he had given me. "He's in your Secret Service. He's very good."

My handbag was lying on the floor. Stiffly, I got off the bed, picked it up, and shook out the contents: the lip gloss, the old receipts and lozenges. Rodale's card was wedged into a side pocket. The name, Michael Howard, and a number were written in Rodale's scrawl. I read it twice, then lifted the receiver of the landline phone by the bed. Dialed the number, and was asked to leave a message.

"You don't know me," I began, "but a colleague said to call you if I was in trouble. He has a country place in Wiltshire. His London house is in Upper Brook Street. I'm in New York, in the city, and someone just tried to kill me. Please call me at this landline number."

It was done, the step was taken. I went into the bathroom, splashed cold water on my scraped face, and limped to Delsey's office.

"You're supposed to be resting," she said.

"I tried, but I remembered I had the name of a man in our Secret Service. I called him, asked for help, and left a message."

"The Secret Service? I thought they mostly protected big names." She swiveled around in her chair and went online. "Here it is. Secret Service comes under the Department of Homeland Security, a branch of the US Treasury. Over a hundred field offices in this country. They're also into financial crimes, telecommunication fraud, fund transfers, computer crime—I didn't know they did all those things."

"Neither did I. Anyhow, I'm not getting my hopes up. He may not get the message. He may not answer. He could be out of the country or on assignment in Alaska or Oshkosh. If I don't hear back, I'll have to make another plan. Maybe get a bodyguard for whenever I go out."

Four hours later, the landline phone on the bedside table began to ring. I took a deep breath and picked it up.

"Is this Mrs. Streat?"

"Yes, it is."

"Agent Howard here. I got your call and I've talked to your colleague. You say the situation is urgent. Maybe I can help. Where are you now?"

"In an apartment on Fifth Avenue."

"I'm not too far away. I could be with you at eight tonight."

"That would be . . . thank you."

"Give me the address. By the way, I'm using the name John Morton."

"I'll be expecting you." I gave him the address, replaced the receiver, and hurried to find Delsey. "He called. The agent actually called. He's coming here at eight."

"Good." She hesitated. "I've been thinking. You shouldn't be alone tonight. I can leave now, get my mother settled with a neighbor, and be back by seven."

"Oh, Delsey. Are you sure?"

"I'll tell them downstairs no one is to come up while I'm gone, no matter what reason they give."

"I won't open the door to anyone but you."

"You need to eat. I'll leave soup on the stove. There's salad in the refrigerator."

She left. I put the kettle on and sat down at the kitchen table. The Secret Service agents I had seen on television wore dark suits. Their faces were expressionless, their eyes darted from side to side. Agent Howard had sounded competent and pleasant. Whatever Rodale told him hadn't stopped him from coming.

Waiting was never easy for me. At six, I ate a little soup, then paced through the big rooms. I could take him into Caroline's drawing room with its group of gilded Louis XIV chairs—no, it had better be the library and I must be professional and precise. Lay out the bare bones of the situation, not babble a lot of extraneous facts.

When the landline phone rang, I grabbed it. "Yes?"

"Mrs. Streat, it's the concierge. Mrs. Delsey Whitten is on her way up. She said to tell you."

I went to the front door and looked through the peephole. She came in carrying a small suitcase and a bag of groceries.

"I stopped at the deli and got more food. Plenty for breakfast. If there's nothing you need me to do, I'll make up the bed in Minnie's room. I'll be in my office while he's here."

"Delsey, you've done so much. Oh God, I don't want to act like a drama queen, but it's like history repeating itself. First Caroline, now me. Someone wants both of us dead—and we don't know *who* or *why*."

CHAPTER TWENTY

It was ten after eight when the concierge called to say that a Mr. Morton was at the desk. "Please send him up," I said, and went to let him in.

The man who stood there was about my height, thin, with pale skin and very dark hair and eyes. Instead of the standard navy suit, he was wearing a tan jacket and a black T-shirt. He looked like an actor or an artist, a creative type who would read the *New Yorker* from cover to cover, and he was carrying a dog the size of a large cat. Its button eyes were bright under a fringe of black hair.

"Mrs. Streat? I'm Agent Howard and this is Ralph. I hope you like dogs. Taking him with me is good cover and his feet won't touch the floor."

"I love dogs," I said and rubbed Ralph's ear. He wriggled and licked my hand as if I was his new best friend. "What kind is he?"

"A Havanese. There are quite a few of them around."

"He's very welcome," I said, and led the way to the library.

We sat down. He kept Ralph on his knee and looked at me. "I was told that you were with a cybercrime operation in France and have had some experience in the intelligence field," he said. "Tell me what happened today. From the beginning."

"It's complicated, the background story, but this morning at about ten thirty I was standing near the front door, trying to get a taxi. A man—a jogger—came by and pushed me into the street.

He meant to kill me, or at least make sure I was badly hurt. I wasn't, but I'm afraid he may try again."

"Would you be able to recognize him?"

"I doubt it. He was wearing a cap pulled down over his face, but he was tall and strong."

"I see." He hesitated. "You say the story is complicated, but I'd like to hear it. Take your time and give me the full picture."

His easy manner went a long way to ease the stress. I went through the list of disasters. The blackmail note. The attack on my godmother. The fact that I got no information from her ex-husband in France. My determination to go on with the investigation, using her detective agency. Today's attack on me.

He listened, stroking Ralph's ears. "What you say indicates that you've been tracked. For instance, who knew you were going to use a detective agency?"

"No one except Delsey, my godmother's assistant. I called her from Boston to get me an appointment."

"You called her from a phone you've been using for some time?"

"Yes. I did."

"Tracking can start by contaminating a phone. May I test the one you're using?"

I picked it up from the table and gave it to him. He wrapped it in a handkerchief, put it in his pocket, and handed me another. "From now on use this, but keep in mind that all your communications will be changed into military-grade cypher text, unreadable except with a code which I'll give you. We'll monitor your incoming and outgoing calls. With your permission, of course."

"Of course. But why should anyone want to silence me or my godmother? That's what I can't understand. It all started when she got that blackmail note."

"That may be, but you answered her call for help. You went to France to ask questions and became involved in a high-level cybercrime investigation. You returned and went on asking questions. Keep in mind that these people want to cover their tracks. Their greatest fear is exposure. If they see you as a threat, they'll go to great lengths to keep that from happening. They have advanced electronic surveillance tools. They hire hit men."

"So asking questions about the blackmail note could make me a threat to cybercriminals?"

"It's possible. Too soon to tell, but I'd say your situation has more to do with money than terrorists or international bad actors. Cybercriminals make billions out of extracting money, laundering it, and lining their pockets." He paused. "How was the blackmail paid?"

"My godmother ordered her money manager to pay the million." I hesitated. "If you think this is a case of following the money, it wouldn't hurt to run a check on him."

"Why?"

"Several things. For one, she told him she was being blackmailed and that she was going to a detective agency to see if her ex-husband was behind it. He was quite defensive. Insisted his firm could handle the investigation better."

"Did she contact the agency?"

"No. She didn't have a chance. That night she was attacked. This morning when I was on my way to that agency, I was attacked."

"This manager. What's his name?"

"Breck Langer. He works for Nickerson and Haversat. It's an old brokerage firm. Very respectable. Lots of rich clients."

"Do you happen to have the blackmail note or a copy?"

"Here." I handed him the copy Delsey had made. Watched his thin, finely shaped hands as he read it. He didn't look like a man who could wrestle an opponent to the ground, but maybe brains made up for brawn. He had a quiet way of drawing people out that evoked confidence.

"I'll keep this." He put it in his pocket and looked at his watch. "I must be off, but I'll have a smart young techie check your phone, then see what he can dig up about tracing that million."

"Will it take long?"

"Not for this young man. Perhaps a few hours. I'll get back to you with any results."

"Thank you for coming," I said as we stood up. "To be honest, I didn't know what to do, then I remembered I had your name. I was afraid I might not hear from you at all."

"I respect our mutual colleague. Aside from that, I don't like it when women are knocked into the street." He handed me a card. "This number will reach me twenty-four seven. Don't hesitate to use it."

"I won't," I said, taking it. He reminded me of a memorable coach I'd worked with years ago. I hadn't expected to find as much empathy in a federal agent.

We walked to the elevator. Ralph squirmed around and looked at me. "I'm glad to have met you, Ralph," I said. Reached out and patted the soft little head. He licked my hand, the button eyes begging for friendship.

"He likes you," Agent Howard said. "I know it's not easy, but try not to worry."

"I'll try." We shook hands. The elevator came up, he stepped in and was gone.

Delsey was still at the computer, dealing with Caroline's numerous boards and properties. She turned. "How did it go?"

"You won't believe this," I said, "but he was dressed like an actor and he was carrying the most adorable little dog. Good cover, he said, and it works. No one would ever take him for an agent."

"Was he any help?"

"God, yes. Far more than I expected. He listened to the whole story, start to finish. He took my phone to see if it was contaminated, one way to follow me, and he's going to look into that blackmail note. It may only take a few hours."

"They'll have resources." She closed the computer and stood up. "How are you feeling?"

"A little bruised. I'm going to take a long, hot bath, get into bed and read, and hope that he calls. Thanks, thanks again for staying with me."

"Well, it seemed best. I'll see you in the morning." A self-contained woman whose expression seldom changed. In the past two weeks she had become a good friend.

Once in bed, I tried to read, but the meeting with Agent Howard kept revolving in my head. Where had he grown up? Did he have a family? He looked as if he might have Spanish blood. There was something of a matador about him, the taut thinness, the quiet authority, but I'd be naïve to expect too much. When push came to shove, it was action, not empathy, that counted.

It was after eleven when my new phone rang. I reached for it and pushed a button. "Yes?"

"Agent Howard here. To start, your phone was contaminated, which is why you could have been tracked."

"Oh, shit."

"Exactly, but there's more. We checked the lead you gave us on Mr. Langer. Preliminary findings, but you were right to want him investigated. He collected the million dollars that was supposed to go to a bank."

"My God." My hand went to my throat. "Oh my God. Are you sure?"

"I won't go into specifics, but it looks as if he's taking money from Mrs. Vogt's accounts—and others—and sending them to an offshore bank in the Channel Islands. Illegally acquired money laundered there often comes back to shell companies here."

I sat straight up in bed. "This is bad. *Really* bad. What happens now?"

"What happens is that Langer is a person of interest. His phones will be tapped. He'll be put under surveillance. He's probably not working alone, and we want names that may lead us to bigger fish."

I threw off the covers as anger surged. That miserable, rotten, smooth bastard—I could see him sitting in the library, eating cucumber sandwiches and lying through his teeth.

"This is hard to believe," I gritted. "Hard to believe he'd take such a risk."

"It's likely that he's following orders. We'll use him to try to infiltrate what could be a significant network."

I swallowed. If Langer was taking orders from a cybercrime network with resources, the job of outing them was just beginning—and the case might not have priority in an overworked agency.

"I understand," I said, "but that could take weeks, even months. He has to be stopped before he can do more harm."

"We'll do our best. In the meantime, we'll lay on security for you."

"Wait." I pushed back my hair. My mind was working fast. "I just had a thought. Never mind security. You want names and I might be able to get them."

"How?"

"We talked earlier before the attack. He asked me to have lunch with him today, but I said maybe tomorrow, I'd let him know. So we have lunch. I bring up the matter of the blackmail note. He'll tell me again not to worry, he's already made enough money to cover the loss. That's when I go for the jugular. I'll say I'm sorry, but detectives are already looking into that million. Do it in a friendly way and assume he's willing to help. Ask if they've called him yet with questions. Not what he wants to hear. Wouldn't that send him hurrying to pass on information?"

Agent Howard cleared his throat. "I'm not saying it can't be done, but there are risks."

"Such as?"

"It wouldn't be easy to pull this off. You could end up being even more of a threat."

"I know, but when I think of my godmother lying drugged in a rehab place, I'd risk a lot more than this. Besides, I used to be on the stage. If it works, it would save you a lot of time and effort."

Silence. I could sense wheels turning. "Okay," he said at last. "You raised the red flag, so you should be given a chance. Call him in the morning. If lunch is on, let me know and I'll arrange for security and give you instructions. This has to be done well or not at all."

It was getting late, but Delsey must hear this startling news. I went through the kitchen and knocked on Minnie's door.

"I'm sorry if you're asleep, Delsey, but Agent Howard just called with something you have to hear."

Delsey put her head around the door. She had taken off the heavy makeup, and her white hair, no longer in a ponytail, fell to her shoulders. She was wearing a long nightgown printed with butterflies.

"You won't believe this," I said, "but Breck Langer took that million and maybe more."

Delsey's hand went to her mouth. "What? Are they sure?"

"They must be. He's a low-life, sneaky, miserable bastard, but at least now we know about him."

"But to risk losing his job when he's got that sick boy on his hands—"

"What's wrong with his boy?"

"Some kind of seizures. Treatments cost a fortune. His mother takes him to a lot of different specialists. What will they do to Mr. Langer?"

"They think he's working for a network. They want names. Anyhow, we'll know more tomorrow." I touched her shoulder. "There's nothing we can do tonight—I should have waited, not upset you."

"No, it's better to know."

By now it was nearly midnight. I got into bed and lay there, unable to sleep, but resisting the temptation to take a sleeping pill. If we met for lunch tomorrow, I must have a clear head. Be ready to eat, smile, and extract evidence that would rip that rotten bastard to pieces. Tiny little pieces.

CHAPTER TWENTY-ONE

April 10

I woke with a sense that my mission had taken on a new dimension. No more working blindly on my own. Agent Howard could provide important resources, but first I would have to convince him that I had the necessary skills—and that it was in his best interest to support me.

It took willpower to wait until nine thirty before calling Langer to tell him I was free for lunch today.

"I'll look forward to it," he said. "There's a restaurant called Geraldine's on East Sixty-Eighth Street. It's quiet and the food is good. Will one o'clock suit you?"

"Fine. I'll be there."

Agent Howard was quick to respond. "I'll arrange for an agent to come to your apartment. He'll drive you there and back. By the way, there'll be a tail on Langer, a dapper young fellow. Don't look around for him."

"I hope I know better than that."

"Sorry. Your looks are a bit deceptive. One last word. Don't worry if Langer doesn't react. We'll find other ways to smoke him out. No need to push him too hard."

"We'll both be putting on an act. Remains to be seen who does it best."

"Call me as soon as you're back in the car."

"I will," I said, deeply relieved. Most agents would have tried to talk me out of this meeting or insisted on getting a green light from someone higher up. Agent Howard had proved that he could turn on a dime. Think out of the box.

My driver, Duncan, had a square jaw and the military look of an ex-Marine. At ten after one, I took a deep breath and walked into Geraldine's. Langer was waiting at the small bar near the entrance. As I came in, he smiled and came forward.

"Sorry if I'm late," I said. "The taxi driver went two blocks out of the way and couldn't turn."

"It happens. Glad you could make it."

The maître d' appeared. "*Bonjour*, madame, monsieur," he said, and led us to a table halfway down the narrow room. I slid onto a velvet banquette and put my bag on the floor. The elegant gilded mirrors and dark red brocade walls reminded me of Paris.

Langer settled himself opposite. He was wearing a dark suit, blue tie, and a striped blue-and-white shirt. A good-looking man with hazel eyes and a strong chin with a cleft. A model of success. The best I could do in the way of clothes was the old black trouser suit, but a quick rummage through Caroline's lesser jewelry had produced an eye-catching pin shaped like a tiger's head.

"What will you have to drink?" he asked.

"Just a spritzer with lemon."

"Two spritzers with lemon," he told the hovering waiter.

Our drinks came, along with a large menu written in French with no prices. I studied it with steady hands.

"The mussels here are good, if you like mussels," he said. "What about an appetizer?"

"Just the coquilles Saint Jacques and the *salade frisee*. This is a treat after fending for myself in the apartment."

"You must be missing Mrs. Vogt. What's the latest news?"

"She's doing better, thanks."

"Quite an amazing lady. Any word when she'll be back?"

"Soon, I hope, because I need to get home." Was he the one who had called Woods House pretending to be her brother? How had he known she was there?

The waiter placed food before us as if offering gifts. I picked up my fork and took a few bites. "Delicious. I love French food. Luckily Boston has some very good restaurants."

"A very manageable city, but do you ever think about moving to New York? If I remember, your boys are both away in college."

"They are." I smiled. "Tell me about *your* boys. I know one plays squash, but you said something about the other not being into sports."

"Understatement. Jimmy has a disease that gives him seizures, a rare kind of epilepsy. Most people have never heard of it. One specialist after another. He's a brave kid, hardly ever complains."

"So difficult for you and your family."

"These things can bring couples together. Not in our case. My ex-wife pretty much spends all her time with Jimmy. I pay the bills and try to keep Davey on an even keel. Be available to take him to games." He shook his head. "Sorry. I shouldn't talk about my problems, but my boys mean a lot to me."

"No need to apologize. I've never had to cope with anything as painful, but my boys mean a lot to me, too. Top priority since my husband died."

"How long ago was that?"

"A little over a year. Caroline has been a big support, she's been like a mother, but it takes a while to adjust. Move on."

"Well, you seem to be managing."

Around us, well-dressed people were talking quietly. No one seemed to be on display or watching for the next celebrity to make an entrance.

"Do you come here often?" I asked, wanting to change the subject.

"Only with clients or their goddaughters. To be honest, I'm a boy from the wrong side of the tracks in New Jersey. Brought up on macaroni and cheese."

I laughed. "Can't beat macaroni and cheese." My initial assessment was right. He had worked his way up to an enviable job—one with temptations as well as rewards.

"What about you? Where did you grow up?" he asked as if deeply interested. The charm was being turned on. I told him about my family, but as we finished the main course, my neck began to tense. It was time to make the plunge.

"Dessert? Coffee?" he asked.

"Just coffee. Oh, before I forget, I'd better give you this," I said, and retrieved a tax form from my bag. "My godmother's assistant wanted you to have it."

"Thanks." He hesitated. "When you see Mrs. Vogt, tell her not to worry about that money she paid to the blackmailer. I went ahead and asked our experts to investigate. There should be a report from them soon, another reason I wanted to get in touch with her."

The arrival of the waiter with coffee gave me a few seconds to think. I put my elbows on the table and went for the jugular. "I'll let her know," I said, "but I'm afraid you'd be wasting your time. She called in that detective agency she uses."

"She did?"

"What's more, her assistant had a call from a Secret Service agent. For some reason they're investigating that transaction."

Langer's expression didn't change, but his shoulders tightened. "I wish I'd been told right away."

"I figured it could wait until lunch. Besides, Delsey and I assumed the agent had already been in touch with you. After all, it's your account."

"He hasn't, but if he does, he'll get the same answer. Except for the blackmail and the threat, it was a simple transaction."

I shook my head. "Maybe so, but Caroline doesn't see it that way. Knowing her, she'll call in the marines, to find out who took that million. This is only the start of what she's prepared to do." I sat back and took a sip of coffee. I mustn't overplay my part.

Langer put a lump of sugar in his cup and drank it down with a steady hand. "More coffee for you?"

"No, thanks."

"If you're sure." He looked at his watch and motioned to the waiter to bring the bill. "That's the trouble with lunches, they always end too soon. It's half past two and I have a meeting at three."

"I understand. By the way, where *is* your office? Caroline never told me."

"Rockefeller Center. Opposite direction from you, but I'll see you into a taxi."

"No taxi. I'm going to walk off that good food. Thanks so much."

"My pleasure, as they say. We must do it again soon."

I picked up my bag and stood up. The maître d' bowed us to the door. As we passed the bar, I saw a young man get down from his stool.

A taxi was coming down the street. Langer waved at it and turned. "About that tax form. I'll look into it and be in touch." He jumped into the taxi and was gone.

Seconds later, the inconspicuous blue sedan slid to the curb. Duncan leaned around and opened the door. "Any problem?" he asked. "That guy sure left in a rush."

"Yes. He sure did." I pulled out my encrypted phone and pressed the number for Agent Howard.

"Where are you now?" he asked.

"With Duncan. Heading back to the apartment."

"How did it go?"

"He talked about his boys. Unless he's a superb actor, he loves those boys. All very normal until he said he'd asked the experts in his firm to look into the blackmail note. That gave me an opening. I told him my godmother had already called in detectives. Then I went out on a limb and told him that the Secret Service was investigating the transaction."

"And?"

"He never lost his cool, but I think it hit a nerve. He swallowed his coffee, said he had a meeting with a client, and dashed off. What happens now?"

"We'll listen to see if he makes any calls. Keep him under surveillance." A pause. "Good work. Don't go out. I'll let you know if there are any results."

CHAPTER TWENTY-TWO

There was no one in the apartment when I got back—Delsey had left earlier to look after her mother. I went into the library and collapsed on the sofa. The coquilles Saint Jacques was sitting like a stone in my stomach and I felt sick. When had the stealing started? The man had to be stopped, but he was a caring father, supporting a challenged son. I had tightened the noose around his neck, but it was not in my nature to lay traps and tell lies. My parents would be appalled.

The landline phone beside me began to ring. I picked it up. "Mrs. Vogt's residence," I said, a way for me to avoid unwanted calls.

"It's Breck Langer. Are you alone?" He sounded out of breath, as if he'd been running.

My queasy stomach did a quick roll. "I'm alone in the library," I said cautiously. "Thanks again for taking me to Geraldine's. It was a real treat—"

"Oh Christ, forget the act. There's going to be an accident."

I sat up, every sense on high alert. "To me?"

"To me. That way my boys get the insurance. They won't have to see their father go to prison."

My hand went to my head. There was no mistaking his meaning. "Wait. Where are you?"

"At a phone bank. I'm being followed. I'll have to talk fast, but there are things you should know. Jimmy needed special treatments. I was over my head in debt. There's a place that does loans, no questions asked, but it must have sold my name to a network of cybercriminals. Last October I got a call telling me to skim accounts. Send the money to a bank in the Channel Islands or Davey would be hit by a car on his way to school. They knew the school. Davey always walks."

"My God," I said. "That's . . . that's blackmail."

"I had that note delivered by hand to Mrs. Vogt, then it all went wrong. I couldn't let her call in a detective agency. Or you. I hired a hit man. He failed, but you're still a target. They got into your phone. Recorded every call except for a gap when you were in France. They know where you are at all times."

I clutched the receiver. Somehow, I must keep him talking. "They? You must have a name—something—"

"It's a big organization with thick firewalls, but I have one name. Lonny Mariano. He operates out of a school in New Jersey. Find him." A pause for breath. "I'm telling you because you have boys. Do what you can to make this look like an accident. It has to look like an accident." The line disconnected.

I dropped the phone and stood there, telling myself not to panic. How would it happen? Gas oven? Slit wrists—no, that wouldn't be an accident. I pulled out my new phone and punched in the number for Agent Howard.

He answered. "I just had a call from Breck Langer," I said, struggling for a calm voice. "He's about to kill himself, I don't know how, but he wants it to look like an accident. For the sake of his boys, but I don't understand. I thought he was being followed."

"The tail lost him. Any idea where he was?"

"He said he was calling from a phone bank. He wanted me to know he was being blackmailed to skim accounts—"

"A phone bank. Tell me later."

I put down the phone and walked over to a window. Took hold of the brocade curtain and ran my nails along the fabric. Less than two hours ago Breck Langer was sitting in a restaurant, eating mussels, talking to me about his boys. Now this. I might have helped drive a man to commit suicide, but he had called and given me a lead to follow.

It was after five when the phone rang. It was Agent Howard. "Bad news, but we were expecting it. After he left you at the restaurant, he went to his office. Stayed a few minutes, made no calls, then left by the main entrance to Rockefeller Center. Crossed the side street and ducked into a building. Knew where to find a bank of pay phones, not many of those left. That's where the tail lost him."

"Where did he do it?"

"The subway station at Forty-Second Street. Times Square. A busy place, always crowded, why he picked it. He fell off the platform in front of a northbound train. The police questioned bystanders. No one was sure whether he was jostled, but that can happen."

I swallowed. Like a camera rolling, I could see him standing on the platform surrounded by people, the headlight of the oncoming train coming closer. There would be a few seconds of doubt as he gathered the will to jump. A few seconds of agony, then nothing.

Agent Howard cleared his throat. "He called you. What did he say?"

"A lot. He was in debt, he went to loan sharks. A man named Lonny Mariano contacted him and gave him orders to skim accounts and send them to a bank in the Channel Islands. If he didn't, one of his boys would be killed on the way to school—oh God, those poor boys. I was furious about the way he fooled my godmother, I wanted to punish him, but I lied when I told him that the Secret Service had contacted Delsey. I may have pushed him over the edge."

"No guilt. You saw a disconnect and acted on it. He was facing prison. Disgrace on every level. Now we know he was linked to cybercriminals who use an offshore bank. That's a start."

"Are the police calling it an accident?"

"So far they're treating it as an accidental death, but the insurance companies will have to investigate. In the meantime, we'll start work on that name and the location of the school. Did he say anything else?"

"He said that I'd been followed, and I was still a target. Why am I such a threat?"

"We've been over the reasons. Now there's another. Langer gave you information before he jumped. That hit man is still unidentified. Until we round up these people, you should have around-the-clock protection."

"You mean, a bodyguard living in the apartment?"

"Well, someone who has training. I know a woman who's on leave from the NYPD. Her name is Peggy McCarthy. Her husband was a detective, killed in a drug raid a few months ago. She has a gun permit and a black belt in karate. I can contact her and see if she's free to come pronto. Okay?"

"I guess so."

"In the meantime, don't take on guilt." He hesitated. "I once had to organize an entrapment. It wasn't pretty. I got through it by putting myself in the shoes of the victims. The ones who'd already suffered. The ones who would suffer if the perp wasn't taken down. Hold that thought." He clicked off.

I closed my eyes. Would I be a prisoner in this big apartment for weeks? Not even allowed to run in the park? Not long ago, I had taken my boys skiing on their spring break. Dear God, I would sell my soul to be sweeping down the slopes in great curves, snow flying. Breathing in the cold pure air until I felt clean again.

CHAPTER TWENTY-THREE

At five o'clock, Delsey came back. I waited until she was in her office, then went to tell her the news about Breck Langer. She listened in stoic silence, then shook her head. "I think he did the right thing for his boys. Avoided a big scandal."

"As long as the media doesn't hear about it. Delsey, there's more. Agent Howard wants me to have protection around the clock. An armed ex-policewoman may be coming to stay. I hope it won't be for long, but at least you won't have to spend the night."

"An armed policewoman. Well, she can have the yellow guest room. I'll make the beds and get in more food."

I was back in the library when my phone rang again. "Mrs. Streat? It's Peggy McCarthy. I just talked to Agent Howard. I can be with you at seven, but I want to make sure you're expecting me."

"Oh. Yes, I am. I'll see you later." The woman had a Queens or Brooklyn accent. I would have to be pleasant and make polite conversation, but I wanted, desperately, to curl up in a ball and sleep.

At a little after seven, the concierge called to say that Mrs. McCarthy was at the desk. "Please send her up," I said and went to the elevator to meet her.

The woman who stepped out was about my height. A tough-looking tinted blonde with brown eyes and a pointed chin. She was wearing a fitted dark suit that looked like a police uniform without the insignia.

"Mrs. McCarthy," I said, holding out my hand. "I'm glad to see you. Please come in."

"Thanks, but you can skip the Mrs. McCarthy. Peggy will do." She looked around. "Nice. I've always wondered what these places looked like."

"It's my godmother's apartment, I just come to visit. I'll show you to your room, then take you to meet Delsey. She's my godmother's assistant and she really knows the place. She can answer any questions."

"Good, because I should have a look around."

I waited in the kitchen while Delsey showed Peggy the various security panels. Peggy wasn't impressed. "You don't have an up-to-date alarm system," she said to Delsey.

"After a man broke in two weeks ago, I started looking into one, but it's still not installed." Delsey turned to me. "There's food for two ready to heat up. If that's all, I'll be going along."

"Of course. See you in the morning—and thanks for everything."

She left. I took a deep breath and looked at my watch. "Would you like a drink? Or shall we eat? It won't be anything fancy, just soup and salad. We can take trays to the library."

"Whatever you say." She put a hand on the kitchen table. "Let's get one thing straight. I've never done this kind of work before, but I owed Agent Howard a favor. From what he told me, the last thing you need is more stress. What I mean is, I won't be in your hair. I've got my iPad. I can watch movies in my room, and I'll get up and check things during the night. You just rest and forget about me."

It was hard to hide a surge of relief. The tough-sounding woman had sensitivity. We would get along—and I should have had more faith in Agent Howard's judgment.

"I have to admit, I've just about had it," I said. "I'll get something to eat and then crash. Do you mind if we forget about trays and just eat here?"

"Suits me."

We made tea and sat down at the table with the deli soups and salads. The tension between us was disappearing. I learned that Peggy had trained at a police academy. Her father was a police sergeant in Hoboken and an uncle was a "loot" in this city's eighth precinct. Police work was in her blood.

"How long have you known Agent Howard?" I asked.

"About three years. It started when he and Al, my husband who was killed, were on a drug bust. Michael used to come to our house. Watch the Yankees, drink beer."

"Does he have family?"

"If he does, he never talks about them. It's just the dog and his work on cybercrime. He takes on a lot. Maybe too much. He doesn't follow the rules, but the brass goes along because he gets results. His cases get priority."

"Let's hope this one does, and he can locate that school."

"Let's hope. You try to sleep. Call me if you need anything."

"Thanks. I will." I almost staggered back to my room and lay down. Exhaustion was setting in along with an avalanche of emotions. Guilt about Langer . . . pity for his boys . . . the sense of being caged for weeks on end. I had been in painful situations before, but this one had a new dimension: the power of technology in the hands of cybercriminals. I had lost control of my life—and there was no way to know if or when I would get it back.

CHAPTER TWENTY-FOUR

April 11

It was one of those long, white nights. I turned restlessly from side to side, unable to silence my brain. My legs cramped. At a little after nine in the morning, I got out of bed, took a long shower, put on my neglected running sweats, and went into the kitchen.

Delsey and Peggy were sitting at the table, drinking coffee and scanning the newspapers. "Anything about Langer?" I asked, reaching for a mug.

"Not much," Peggy said. "Just a paragraph about a broker falling under a train."

"Well, at least they're not calling it a suicide."

Delsey shook her head. "His firm will be upset. I'll have to call Mr. Haversat, one of the partners, and see who's going to replace him."

I nodded. "When you do, ask about funeral arrangements. Caroline would want to send flowers or give a donation."

"How are you going to break the news to her?" Delsey asked.

"Oh Lord. I'll call Woods House and get a report. If she's still sedated, she won't be reading the papers."

"Maybe that's just as well," Delsey said and left.

Peggy folded the papers and looked at me. "How are you feeling? Did you sleep?"

"To be honest, not too well. I'm just beginning to realize that cybercrime has a long reach and I was stupid. I was warned about being followed, but I never thought it could happen to me."

"No, you never do." She stood up. "Your breakfast. What would you like?"

"Just toast and fruit. I'll get it." I hesitated. "I'm sorry if I spoke out of turn. Agent Howard told me your husband was killed not long ago."

"He left in the morning and never came back. Everyone in the force knows it can happen, but you're never prepared."

"No, you're not. Mine was run down near our house in Connecticut. It was looking for his murderer that got me started with intelligence agencies."

"Agent Howard told me you had some experience. Well, they say it gets easier with time." A pause. "I did a couple of tours during the night. This place, it's like a museum, all the paintings."

"My godmother collects. She's quite a character. Everything seems empty without her. In fact, I'd better go and make that call to Woods House. See how she is."

"You do whatever you have to do. Forget I'm here."

Back in my room, I called Woods House, and after skirmishing with a nurse, I was put through to Caroline's room.

"Caroline," I said loudly. "It's Emma."

"Who?"

"Emma. Your goddaughter."

"No. My goddaughter's name is Emma. She never comes to see me." A slurred voice. "I want to go home." Her voice trailed away.

"Mrs. Streat?" The nurse again. "I'm afraid Mrs. Vogt has gone back to sleep."

"She must be getting too much medication."

"We have to follow her doctor's orders, Mrs. Streat. You could speak to him."

"I will," I said, tamping down additional guilt. I should be going to Woods House and throwing my weight around.

The day dragged on. I contacted my boys to say I was staying in New York for a while. Answered neglected emails and waited for Agent Howard's call.

It came at three o'clock. "Good news. We've located that school. It's listed as a rehab place for troubled boys. There's a plan, and I'd like to come by around five and talk."

"Fine. I'm not going anywhere."

He arrived at a little after five looking like a successful Wall Street broker. White shirt open at the neck, tailored blazer with a logo on the pocket, polished Gucci loafers. Ralph had on an African bead collar that matched his lead.

"I see you've changed your cover," I said as he stepped out of the elevator. "You look like you're coming to buy the apartment."

"That's the idea. Not to be recognized."

As Peggy appeared, Agent Howard gave her a mock salute. "Hardship assignment?"

"Ghetto duty. Do you want me in on this meeting?" The easy exchange of old friends.

"By all means."

We walked down the hall to the library. "Something to drink?" I asked.

"No, thanks, can't stay long."

We sat down. "Here's the situation," he began. "It'll be a raid, using a number of resources including the FBI and a SWAT team. We'll take whoever is there into custody. Begin investigations. Collect evidence."

I nodded.

"This is where you come in, Mrs. Streat. I realize it's asking a lot of you, but we'd like you to be there on the chance that you could identify the attacker."

I hesitated. "That's not likely, it really isn't. I never saw a face, only a shape."

"Understood, but it's worth a try. Even a shape can lead to

questions. An agent can pick you up here, take you to the school, and be with you in a car when we bring out the perps. Give you a good chance to look. There wouldn't be any danger."

"As long as you don't expect too much. I'd do almost anything to get out of this apartment—no offense to Peggy. She's been great."

She smiled. "No offense taken."

"Right. An FBI agent will pick you up at the back elevator at eight thirty. Eat a good breakfast and bring extra food and water. If all goes well, you should be back here by midafternoon." He turned to Peggy. "Any questions?"

"Plenty. What more can you tell us about the operation?"

"We'll meet at a designated place for briefing. The plan is for me and a second agent to go in posing as state school inspectors. We observe the layout. Make an assessment. We leave and the SWAT team takes over."

"Makes sense," Peggy said.

"Good." He looked at his watch, tucked Ralph under his arm, and stood up. "I'm off. Still a lot to do."

"I can imagine," I said. "I'll see you to the elevator." As we walked down the hall, I could see that he was very tired. Not surprising. A lot was resting on those thin shoulders.

We reached the elevator. "You seem to have thought of everything," I said, wanting to reassure him.

"Remains to be seen. It's always the unexpected, the one missing detail that can kill an operation."

"But not tomorrow."

"No." He frowned. "There's no margin for error tomorrow."

CHAPTER TWENTY-FIVE

April 12

It was going to be a long day. At six in the morning, I turned on the radio and listened to the weather report. Sunny, then afternoon showers. Temperature in the fifties.

Dressing for a raid suggested something inconspicuous. I pulled on the black trousers and a black sweater. Packed my carryall with three energy bars, two bottles of water, my phone, and a small hairbrush.

At eight twenty-five, I went down in the freight elevator with Peggy. A gray Toyota sedan was waiting at the back entrance. A man got out. He had dark hair, cut very short, and a nose that was out of proportion with his face.

"Special Agent Roehm, FBI." He pulled out a wallet and showed his badge. "You might as well sit in front."

We didn't speak as Agent Roehm negotiated his way through the traffic. I stared at the crowds of people hurrying to work, the life's blood of the city. People who would never in their lives be asked to take part in a police raid.

Travel by car seldom took me south of New York; it was over a year since I had crossed the George Washington bridge, high above the wide sweep of the Hudson River. As we reached the New Jersey side, I turned to Agent Roehm. "Where do we go from here?"

"I take the Garden State to 287, get off at the Bedlington exit. Not far from there." Not a talkative fellow.

We passed through endless sprawls of factories and commercial buildings. After a while I decided to break the silence. "What happens when we get there? Do I stay with you?"

"My instructions are to hand you over to another agent." From the tone of his voice, no more questions. I'd have liked diversion, but this was an operation for professionals only. I must stay out of the way and let them do their work. In the end, I might have nothing to contribute, but my tension was growing. Operations could go wrong, as I knew all too well. SWAT teams from New London hadn't saved my house on the Connecticut River from being blown up—but this was not the moment to dredge up disasters.

Suburbs with small houses gave way to undeveloped stretches; I hadn't realized there was so much untouched land in this heavily populated state. Another long stretch of woods. As we reached an exit sign, Agent Roehm spoke into a device. "Agent Roehm at the Bedlington exit. I need instructions."

A man replied: "At the end of the ramp, turn right onto River Road. Go two miles to an overhead light. There's a gas station and convenience store on the left corner. Go to the back of the parking lot."

I reached into my bag, pulled out my water bottle and took a long swallow. A convenience store meant a chance to find a restroom before what might be a very long wait.

River Road was straight, bordered by a few small houses. At the crossroads, the overhead traffic light was green. We turned into a big Exxon station, passed the pumps and went to the far side.

A number of cars and other vehicles were parked together. Agent Howard was standing with a group of men. They were talking, their heads close together. One raised his hand, fist clenched. Something about the body language spelled trouble.

Agent Roehm turned off the engine and looked at the group. "You stay here. I'll go see what's going on," he said. I watched as he went over to speak to Agent Howard. After a moment, Agent Howard turned and walked to the car.

"Bad news. The operation is on hold, maybe for good. The agent who was going in with me had to leave. Her child has been in an accident and was taken to a hospital."

"Oh, no," I said. "But—can't you go in alone?"

"Against the rules. We have to work in pairs. Back each other up. Compare notes and corroborate in case we have to be witnesses."

"I know that, but why not use one of these men?"

"Because the inspection permit lists a man and a woman. These people can smell cops a mile away. Women are less threatening than men." His voice was tight. He was feeling the strain. "There's no margin for error tomorrow," he had said last night. He had worked so hard, but it had happened, this unforeseen snag.

There was one solution. I opened the door and got out of the car. "Let me get this straight," I said. "You were going to go in with a woman agent, make an inspection, and leave."

"Correct."

"Then why not take me? I've been in other operations. I've got eyes in my head. I can observe. Take notes."

"Out of the question."

I took a deep breath. "Look. It's not rocket science—and don't give me crap about taking risks. I'm at risk until these people are locked up. Believe me, I want this operation to succeed."

Silence. I could sense wheels start to turn. "Right," he said at last. "You outed Langer. You've worked on other operations. Wait here," he added and went over to the group. There were glances in my direction, talk in low voices. In a moment he was back.

"There were objections, but I told them you gave us the first lead. No argument after that. The raid's on, the SWATs are in the air. You'll have to change your clothes."

I watched as he went to a white van. Pulled out a plain navy blue shirt and jacket. "Agent Stokes left these. The skirt's too small, but the jacket with your pants should do. You can use the restroom over there. Here." He handed me a hat with a visor. "Try to hide your hair."

The restroom was reasonably clean with a strong smell of disinfectant. I piled my hair on top of my head and jammed down the cap. Without the mane of auburn hair, my face looked thinner.

Agent Howard was waiting outside in the white van. We drove out of the parking area and started down the straight road.

"I'll save the thanks for later," he said. "For a few moments I thought we'd have to abort or at least delay."

"No need for thanks. Just tell me the plan."

"Agents will be posted around the perimeters to make sure no one gets away. We go to the front door. I show my credentials, we go in, and I do the talking. Shouldn't be trouble, but any sign of aggression, I use my Glock or call in the SWATs. We look around and leave, the SWATs pile in and round up whoever's there. Okay?"

"Okay."

We drove on. The day was turning warm and sunny. Horses ran about in fields, kicking up their heels, full of spring energy. Thoroughbreds, not backyard ponies.

"This looks like Virginia hunting country," I said, trying for lightness. "The openness. Not what you'd expect."

"These people were smart to buy an estate with land. No close neighbors."

In the next field, a man was mending a three-rail jump, unaware that a massive operation was gathering a few miles away.

The macadam road changed to packed dirt. Agent Howard glanced at the GPS. "Getting close." He turned to me. "Remember, you work for the state. Think of this as just another boring job. You'd much rather be out on a date with your boyfriend."

"Do my best," I said, and meant it. If I did well, we might continue to work as a team in the future.

A sharp turn took us over a small bridge spanning a narrow stream. Ahead on the right were two white gateposts. A name—Longfields—was painted in black letters on a small sign.

Agent Howard flexed his fingers and slowed. "That's it. Ready?"

"Ready."

CHAPTER TWENTY-SIX

The short gravel drive was blocked by a heavy iron gate. It was set in a high brick wall that looked as if it had been recently built. Agent Howard stopped and turned off the engine. "Walls can be a problem. There may be cameras."

He got out and pressed a bell set in the brick. We waited. At last a woman answered.

"Yes?"

"It's the state health inspector. Here for the annual check."

"No one come before. What is this check?" The woman had a thick accent.

"Regulation. All schools in this state must be inspected every year."

"You have a permit?"

"Yes."

"Hold it up. Facing the gate."

He reached into a briefcase, pulled out a paper, and held it up. After a moment the gate swung open.

The drive ended in a circle beside a large house. It was built of older, mellow brick, fronted with tall white pillars. A family with money would have lived here. A family that kept a stable full of horses and rode out with the hounds.

I looked around, noting weeds pushing up through the gravel. Flaking paint around the windows.

Agent Howard picked up his briefcase, then handed me a

small black notebook and retractable pen. "We're off. Remember, I'll do the talking."

I nodded and straightened the visor cap. Ski racing years ago had taught me the importance of focus. My job now was to concentrate on my notes. Observe locations.

The middle-aged woman who opened the door was sturdy, with blunt features. Her faded blonde hair was pulled back into a ponytail. She was wearing a blue-and-white striped shirt and a black skirt, suitable for the matron of a school. She looked us up and down.

"No one tell me about this inspection." A sullen voice with what sounded like a Nordic accent. "What is it that you do?"

"We make a tour of the premises and file a report." He gave her a sharp look. "Noncompliance means penalties. More inspections." She stepped back.

The front hall was as imposing as the pillars outside, but the parquet floor showed signs of wear. Agent Howard took a clipboard from his briefcase and turned to the woman. "You are?"

"Maria. Housekeeper."

"We'll start with the classrooms, Maria." I followed with my notebook.

The paneled room had once been a fine library. Shelves of leather-bound books lined the walls. The portrait of a woman hung over the carved fireplace. She was wearing a black lace dress and holding a child with long, fair curls.

Two rows of scruffy-looking teenage boys were seated at large desks, heads bent over computers. A burly man with a shaved head was standing by the window, jingling the change in his pocket. He turned as we came in. The jingling stopped. His expression changed. "What the—"

Maria spoke quickly. "The health inspector from the state."

"What?"

"He showed me a permit." A look passed between them, as if

conveying a message. I glanced at Agent Howard, hoping he had noticed, but he was making a check on his clipboard.

The boys twisted in their chairs, mouths open as if this was the first time they had seen visitors from the outside world. Surprise ran like a fever through the room.

The burly man walked toward them. I could see that he was not my attacker. Not as tall and with more bulk around the shoulders. "Manners," he barked. "On your feet for visitors."

The boys shuffled to their feet, eyes lowered. I made a quick count. Fourteen—and I knew enough to see that these supposedly troubled boys were in a bad way. Abused or on drugs or both.

"What is it you want now?" Maria asked as went back to the hall.

"The main rooms, please."

"I show," she said and began to open doors. What used to be the drawing room was empty, with a strong smell of dead mice. The dining room was dark, filled with sheeted furniture. A long table had been pushed to one side. We passed through quickly and back into the hall.

"Second floor, please," Agent Howard said, and we started up the stairs. The arched window on the landing was hung with faded yellow damask curtains, probably as old as the house itself.

The bedrooms were eerie reminders of a departed family. I did a quick inspection. One must have been a girl's room; it was papered with faded roses on a trellis. Some were partitioned in half, and all had barred windows. Beds were made, but there were no photographs on the bureaus. Two bathrooms were far from spotless, but not grubby enough to warrant a complaint.

As we walked around, Agent Howard made checks on his clipboard. "These barred windows," he said to Maria. "They could be a hazard in case of fire."

She shrugged. "This is a school for boys with—how you

say—special needs. Many having treatment. They cannot be running off in the middle of the night."

"Has that happened lately?"

"No, but care is taken."

"Supervision requires a large staff. Where are those rooms?"

"Over the garage."

"These special needs boys are alone at night?"

"One person stays," she snapped. The sullen voice matched the thin-lipped mouth. I pinched my wrist to fight mounting stress. There was something unnatural about this place, something in the fetid air that was affecting my breathing.

Agent Howard made more checks on his clipboard. "Now show us the kitchen," he said.

The kitchen, like the rest of the house, was old-fashioned. The stove and two refrigerators were avocado green, a popular color in the 1960s. I made a show of looking in a refrigerator. Food was stacked neatly in containers. There were no dirty dishes in sight. A dishwasher hummed loudly.

Agent Howard crossed the room. He unbolted the door that led to an outside porch, looked out, and came back. Maria was watching him closely.

"I now show you the cellar," she said, as if wanting to keep us here longer. I clenched my fists and tried to catch Agent Howard's eye. Every instinct was sending me signals that we should leave immediately using the kitchen door—but this wasn't my operation. It wasn't up to me to break the cover.

"That won't be necessary," Agent Howard said and put the clipboard back in the briefcase.

She shrugged, turned, and led us through a pantry, through the dark dining room, and into the hall. I followed and began to breathe again. A few more steps and we would be in the van.

"Stop right there." A loud voice. The big man was standing squarely in front of the heavy door, arms crossed over his chest.

Agent Howard walked toward him. "We're leaving. We're late for our next appointment."

The man stepped forward. "You're not going anywhere. Stand against the wall and put your hands up."

"What?"

"You heard me. Hands in the air. The boss called the state office and checked with the officials. You're no goddamn inspector."

"Then someone made a mistake. Here's my permit." He pulled the pistol from his pocket. Not fast enough. The man lunged forward, and the Glock clattered to the floor. I jumped to get it, but Maria had her hands on my shoulders. She pushed me against the nearest wall, pressing her solid thickness against my back.

I tried to kick. She pressed harder, grinding my face into the wallpaper. Behind me, there were gasps. Grunts. Fighting that seemed to go on forever. Then a thudding crash.

"He's down," the big man shouted. "Let her go." Maria gave me a sharp jab in the ribs and stepped back. I spun around. Agent Howard was lying on the parquet floor, his head twisted at a sharp angle. The man gave him a vicious kick. He didn't move.

I stared, speechless, as if every drop of blood in my veins had stopped running. The big man caught my arm, slapped me across the mouth, and turned to Maria.

"Take his pistol and get your fat ass to the boys. Tell them if they move out of their seats, you'll shoot them all." She picked up the gun and disappeared.

"Now for you, bitch." His hands went up and down my body, pausing to feel my crotch. He pulled out his phone.

"It's done, boss. He's down for the count." A pause. "For Chrissake, Lonny, he had a pistol." Another pause. "Okay, okay, I won't hurt the woman. We're on our way."

CHAPTER TWENTY-SEVEN

The back hall was long and dark. At the end, a door stood open. A man was standing by a desk, throwing papers out of a drawer. A small man with dark hair and pockmarked skin. As we came in, he turned and looked at me. "What are you? Police? FBI? Quick. No lies."

"I . . . I . . ." The words wouldn't come. Blood was dripping from the cut on my lip.

"Tell him, bitch." The big man slapped me again.

The small man raised his hand. "Enough of that. Listen up. Those two wouldn't have come without backup. We have to demolish the place before they're missed, then make tracks."

"How the hell do we—"

"Get the boys together. Put them and the computers into the wine cellar. Maria can help you. I'll have to send a signal to Atlas."

"Jesus, Lonny. We'll be killed for messing up."

"Only if we leave footprints. First you lock the boys, computers, and those two in the cellar, then you throw in gasoline. Torch the place. You got twenty minutes max, maybe less, so move it."

Once again, I was dragged down the hall, his fingers clamped around my arm. I gagged and swallowed back bile. How long would a SWAT team wait out there? How long would it take to round up those brainwashed boys? How long would it take to die from being burned alive?

We reached the kitchen. He pulled me through the dining

room. Pushed at the double doors that led into the front hall and stopped.

"Jesus," he said. "Oh Jesus."

Maria the housekeeper lay on the floor, screaming, her hands over her face. Boys were leaning down, beating her with a chair. One boy looked around and saw us. "There he is," he shouted. The crowd picked up the chair and rushed toward us. The big man swiveled and pushed through the dining room doors, slamming them behind him.

A boy grabbed my shoulder. He was holding the Glock pistol. He stared at the blood on my face.

"Who are you?" he yelled.

"I came with a man—you saw us. The big guy hit him. Now they—those two—they want to burn us all alive."

"Not going to happen." He pointed the gun at me, shot over my head, and skipped back to the others.

I shuddered. The abused boys had gone mad. A woman was being killed in front of my eyes, but while they were killing her, I might be able to pull Agent Howard to safety.

I inched my way along the wall until I reached Agent Howard. That terrible crash—he was unconscious, his breathing was shallow, but he was alive. I took hold of his feet and began to pull. If I could reach the door without being noticed, I could open it and scream for help.

Maria's screams were growing fainter. Suddenly the shouting stopped. I looked around. A red-haired boy was running down the stairs. He was carrying a burning cloth on a stick. As he came to the landing, he reached up and held the fire against the tattered damask curtains. They caught fire. He ran faster, swinging the stick, sparks flying in all directions. "Burn it," he yelled. "Burn down the fucking place."

After a few seconds, the chant began. "Burn, burn." As the flames swept down the stairs, growing higher, the hall began to fill with smoke. The chanting turned to coughs as boys pushed by me. Agent Howard was heavier than he looked. As the smoke thickened, I tugged at his ankles, trying not to inhale.

The flames were licking at the walls. I had no idea fire could move so fast. Another minute and we would both die. I choked, desperately trying to move the inert body toward the open door. So close…so close, but I would never make it. My lungs were filling up with smoke.

"Quick. Out." Two men in camouflage were kneeling beside me. One heaved Agent Howard over his shoulder, the other lifted me to my feet.

"Two men in the back," I croaked. "Don't let them get away."

CHAPTER TWENTY-EIGHT

The medical world was there to receive me. As I was lifted into an ambulance, the young EMT took my hand. "You'll be fine, ma'am, but we're taking you to County Memorial Hospital. Just a precaution."

By now I was familiar with emergency rooms: the bays, the battery of equipment around the beds. Technicians in and out. Shock and smoke inhalation, I was told. Nothing worse. When I could talk, an FBI agent was waiting to see me.

There were more technicians, more evaluations, but in a few hours the pain in my lungs had eased. The FBI agent was allowed in, an older man with craggy features, graying hair, and a puckered scar on his left cheek.

"Special Agent Strader," he said and sat down, wincing as if his back hurt.

"Agent Howard," I whispered.

"A head injury. He's in intensive care, that's all I know. About those two men. They were picked up at the edge of the property. They're now in our custody." A pause. "If you can, tell me about them."

I took a sip of water through a straw. "The one called Lonny—he was sending a signal to something he called Atlas. That's where he got his orders."

"Atlas. I'll pass it along." He made a note.

"He told the big one to throw us all into the wine cellar and torch the place. I'm alive because those boys went mad. Killed the housekeeper and set the fire, but they've been abused. Agent Howard—it shouldn't have happened." My voice choked.

He shifted in his chair. "We'll want to hear more details, but they can wait."

"What about the boys?"

"Right now, they're getting medical attention." He glanced at his watch and gave me an assessing look. "I'm told you'll be released soon and that you live in New York. Until we know who runs this operation, we think you should have around-the-clock protection."

"I already do. Agent Howard arranged it."

"Good. I'll arrange for an FBI car and driver to take you back." He reached into his vest pocket and handed me a card. "I'm your contact as the case develops. This will always reach me."

"Thank you. Please let me know about Agent Howard."

"I will." He stood up slowly, as if he was favoring his back. "You've had a distressing experience, Mrs. Streat. You need to take care of yourself. We'll talk tomorrow."

I lay back on the pillows and sipped more water. Not an Agent Howard, but he'd been kind and competent. I had the feeling he'd been involved in a lot of operations in his time.

A few minutes later a young doctor appeared. She stood at the end of the bed and looked at me. "You're a very lucky woman. How are you feeling now? Any pain?"

"No pain. I want to go home."

"Your oxygen level is nearly back to normal. I'll do the paperwork and give you a prescription to soothe your throat. Just keep in mind that you've had a shock and sometimes the effects are delayed. I'll give you a sedative and you'll need to rest."

At five o'clock an aide strapped me into a wheelchair and pushed me down to the entrance where a car and a driver wearing plain clothes were waiting. I got into the back. "I'm not supposed to talk much," I said. "I think I'll try to sleep."

"You do that. I'll wake you up when we get there. Traffic may be bad this time of day."

It was, but at last we pulled up in front of Caroline's building. The driver stopped.

"Already," he muttered. "Someone must have given them your name."

I looked. There was a crowd of people standing on the sidewalk, holding equipment. Charlie came forward and opened the door. I stepped out. A woman thrust a microphone into my face.

"What happened at that school, Mrs. Streat? Are you working undercover for the FBI?"

Between them, Charlie the doorman and the driver hustled me into the lobby. Residents passing through looked stunned as several reporters chased me to the elevator.

Peggy was waiting outside the door. "I'll take care of her," she said and shut the door. Looked at me.

"Those filthy clothes—but you don't look too bad. I've talked to the hospital. You're for bed."

"After I take a shower and get the smell of smoke out of my hair."

"When did you last eat? I'll bring tea and maybe something soft like a scrambled egg."

It didn't take long to shower, put on a T-shirt and a sweater and climb into bed. I felt shakier than I wanted to admit. Peggy came in with a tray set with Caroline's best china. She put it down and stood back. "Someone must have leaked the story to the press. That's how I heard about Agent Howard. It sounded bad. Do you want to talk, or would you rather wait?"

I swallowed. "Talk. He was hit on the head, a terrible blow. He's alive, barely, and he's in intensive care. Oh God, it happened so fast—it's beginning to sink in. I keep seeing him here last night, looking like he'd made a killing in hedge funds. He seemed to have thought of everything, but shit happens. The partner he was going in with had to leave. To keep the raid from aborting, he took me instead."

"So that's why you were with him. I couldn't figure it out."

"A dragon of a housekeeper let us in. It was someone's beautiful old place—there were even portraits on the wall. There were fourteen kids, teenagers, in the library sitting at computers. A big man who looked like a jailer. He was the one who hit Agent Howard." My voice faltered.

"You don't have to go on—"

"I must." I clutched the sheet and let the story pour out. The sound of Agent Howard's body hitting the floor. Lonny's order to pour on gasoline. The housekeeper's screams. The boy running down the stairs and lighting the house on fire. "What they did was bad, but those boys saved my life," I ended.

Peggy reached out and took my hands. "Terrible. Terrible. But at least you're alive."

"That's what I keep telling myself, but I blame myself for not following my gut instinct to get out sooner. I almost broke our cover and begged him to leave. If I had, he wouldn't have been hit."

"You can't take on blame."

"But I do. What if he never comes out of the coma? The waste—the awful waste. I only met him three times, but he always saw what needed to be done and did it quickly. He could think out of the box. He had empathy." I coughed and took a sip of tea. "His little dog. What will happen to Ralph?"

"He always had a friend take him when he went off on an assignment—"

"But what if he never comes back—sorry, I'm sorry. I did it again. I keep forgetting about your husband."

"That's all right." Peggy let go of my hands and stood up. "I'll tell you something. When Al died, I fell apart. Couldn't keep going. Mike Howard came to our house one night. He gave me a message. I kept it. I think you should have it."

She left. When she came back, she was carrying a piece of creased paper. She handed it to me. The message was written in large block letters:

> *You gain strength, courage, and confidence by every experience in which you really stop to look fear in the face. You are able to say to yourself, "I lived through this horror. I can take the next thing that comes along." You must do the thing you think you cannot do.*

I read it again and put the paper down. "Who wrote this?"

"Eleanor Roosevelt. It was in a book she wrote. It still helps me. Listen. Doctors do amazing things these days. We just have to hope that Mike Howard is going to recover. Not give up on him."

"You're right." I blinked back tears. "We have to hope. Hope and pray. I'm not much good at that, but at least I can send out good vibes. That's all we can do for him now."

CHAPTER TWENTY-NINE

April 13

For media bored with self-serving political spin, the school story was manna straight from heaven. Young boys held captive on a New Jersey estate. Building torched. Federal agent injured. One woman dead. Another nearly burned alive as she ran from the house.

Who was this woman? Enterprising journalists dug up her bio: Emma Metcalf Streat, forty-eight. Former opera singer. Married to a CEO who died in a tragic accident. Two sons. There were pictures of Lewis and me in Davos, mingling with the international elite.

Charlie turned away a reporter pretending to deliver flowers. Delsey composed a polite answer for media requesting interviews: "Mrs. Streat thanks you for your interest, but she's not available at this time." There was a deluge of calls from friends and family, all wanting to know the story behind the media blitz.

Generalissimo Peggy kept me in bed while Delsey fielded the calls. There were calls from my boys. Jake's concern was predictable, but Steve's was both a surprise and a relief. I had expected anger, but instead he suggested I should be paid and get a badge.

At noon a call came from FBI Agent Strader. He had important information and wanted to see me that afternoon. Peggy shook her head.

"You're still shaky. Are you sure you're up to this?"

"Yes, but I'd like you to be there. Another pair of ears. Besides, you have the background. You know how the FBI works better than I do."

When he arrived, I was dressed and sitting in the library. I introduced Peggy as my security, on leave from the NYPD.

He nodded and eased himself into a straight chair. The craggy face looked tired. "I see the press is making quite a meal of you," he said. "How are you feeling?"

"Much better. What about Agent Howard?"

"Still in a coma, but vital signs are better. It's a serious skull fracture. He'll recover, but it will take time."

"Thank God. It's so unfair. He was so careful, tying up all the loose ends. Have you found out what went wrong, how they knew we weren't inspectors?"

"We have. When called, the person in the state office knew nothing about an unofficial permit. Bad communication on their part."

"Big time. Unforgivable. What about those two men?"

"We're working around the clock." He took out his notebook. "We're beginning to see a pattern of blackmail and extortion. So far, this outfit called Atlas seems to be calling the shots. Specializing in locating vulnerable individuals and then shaking them down for money. A great deal of money, and those two were victims."

"What do you mean, victims?"

"Lonny Mariano's father was a bill collector in Hudson County, one of New Jersey's toughest areas. The son grew up with connections to the crime underworld and is now deep into cybercrime, along with drugs, gambling, prostitution. If his part in a murder had been discovered, it would have meant prison for life. That was Atlas's hold on him."

"What about the one who nearly killed Agent Howard?"

"An underling known as Speedo. His job was to find boys

who had run away from home. Incarcerate them in that school and force them into hacking accounts. Millions were laundered through a number of offshore banks. We'll try to trace that money to shell companies and eventually to Atlas. It's a crack in their firewall, and Mariano is singing like a canary, hoping for leniency."

For the first time Peggy spoke. "What about Mrs. Streat? Is she still a target?"

Agent Strader shifted in his chair. "Here's the situation. The hired mafia hit man who attacked her has been taken in, but the fact remains that Mrs. Streat was in that school. She saw Agent Howard taken down. She heard Mariano talking. When the case comes to trial, she'll be called as a key witness."

Peggy frowned. "Meaning?"

"We don't know what the Atlas group has in mind. They may decide to leave her alone, but there's a long history of witnesses who disappeared or were killed before they could give damaging testimony."

"True. How long until that trial?"

"The wheels of justice grind slowly. Lawyers will be brought in. Evidence collected. My guess is, five or six months." He cleared his throat. "We can provide a safe house, but otherwise she'll need security around the clock." He put away the notebook and looked at me. "You did well in a difficult situation. I'm extremely sorry you're still involved."

I didn't answer.

He got to his feet with an effort. "Let me know what you decide about security. I must go, but the investigation now has top priority. I'll keep you informed at every turn."

"I'll see you to the door," Peggy said, and they left.

I picked up a cushion and began to turn it around in my hands. Like a fool, I had let myself think that once those two men were in custody, I could go back to my normal life. That wasn't going to happen, but the question remained: Would these bad actors keep after me? I wasn't an enemy nation or a big company. Right now, all I wanted was to walk around without wondering if someone was going hit me over the head or push me under a car. To be free of the dark world of cybercrime.

In a moment Peggy was back. She straightened her jacket and stood straight. "You're upset. Needing more security was the last thing you wanted to hear, but Agent Strader is right. Key witnesses need protection." She put her hands behind her back. "Look. Here's the thing. I'm on indefinite leave. I don't have any children. We get along and I'm qualified. If it's any help, I can stay as long as you need me."

I put the pillow down. "Oh God, Peggy, I *am* upset. I'm ready to pull the covers over my head. Of course, I want you to stay, it would make all the difference, but are you sure?"

"I'm sure or I wouldn't have offered. Will you keep living in this apartment?"

"I don't know. I just don't know. I'd like to go back to Boston, but that depends on when my godmother can leave that fancy nursing home. I have to get her back here and settled in. Then we'll see," I said, and went into a fit of coughing.

"You've talked too much. Sit still and I'll bring you something hot to drink."

"You're getting very bossy."

She left. I pushed back my hair and went to the window. The newly leafed trees in the park swayed in a gust of spring wind that was testing their strength. In the past few weeks my strength too had been tested to its limit. On the other hand, I was alive. I was back on good terms with my boys. Peggy was going to stay with me—and I had a new mantra to apply when challenges loomed.

I have lived through this horror . . . I can take the next thing that comes along.

PART TWO

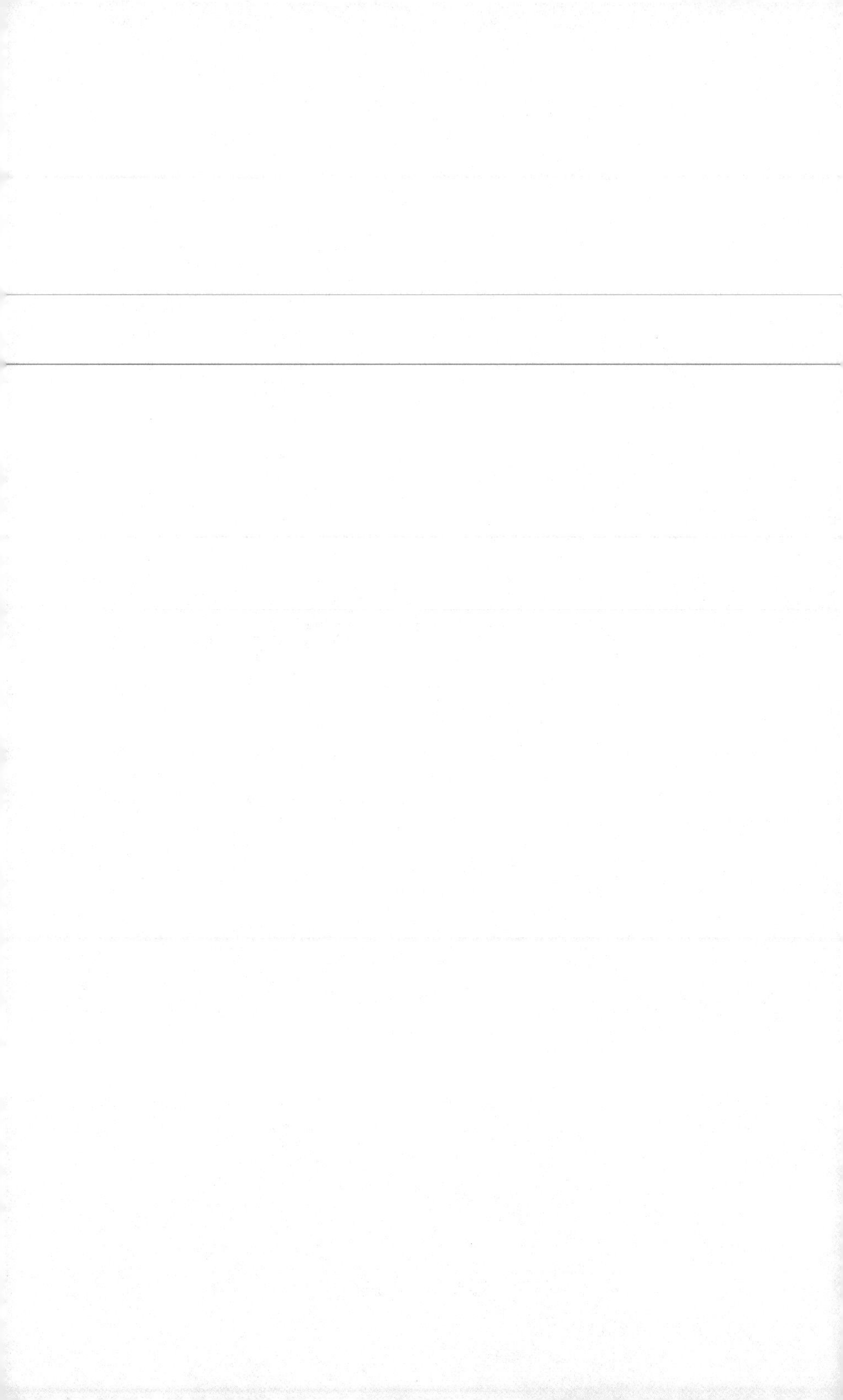

CHAPTER THIRTY

September 15

It was late afternoon when Caroline's Gulfstream V landed at Florence's Amerigo Vespucci Airport. Italy is one of my favorite countries, but I'd never been to Florence—and until last week there wasn't the slightest reason to be there.

I should have known that calls from Caroline had unexpected consequences, but this time there was no cry for help, just a surprising invitation.

"Darling girl, you won't have heard, but a famous Renaissance painting was found inside the wall of an old palazzo in Florence. There's a special two-day program laid on for big collectors like me. I know what you'll say, but I've made up my mind. You can come as my guest, but whatever you do, I'm going."

Alarm bells went off. Caroline had never really recovered from the attack. Her legs were shaky. Worse, although she denied it, at times she seemed to be losing her short-term memory and there were mood swings. Her feistiness could turn into belligerence, hard to manage.

A stream of consultations followed. No way could Caroline travel by herself. As the designated caregiver, I did my best to persuade her not to make this trip, but being Caroline, she tanked right over me. There were other problems. As a key witness, I was scheduled to appear in court on October 5. So far there had been no threats, but security was still an issue. The authorities were against my leaving the country without security, even though it was only for a few days and I would always be with a group.

An impasse, but it turned out that Caroline's detective agency provided trained operatives who could double as caregivers. A young woman named Bailey was just finishing a job as nanny to the child of a Brazilian billionaire. For a price, she would wear a gray wig and come as Caroline's personal maid. In the event of any threat to me, she would contact the FBI's legal attaché in Rome.

So far, Caroline had raised no objections. In fact, the idea of bringing a personal maid seemed to amuse her.

We met Bailey at the plane, a thin gray-haired woman wearing a plain gray dress. She had a pleasant voice, and during the flight she sat quietly in the back, saying little. She understood that Mrs. Vogt needed careful handling. Between us, with any luck, we could manage Caroline's lapses into a shadowy world.

Travel with Caroline was never a hardship. As usual, a car and driver waited on the tarmac. One of the faithful crew brought out her Vuitton bags. I took her arm, and we walked slowly toward the black Mercedes. Bailey followed with an old-fashioned case.

Suddenly Caroline's head swiveled around. A small white-haired man and a younger woman were disembarking from an even larger jet. Another man with bulky shoulders followed close behind.

"Cyrus Liden *and* his mistress *and* his bodyguard," Caroline said loudly. "You know who *he* is."

"Of course, I do. Early Silicon Valley breakthrough, one of the world's richest men. But I read somewhere that he never leaves California."

"Well, he's here, a tasty dish for kidnappers. Italian security will have their hands full. Every time we step out, there'll be little men in dark suits hovering."

"Pretending not to be there," I said and made a quick mental adjustment. Security laid on for Cyrus Liden meant even more security for me.

After months of restricted living, I was looking forward to a change of scene, a chance to be in the center of Renaissance art. My first sight of the city was the mass of red tiled roofs, gilded domes, and the wide, curving river. We crossed on a graceful bridge and entered a maze of narrow streets lined with yellow stucco buildings. Little shops were compressed into ground floors. Tourists filled the sidewalks.

Caroline shook her head. "Worse in July and August."

"Like Venice. What happens tonight?" There was a long pause. "Never mind," I said quickly. "It doesn't matter." I was learning not to ask direct questions, but it hurt to see Caroline, once so sharp, struggle to find an answer.

"Wait. I have it," she announced. "It's a dinner at the Palazzo Bracciolini. My friend Maisie tells me the countess comes from the plains of Kansas, married up, and has a wicked tongue. Never mind what she's being paid for tonight. Tomorrow she'll be calling her friends and ripping us to pieces. Best foot forward, Emma."

"I'm warned," I said lightly, glad that at least parts of her memory were still functioning.

She turned and looked at me. "Did I tell you to upgrade your clothes? That underdressed look won't do for this crowd."

"Loud and clear. Big money was spent in Newbury Street boutiques."

"About time."

The car passed through a large piazza, dominated by a gleaming white church. A young woman with flying dark hair and a bored look buzzed by on a Vespa motorbike.

A moment later our driver slowed and began to inch along a dark passage, so narrow there was barely room for a pedestrian to pass. Rectangular blocks of rough gray stone loomed on either side like a prison. The driver slowed again, then swung sharply through a small entrance and into a paved courtyard banked with flowers. There were lemon trees in huge terra-cotta pots. A marble mermaid stood in the middle of a fountain, washing her long hair.

According to the brochure, the distinguished group of art collectors would be staying at an old palazzo. Fifteenth century converted into a five-star hotel. Each guest would have a private concierge. As I stared, a young man in white livery came hurrying from the open loggia.

"Welcome to the Palazzo Otterini," he said in stilted English and opened the car door with a flourish.

Ignoring his outstretched hand, Caroline got out stiffly. We followed him across the open loggia and into a large frescoed anteroom.

An elderly man wearing a morning coat and striped trousers rose from behind a carved table and came forward with the air of a family butler.

"Welcome, signoras. I am the manager, Signor Fosco. It will be my pleasure to assist you in any way. For Signora Vogt and her maid, we have reserved the Brunelleschi suite. The other signora will be in the next room." He snapped his fingers, and two porters jumped forward. He spoke to them in staccato Italian, then escorted us to a paneled elevator concealed behind a high leather screen.

"Not bad," I said to Caroline as we went up.

"You wouldn't believe what it costs. I think I'll have a little toes-up before this dinner. Did I tell you to get new clothes?"

"You did and I did. Big time," I said, relieved to hand her over to Bailey.

The hall was long and dark; marble busts of ancient men with short curled hair stood in niches along the wall. The liveried minions were waiting for us. Mine bowed and handed me a large key hung with red tassels. I gave him a few euros and went into the room.

"Cripes," I said aloud. The windows had shutters. Frescoes of flying cherubs covered the high ceiling. A faded tapestry on the wall depicted a stag hunt. An enormous bed stood in an alcove. History seeped out of every corner.

Needing to take possession, I kicked off my shoes. Went to a carved chest where bottles of wine and mineral water stood chilling. A large basket of fruit stood on the table, complete with linen napkin and pearl-handled knife. Compliments of the management, no doubt. I poured myself a glass of water and went to check out the bathroom. The floor was green marble, and the gold fixtures were shaped like swans. All mod cons. No expense spared.

Back in the room, I walked around, sipping water, letting my imagination take over. I could be a Renaissance princess, about to marry a duke from nearby Padua. Or the wife of a Medici banker, the patron of Michelangelo. For the past several months I had been caught up in the ongoing case and worries about Agent Howard, who was making a slow recovery. For the next two days I must make the most of this intriguing place. Immerse myself in lavish and historic surroundings.

CHAPTER THIRTY-ONE

The schedule politely requested that guests meet in the anteroom at eight o'clock. Moving leisurely, I took a shower and put on a new dress, a Valentino knock-off cut low in the back. Last spring Caroline had given me a necklace made of brilliant semiprecious stones set in gold. Wildly pretentious and never worn until now.

I clasped it carefully and studied the overall effect. There were fine lines around my mouth and eyes, but there was no gray in that mane of auburn hair, and my long legs were exceptional. Rubbing shoulders with highfliers could be a challenge, but I had credentials. Emma Metcalf had been a rising name in the opera world. My dead husband had been the CEO of a large international company, but my status didn't matter. My one job was to support Caroline in case she became confused—and mind my manners in front of the jumped-up countess.

For once, thanks to Bailey, Caroline was ready in full war paint, clanking with bracelets. She gave me the once-over. "You'll do. Italian men love dark red hair and blue eyes. Shades of Botticelli."

"With clothes. That monster key—they must want to keep tabs on us. Check to see who's in and who's out."

When we arrived, the frescoed anteroom was filled with guests. "Signora Vogt?" A young woman clicked toward us across the tiled floor. She was wearing a smart black suit and high heels. There were blonde streaks in her dark hair. "I am Luisa Respigli, your personal concierge," she said in accented English. "I am here to assist you during your stay." She looked at me. "And this is?"

"My guest, Mrs. Streat," Caroline said.

Luisa gave me a brief nod and consulted her clipboard. "Please note that important members of Florentine society have been invited to meet you. The dinner will end promptly at eleven thirty. I will be here when you return to give you the details of tomorrow's program." She tucked the clipboard under her arm. "I will now introduce you to others in your group."

Caroline's bracelets rattled ominously. "That won't be necessary." She turned to a couple standing nearby. "Henry. Genevieve. I saw your names on the list. This is my goddaughter, Emma Streat. Emma, the Trains are old friends."

We smiled and nodded. He was built on a large scale with an air of authority. She had curly gray hair and looked as if she spent a lot of time in her garden.

"Hi there, Mrs. Vogt." A woman with long platinum hair pushed forward. She was wearing a skin-tight silver dress. "Lorraine Kegler. We met at that dinner for saving the library. My hubby, Matt, was a major sponsor."

The husband was small and dark with shiny blow-dried hair. I braced for one of Caroline's cutting snubs, but the woman shrilled on.

"Hey, look over there. It's Cyrus Liden and the woman he lives with. He's twice her age so he can't be up to much—"

"Sugar." There was a warning note in hubby's voice. Lorraine shrugged and was silent.

I turned my head for a closer look at Cyrus Liden, the Silicon Valley legend. His fragile build and gray goatee reminded me of an elderly Harvard professor, one of my father's colleagues. The woman was wearing a simple red dress. She took his arm as they went out to the loggia. The bodyguard with heavy shoulders followed.

"Signora Vogt, your car is here." Luisa motioned us toward the door.

"Cow," Caroline muttered.

A small black Mercedes was waiting in the courtyard. Just ahead, men in double-vented dark suits were jumping into a car behind the Liden limousine. The Italians weren't taking any chances.

As we drove down the narrow street, I looked at Caroline. "I need a heads-up about these people."

"Henry Train is the head of a New York bank. Genevieve's one of those born organizers, but she stays mostly in the country with her King Charles spaniels."

"What about—uh—Lorraine?"

"Trophy wife, God knows from where, clawing her way up, trying to get on boards. Matt made big money in hedge funds. Now he's into buying art."

"What does Cyrus Liden collect? Titians and Rembrandts?"

"Nothing, as far as I know. He's a farm boy who went into computers early on and made billions. His wife died. No children. Anna Deglos is a widow, her husband was one of Liden's lawyers. They've been together a few years. Maybe *she* wanted to come."

We crossed the river Arno, peaceful in the soft evening light, and drove along the embankment until the driver slowed and turned into a narrow passageway. It was blocked with cars. People were getting out.

"*Scusi*, Signoras," the driver said. "From here you walk."

Caroline stiffened. "Walk? He wants us to walk?"

"It can't be far," I said and took her arm. Those pencil-thin legs were apt to collapse and she refused to use a cane.

The passageway was paved with rough cobbles. Dim circles of light from old lamps barely touched the high walls. Behind us, the trophy wife was complaining about her high heels. A few yards ahead, the Liden bodyguard was looking from side to side as if suspecting a trap. Not surprising. I could picture men with daggers sliding along in the shadows, waiting to pounce on rich nobles wearing doublets and pointy shoes.

"This is outrageous," Caroline said loudly. "Hot dogs and corn on the cob, that's all we can expect from a jumped-up countess from Kansas."

"Hush," I said, tightening my hold on her arm.

At last a servant in black livery with gold buttons appeared. He led the now silent group through a door and across a vast echoing space; several bicycles and two small cars stood in a far corner.

Still in silence, we straggled up a long flight of stone stairs. At the top, he marched us up to a pair of gilded doors.

"Palazzo Bracciolini," he announced, and flung them open.

CHAPTER THIRTY-TWO

The change from dimness to brilliant light was dazzling. A large number of Florentines had already gathered in the vast *salone*, pressed, no doubt, into meeting the rich collectors.

Count and Countess Bracciolini were receiving near the door. He was slight and held himself very straight. His black dinner coat was sharply nipped in at the waist. He raised Caroline's hand and kissed the air.

The countess was tall and blonde, with even features and a cold smile. "Good evening," she said to me, assessing my dress like a woman who would know the price of everything.

As always at large parties, people seemed to resist open spaces. A waiter wearing a peach silk jacket and white gloves approached with champagne in fluted glasses.

Caroline took one, sipped, then put it back on the tray. "Quite a leap from the yellow brick road to here. That forced march—my feet hurt. I have to sit down."

"I'll try to find you a chair," I said. Caroline was starting to be difficult, and I was relieved to see Henry Train coming our way. "Genevieve wants you to join us," he said. "She doesn't speak Italian and she needs support."

"Ghastly-looking people," Caroline said, taking his arm. "Come along, Emma."

"After I have a quick look at the river." I walked to the long open windows, needing to think ahead. Mr. Train seemed kind. If

Caroline began to slip and make a scene, maybe he would help me find a car.

Across the water, a lighted dome rose above the roofs. I looked out, wishing I knew more about this ancient city. I might meet a few Florentines tonight, but I'd never know what lay under the surface.

It was time to get back to Caroline. I turned. A handsome young man had come up and was standing in front of me. "Nando Bracciolini, son of the house," he said with a small bow. "And you are?"

"Emma," I said.

"Are you married to one of these rich Americans?"

"Actually, I'm not."

"Excellent." With a hand on my elbow, he led me to a row of gilded chairs. Pulled one out and sat down close beside me. "Allow me to say that you are the most beautiful woman in the room."

I took a sip of the champagne I was holding and tried not to laugh. The son had his father's slight figure, but he had a merry face under a mass of dark curls. In a Henry James novel this cheeky boy, not much older than my sons, would be the terror of mammas and chaperones.

"Your palazzo," I said, wanting to change the subject. "How old is it?"

"Trecento. Fourteenth century. In the old days my family moved to a different part each season. You must understand that Florentines are survivors. We turn ground floors into shops, live in upper floors like the Otterini family."

"Do they still live in that palazzo?"

"Where else? They have their own entrance. With the prices they charge, they have never been richer. There's one of them now, the man in the black wig. He owns a string of brothels in Milano."

This was no longer amusing. I stood up—and saw that the countess was hurrying toward us. She gave me a furious look, spoke to her son in rapid Italian, and marched away.

"She doesn't seem pleased," I said, and began to walk toward the others.

He shrugged, a mock gesture of despair. "She is angry because I had orders to keep my aunt away from Signor Liden. My aunt will do anything to sell him one of her terrible paintings."

"Then you'd better go and find her."

Caroline was annoyed. "Where were you? We're going in to dinner. If that woman from Kansas is making money off us, God knows what we'll get." But as we entered the adjoining *salone*, Caroline was silent. Round tables were covered with apricot silk and topped with lace. Light from tall candelabras shone down on cut glass and silver. The air was heady with the scent of flowers and perfume. A harpist played softly in a corner.

A bowing footman handed me a rose that matched the color of a centerpiece. Caroline was escorted to another table. I went to mine. Nando was standing there. He motioned me to the empty seat beside him.

"For you, I have changed my place," he said, looking triumphant.

"You did *what*?"

"My mother shouldn't have put me beside Aunt Gina. And you wouldn't have liked the *dottore*. He's sleeping with his daughter-in-law."

There was nothing I could do. I sat down, unfolded my napkin with a snap, and turned to the man on my right. "I'm Emma Streat," I said.

"Thomas Mellinton. I believe you're with our group. I saw you in the distance as we were leaving."

"I'm with them, but I'm not a collector. My godmother is, and I'm with her," I said, taking stock. British accent. Middle-aged, with carefully combed gray hair. Neither handsome nor plain. In a precise way, he went on to tell me that he had come ahead to learn more about the city, that he lived in Hong Kong, and had made an extensive study of white jade.

Keeping my back to Nando, I did my best to draw out the small talk. I learned that Thomas Mellinton had spent most of his working life in the British Civil Service but had stayed on in Hong Kong after the handover to the Chinese.

"It's a long flight from Hong Kong to here," I said, reaching for yet another conversational straw.

"Very long, but I broke the trip by going to see a cousin who lives on the west coast of Ireland."

"Lovely green fields and hedgerows. I've only been once, but I want to go back."

Gold-edged plates were removed for the next course. There was no way to avoid the inevitable. Thomas Mellinton turned to the large, bejeweled lady on his right.

Nando was waiting to pounce. He twisted his head and looked into my eyes. "You waste your time with a man who looks like a lawyer. He barely moves his mouth when he talks. Do you believe in love at first sight?"

"No," I said coldly and took a sip of wine. There was only one reason for this unwelcome attention, and that was my glaringly expensive necklace. It was known that some rich American women had a taste for young Italians, a taste that provided their toy boys with much-needed funds.

"You reject me." He pulled at his curls. "But I do not give up. Observe, please, the security types here to guard Signor Liden and pretending to be waiters. My father cannot complain that the silver will be stolen." He launched into slanderous accounts of the Florentines sitting near us. Their venal lifestyles and scandal-ridden love affairs.

A delicate gelato was served with tiny cups of coffee. I talked to Thomas Mellinton again, ignoring Nando. At last it was eleven thirty, time for the captive Florentines and the jet-lagged guests to leave. People were rising to their feet.

"*Bellisima*. You must listen to me." Nando motioned to the

waiter to fill his wine glass and ran his hands through his curls, a despairing gesture. "You are silent, you are cruel, but I forgive because of the hair. The mouth."

I turned to Thomas Mellinton. "This boy is being a nuisance," I said. "Would you be very kind and go with me to my godmother?"

"With pleasure. I couldn't help overhearing his libelous stories."

The countess was standing by the door, receiving compliments. But as I went by, murmuring a thank you, she gave me an angry look. Did she actually think I had asked her obnoxious son to change the place cards? Either she was overprotective, or she was clueless about her precious boy. I could only hope she wouldn't be on the phone tomorrow, telling her friends about a Mrs. Streat who had made a play for her son.

Luisa, the bossy concierge, was waiting in the anteroom, clipboard in hand. "I trust you enjoyed your evening. Tomorrow you go to Villa I Tatti, once the home of Bernard Berenson, the well-known art dealer. The villa is situated in Fiesole, a few miles from the city. Your bus will leave promptly at noon. For those who wish to make a visit to the church of Santa Croce, a guide will be here at ten thirty. Do you have questions?"

Caroline's bracelets rattled. "Emma, get those damned keys."

"I will," I said, but as I reached the desk, an arm went around my shoulders. "*Bellisima*, I am here. We go now. The evening is young."

I whirled around. "For God's sake—"

"First we go to a bar with dancing, then to a party with my friends."

"Certainly not. I'm taking my godmother to her room." Conspicuous attention from a randy young Italian would do nothing for the image of the quiet caregiver I was trying to achieve.

"But my great wish is to please you—"

"The keys. Quickly," I said to the young concierge. He handed me the tasseled keys. I turned on my heel and walked back to Caroline.

Nando followed. He bowed and kissed Caroline's hand. "Signora, allow me to introduce myself. I am Nando Bracciolini."

Caroline stared. "Who?"

"We did not meet at my mother's dinner, but I see that you are not the strict godmother in the fairy stories. Signora, I throw myself on your mercy. Please allow me to show your goddaughter the beauty of Florence at night. I promise to be a reliable escort." He smiled at her, looking like a Christmas card choirboy.

Caroline turned to me. "What on earth is he talking about?"

"Nothing. He's leaving."

"Why does he want to take you out?"

"Pay no attention. He's just being ridiculous—"

"Well, I'm tired. I want my bed. Do what you want," she said and walked toward the elevator.

"Wait." I started to follow, but Nando stood in my way. "You see? She gives permission. You cannot refuse." He raised his hands and looked around as if to enlist help.

People nearby were watching with interest. Lorraine Kegler moved closer. I could feel my face grow red. "*No*. For the last time, I am not, repeat *not*, going anywhere with you."

"But I wish only to give pleasure. Pleasure you."

This was beyond annoyance. It was almost as if he was trying to create trouble—and it had to stop. I motioned to one of the porters. "This man must leave at once. Help me see him to his car," I said loudly. After a second the porter came forward and stood on the other side of Nando as I herded him toward the loggia.

A blue Alfa Romeo was parked at the entrance. Nando shook his head and looked at me. "Why do you, how you say, throw mud in my face?"

"What I say is this. I'm old enough to be your mother. In fact,

I have two sons your age and thank God they have more sense. Get lost. Go home. I never want to see you again."

He raised his hand. "Please. You don't understand."

"Understand what?"

"I want you to like me. You are meant to like me."

"You're out of your mind if you think I'm going to pay for sex. There are plenty of rich women around. Try one of *them*."

"But it's you I need." The pleading voice of a little boy who was deeply hurt.

"You do not. Just get in your car and leave."

"May I call you tomorrow?"

"No."

"The next day?"

"*No*. Leave now or I'll call for security and have you thrown out on your ear."

The threat seemed to resonate. He hesitated, then flung himself into the car. Zoomed off through the narrow entrance with a roar.

CHAPTER THIRTY-THREE

I stood still, breathing hard. No way could I go back and face curious looks, the assumption that I must have done *something* to attract that handsome young Italian.

There was a small walled garden on the left of the court, lit by tiny lights in the lemon trees. I pushed the gate open and sat down on a marble bench. In a few moments people would have left the anteroom and I could slip upstairs. The canopied bed would be turned down, waiting for me to crawl in and crash.

The air was cool on my hot face. Not surprising that the boy had a problem, given such a disagreeable mother, but just now he had sounded almost desperate. Why? Somehow, I should have handled the situation better. Brushed him off with a joke and a laugh.

The tangy smell of lemon was soothing. I closed my eyes, then opened them. Men were shouting on the other side of the wall, a furious outpouring in Italian. Not a pleasant sound. I got up to leave, but suddenly the voices stopped. There was a heavy thump, then footsteps running away.

"*Gesu, Gesu, Gesu.*" A primal scream, then a choking sound. I stood still, my hand at my throat. It would be madness, sheer madness, to get mixed up in a fight, especially in another country. But what if Jake or Steve were attacked and nobody went to help?

A small door in the ivied wall lead to a narrow alley. The light from the garden was dim, but it was enough to see a stocky man lying on rough gravel. His legs were spread wide. His hands clutched the air as he fought for breath. Blood was spreading in a dark pool under his back.

I leaned down. His eyes took on focus as if he saw me. His mouth moved as he tried to form words. A trickle of blood ran down his chin. I told myself not to faint or be sick. Turned and raced through the garden, across the loggia, and into the deserted anteroom.

The young concierge was sitting behind the desk, reading a sports car magazine. He put it down as I stumbled in.

"Two men were fighting in the alley," I gasped. "The alley behind the garden. One of them is hurt. Badly. Get an ambulance. A doctor."

The concierge stared. "The signora saw this?"

"One man ran away. I think the other is dying."

"A man is dying?"

I clenched my fists. "Dying, do you hear? *Dying*. I'm going back. Make that call, then send the manager or whoever is in charge here. Do you understand?"

"Si, si." He picked up the phone. I grabbed a cloth from a nearby table, upsetting a vase of flowers, and ran.

In that short time, the man had stopped waving his hands. His eyes were closed. The pool of blood was wider.

I kneeled down and took his hand. Lewis had been killed by a hit-and-run driver, but he was already dead when I found him on the road. This man was still alive, but the rattle in his throat was ominous, the final sound before the passage from pain into peace.

He needed to know he wasn't alone. I pressed his hand harder and began to pray—any prayer would do. "Our Father who art in Heaven," I began, "hallowed be thy name . . ." The rattling grew louder, then stopped.

I placed his hand on his chest, took several deep breaths, and sat back on my heels fighting shock. Who was this man? Did he have a wife? Children? Why had he been killed?

Voices broke the silence. Two of the liveried porters erupted into the garden. There was a burst of exclamations. The name Mario was repeated, accompanied by signs of the cross.

The dignified manager appeared, buttoning his coat. He bent down, looked at the man, then turned to me.

"Signora, help is coming. You must leave. Allow me to escort you to your room." He grasped my arm and led me away. As we reached the loggia, an ambulance swung into the courtyard. Two men stepped out. They were wearing black hoods and looked more like hangmen than medics.

I stared. "Who—"

"They are Misericordia. An ancient Florentine organization that assists those in trouble. They are often the first to respond." He paused. "Signora, you must see a doctor. There is shock. Bleeding."

I looked down. I hadn't felt pain, but my hands were covered with blood. Blood was trickling down my legs, cuts from kneeling on the sharp stones. "I don't want a doctor," I said. "I just want to go to my room."

"We go, then I will send a maid to assist you."

The carved wooden shutters in the high-ceilinged room were closed. The silk coverlet on the large bed had been turned down and a white linen square placed on the floor. I opened the door to a small, dark-haired woman wearing a black dress and a white apron.

"Ah, ah." Making little clucking noises, she helped me take off the stained dress and led me to a chair. "Rest. I go for what is needed."

In a moment she was back with a basin of warm water and towels. Moving like a little bird, she washed the gore off my knees and applied antiseptic. "*Povera, povera.* Now hold out the hands." And finally, "It is done."

I looked down. No signs of the dead man's blood. My hands were clean, and the cuts on my knees were superficial, no worse than scrapes when the boys were learning to ride their bicycles.

"You've been very kind," I said. "Very kind. What is your name?"

"Viola." She picked up the basin. "The signora is cold. I bring the signora something hot to drink. Soup? Coffee?"

"Tea, please. Strong. No milk."

"I regret the wait, but I must go to the kitchen. There will be no room service tonight."

"No room service?"

It was the wrong thing to ask. Viola crossed herself. Her eyes filled with tears. "Mario, the waiter, he is *morte*. Dead."

"That man was a waiter here? You know—knew him?"

"His wife, she a cousin of my cousin. Mario a good person. He did wrong to go into a suite tonight, but who would kill him for that?" Tears were running down her cheeks.

I shook my head to clear it. "But if he was a waiter, why was that wrong?"

She rubbed her face with her apron. "It is not for you to be concerned, Signora. You must not be troubled."

"But I *am* concerned. I heard the fighting. I held his hands while he died. I *prayed* for him. I *need* to know why he was killed."

She looked away, twisting her apron. After a moment she spoke. "You a kind lady, very kind to stay with a dying man, so I tell you." She took a deep breath. "Francesca, she the maid tonight in the suite of Signor Liden. She go with towels to make ready the rooms before the signor and the signora come back from the dinner. She see Mario standing in the bedroom, but no one else is there. No one has called for him."

"What did she do?"

"He beg her to say nothing to anyone. Nothing at all. Then he go out and he is—" She stopped. Someone was knocking on the door. She went to open it. Spoke in Italian to whoever was there, shut it, and came back.

"*Dio mio*, now it begins. A *commissario* from the *polizia* wishes to speak with you, the person who found him. He is in the manager's office. A porter is here to take you."

"Now?" I swallowed. This was too much. As Caroline often said, I was too quick to step forward. I had done it again, acted on impulse, played the good Samaritan with no thought of consequences.

"I find you something to wear," Viola said. She pulled my black jacket and trousers out of the armoire and helped me ease my legs into the trousers. I winced as the cloth touched my knees. "Signora."

"Yes?"

"When the *polizia* ask you about Mario, tell them he a good person. A good person with a sick wife."

The knocking on the door was louder. Again, Viola went to open it. "Have patience. The signora comes."

It was one of the young liveried porters. He made the customary little bow. I followed him along the hall to a flight of winding stone stairs; the centers of the steps were worn hollow with age. I went down clutching the red velvet rope. The passage below led to another and then another. The porter stopped in front of a heavy door studded with nails and knocked.

We waited. One minute. Two. The porter knocked again. At last a voice called out. "*Avanti*."

CHAPTER THIRTY-FOUR

The manager's office was small, with filing cabinets and notices tacked to a board. The air was thick with cigarette smoke. The man sitting behind a desk got to his feet. He was wearing a badly fitting brown suit.

"You are Signora Streat?"

"Yes."

"Commissario Santello." He gestured to a straight chair facing the desk. I sat down. The *commissario* in charge of the Venice murder I'd uncovered had been rotund and middle-aged. This one was young, with a thin face. His dark hair was receding, leaving two sharp V shapes on his scalp.

"Thank you for coming," he said. "With your permission, I ask a few questions."

I nodded. His English was heavily accented, but not hard to understand.

"You arrived in Florence when, Signora?"

"This afternoon." I went on to describe the dinner with no mention of Nando.

"You returned from this dinner, you left the anteroom, and went to the small garden next to the loggia. Why was that?"

I hesitated, but staff as well as guests had seen the confrontation with Nando. "The Bracciolinis have a son named Nando," I said. "He followed me here from the dinner. Made a scene and embarrassed me in front of the other guests."

"In what way?"

"He wanted me to go with him to nightclubs. He was . . . persistent. He left, but I was upset. I went into the garden to calm myself."

"Nando Bracciolini. I recognize the name." His phone beeped. He picked it up and listened, tapping his nicotine-stained fingers.

The smoke was hurting my throat. I waited, trying not to cough. The less I said the better, but the police must be treated with respect.

"*Vero. Grazie.*" The call ended. He picked up a pack of cigarettes, then pushed it away. "Continue, please. The young man leaves and you are in the garden. What then?"

"I heard men's voices in the alley on the other side of the wall."

"How many?"

"Two, but I can't be sure."

"You understood what they were saying?"

"No. At first they talked loudly. They began to fight. There was a thump. Footsteps running away. A man cried out."

"Ah. And then?"

"There was a door in the garden wall. I went into the alley. He was lying on the gravel. There was blood coming from his mouth and from under his back. I ran to the concierge. I made him call an ambulance."

"My report says you went back to the man. Was that necessary?"

"I thought of my two sons lying hurt and no one helping them. I held his hand while he died and said a prayer."

"That was good of you, Signora."

"It seemed like the right thing to do. I went back to my room. I was going to bed when the porter came to bring me here."

The *commissario* reached again for the pack of cigarettes. This time he pulled one out and lit it.

"*Grazie*, Signora, you may leave, but there will be more questions."

"More questions? I've told you all I know."

"Because, Signora, it appears that you are the only witness to this crime."

A warning flag went up. I leaned forward. "But that's not true. I mean, I wasn't a witness. I didn't see the fight. Nothing except the man lying there."

A long pause. He drew deeply on the cigarette, then laid it in the ashtray. "Signora, when we have a suspect, it is possible that you will recognize a voice."

"No," I said quickly. "It is not possible. I was on the other side of the wall. There's no way I could recognize a voice." I shifted in the chair. "I'm very tired, sir. May I leave?"

He frowned, then smoothed his thinning hair. I could see that he was wrestling with a problem. "Signora," he said at last, "there is a difficulty, and I now ask for your cooperation."

"Oh?"

"It so happens that Mario Capuciati was a room service waiter. He entered the suite of Signor Liden while the occupants were away and went into a bedroom. For what reason? He may have been working with another. They meet. They have a disagreement which you alone heard. Minutes later he is dead of a knife wound in the back."

"But I have no idea what they said."

"Even so." He raised his hands. "Signora, the presence of Signor Liden in Florence is a sensitive matter. It requires much vigilance. Every step must be taken to find the motive for an incident involving Signor Liden."

"I understand. I'm sorry that this happened."

"It is a situation that must be resolved." He got to his feet. "That is all for now, but I must ask you to say nothing to the other guests. A disturbance of this kind requires much discretion."

"I'll say nothing, but the maid who found this Mario in Liden's suite has talked. Many in the staff know."

"Steps will be taken to contain the damage. Good night, Signora."

The porter was waiting to take me back to my room. Viola was still there. She hurried forward. "Shall I help the signora undress? Was the signora able to speak well of Mario?"

"There wasn't a chance." I sat down. I had reached the end of my endurance. "Thank you again for fixing my knees."

"The signora was very brave. I hope the signora rests well."

She left, closing the door gently. I pulled off my clothes, did a token wash, and climbed into the big bed. The heavy linen sheets were cold. I curled into a ball and rubbed my feet together to warm them. Was there some strange chemistry in me that attracted trouble like a magnet? I had been in this country for a few hours, and already I had become the target of a malicious young Italian and involved in a murder.

What else could happen? I had better talk to Bailey, but what could she do? No one was threatening my life, but the sense of escalating trouble was as tangible as the smell of escaping gas or the sound of ice cracking in a pond.

"Shit, shit, *shit*," I said, and put my head under the covers.

CHAPTER THIRTY-FIVE

September 16

The clanging of church bells woke me from fathoms-deep sleep. Sunlight streamed under closed wooden shutters. I stared up at the gilded ceiling and tried to concentrate on the coming day. Useless to fixate on what was out of my control. What mattered now was to keep a firm grip on Caroline and correct the impression that I was involved with Nando.

At nine, Bailey reported that Caroline had slept well and was about to order her breakfast. "I'll get mine and be along later," I said.

The wheels at the palazzo were oiled again and running smoothly. A smiling waiter wheeled in a table with a rosebud in a crystal vase and several English papers.

At ten, I went down the hall to Caroline. She was doing her nails and wanted to talk. "That dinner last night," she began and launched into descriptions of charity benefits she had chaired in New York. No mention of Nando.

"About today," I said during a pause. "Where is this Villa I Tatti?"

"It's up in the hills beyond Fiesole. Bernard Berenson was the son of a tin merchant in Boston. He became an expert on Renaissance painting and left the place to Harvard."

"There may be a lot of walking. Have you got any sensible shoes? You don't want to wobble around in high heels."

"I never wobble." A pause. "Do me a favor. Take off that black pantsuit. It must be growing mold." In the end we settled for my new green jacket over the old trousers. Bailey wished us a good day. She planned to go out and walk around the city.

At noon, the anteroom was filled with guests exchanging greetings. No one gave me curious looks. Now, after studying Caroline's list, I was beginning to put names to faces. I had met the Trains, the Keglers, and Thomas Mellinton. As well, there was the New York gallery owner, Nathan Rennie, who had a thatch of white hair and looked like a clever monkey. The bejeweled lady from Rio. A young French couple, two dark-skinned men from Dubai. Cyrus Liden and his friend Anna Deglos. A mixed bag if ever there was one, thrown together by art and money.

Our take-charge concierge, Luisa, came hurrying to meet us. "Good morning, ladies. At Villa I Tatti there will be a luncheon, a tour, and you will be back by four. At eight o'clock, your car will arrive to take you to La Serena, a fourteenth-century palazzo seldom open to the public. Dignitaries from all over Europe will be attending. Dinner will be followed by speeches and the unveiling of the painting. A very prestigious event. I wish you a pleasant day."

A large brown Mercedes bus waited in the courtyard; there was a circular bar in the back and the seats were made of expensive leather. I staked out a window seat for Caroline near the front and sat down beside her.

The motor was running, but we didn't move. "Who are we waiting for?" someone asked.

"Cyrus Liden and his friend," someone else answered. A moment later Anna Deglos came hurrying from the loggia, but the man with her was not Cyrus Liden. I stared as they came up the steps and took the front seats near the driver.

"Younger and better looking," Caroline muttered. "I wonder who *he* is."

I hesitated, then made a decision. "Actually, I used to know him," I said.

"When? Where? Tell."

"Not much to tell. It was over thirty years ago."

"Never mind. What's his name?"

"Richard Redson. I met him in Maine the summer I was fifteen. I was staying in North Haven with my cousin Sally. He was studying at MIT, visiting his girlfriend."

"Are you going to rush up and say 'Remember me?'"

"Certainly not, and he won't. I was a skinny little kid always trailing after the older ones. Getting in their hair."

We rumbled over the Arno River, calm in the noonday sun. As we wound our way past villas enclosed by walls, the man sitting behind the driver got to his feet. He was holding a microphone and looked like a tall bird with an elongated neck.

"Good day, ladies and gentlemen. I am Dr. Klarnet, director of the Florence Foundation, and I welcome you to a memorable occasion."

Polite murmurs. Caroline closed her eyes.

"We are now on our way to Villa I Tatti, once owned by the late expert on Italian masters, Bernard Berenson."

Richard Redson turned his head to listen. I folded my hands in my lap. I must have written his name a thousand times: Mrs. Richard Redson. Emma Redson. Emma Metcalf Redson.

The lecturer droned on, ". . . B. B., as he was called, taught himself by visiting little churches and monasteries. In this way, he learned how to spot certain artists by the feet, the folds of a Madonna's dress. The words *tactile values* was one of his favorite phrases . . ."

My wedding to Richard was going to take place under the arbor in my grandmother's New Hampshire garden. Our children would be named Richard, Peter, Amory, and Molly, named after my grandmother. Molly was going to be a three-day eventer on the US Olympic team.

". . . by the beginning of the twentieth century, B. B. had acquired a number of wealthy clients who appreciated his talent—shall we say genius—for attribution. He had an eagle eye for copies and forgeries and an encyclopedic memory . . ."

The Motley family had a yawl, the *Neptune*, and on that particular day we had sailed out to picnic on an island. I was running down the beach when my foot hit a piece of buried glass. My cousin Sally took one look at the blood and screamed. Richard came to the rescue. He pulled a dish towel from the picnic basket and wrapped it around my foot.

"It's okay, kid, nothing deep." He sat me down on a rock and put an arm around my shoulders. I stared at the long, muscled legs in the cutoff khakis, knowing that I would happily bleed to death as long as he was touching me. Years later I heard that he and Alison were married and living in California.

". . . it was a time when new millionaires like J. P. Morgan and Henry Clay Frick competed to own the great masters, Giorgiones, Raphaels. A Golden Age for art dealers, among them Joseph Duveen . . ."

Richard's hair was still thick and dark. Why on earth was he here? Had Liden decided that the art group was not worth the effort and Richard had come to act as Anna Deglos's escort? Were they more than old friends? It didn't matter. The teenage pain was long gone, but I must never let Caroline know that this was my first love, or she'd work at it like a dog with the proverbial bone. With a history of four husbands and a number of lovers, she considered herself an expert.

". . . drinks will be served on the terrace, followed by a light luncheon and a tour of the villa. You will be privileged to see a number of resident scholars at work . . ."

Caroline rolled her eyes. "Braying like an ass. I need a drink."

"Hang in, I think we're there," I said as the bus made a final turn and stopped.

The long, low villa was painted a tawny yellow with faded green shutters. Still talking, Dr. Klarnet led us to a wide graveled terrace. Like salmon leaping upstream, the group headed for a table set up as a bar. I took Caroline's arm as she teetered on the rough gravel and led her to a row of chairs against the wall.

"What do you want? I'll get it."

"A Bloody, if they have them. Plenty of vodka."

When I came back, Nathan Rennie was sitting with her. I handed her the drink and took mine to the edge of the terrace. Furrowed vineyards sloped below. Dark cypress trees, standing straight as pencils, punctuated distant hills.

Henry Train appeared, followed by Anna Deglos and Richard. "Beautiful view," Anna said to us. "I'd like you to meet an old friend, Richard Redson. So nice he could fly over at the last minute." She smiled at me. "I'm Anna Deglos. I don't think we met last night."

"Emma Streat," I said. Anna wasn't a beauty, but there was warmth and humor in her face. Her dark hair was streaked with gray. The short green dress could have come from a catalogue, not a designer's atelier.

Richard and I smiled and nodded. I took a sip of wine, annoyed that my heart was doing a fast tattoo. There were new lines in his face, but the eyes were the same blue bordering on hazel. What had happened to Alison? Had they escaped from her tight little circle of schools and cousins and clubs? I remembered swinging on a porch glider and overhearing her mother say that she liked Richard even though he came from Sacramento.

"Quite a view." Thomas Mellinton joined us. Not the most exciting man, but he had rescued me from Nando.

"Hi, how you all doing?" Lorraine Kegler was wearing a tight red dress, so short it barely covered her bottom. She reached out and touched my arm. "Honey, is it true you found a dead man in an alley last night?"

The others looked at me. "A man did die," I said carefully.

Lorraine waved her drink. "Is it true his throat was cut from ear to ear?"

I stiffened. "It's all in the hands of the police."

"Sure, but did you see him?"

Henry cleared his throat. "Whatever happened, the police will take care of it."

"I agree." Thomas Mellinton turned to me. "You should see the garden," he said and led the way toward a few squares of boxwood containing scraggly grass. The marble statue of a girl looked down with hollow eyes. "Dreadful woman," he said. "No manners whatsoever."

"But a man did die. How did she know?"

"It's hard to keep people from talking. I was told that you found him and saw the killer before he ran away."

I pushed back my hair. "But that's not true. I only heard men shouting, and I don't speak much Italian. When I realized someone was hurt, I went to get help, but he died. That's all."

"Most unfortunate, how stories become exaggerated. Have the police found a suspect?"

I hesitated. "To be honest, I have no idea."

"And you may never hear, not in a foreign country. As a lawyer, I would advise you to say as little as possible. By tomorrow people will have other things to gossip about." A pause. "Perhaps we should go back. I see people are moving into the house."

Lunch was served at long refectory tables. I picked at the pasta and made conversation with Nathan Rennie. One thing was clear: I was now a topic of conversation for two reasons.

Dr. Klarnet was on his feet again. ". . . the Germans blew up bridges, bombs were dropped, but Florence has survived disasters ever since Etruscans lived at a bend in the river. Then came Romans with forums and temples, followed by Renaissance builders set on creating a new Athens. At the turn of the twentieth century many foreigners came here to live, which created the phrase *a sunny place for shady people*." There were a few forced smiles.

Gelato, coffee, and finally the tour. We walked through dim rooms where scholars were bent over their desks. Dr. Klarnet kept up a running commentary: "Herbert here is devoting his life to a little-known Renaissance humanist, George of Trebizond . . ."

A painting of the Madonna hung on one wall. I stopped, struck by the expression on her face as she stared down at the swaddled baby. I too had held a newborn son, wondering what life held in store for him.

"Does she have the faintest idea of what lies ahead for that child?" I turned. Anna Deglos was standing beside me.

"Strange. I was thinking the same thing." We smiled at each other and moved on. I was beginning to like this woman.

After hours of togetherness, the trip back was made in near silence. Caroline was tired. "Italians have no idea how to make a good Bloody," she complained. "What's happening now? Where are we going?"

"Back to the palazzo." Recently, a friend had given me a heads-up about the progression of dementia: "At first, they fight it tooth and nail, but there often comes a kind of acceptance. They can't remember where they were five minutes ago, but they can name their bridesmaids."

Caroline was still in the fighting stage, but the cogs were slipping. If she was still tired at seven, I must cancel the unveiling dinner. Not risk bad behavior.

At last the bus crept slowly between the narrow fortress walls, turned, and came to a stop in the courtyard. The group disembarked. As I walked with Caroline to the loggia, Genevieve Train came up.

"Caroline, I've set my heart on Pratesi sheets. My concierge says she knows the best places, and there won't be another chance to shop. Are you interested?"

"My feet hurt, but take Emma. She can see me to my room and then come back."

I hesitated. Until now I'd been in the palazzo or with people—no need for Bailey. This would mean going into the streets, but Genevieve and the concierge would be with me. "Well, I could use some shoes," I said.

"Good. We'll meet in the anteroom in, say, twenty minutes."

As Anna Deglos walked by, Genevieve spoke to her. "Anna, Emma and I are off to do a quick shop. Would you like to join us?"

She stopped. "Let me think. I've deserted Cyrus all day, but I need to get presents in the worst way. How soon?"

"The anteroom in twenty minutes."

"I'll try, but please don't wait for me."

As we went up in the elevator, I spoke to Caroline. "Have a good rest. If you don't feel up to that unveiling dinner, we can cancel. Order from room service."

"Nonsense, and I won't be treated like a doddering old trout. All I need is my little toes-up. Go off, and for God's sake get yourself some decent shoes."

CHAPTER THIRTY-SIX

When I returned to the anteroom, Genevieve Train was turning in her key. "A nuisance, but I suppose electronic things don't work in these old doors. My concierge is waiting for us on the loggia. Her name is Rosa. She says she'll lead us to some great bargains. We'll give Anna a minute more."

Several men were standing nearby, debating whether to make a quick trip to the Bargello Museum. Nathan Rennie detached himself and came over to us.

"Let me guess. You're off to shop for shoes and table linens," he said.

Genevieve laughed. "It's easy to see why you're the sharpest art dealer in town. Here's Anna," she said as Anna came hurrying from the elevator.

"Sorry if I kept you waiting."

"You didn't. Off we go."

Rosa was middle-aged, wearing the standard black concierge suit. Like schoolgirls on a field trip, we followed her along the narrow pavements, stopping as she held up her hand.

"Ladies, in 1325 a law was passed forbidding sewage to be tipped into the street. Before that, it was the custom to call out three times before emptying the pots." As we emerged into a large square, Rosa stopped again. "We are now in what was once the civic center of Florence, the Piazza della Signoria."

At this hour, the piazza was crowded with tourists. The outdoor restaurants were filled with people reading newspapers and eating as waiters darted between the tables. Rosa raised her hand again. "The building in the center, the Palazzo Vecchio, once belonged to the Medici, the great family of Florence. Across the piazza lies the stone where the monk Savonarola was burned at the stake."

"Enough history," Genevieve muttered. "If we weren't in a hurry, I'd ask her where the man was stabbed in that movie."

The sun was still hot. I took off the green suede jacket and let it hang around my shoulders. Nearby, a man was playing a violin, a battered hat lay on the ground for money. Two carabinieri strutted by, handsome in their polished shoes and uniforms.

Our destination, the Via de' Tornabuoni, was lined with expensive shops. In one window, bedsheets were draped over an ornate table. Rosa halted.

"Are these to your taste, Mrs. Train? I know the owner. I assure you that here is the best value in town."

"I'd better have a look. What about you two?" Anna and I shook our heads. They left. Anna laughed. "A nice percentage for our Rosa, wouldn't you say?"

"Definitely, but our Genevieve's no soft touch. I have a feeling she'll give the owner a hard time."

The next shop window displayed a collection of majolica plates, cups, and pitchers. "Those little pitchers would make good presents to take home," Anna said. "Very Italian and they can be used for lots of things."

"Let's go in—oh my God." I swung around. A few yards away, a woman had fallen facedown on the pavement. She was screaming loudly, clutching her head.

"The poor thing," Anna said, raising her voice. "Should we do something?"

"I don't think so. People are stopping. Someone will call for help."

The screaming continued, a steady earsplitting screech. More people were gathering. I heard the words *Misericordia* and *carabiniere.*

Anna put her hands to her ears. "If there's nothing—we might as well go in."

A rowdy group of men came marching toward us, singing loudly. They were wearing backpacks and bright knitted caps. As they passed, one hit me squarely on the shoulder. I stumbled and fell, dropping my bag.

"Watch it," I yelled and got to my feet, preparing to vent annoyance. Too late. They were going fast, almost at the corner.

The woman was still screaming, arms flailing the air. I brushed the dirt off my trousers—the scrapes on my knees were stinging—and went into the shop.

The woman behind the counter smiled. "May I help you, Signora?"

"Those little pitchers in the window," I began, and turned to speak to Anna. She wasn't there. I looked around. "My friend," I said. "Didn't she come in?"

"Only you, Signora."

"Are you sure?"

"Yes, Signora."

In the shop next door, Genevieve was negotiating with a young man. Rosa was standing to one side, looking sour.

"Did Mrs. Deglos come in?" I asked her.

"No, Signora. She was with you."

Back on the pavement, I looked up and down the street, not sure what to do. No one vanished into thin air. Anna couldn't have gone far.

A crowd was still standing around the woman lying on the pavement. Suddenly the screaming stopped. She jumped to her feet and pushed away the helping hands. I stared. What was this?

She didn't seem to be hurt at all, so why fall down and make such a horrendous scene?

The answer came with sickening force. "Kidnappers have a favorite trick," a detective once told me. "They create accidents using decoys. Divert attention from the kidnapping. You'd be surprised how often it works."

My hand went to my throat. First the screaming, then the blow that knocked me to the ground. In those few seconds the men could have seized Anna and carried her off as they sang at the top of their voices. No one would have heard her cry out. Right now, she could be gagged, blindfolded, held captive in a car speeding away.

I ran toward the woman, now trying to free herself from the crowd. "Stop her," I yelled at the top of my long-ago damaged throat. "Stop her. Call the police."

The woman turned. I got a glimpse of her face. Young, not pretty, dark eyes. A flowered scarf hid most of her hair. She lowered her head, charged through the crowd, and dashed into the street. I followed, shouting, but she was too fast for me. She reached the corner and disappeared.

I stumbled back to the pavement and reached for a lamppost. A young couple pushing a stroller passed, followed by a gaggle of teenage girls. I stood there, clinging to the lamppost. Impossible, but it had happened. I could run back to the Piazza della Signoria and find that pair of carabinieri—no. Going to the police meant reports, red tape, delay when every moment counted. Anna's very life could depend on keeping my head.

I hurried back to Genevieve. "Anna isn't feeling well," I said to her. "It's just a headache, but we're going back to the palazzo. She says for you to stay and finish your shopping."

"If you're sure—we're almost done here."

"I'm sure."

Breaking into a jog, I dashed through the Piazza della Signoria. Just minutes ago, Anna and I had been strolling along, listening to Rosa's spiel. At the next corner I made a wrong turn and had to retrace my steps. Finally, I was in the narrow street that led to the palazzo, but as I ran, another thought was racing through my head: Could the kidnappers have made a mistake? Maybe I was the one who was targeted. Not Anna.

When I arrived, breathless from the sprint, the elderly manager was at the desk. It was the first time we had met since the murder in the alley. "I trust you had a pleasant day, Signora," he said.

"Yes, very pleasant. I . . . I need directions. I'm expected in the Liden suite, but I don't know where it is."

"The Da Vinci suite is on the first floor, Signora. Facing the river."

"*Grazie.*" I took my key and headed for the elevator, wanting to bolt to my room. How in God's name could I face the formidable Cyrus Liden? Face him and tell him that Anna wasn't coming back?

The long hall was hung with faded tapestries and ended in a massive door. I knocked. It opened and the big bodyguard stood there.

I took a deep breath. "I'm Mrs. Streat," I said. "I'm with the group here. I need to see Mr. Liden."

"Is he expecting you?"

"No, but I *must* see him. It's—I have bad news about Mrs. Deglos." Something about my distress must have reached him. He hesitated, then opened the door wider and let me in.

CHAPTER THIRTY-SEVEN

The *salone* was the size of a small cathedral; stone chimneys rose to a distant ceiling. Cyrus Liden and Richard Redson were sitting at a table at the far end of the room. The bodyguard spoke to them in a low voice. Richard came forward. His face showed concern.

"We met at I Tatti. Mrs. Deglos went out to shop. Has something happened?"

"We went together. We—she—" The word *kidnap* stuck in my throat.

"Was there an accident?"

"No. That is, it wasn't an accident."

Cyrus Liden got to his feet. "What, then? Speak up."

I swallowed. "She—we—were looking at majolica in a window. A woman near us fell down and began to scream. She lay on the pavement screaming at the top of her lungs. That's when it must have happened."

"What happened?" This from Richard.

"These men came by. A group of them. Singing. They knocked me down. When I got up—at first I thought she'd gone into the shop. When she wasn't there, I realized—but they were so *fast*."

Liden sat down. He put his head in his hands. Richard cleared his throat. "Can you describe them?"

"They were dressed like tourists with backpacks. Knitted caps pulled down. They went swaggering by singing a song. Anna was standing beside me. The next minute she wasn't *there.*" Tears were coming, stinging my eyes.

"She didn't struggle at all? Cry out?"

"I told you, it was so fast. The screaming stopped. The woman was on her feet, she wasn't hurt. She wasn't hurt at all. That's when I knew it was a trick. I tried to chase her, but she got away."

Cyrus Liden raised his head. The little goatee quivered. "You were with her. You should have seen—you could have stopped them."

I stepped back as if he had hit me.

"Wait here. I'll be back," Richard said to me, then he took Cyrus Liden's arm and led him toward a door beside the great fireplace.

I stumbled to one of the stiff chairs. Unbearable—but he was right. I *should* have seen what was happening. Held on to Anna and stopped them.

Moments passed. The bodyguard had placed himself in front of the door, arms crossed over his chest, watching me.

At last the door by the fireplace opened and Richard came out. He pulled up a chair, sat down, and looked at me. "We need to talk. This is pretty bad, but you aren't at fault. Mr. Liden now blames himself for not keeping her here, or not sending the bodyguard with her."

I nodded.

"Mrs. Streat, I was introduced as an old friend, but I'm here because I run a security consulting service in California. We handle criminal investigations, and Cyrus Liden is one of my clients. Luckily, I was in London at a meeting when he called. I flew over last night because he was concerned that a waiter was seen in his bedroom and could have installed intrusive technology. When there's trouble, Liden prefers to use his own people."

I nodded again.

He leaned forward. "I realize that this has been a very distressing experience. You showed good judgment in coming straight here. Now we have to act fast, use every possible asset. Will you answer a few questions?"

"Of course."

"Who suggested the shopping trip?"

"Mrs. Train. In the anteroom. After we got off the bus."

"Who could have overheard this talk?"

"Quite a few people."

"Their names?"

"Henry Train, Nathan Rennie, Thomas Mellinton. I'm not sure about the Keglers."

"What about staff?"

"The young concierge at the desk. Two of the porters were standing nearby."

"So, a mix of guests and staff. How long was it between the time you made plans and when you started off?"

"Twenty minutes, maybe a little more. I took my godmother to her room. It was another twenty minutes before we got to the shop."

"Forty minutes, give or take. Not much time to carry out an abduction unless those men were organized and ready to act on a signal from an informant. How did you get to Via de' Tornabuoni?"

"Through the Piazza della Signoria. Mrs. Train and her concierge went into a shop. That was when the woman started to scream. Caused a distraction."

"Can you describe her?"

"I only had one look, but she was young. She had dark eyes and a flowered scarf tied over her head. And she was a fast runner."

"If she's found, could you identify her?"

"I might, but it would have to be soon. My godmother and I are flying out at noon tomorrow." I twisted my hands. "I still can't believe those men took her. If they hadn't knocked me down, I might have, might have . . ." My voice wavered.

"You acted promptly. Try not to look back. Keep in mind that most kidnappings end well." He stood up. "I must get back. We can talk while I walk you to the door."

As we began the long march, I glanced at him. "You say most kidnappings end well. But being in Italy—what can you do?"

"There's a process, nothing secret about it. I'll set up a command post here. Fly in an expert with equipment for tracing calls when the demand for ransom comes in. Then we start negotiating, but these things can take time. Trickier when you're dealing with Liden's kind of money."

"What about the Italian police?"

"A *commissario* is on his way. We'll have to keep staff out of the suite, stop the talk that anything is wrong." A pause. "It's important that none of our fellow guests hear about this."

"I told Mrs. Train I was taking Anna back to the palazzo because of a headache, but there'll be questions when she doesn't appear tonight. I *could* say the headache is worse. Oh God, this dinner. I'm not one of these rich collectors. I came to be with my godmother who's losing her mind. It's been one disaster after another."

We were reaching the door to the hall. He took my hand. His was warm and strong. "I realize it's hard, but try to act as if nothing is wrong. I'll let you know if there's any news."

"I'll—well, thank you." He was being kind, but showing kindness was part of a good investigator's tool kit.

Back in my room, Viola had closed the shutters and turned on the lights. It was late, already after seven. The red light on my phone was blinking. Caroline's voice resonated in my ear. "Where are you? It's late."

No chance to abort this dinner and avoid having to put on a public face. I fought the compulsion to get into bed and pull the covers over my head. Went to the armoire and pulled out the utilitarian black dress. Caroline's dazzling necklace, the magnet for Nando's attentions, was back in a drawer. I might run into him and his parents, but with luck he wouldn't risk another verbal lashing. In any case, all that mattered now was to hold myself together for the next few hours. Put on a smiling face and hide my inner agony. *Oh Anna, where are you? What are they doing to you?*

CHAPTER THIRTY-EIGHT

There was no "darling girl" greeting for me when I arrived in Caroline's room. She didn't even notice the old black dress. "For God's sake, Emma, where have you been?"

"Sorry, sorry, the shopping took forever, then I went for a walk and lost track of the time."

Once again, the group had gathered in the anteroom. Luisa was waiting. "Good evening, ladies. Your car is here to take you to La Serena. Your driver will return for you at midnight. I trust you will have a memorable evening."

"One thing," I said. "We'll need a car to go to the airport tomorrow, to be here at eleven thirty. Mrs. Vogt's plane is scheduled for a noon takeoff."

"I will make the arrangements."

Genevieve Train touched my arm. "I hear Anna and Cyrus Liden aren't coming tonight. I hope her headache isn't worse."

"She did say she was afraid it might turn into a migraine. She gets them."

"Luckily they don't last long. As for Liden, I don't understand why he bothered to come at all. I've never heard of him buying any paintings. Any kind of art. I suppose Anna talked him into it. By the way, Caroline doesn't look well."

"Too long a day, too much walking. I wanted her to give up tonight, but she wouldn't hear of it."

Once again, we crossed the river and started down the wide

embankment, but tonight we passed through the city and out into the countryside. Caroline's hand, heavy with rings, began to pluck at the skirt of her white Givenchy dress. Not a good sign. "Are we going to the moon?" she asked.

"The cars ahead are barely moving, we must be almost there—oh my God!" I reached across her and pointed. "Oh, my God, Caroline, look at that."

Above and to the left loomed a castle built high with turrets. Tall statues on the roof were outlined against the sky. Torches flamed. A great stream of water rose from an illuminated fountain.

The car slowed and stopped beside a long flight of marble stairs. Motionless footmen stood at attention on every step. They were dressed in bright colored tights and doublets with flowing sleeves.

We got out. I took Caroline's arm and we began to climb. Halfway up, she stopped and looked at me. "What *is* this? Why are we here?"

"To see an old painting. It's why we flew over." My hand tightened. I should have followed my gut instinct not to come. Her mental cog was slipping, but our car had already disappeared.

We reached the top of the stairs, entered the majestic great hall, and stopped. The din from hundreds of guests echoed and re-echoed from the distant ceiling. We stood still, hemmed in by the crowd.

Caroline dug her fingers into my arm. "Who are all these people? I have to sit down," she shouted.

I looked around, feeling helpless, then saw that Dr. Klarnet was coming our way. I waved wildly. He swerved.

"Welcome to La Serena," he boomed. "I will lead you to your group." Like ships plowing through ice, we followed.

The Trains, the Keglers, Nathan Rennie, and Thomas Mellinton, holding drinks and looking appalled, were huddled under giant urns and a faded fresco of gods conferring on Mt. Olympus.

"Mr. Train, I have a problem," I said to him. "Caroline absolutely has to sit down."

"It's a scrum, but I see chairs against the wall over there. I'll bulldoze the way." In a moment Caroline was seated on a gilded chair.

Our little group rearranged itself. Thomas looked at me and shook his head. "At home we would call this a bun fight."

"Bun fight—we'll be lucky if we ever see a bun."

His lips twitched. "I shouldn't care to make a wager. I trust you ladies had a successful shopping expedition."

Genevieve shrugged. "Pricey, but I got my sheets. Too bad about Anna and her migraine, but I'll have one myself if we don't eat soon. That'll shut people up. Can't shout if you have food in your mouth."

Nathan Rennie laughed. "Don't get your hopes up. Emma, you and Caroline need drinks. I see a waiter in a medieval costume coming this way. Will you take whatever's on offer?"

"Anything at all," I said.

"Look, folks," Lorraine Kegler waved her glass. "Over there. It's Countess Bracciolini. Shall we go over and say hi?"

No one moved.

The tall, tinted blonde was standing a few feet away with a group of people. She was wearing a red dress with a huge pleated collar that framed her face. No sign of Nando, but I turned away and spoke to Nathan Rennie.

"I heard you talking about going to a museum. Did you ever get there?"

"There wasn't time—relax, Lorraine. Here she comes."

I looked around. The countess was marching toward us, drink in hand. She stopped squarely in front of me.

"Mrs. Streat. It's a disgrace. You should be arrested for preying on a boy half your age."

I stared. It took a few seconds to process what she was saying. No words came.

"Don't look so innocent. You sold my boy a bad drug. You took him off to some place last night and sold him a bad drug. He's been extremely sick. He could have died."

"*What*?" My hand went to my neck. "Took him off—I did no such thing. Your son is lying."

"My son never lies. Your friends should know what you're doing on the sly, making money off young boys."

"That's quite enough, madam." Thomas stepped forward. "You're quite mistaken. Last night at dinner your son was annoying this lady with aggressive attentions."

"I tell you, she sells drugs."

"Countess." Henry Train, always an imposing figure, drew himself up. "Your son followed Mrs. Streat back to the palazzo. He tried to persuade Mrs. Streat to go with him to a nightclub. She refused. If anyone is out of line, it's your son."

"My son nearly died. The police—"

"Madam." Thomas again. "As a lawyer, I can tell you that what you say borders on slander. Your only evidence comes from your son. You should investigate further before making such accusations."

The countess looked at him and then at Henry. She opened her mouth, then closed it, turned on her heel, and went back to her group.

Lorraine was the first to break the stunned silence. She shook out her long platinum hair. "Jesus H. Christ. We all heard you tell the bastard to get lost." She put an arm around my shoulder. "Hey, if someone pinches you in the ass over here, you shout *che schifo*. That means 'how revolting.' I'll go over and say that to her."

"No. Don't," I said.

"Why not? Listen, honey, you're not a seller. She's had one too many—or maybe she's the one who's using. Now she's talking about you to her friends. They're all gawking at you."

"Let them." I tried to smile, but I knew what she was saying: *You see that woman over there, the one with dark red hair? Her name is Emma. Emma Streat. She pretends not to be a dealer, but she sold Nando a drug that almost killed him.*

Until now Caroline had been sitting quietly on a chair. She got to her feet and looked around like a bewildered old dog. "Emma. I don't like this place. I don't like these people. I want to go."

I took her hand. "We will. We'll find our car—oh no, we can't. The driver won't be back until midnight."

As usual, Henry came to the rescue. "I'll see that you get a car. Mellinton, if you'll escort these ladies through the crowd, I'll meet you out front."

"Right." Thomas offered his arm to Caroline. "Allow me."

I turned to the others. "I'm sorry, very sorry," I said, and hurried after them, aware that the countess and her friends were watching.

The costumed footmen were still lined up on the marble stairs, an incongruous display of pageantry in what now felt like a nightmare.

"Train has gone to find an official who can produce a car," Thomas said as I joined them. "I fancy he's a man who gets results."

"I think you're right. And thank you for speaking up to the countess. For a moment I was paralyzed. I couldn't believe what she was saying."

"Most unpleasant. I've seen similar cases. Mothers blind to their children's misbehavior. I think you have ample grounds to take her to court, particularly if the damaging story spreads."

"Which it will. In hindsight, I had no idea her son would turn out to be such a little rat. I should have left him ranting in the anteroom. Gone upstairs with my godmother, instead of making sure he left and getting mixed up in a murder."

"Well, by now the police have found the assailant."

"I hope so." I wasn't going to talk about the ongoing investigation—and the death of a stranger in the alley paled compared to losing Anna. "Will you be going back to Hong Kong?" I asked.

"I may stay a few more days. A former colleague is arriving in town. He expects me to show him around." He stopped. Henry Train was coming up the steps, accompanied by the Brazilian lady, diamonds hanging from her ears and bosom. She nodded to us and swept on.

"Her driver will take you ladies back to the palazzo," Henry said. "Now, Caroline, Mellinton and I will help you down the stairs. We won't let you fall."

Step by step, we went down the long flight. As Caroline was handed into the car, Henry spoke to me. "For two cents I'd desert Genevieve and go back with you. What time are you off tomorrow?"

"At noon. I can't thank you enough for finding the car. *And* for confronting the countess."

"That boy certainly managed to pull her chain. Something wrong with him, he had no reason to behave like that, cause trouble. Not as if you didn't have enough on your plate."

"I know. It doesn't make sense."

"Well, we'll all be home tomorrow."

The driver was waiting. I joined Caroline in the car and we moved off. The fountain, the turrets with flags all faded into darkness.

The air had grown cool. I rubbed my arms for warmth and thought about the countess. Even drunk, to behave like that was extreme. Worse, she seemed to believe those lies. As for Nando, his behavior last night was bad enough, but why on earth would he want to whip his protective mother into a rage, making me a victim of the international gossip mill? Was it out of revenge for being rejected? His lies would certainly cross the ocean, might even be picked up by the press.

Caroline was plucking at her skirt again. "That woman. I've seen her before. I thought she was going to hit you."

"She had too much to drink." In her prime, Caroline would have pulverized that upstart from Kansas.

At last we turned into the paved courtyard. Caroline looked around. "I know this place. I'm cold."

"It's the palazzo. Before you know it, you'll be tucked up warm and cozy."

I delivered her to the indispensable Bailey, went back to my room, and lay down on the bed, too tired to take off my clothes. Anna—I hadn't thought about Anna for hours. Dear God, let her be found alive. Let this nightmare be over soon.

After a while I pulled myself up and slid out of my dress. I must try to sleep, but there would be nightmares. Men with backpacks swinging along the street. The countess standing in front of me with venom coming out of her mouth. A year ago, I had been sitting outside Florian's in Venice, watching pigeons and caught in the middle of escalating disasters. Then, as now, two words kept pounding in my head: *Get out. Get out. Get out.*

CHAPTER THIRTY-NINE

September 17

Even a few hours of sleep can steady the mind. I faced the day, ready to cope with the process of leaving. In a few hours Caroline and I would be on our way to the airport. The Gulfstream would rise into the sky, away from this ill-starred place, but there would still be the worry about Anna. If I heard nothing from Richard by eleven, I'd have to get in touch.

By nine I was dressed, packed, and on my way to Caroline's room. She was sitting up in bed, wearing her Japanese kimono, drinking coffee. I leaned down and kissed her cheek. "It's a beautiful day for flying. How are you?"

"My legs hurt. I'm going to spend the day in bed."

I straightened the coverlet and looked at Bailey. For the first time, she shook her head as if to imply she could do nothing.

This was a complication no one needed. I took a deep breath. "I'm sorry," I said. "Really sorry. We did too much yesterday, but as soon as we're in the air, you can lie down. Sleep all the way to New York."

Caroline sipped at her coffee, looking mulish. "I'm not leaving. I came to see a painting. I paid the earth to some foundation. Either I see it, or I want my money back."

"Oh, that. Mistakes were made, but don't worry. Delsey will arrange everything. Eat something while I go take care of a few things." Rather than ask Caroline for her credit card, I would have to use mine—and hope it would cover enormous expenses. Between us, Bailey and I would prevail, even if the plane had to wait.

Viola was in my room, changing the sheets. "I'll be leaving soon," I told her. "That dress—the one with the blood stains. Were you able to get them out?"

"I try, Signora. I try, but nothing take away the blood—" She choked and covered her mouth.

"It doesn't matter," I said quickly. "I didn't mean to upset you."

"*Mi scusi*, it's not the signora who upset me. The *polizia*, they come again this morning. They ask the staff questions. I tell them that Mario needed money for his sick wife. Whatever he do wrong, it was because someone pay him money, much money, to go into that suite."

I looked at her. "He was paid to go into the suite? Are you sure?"

"*Dio mio*, he wanted money for his wife. A disease of the stomach. Why else would he do such a thing? Besides, to kill with a knife, this is the work of a mafioso. Bad things are happening in the palazzo, Signora."

"What bad things?"

"Ah." Viola crossed herself and looked around. "When the walls have ears, it is dangerous to speak. I say no more."

I frowned. True, money was a classic reason to kill, along with lust and revenge. If he had failed to do something illegal in the suite, he and the other man might have been arguing about payment, but I had no time—or reason—to dig deeper.

"Here." I opened my handbag and handed her a wad of euros. "For the sick wife."

"Signora." Her hand went to her heart. "So much. I remember you in my prayers. It is good you leave now. There is sickness in the palazzo. The lady in the big suite, she very sick. The maid and the waiter, they told not to go in."

"I hope it's nothing serious." So the plan was to hide Anna's disappearance by spreading rumors of contagion—but how long would it last?

Heavy knocking sounded on the door. Viola went to open it. Mr. Liden's bodyguard was standing there. He glanced at Viola and then at me. "I've come to take Mrs. Streat to Mr. Liden's suite," he said.

Was Anna dead? Every possible disaster streamed through my mind. I must go, even though it would delay dealing with Caroline.

The bodyguard set a fast pace. I followed, almost running to keep up. No use to ask questions. He was just carrying out orders.

As we reached the carved door to the suite, he opened it and waved me into the *salone*. I paused, took a deep breath to steady myself, and began the long march down the worn parquet floor.

CHAPTER FORTY

Three men were sitting around a table at the far end. Cyrus Liden, Richard Redson, and the young *commissario*, whose name I had forgotten.

Richard got to his feet and came to meet me. "Thank you for coming."

"What's happened? Is she—"

"Nothing. No calls, no ransom demand. Liden is leaning hard on the police, but the more people involved, the greater the risk that someone will tip off the press."

As we reached the table, Mr. Liden made a gesture of rising. He had aged overnight, but the intimidating aura remained.

"Sit down, Mrs. Streat," he said abruptly. "The *commissario* has questions."

I sat. The *commissario* picked up a paper with nicotine-stained fingers.

"Signora. Two nights ago, we have the killing of the waiter. Yesterday, the kidnap of Signora Deglos. You were present at both events."

I nodded, not liking the implication. Where was he going with this?

He picked up another paper. "About the abduction. A woman lay down on the pavement and began to scream. This woman. Please describe her."

"She was wearing a scarf over her head. Flowered, mostly red.

It was tied around her forehead, hiding most of her hair. She was young. She had dark eyes. I ran after her, but she was too fast. I've already told Mr. Redson all I know."

"But you saw her. Therefore, you can identify her."

"It was only for a few seconds and unless you've already caught her, I'm afraid I can't help. I'll be leaving Florence at noon."

Cyrus Liden cleared his throat. "Mrs. Streat, so far the only identifiable face is that of the woman—and you are the only person who can make the identification."

"No," I said quickly. "That's not true. There was a crowd around her. People a lot closer than I was. When I called out not to let her go, they saw her run away. They could see she wasn't hurt."

"That may be, but unfortunately appealing to the public would bring in the media and compromise a rescue." Liden paused. "The fact is, you are needed to make the identification. The woman can then be treated as an accomplice. She may be able to give us valuable information."

I stiffened. This was asking a great deal of me—and the police should be handling this situation. "I understand," I said, "but finding her may take days. Weeks. If she's found, and you still want me, I'll fly right back."

"That would take time and time is of the essence." A pause. "Keep this in mind, Mrs. Streat. If you had acted promptly, this might never have happened. Anna might never have been taken." Liden's pale blue eyes were colder than ice.

I dug my fingers into the arm of the chair. He might be one of the richest men in the world, used to having his own way, but to pressure me by applying guilt was wrong.

"Mr. Liden, believe me, I'd do almost anything to help Mrs. Deglos. Anything at all, but I have to take my godmother back to New York. She isn't well, and her plane is waiting. As I say, when that woman is found, I'll come back."

"But that might be too late." He touched the little goatee. "A few hours could make a difference. There is a reason—" His voice broke. "Tell her, Redson. Tell her." He got to his feet and stumbled through the door by the fireplace.

Richard stood up. "Excuse us," he said to the *commissario*, then motioned me to follow him to the arched window.

"Anna means a great deal to Cyrus Liden," he said in a low voice. "She has a way of smoothing his life. He's desperate to get her back, no matter what it takes. That's why he spoke to you like that."

"All the same—"

"I'll try to explain. Five, no, six months ago, Anna Deglos was diagnosed with a rare kind of neuropathy, a disease of the nervous system. He's taken her all over the country, to the Mayo Clinic, the Cleveland Clinic, to every top doctor in that field. It's a severe and unusual case. At the moment she's on daily medications—that's why she could make this trip. Without them her condition will start to deteriorate. Fast."

I swallowed. "Meds. Her meds. Did she have them in her bag?"

"No. By tomorrow she'll begin to feel pins and needles in her arms and legs. Then numbness, then severe pain. At that point every hour counts, or she may become paralyzed. Her organs may fail."

"Oh, my God."

"Every effort is being made to find both women. That may change if we get a call from the kidnappers and can start negotiating. It's a matter of time."

I closed my eyes, remembering heart-wrenching appeals on the news, parents begging kidnappers to return a sick child before it was too late. Right now, Anna needed me far more than Caroline did.

"I wish Mr. Liden had told me straight out," I said. "I'll stay if I convince my godmother to go without me. Give her a reason she can grasp without telling her about the kidnapping. It won't be easy."

"Well, do your best."

We turned away from the window. The *commissario* was standing by the table, pulling at his tie. No doubt he needed a cigarette, but there was no ashtray in sight.

Richard approached him. "Mrs. Streat may be able to stay. Is there any way to accelerate the search for the kidnappers' woman?"

"Every known mafia and terrorist network is being investigated. The Polizia di Stato have been brought in."

"An informer may have been planted in the palazzo. What steps are you taking with the staff?"

"We continue to question. One may come forward. I go now. I will keep you informed." His heels clicked sharply on the parquet floor as he left.

I glanced at Richard, the intermediary between Liden and the police. He looked tired. He must have been up all night.

"There's another problem," I said. "If I stay, I'll have to arrange to stay on in my room."

"I'll speak to the manager. He's a trusted family retainer, determined to protect the palazzo's reputation and stop any leaks to the press. We're using him as a conduit to the staff. They've been told that Mrs. Deglos is ill. Even the maids and waiters aren't allowed to go in."

"No service at all? That must be difficult."

"It is." He handed me a card. "Call this number after you've talked with your godmother."

By now the clock was running—and Caroline hadn't moved from the big bed. "Where were you?" she snapped.

I removed the breakfast tray and sat down. Ever since talking to Richard, I had struggled to think of a valid excuse to stay, one that she would accept. Nothing made sense. I was getting desperate when inspiration came to the rescue.

"Men," I said loudly.

"What about them?"

"You're always trying to find a man for me."

"I'm about to give up. You're not young anymore."

"I know. Believe me, I know. Why I'm asking you for a big favor. A very big favor. That man with Anna Deglos when we went to I Tatti. I told you I used to know him, but I didn't tell you that he was my first love. Once upon a time I was crazy mad in love with him."

Caroline pulled herself up. Her eyes brightened. "Go on."

"One summer in Maine was very intense. I never saw him again until yesterday, but I never forgot him. Now it turns out he has never forgotten me."

"He told you? When?"

"Yesterday. Just before I went off to shop. It was the first time we'd had a few moments alone. I can hardly believe it, but the vibes are still there after all these years. Really there."

"I suppose he's married."

"Divorced. Here's the thing, the big favor. He wants me to stay on with him. Be with him for a few days in Florence."

It took Caroline a moment to process the thought. "Stay with him? In Florence?"

"I said I'd talk to you. Explain that we want to see if we have a future together. I told him that you would understand, that you were always trying to find the right man for me."

"*That's* true. A lost love. How sweet—but I need you to go back with me."

"Don't worry, you'll have Bailey. I'll take you to the airport and Delsey will meet you at the other end. But if you don't think you can manage, I'll tell Richard it's all off."

More processing. I held my breath. "Oh, Emma," she said at last. "I want you to have a life, not spend it getting mixed up in everyone else's troubles. Tell what's-his-name it's settled."

"You're a treasure." I leaned over and kissed her. "I can never thank you enough."

"Not so fast. Where are you and this man going to stay?"

"I'm . . . not sure. He's making the arrangements."

"As long as it's not one of those little *pensiones* where they charge extra for a towel."

I laughed. "How would you know? You've never stayed in that kind of place in your life."

"No, and I don't plan to." She hesitated. "Darling girl, he may have changed and not for the better. I'd hate you to go out on a limb and fall off. Break bones."

"You mean, break my heart. That's always a risk, but here's the bright side. We both know where we come from. We have the same sort of background. That's important." With Rodale, I was always the outsider.

"Well, be careful. I'll be expecting a call. A full report, and I mean full."

"You'll have it. Now it's time to get dressed."

"Don't rush me," she snapped and went into the bathroom.

Bailey had been silent. Now she looked at me. "I'm not sure about this. My job is to provide security for you, not leave you here alone."

I reached out and touched her arm. "You've been great. I couldn't have managed without you, but there haven't been any threats and it's important for me to stay. I'll be careful. I won't go anywhere alone."

Back in my room, I talked to Delsey, then called the number Richard had given me. "It's done," I said. "I can stay. I just have to take her to the airport."

It took the combined efforts of Bailey, two maids, and a porter to collect and transport Caroline and her clothes. When we arrived at the airport, the head pilot, Sam, was standing on the tarmac beside the Gulfstream V.

"There's Sam," I said as we got out. "He'll look after you. Have a good flight."

Caroline blinked. "You're not coming?"

"No, because you're being an angel, letting me stay with my first love. Wish me luck."

"Oh. Yes. Don't forget to send reports. I want to know how he is in bed."

Sam came forward, a capable man with the air of a seasoned Marine. "All set for takeoff, Mrs. Vogt."

"The sooner the better. Ghastly place. People you'd never want to lay eyes on again."

"Sorry to hear that." He took her arm and they walked up the steps to the cabin.

I waved as the plane taxied down the runway, then turned to the driver. "Back to the Palazzo Otterini," I said to him. No shopping or sightseeing. It was beginning to sink in that I was now on my own—for how long?

CHAPTER FORTY-ONE

The day was getting warmer. People on the streets were wearing coats slung over shoulders. When I got back to the palazzo, the manager was waiting to see me.

"Do you wish to have the signora Vogt's suite?" he asked. "It can be arranged."

"Thank you, but I'd rather stay where I am. For the moment, anyhow."

I went to my room, poured myself a glass of mineral water, and thought of the moment when Anna and I were standing in front of the Madonna painting, wondering what lay ahead for the baby Jesus. Without her medications, even Cyrus Liden's billions couldn't save Anna from pain. I must remember that I was only a small part of a rescue effort, available when needed, but otherwise out of sight.

Running was an antidote to stress, and I had been two days without exercise. I went into the marble bathroom and collected two thick towels. Laid them on the worn parquet floor and took off my shirt. First the push-ups, then power yoga. Even in this short time I was getting out of shape.

As I began the push-ups, I thought about my boys. I must text them that I'd been delayed in Italy. Not why.

Ten, twenty, thirty push-ups, ending with a yoga workout. I was winding down when a knock on the door brought me scrambling to my feet. I reached for a towel to wipe my face, and went to open it. Richard was standing there.

My stomach did a steep dive. "Has something happened?"

"No. Sorry if I surprised you. To be honest, I was afraid you might have changed your mind at the last moment and hopped onto the plane." He looked from me to the towel.

"Working out. I'm a dripping mess."

"You said it, not me. Look. I'm taking a short break for lunch. If you feel like joining me, I'll give you an idea of what's going on in the suite."

"I'd like that." I hesitated. "Actually—it seems years ago—Anna and I walked through the Piazza della Signoria and I wanted to sit down in one of those outdoor cafés. Drink wine. Watch the people going by."

"Piazza della Signoria, then."

"I need to take a shower and change. Give me ten minutes."

"Back in fifteen."

"I'll be ready," I said and closed the door. This was an unexpected turn of events, but it made sense for him to combine eating and business with a woman who was on his hands for the foreseeable future.

At the crowded Piazza della Signoria, bands of children were running around the massive gray walls, shouting and waving flags. Rows of teenagers sat on the steps, laughing and smoking. Overhead, the sun shone brilliantly in a deep blue September sky.

The outdoor restaurants were filled. "Now to get a table," Richard said. "No, we're in luck. That couple is leaving."

We sat down at a small table made of imitation wicker; the brown plaid cloth was covered with cups and leftover plates of food.

"*Buon giorno.*" A waiter in a tan jacket and black bow tie swept the litter onto a tray and stood waiting for our order.

"What would you like?" Richard asked.

"A sandwich. Maybe a gelato after."

"*Due* panini," he said to the waiter. "Chianti Antonelli, *per favore.*"

"*Litro*?"

"*Litro*."

"*Si*, Signor." Raising the tray above his head, he slid off like a dancer, not missing a beat.

I had changed into a white shirt and the green suede jacket. Richard was wearing khakis and a blue button-down shirt, comfortable clothes that reminded me of Maine. As he spoke to the waiter, I made a closer survey. He was still in good shape, a little taller than me. Dark hair. Good looking, not handsome. The real change was in his voice. It was measured, as if he had learned to be careful with words.

"You seem to know your way around," I said.

"I've spent time in Italy. Mainly business. How about you?"

"A few visits. My first time in Florence." I leaned back and studied the huge statues under the colonnades. "I wish I knew more about its history."

"Well, you're in the old civic center. At the sound of bells, all Florence would come running. Mob scenes, stonings, the burning of the monk Savonarola."

"What about that ugly tower?"

"The town house of the Medicis until the Grand Duke built the Pitti Palace. Never underestimate the power of the Medicis. Even the statues over there were symbols. Will that do you?"

"That'll do me."

The panini arrived, along with a bottle of wine.

Richard filled the glasses and tasted. "Drinkable. By the way, what did you say to your godmother?"

I took a bite of crusty bread. "I'm not sure I should tell you."

"Why not?"

"Besides being a pack of lies, it's embarrassing."

"Try me."

I picked up the glass, then put it down. "First of all, you have to understand that my godmother is forever trying to set me up with men. Worse since my husband died, that was almost two years ago."

"Sorry to hear that."

"Anyhow, when I went back, she was still in bed. I had no idea what I was going to say to her. Then—a brainstorm. My godmother has had four husbands and a string of lovers. She considers herself an expert on men. Don't laugh, but I told her that you and I had a wild fling years ago. I said if she let me stay, there might be a chance to find out if the vibes were still there."

"She bought that?"

"Yes, and one part is true." I ran my finger over a spot on the brown tablecloth. "You don't remember, but we *have* met before."

"We have? Where?"

"In Maine. One summer. You were at MIT, visiting Alison Motley. I was staying with my cousin Sally Amory."

He frowned. "I'm pretty good with faces—it's part of my job. I should have remembered yours."

"I'm glad you didn't. Fifteen, skinny, all legs and braces. I thought you were God's gift, why I was always tagging along, getting in everyone's hair. My big moment was when we sailed out to one of the islands. I cut my foot on a piece of glass. You wrapped it in a towel and said I was going to live."

He began to smile. "It's coming back. That picnic. The brat. Sally's little cousin. No wonder I didn't recognize you at I Tatti."

"I heard later you and Alison got married. I thought you were very brave to cope with her ultraconservative family."

"It wasn't easy. We got divorced eight years ago. No children, faults on both sides. Mine was getting too involved with work. Silicon Valley tech burnout, then I started the security company." He paused. "Allie never wanted to leave Boston. In the end she went home and married a State Street banker. It might have been better if we'd stayed in Boston, but you never know what's ahead."

"Maybe that's just as well." I took a sip of wine. Instead of making polite conversation, we were beginning to talk like friends.

He picked up his panini. "Enough about me. What about you?"

"I went to music school. Studied singing. Opera. I was making a name for myself until I had an operation and lost my voice. That hurt, but I got married. Like you, Lewis was an engineer who went to MIT. When he died, he was the CEO of a big international company."

"Any children?"

"Two boys. In college. Empty nest." This wasn't the moment to tell him about my work with intelligence agencies.

An American family was sitting at the next table. The mother was hanging on to her temper by a thread.

"Christine, you wanted spaghetti. No, you can't have a gelato."

A toddler in a stroller was smearing banana on her little shirt. As the mother turned away, she started to slide to the ground. Instinctively, I leaned over and grabbed her.

"Whoa there, monkey."

The child reached up and rubbed banana on my cheek.

"Oh God," the mother said. "I'm so sorry."

"No harm done. How old is she?"

"Fifteen months. Greased lightning."

"I know that age. Where are you from?"

"Idaho. We're with the army in Germany. We wanted to see Florence, but with three kids it's turning into a hassle."

"I can imagine," I said, patting the toddler's head.

The father was on his feet. "Okay, Christine and Micky, pick up your knapsacks. No arguments." In moments the toddler and two mutinous children were being herded across the piazza.

"They've got courage," Richard said, shaking his head. "You were quick to catch that baby."

"Practice. I was a stay-at-home mother. Car pools, every kind of sport. We had a big house on the Connecticut River."

"Sounds like a good life. I'd like to have children, but in a job like this maybe it's better not."

"How do you mean?"

"I'm away for weeks. There's a certain amount of risk."

"In this case?"

"It would help to know if we're dealing with experienced pros or amateurs." He shifted in his chair. "Gelato?"

"Just a cappuccino, if there's time."

"There's time." He turned and signaled to the waiter. "*Due* cappuccini. *Subito, per favore.*"

"Signor," he said and then he was off, the tray balanced precariously on one hand.

I put my elbows on the table. "You said you'd fill me in on what's happening."

"The good news is that Liden sent a plane to London and we now have an expert in electronics who was just finishing a job there. Boysie comes from darkest Appalachia, learned technology in the army, and can trace calls. Goes without sleep as long as he can play Patsy Cline on his iPhone. He's in place with the newest tools. Could be that they're quarreling about how much to ask or who's to do the negotiating, but by now they should be demanding ransom."

"How does that work?"

"When a kidnapper calls, the conversation starts. Maybe with a warning not to call the police. A password at the start of each call. We demand proof that the victim is alive and well. The aim is always to bring the victim back without violence or publicity. The most dangerous moment is the handover. That's when things can go wrong."

"You make it sound like a formula."

"Well, you could compare it to buying and selling a company. The seller sets a high price. The buyer comes back with a counterproposal. They meet somewhere in the middle." He paused.

“Kidnappings are apt to bring out the best and the worst in people. Having to find large amounts of money can ignite family fights. Part of my job is to keep emotions under control. Tamp down on high drama and hysterics that don’t help.”

I nodded. In fact, I could relate. His calm competence had steadied me in my stress-filled confrontations with Cyrus Liden. “How is Mr. Liden coping?” I asked.

“Not well. Aside from organizing the ransom money, he just sits there listening for the call. It’s hard for him to accept the fact that he can’t just pull levers. Get results.”

“How are you managing without help?”

“The laundry situation is pretty dire. Al the bodyguard takes a bundle to the manager. Food is brought to the door, but we can’t go on much longer.”

The cappuccinos arrived along with the bill. Richard paid with a tip that brought a deep bow from the waiter.

“*Molto grazie.* Have a fine good day.”

We drank quickly and got up. As we crossed the piazza, he looked at me. “I still can’t take it in, that you’re Sally’s little cousin. She and Alison weren’t too nice to you.”

“Can you blame them? Right now, I’d like to be out sailing or going into town to meet the ferry. I loved the islanders. Short on words, always raised one finger from the steering wheel in passing.”

“I remember. Seems like another world.”

“It does.” For a moment we walked in silence, but it was the friendly silence of recollections shared. Maine had moved us to a new level of connectedness, but this could change once he switched back to professional mode.

As we reached the narrow street, he slowed and looked at me again. “I’ve been thinking. You’re involved in this operation. You’ve shown you have a good head on your shoulders. I may have to visit someone of interest near Florence. I’ll need to take someone with me for backup and as a witness. Would you be willing to do that?”

I didn't hesitate. I always claimed that I didn't want to be involved in trouble, but there was a part of me that seemed to crave the rush of adrenaline, the satisfaction of putting pieces together.

"Of course," I said. "Better than just waiting."

"There may not be much notice and someone in the palazzo may be an informer. Don't talk freely in case the rooms are bugged."

"My maid Viola is really afraid. She thinks the walls have ears."

"She has a point. By the way, the story you told your godmother might work for the staff if you go along with what I'm about to do."

We crossed the courtyard and went into the anteroom. The young concierge was sitting behind the desk. Two liveried porters stood nearby.

"Mrs. Streat's key," he said to the concierge, then leaned over and kissed me lightly on the mouth.

"See you later, babe," he said loudly. "Your room or mine?"

CHAPTER FORTY-TWO

The room was dark after the sunlit piazza. I took off my shoes and lay down on the bed. That kiss in front of the concierge and the porters—the feeling of his mouth on mine meant nothing. Deception was part of his job.

Sun and wine had made me sleepy. I drifted off, trying not to think about Anna. Was she begging the thugs to call Liden? Promising that he would pay anything if they would let her go? A kind God would hear and send her back.

When the landline phone beside me rang, I rubbed my eyes and picked it up. "Yes?"

"Hi, babe. We talked about going for a drive. How about now?" A calm voice with only a hint of urgency.

"I'd like that. Where shall I meet you?"

"In the anteroom. Bring a coat."

"On my way," I said, then ran into the bathroom and splashed cold water on my face. Put my shoes back on, pulled the quilted jacket from the armoire, and hurried to the elevator.

He was waiting for me by the front desk, wearing a dark suit and tie. The usual cluster of staff was standing nearby.

"Hey, babe," he said, taking my hand. "How'd you like to go up into the hills beyond Fiesole? Stop in a little town and have a drink?"

"Love to."

"Off we go, then." He put his arm around my shoulders, and we strolled out to the loggia, followed by one of the porters.

A small blue Peugeot was drawn up by the entrance. The porter opened the door, then stepped back. I saw him look at the plates.

We got in. "Is this your car?" I asked.

"A rental. They sent it around." He started the engine and we left the courtyard.

"That porter was looking at the plates," I said. "Is this drive to do with Anna?"

"It's complicated. Once we get out of town, I'll explain."

As he navigated through Vespas and tourists, I saw that we were heading away from the water.

"I thought Fiesole was the other side of the river," I said.

"Deliberate misinformation. We're not going to Fiesole."

We passed through the commercial district and emerged into the classic Tuscan countryside, so loved by foreigners. There were landmark silvery olive trees and tall cypresses. In the distance, white ribbons of roads wound between yellow dots of houses and green vineyards.

His hands on the wheel were strong and competent. The road was wide, with very little traffic. We passed a roadside shrine with a crude statue of the Madonna; a jam jar of flowers had been placed at her feet.

"Nice country," I said, "but I still haven't a clue why we're here."

"As I said, it's complicated. Cyrus Liden doesn't collect art. He didn't make this trip to see an unveiling."

"I'm not surprised. My godmother said he's never been known to buy a painting. Was it Anna's idea?"

"No. His." A pause. "How much do you know about cybercrime?"

"Cybercrime?" I hesitated, not sure how to answer. "I know it's a growing threat."

"Understatement. We're here because Cyrus Liden is in a race to buy a cutting-edge program, one that could penetrate all our present security measures and firewalls. Whoever gets this program will have a powerful new tool. It's a global threat and the stakes couldn't be higher."

I folded my hands. Cybercrime again, an unwelcome misery in my life. "That sounds bad," I said. "Are there others in the race?"

"Attribution is hard to prove, but China is the chief suspect. Could be a consortium of princeling billionaires—there's a system called *guanxi*, a mix of relationships and favors that opens doors. Could be the military with government backing. Worst case, it's a bunch of terrorists working under the radar."

"Nasty, but why this dash into the country?"

"Because of an Italian physicist named Bruno. He never won a Nobel, but he was one of the early pioneers in cyberspace technology. Respected and consulted by companies like Liden's in Silicon Valley. That ended when he came back to Italy and was lost from sight. By now he must be well into his eighties."

"Interesting, but why are we going to see him?"

"Because a few weeks ago Liden learned about this breakthrough program. Because of his achievements, anything Bruno does has to be taken seriously, but there's a problem. The program is up for sale. To the highest bidder."

"But why is that a problem for Liden? Can't he just outbid everyone else?"

"It's not that simple. Bruno has gone eccentric. Sees himself as a present-day Galileo, persecuted by the scientific world. If you remember, Galileo was a sixteenth-century genius. Chief mathematician to Grand Duke Cosimo de' Medici. For a while, he lived in a villa called Bellosguardo near Florence. Bruno has named his villa Bellosguardo." A pause. "Liden should be handling this, but he won't leave the palazzo in case there's a call. I'm to negotiate."

"Not easy if the old genius is over-the-hill and senile."

"It's not the old man, it's his assistant, a young Italian named

Enrico who figures he'll make a fortune with this. He's asked for bids, like an auction, and he's set a deadline for submitting them. The stakes are high, and you can bet the Chinese are here too."

"I haven't seen any except a few in tourist groups. Can't the *commissario* investigate?"

"Far too sensitive for the police. Besides, the Chinese may be using mafia as front men. They could have paid that waiter to put listeners in Liden's suite, then had him killed to keep him quiet."

"What about Anna?"

"Hard to say. It took organization to grab Anna, but they may have thought kidnapping her would shake Liden up. Put him out of the race."

"But it hasn't."

"Just the opposite. He's even more determined to get hold of that program. Not for profit, but to keep it from falling into the wrong hands." Another pause. "I've thrown a lot at you."

"I'll try to wrap my head around it. One question. When we get there, what do you want me to do?"

"Stay in the car. If someone sees you and asks questions, you're my girlfriend. I'm showing you the Italian countryside, just stopping to make this call. You know nothing about my business."

"Got it," I said, but this was too much like history repeating itself, like acting as Rodale's girlfriend at the mill. At some point I would have to tell Richard that I'd been involved in police work and cybercrime.

We were coming into a small town; the main street had a yellow brick post office and a gray concrete bank. A curtain of brown chenille ropes hung across the door of a shop.

He pulled to the curb beside a place called the Jolly Caffe. Reached into his pocket and pulled out a piece of paper. "Directions. They look easy enough. Go straight for two miles, then turn right, go up a hill another mile. Bellosguardo is the only villa on a dirt road."

"One thing," I said. "This Enrico doesn't seem to play by the rules. What do I do if you go into the villa and don't come out?"

He turned his head. "Look. If you're having second thoughts, you can get out and wait here."

"I'm not. I just like to cover all the bases."

"Have you got your phone?"

"Yes."

"I'll give you the car keys. Enrico would be a fool to threaten me, but if I don't come out in an hour, come back here and call Boysie at this number. Use it only in an emergency."

We left the town and picked up speed. Richard's hands tightened on the wheel. Two miles. A right turn. We started up the steep hill. He turned his head. "Almost there. Try not to worry. Okay?"

"Okay."

CHAPTER FORTY-THREE

The villa was a low stone building, painted a dark shade of ochre, the small windows covered by closed shutters.

Richard pulled into a dusty area a few yards away. He flexed his fingers, then pulled his briefcase from the back seat. "See you," he said, and started up the worn dirt path. Knocked on the scarred wood door. It opened. He disappeared.

I looked at my watch. It was exactly four thirty. I rotated my shoulders to ease the strain, got out, and looked around. No flowers. Unpruned fruit trees. A broken jug lay on the straggly grass. At one corner of the house, a telescope stood on a platform, an eerie reminder of Galileo.

By now the sun was losing strength. Shadows moved over the vineyards, making long stripes across the valley. Suddenly the quiet was shattered by deep-throated howls. I jumped back into the car. No vicious watchdogs raced toward me, but this showed that a canine alarm plan was in place.

Four forty-five. I shivered and buttoned my jacket. A heavyset woman came out of a side door and hung a rag rug on a line. She didn't look in my direction, but she could have seen me get out of the car.

Five o'clock. I tried to fix my mind on harmless things. A present to take home to Peggy. Thanksgiving plans for my boys—anything to distract my mind from being in this dismal place.

Footsteps on the path jolted me back to the present. Richard opened the door and threw the briefcase onto the back seat. "No luck. The little shit wants another round of negotiations. He heard the dogs and spoke to the woman who works here. He wants to see you."

"See *me*?"

"Probably wants to check you out, make sure you're not a technician with surveillance equipment. I think he's beginning to realize he's in way over his head and he's running scared. No need to worry, just be the brainless girlfriend. I'll do the talking."

"Brainless. I can do brainless."

More blood-curdling howls as we went toward the door. Richard pushed it open. We walked into darkness and an overpowering smell of damp and cat.

"This way." He took my arm and led me to a low-ceilinged room. The walls were rough and whitewashed. The floor was brick. A long table and a few straight chairs stood in the center.

Two men were sitting at the table. One stood up and came forward, smiling. "My name is Enrico. You are?"

"Emma."

"Ciao, Emma. Allow me to present you to the Maestro." He turned. "Maestro," he said in a loud voice, "we have another guest."

The old man had a halo of white hair and very dark eyes under jutting eyebrows. His brown jacket, worn over what looked like a soiled undershirt, was frayed at the edges. He nodded, then stared up at the ceiling as if it was too much effort to speak.

Enrico pulled out a chair for me. "It is our custom to have a glass of wine at this hour. Lucia," he shouted. "*Avanti.*"

A door on the opposite wall opened. The heavyset woman came in carrying a tray. She thumped it down on the table and left.

I studied Enrico as he poured wine into glasses. He was short, running to fat, with dark hair down to his shoulders and eyes that moved rapidly from side to side. A shirt with a designer logo indicated an expensive taste for fashion.

He handed the glasses around, then seated himself and raised his glass. "To your good health," he said smoothly.

The glass looked scummy, as if it had been wiped with a dirty towel. I took a sip, barely touching it with my lips.

Enrico turned to me. "Your friend says you are visiting Florence."

"That's right. For the very first time," I said, reverting to the high little voice I had used at the mill.

"I trust he is showing you our treasures. What have you seen so far?"

"Lordy, there's so *much*. The Uffizi, the Duomo—everything is so *old*. I'm from a small town in Massachusetts. We think history started with the Pilgrims."

"And what small town might that be?"

"Manchester. Outside Boston." Not quite a lie. I had permits for building a house in Manchester. "I've known Richie since we were kids in high school. Poor guy, I pity him having to take me around, show me the sights." The fetid air was affecting my breathing.

The old man at the end of the table took a sip of wine, pushed his glass away, and coughed. A rattling cough, deep in his chest. Phlegm came up. He spit into a filthy rag.

Richard finished his wine and looked at his watch. "We're expected back in the city," he said, and walked around the table to Bruno.

"It's good to meet you, sir. Your name is still legendary in Silicon Valley." The old man lowered his gaze from the ceiling. He made a vague gesture with his hand.

Richard moved closer and raised his voice. "Mr. Liden regrets he wasn't able to come here today. He hopes to reach an agreement with you. Soon."

The old man seemed to hear. He nodded. "I have much respect for Mr. Liden. I will see him tomorrow afternoon." He coughed again, a violent spasm that shook his body.

Enrico came forward and motioned us toward the door. "It is not good for the Maestro to talk," he said in a low voice. "That is why all arrangements must be made by me."

"Not always. The Maestro made it clear that he wishes to see Mr. Liden tomorrow."

"That may not be convenient—"

"Expect us at four." He put his hand on my shoulder and led me to the dark entry and out into the cold air. As we walked toward the car, he put his arm around my shoulders. "In case the little bastard is watching."

As we started down the hill, I pushed back my hair. "That little shit, that smarmy voice—but listen. I think Bruno is very sick. If it's pneumonia, he needs antibiotics right away. Who is Enrico, anyhow? You must have had him investigated."

"We have. No criminal record, he's just a bloodsucking little leech who studied physics at the University of Bologna and has made himself Bruno's keeper. Still, there's hope. You saw Bruno give him a put-down. That tells me the old boy is holding on to a key part of the project. Without it, no deal. Otherwise it would be done by now."

He slowed as we turned onto the main highway. "That cough. You think it could be pneumonia?"

"I'm not a nurse, but I'd say if he doesn't get help soon, he may not be able to see you tomorrow."

"That bad. I'd better alert Liden." A pause. "By the way, thanks for coming. I didn't expect you'd have to go in, but you managed it well."

It was time to be open about my investigative past. I folded my hands. "Actually, I've handled situations a lot worse than that. There's something I should tell you."

"Besides Maine?"

"Besides Maine. It started when my husband was run down in broad daylight near our house. I had a feeling there was something wrong. I tried to find answers. In the end, the killer was found, but since then I've been involved with several intelligence agencies. The FBI. Our Secret Service. An undercover agent in the British Secret Service. I'm not trained, a pro, but I see remote connections that might otherwise fall through the cracks. Now there's a problem on my plate."

"What?"

"Last March my godmother was attacked in her New York apartment. It's a long story, but it turns out that a big cybercrime network was responsible. I'm to be a key witness in a trial, and until then I'm supposed to have security. My godmother's maid was really here for my security and she left with my godmother."

"Good Lord. Why didn't you tell me before?"

"It didn't seem relevant. But now—I thought you ought to know."

We passed the shrine to the Madonna. Richard cleared his throat. "Here's what I think. We're beginning to be an item, which gives us cover. Keep in mind that the kidnapping started with someone in the palazzo who knew that Anna was going out. Passed along the message to those organized thugs. You can't go out alone, but you can use your eyes."

"I will."

The drive back seemed shorter. As we went down the narrow street, rain began to hit the windshield. Richard turned into the courtyard and pulled up to the loggia.

"I'll let you out, then get rid of the car. You'll be on your own tonight. All right?"

"All right."

The tall porter was there with an umbrella. Richard leaned over and touched my cheek. "Ciao, babe. See you later."

I collected my key and headed for the elevator, telling myself to ignore the growing sense of rapport. This deception was over, but there were others. Layers and layers of not knowing who could be trusted.

Once in my room, I went to the chest and poured myself a glass of mineral water; the cheap wine had left a bad taste in my mouth and it would take a long shower to wash the smell of the villa out of my hair.

The card propped against the wall near the table was so small I hadn't noticed it when I came in. I leaned down, picked it up, opened the envelope, and pulled out the stiff piece of paper. Four handwritten words in black ink:

Leave tomorrow or die

CHAPTER FORTY-FOUR

I held the card with the tips of my fingers as if it might explode. Very few people knew I had gone out for the afternoon. Even fewer had a key to unlock the door, but panic was not an option. This time I could get help.

A quick survey showed that nothing was missing. I took several deep breaths and clicked Richard's number. This qualified as an emergency. "A note was in my room telling me to leave tomorrow or die," I said, trying to keep my voice steady.

"You'd better come here. I'll send Al."

In moments Al was at my door. In silence, we walked through the halls. It was clear that he considered me a loose cannon. A person who needed to be watched.

Richard was alone at the end of the cavernous *salone*. I handed him the envelope. "I've touched it as little as possible."

"Good. We might be able to get prints. Boysie will have a look. Who knew you were going out?"

"It could have been the porter who saw us leave. The manager. Maids. Anyone."

"You look shaken. Brandy." He went to a side table and poured from a bottle. "Get that inside of you."

I swallowed and coughed. I had forgotten the fire in the throat, the warmth in the gut.

"Steadier? Here's what I'm thinking. It's no good speculating about who wants you to leave and why, but I'm going to call my friend the manager. You should move into a suite where there's a room for security. In the meantime, stay here. A waiter is bringing food and you can eat with us."

"Is that a good idea? I have a feeling Liden still blames me for the kidnapping."

"He may not join us, but there's no longer any blame. You stayed in Florence. You went with me this afternoon."

I watched as Al pulled a round table from the hall and trundled it across the room. There were a number of covered dishes. China, knives and forks.

"Make yourself useful and set the table while I make that call," Richard said and left.

I put out all the forks and knives and looked under the silver covers. There was veal scallopini, a chicken dish, two salads, bread, and a plate of pastries.

The small door opened and a tall, thin man with flaming red hair came through. He was wearing green khaki pants and a matching shirt.

"Hey, there. I'm Boysie."

"Hi. I'm Emma."

"Richard told me about you." He filled two plates and turned. "Take care," he said and left.

Richard and Mr. Liden appeared. He looked very tired and smaller, as if intense stress was shrinking him. "Good evening, Mrs. Streat," he said and sat down.

Richard placed a small helping of veal scallopini on a plate, added salad, and handed it to him. "For you, Emma?"

"The same. Not too much." I picked up my fork. It wasn't my place to rush in with chatter, not when the atmosphere was palpable with pain.

Mr. Liden took several bites, then pushed away his plate and looked at me. "I hear you went with Richard this afternoon," he said in a stronger voice. "You saw Maestro Bruno and you're concerned about his health."

"Very concerned. I think he may have pneumonia and in old people that can be fatal. He ought to be in a hospital, getting antibiotics. Without them, he could die in that miserable place."

"Then steps must be taken. The man is a true genius. To lose him—" He stopped as a phone in the other room began to ring. In seconds, Liden and Richard were on their feet and through the small door.

I sat back as every grim scenario streamed through my mind. Anna had been found dead beside a country road. The body would go to a morgue or whatever it was called in Italy.

At last the door opened and Richard came out. His face had the set look of anger barely contained. "Sorry to be so long. That was Enrico to say Bruno can't see us tomorrow."

"I was afraid it might be bad news about Anna."

"No, but it lit a fire under Liden. He moves fast. A medical van will go to the villa tonight with an emergency crew and oxygen. They'll bring Bruno here to the suite. There's plenty of room for nurses and the necessary equipment."

"Thank God. Keeping him there really was criminal."

"I'll take my car and lead the van to the villa. By the way, the manager says you can have your godmother's suite. He'll send a maid and porter to help you move."

"Wait," I said and stood up. "You'll have to deal with Bruno and Enrico and that woman. You'd better take me for backup.

He didn't hesitate. "Right. Get a coat. Al will go with you and we'll meet at the Otterini's private entrance. Using that keeps us under the radar."

"I'll be quick." His ability to sum up a situation and move forward reminded me of Agent Howard.

A maze of halls led to the back of the palazzo. An ambulance with two attendants was waiting in a small walled courtyard, along with a small green Fiat.

"Your car, Signor," the manager said to Richard. "Be so kind as to call me when you return. Do not ring the bell. I will come and unlock the door."

We left the courtyard. The ambulance followed. At eight o'clock there was less traffic and many of the shops had closed. Once on the long straight road, Richard drove faster. By now it was raining hard.

"How much trouble can Enrico give you?" I asked.

"My guess is he'll crumble if I threaten to bring in the police. Once Bruno is on the way to Florence, I'll apply major pressure. Try to find out who else is after that program. I need you to listen."

In the higher altitude, the rain had changed into heavy mist. We passed through the little village. "Two miles. Here's the turn," Richard said, shifting gears. "Can you see the van?"

"Foggy, but it's there."

Slowly, the ambulance followed us up the steep hill and into the flat area. Richard turned off the engine and took a small device from his pocket. "Latest thing in taser. Better than using a gun on the dogs if they're loose. I'll speak to the medics. Then we'll go in. Surprise the little shit."

CHAPTER FORTY-FIVE

No lights showed through the shuttered windows. There was a chorus of howls as we went up the path, but no dogs came running out. Richard pounded on the door. We waited. He pounded again. At last bolts were pulled back. Enrico stood there. He was wearing a crimson brocade dressing gown.

"What—"

Richard stepped forward. "Cyrus Liden was concerned to hear about the Maestro's illness. Even more concerned when you canceled the meeting."

"There is a cough. Nothing more."

"We would like to see the Maestro."

"He is sleeping. He must not be disturbed. I wish you good night." He started to shut the door.

Richard put out his foot. "We see him, or I call a *commissario*. Mr. Liden has influence. The *polizia* will be here within the hour."

The light was dim, but I could see the change in Enrico's expression. He tightened the brocade sash and turned.

We followed him through the damp passage that smelled of cat and into the low-ceilinged kitchen. At the far end a door was open. Enrico motioned us to go in.

The strong rank smell of sickness in the small room caught in my throat. Bruno lay on a large bed with a black iron headboard. He was wearing the same rumpled clothes. The woman was standing over him, wiping his face with a dirty cloth. She saw us and shrank back against the wall.

Richard went to his side. "Maestro?"

No answer. I walked closer and touched his forehead. It was burning hot. "Fever," I said. "Very high."

Richard leaned down and spoke in his ear. "Maestro, can you hear me?" His eyelids moved. He coughed and a thick greenish fluid trickled down his chin.

I sat down on the edge of the bed and took the blue-veined hand. "Maestro, we're here to help you," I said loudly. "We're taking you to get the care you need."

No response.

Enrico came forward. "What is this you say? He goes nowhere."

Richard turned. "The Maestro is extremely ill, far worse than when we saw him this afternoon. If he dies, I'll see that you're charged with negligence among your other crimes. A medical van with two trained attendants is waiting outside to take him to Florence. I'm bringing them in." He brushed past Enrico and disappeared.

"*Ecco.*" Enrico hurried after him. The woman sobbed into her apron. The Maestro coughed, a deep, racking cough. He seemed to be drifting in and out of consciousness. I waited, holding his hand.

The two attendants who appeared were young, wearing green scrubs. The Maestro was lifted onto a stretcher and covered with a blanket. Enrico screamed at them in Italian and tried to remove the blanket.

Ignoring him, the attendants picked up the stretcher and made for the door. Enrico tried to follow. Richard took his arm, pushed him into the kitchen, and shoved him into a chair. A moment later we heard the sound of an engine starting up.

I sat down on a chair at the end of the table. Took a deep breath and tried to center myself. From now on, I must observe details like the snuffling of dogs on the other side of a door. Remember every word that was spoken.

Enrico was spluttering what sounded like curses in Italian. Richard leaned forward.

"Be quiet and listen to me. You are in very bad trouble. You played a bidding game with people who know how to protect themselves. When they find out that the Maestro has been taken away, they will have to silence you. Do you understand?"

"*Dio mio*. Not that." He put his head in his hands.

"Yes, kill you, but you have one way to save yourself." He paused. "Give me their names, and I may try to help you."

Enrico let out a groan. "I cannot. I have no names."

"No names? How do you communicate?"

"There are letters from Florence. No phone. No email. I was told to burn their letters."

"How much did they pay you in advance for the program?"

Enrico shook his head. "Nothing."

"You're a stupid liar." Richard hit the table. "How much?"

"Forty—it was forty thousand euros." A whisper. "Another forty thousand when they receive it, but much is still in the Maestro's head. He is stubborn, the old man. He refuses to give it up."

"How was the forty thousand paid?"

"A money order from a bank in Hong Kong to the bank in the village. That is all I know." He put his head down on the table and sobbed.

I sat still, but my mind was moving fast. By putting Enrico's feet to the fire, Richard had extracted a piece of hard evidence. One that could be investigated.

Richard must have come to the same conclusion. A muscle in his cheek twitched. "Very well. Pay attention. You have a car?"

"*Si.*" A muffled sob.

"Leave at once. Go to family or a friend and call me at this number with the address. The woman who was with the Maestro. Does she live here?"

"*Si*, but she knows nothing."

"Let her stay. Give her money to feed the dogs," Richard said. He came around the table, took my elbow, and we walked to the door. Enrico didn't follow, but as we left, we could hear a cry of pain.

CHAPTER FORTY-SIX

The mist had thickened. I shivered as Richard turned the green Fiat and started down the hill.

"The smell—I never thought Bruno could be so much worse. I think we came just in time."

"Let's hope. He may never be able to give us the program, but it won't go to cybercriminals. And now we have a lead, the fact that he was paid by a bank in Hong Kong."

"Yes." I glanced at him, impressed once again by his intelligence. His inner and outer strength, but I must try to keep the old attraction from showing. I was carrying a legacy of emotional baggage. He wasn't.

We were back on the main road. I folded my hands, as disconnected incidents began to insert themselves into my mind. A series of links was forming, but it was hard to know if they were valid.

As we passed the Madonna shrine, Richard glanced at me. "You're very quiet. Is something wrong?"

"Not wrong." I hesitated. "I'm supposed to be good at putting unlikely facts together, and that's what I'm trying to do."

"Go on."

"Okay. This bank in Hong Kong points to the Chinese being here. You once said they were probably using a front man."

"It would make sense."

"Someone with links to China. I know it's a stretch to think of him as a suspect, but do you remember meeting Thomas Mellinton at I Tatti?"

"The quiet Brit. Why him?"

"Because Mellinton lives in Hong Kong. He told me he came to Florence several weeks before the unveiling, which would give him time to contact Enrico and organize a bunch of thugs and informers. The night before the group left, he told Henry Train he was planning to meet a friend and stay on. I haven't seen him at the palazzo, but he may still be in Florence."

"I see where you're going, but it's not enough to make him a suspect."

"No." I hesitated, feeling my way. "It's not, but I'm putting pieces together, pieces that might possibly make a complete picture. Do you remember when we were standing on the terrace at I Tatti? Lorraine Kegler began to talk about my finding a dead man in the alley."

"Making a meal out of it."

"Mellinton cut her off midstream. I thought he was being kind, but he took me off into the garden and asked if I had understood what the two men were saying. I told him I didn't, but later he asked me if the police had made any progress. He seemed a little too curious, the reason it stuck in my mind."

"Anything else?"

"He was standing in the anteroom when Anna made plans to go shopping. He *could* have been the informant, the one who passed the word."

"You're connecting him to the waiter and then to the kidnapping. I hear you, but that's still not enough evidence to make a case."

"Except that Enrico says his letters came from Florence and there was a transaction from a bank in Hong Kong to a local bank in the village. Forty thousand euros. Wouldn't there have to be some identification on that transaction?"

"Point taken. I'll look into that transaction, but it's going to require a lot of pressure and cutting through red tape. Not easy to do over here."

We were entering the outskirts of town, wipers scraping the glass as the rain subsided. Richard cleared his throat.

"Thanks for coming and for the input. I'd never have guessed that you've worked with agencies."

"It's not something I go around advertising."

"No, but you're part of the team. About that note. As I said, Boysie can check for fingerprints, but do you have any idea who or why?"

"None. It seems farfetched for cybercrime to wait this long to threaten me. On the other hand, maybe I'm paying the price for being the good Samaritan to that waiter and then being connected to Anna's kidnapping. Maybe someone assumes I'm working closely with the police and that I know more than I do."

"That makes more sense. We'll have to be careful. Maybe lay on more security for you. In any case, it won't be for long. The kidnappers are going to realize they've got a sick woman on their hands and make a move."

We reached the palazzo and the private courtyard. The manager was standing at the door, still dressed in his striped trousers and morning coat. In a room nearby, someone was playing a Chopin mazurka and playing it very badly.

"The sick man arrived and was taken to the suite," the manager said in a low voice. "The doctor is with him. Signora Vogt's suite has been readied, but Signora Streat's clothes have not been moved in yet."

"I'll go up with her," Richard said.

Back through the long halls to my old room. I turned on a light. Richard looked at the tapestries, then up at the high painted ceiling. "Quite a place. Full of history."

"That's what struck me when I first walked in. Why I hate to leave. Luckily, I did most of the packing this morning. Not much left to do."

"Shout if you want help," he said and went to lean against a shuttered window.

I walked over to the bed, picked up my little alarm clock and put it in a carryall, aware that he was watching me intently, arms crossed. "Done," I said. "If you carry the duffel, I'll take the rest."

There was no one in the hall as we went into the Brunelleschi suite. He laid the duffel on a chair and looked around. "Overdecorated, no history, but it has two bedrooms. We can spare Al tonight, then find someone for tomorrow."

"Al won't like that at all. He thinks I'm bad news and I don't blame him. I was the one with Anna, I should have been quicker and by now she's hurting. It's so unfair, so cruel—" My voice broke.

"No." He put an arm around my shoulders. "You're not to blame."

"But I am. If no one calls, if nothing happens, if she dies—"

"Hush." He raised my head and put his mouth on mine.

I stood still, startled by the surge of sensation that numbed the brain and heated the blood, then let myself sink into the tumultuous world of the senses. The craving for the hot center. If he moved toward the big bed, I would go with him.

He lifted his head. "Sorry. Strange, when we met at I Tatti, I liked your eyes. The way you stand very straight. Anna said you had heart. At lunch in the piazza, I felt that we were in sync. I wanted to know you better. No need to do a kabuki dance around you."

My legs were shaking. I held on to his arms. "Until then I thought you were still married to Alison. When you kissed me in front of the concierge—it was just a game for you, but it brought back those old feelings."

"And now?"

"I'm confused. So much has gone wrong."

"We'll get through this. I promise you." He touched my hair. "I don't want to leave you, but I have to get back."

"I know."

"Try to sleep." He took my face in his hands. "You've turned into a beautiful woman, but don't let it go to your head. You were a repulsive kid, and no one wanted you around. I'll send Al." He turned abruptly. In a moment he was gone.

My legs were still shaking. I stumbled across the floor and collapsed onto Caroline's canopied bed. Nothing in life was predictable. If I'd left with her this morning, I might never have seen him again—and Caroline was right. I needed a man in my life. One who was caring and sensitive in spite of his demanding work.

I lay there, holding on to the feel of him, and began to compose the progress report I had promised Caroline:

Hi, by now you're back, but bless you, bless you for letting me stay. I'm not sure yet, but I may be in love again. Really in love.

CHAPTER FORTY-SEVEN

September 18

I woke in a state of painful uncertainty. Richard was regretting the professional lapse, a reaction to tension, the intimacy of the dimly lit room. Anna was dying in the hands of the kidnappers. Bruno was dead. Changing rooms did not guarantee my security.

It was too early to call Delsey in New York—and the way things were going, I might well be spending the rest of the day in my room. I ate breakfast and was about to get down on the floor and start push-ups when the landline phone rang.

It was Richard. "Morning, babe. I hope I didn't wake you."

"Heavens, no, I've been up for hours," I said, remembering that the phone could be bugged.

"I'm going out to get a breather. Meet me in the loggia?"

"Sounds good. Give me a few minutes."

I threw on the white shirt and black trousers and went down. In the anteroom, guests were arriving. An elderly couple speaking German. A young pair talking in French, the image of haute couture. No sign of a mounting crisis in the Liden suite.

Richard was on the loggia, wearing the same blue shirt. I walked forward, telling myself to keep it light. Assume nothing.

He picked up my hand. "Turning out to be a good day," he said loudly. "You haven't had a chance to see Florence. Want to do a quick tour of the Duomo? The Bargello?"

"Actually, I'd rather walk along the river, not shuffle in lines with the tourists."

As we went into the street, I looked at him. "Any news?"

"Not about Anna. The Maestro is hanging in by a thread. There are doctors and nurses underfoot all over the place." A pause. "By the way, I pulled some strings about the Hong Kong bank transaction. As we speak, the *commissario* is working on the manager at the village bank. I should be hearing from him soon."

"Well, it can't hurt."

"No." He hesitated. "Look. About what happened between us last night. For me, it was important, but it can stop right there. You may have someone in your life."

I swallowed. Richard deserved a straight answer. "I did have someone," I said, "but it's over."

We reached the Ponte Vecchio, a bridge lined with shops. The area was thick with people, but there was a sidewalk café nearby. He took my elbow and steered me to a table. "We need to talk. Coffee?"

"Caffe latte."

"*Due* caffe latte, *per favore*," he said to the hovering waiter, then put his hands on the table. "My turn to be open. I've had a few relationships, but nothing serious since my marriage fell apart." A pause. "Did you have a good marriage?"

"That's hard to know," I said slowly. "To be honest, mine started on the rebound from losing my voice, but we worked at it. We respected each other in and out of bed. After Lewis died, I had an on-and-off affair with a brilliant man, but it ended last spring."

"I see." He turned his head and looked at me. "Back to last night. I was afraid you might be having withdrawal symptoms."

"Not exactly, but I woke up telling myself that the stress of dealing with Anna and Bruno had thrown us together. That last night meant nothing to you."

"Wrong. It meant a great deal. I want to know more about you. Little things as well as the big ones." He stood up and held out his hand. "Come."

"What about the coffee?"

"It can wait," he said, and propelled me onto the bridge and the long line of open booths. Stopped in front of a counter displaying gold jewelry. Necklaces. Bracelets. Rings.

A pretty young woman with a deep cleavage in her dress smiled at us. "All eighteen-carat gold. The finest in Florence."

"I'm looking for a ring. For the lady."

I swiveled around. "What?"

"Just a hello present. No strings attached."

"*Si.* I show," the woman said. She pulled out a tray of gold rings, some plain, some intricately woven.

"Left or right hand?" he asked.

"Uh—the right."

"Which finger?"

"I guess—the little one."

He studied the tray, then picked out a small ring made in two twisted circles. "Hold out your hand," he said. He slipped it onto my finger. "It fits. Wear it or not, it's there. Not a commitment. Just a token that you won't disappear when this job is over."

"I won't. This morning—I felt so isolated. Then you called. Now we're able to talk. Be open with each other, and the ring is lovely. Thank you."

We went back to the table. The waiter brought coffee. Richard handed him a few euros.

The sun was warm. Nearby, an elderly woman was kissing a small fat baby on both cheeks. A bunch of teenagers wearing backpacks swaggered by. I sat there, remembering the moment last night when teenage dreams became a primal wish to be joined to another person. A longing to touch and be touched.

"Emma." He took my hand. "When Anna is safe, I'm not

going straight back to California. I want to spend a few days with you. Go to Rome, or Vienna, or Paris. Your choice. A chance to see if we have a future together."

"Exactly the excuse I gave my godmother for staying." I touched the ring. "I'd gladly, happily, go off with you for weeks, but there's a problem. I have to get ready for that trial."

"Of course. I forgot." His phone rang. He let go of my hand and pulled it out. "Yes?"

The person on the line talked fast. Richard's eyes narrowed. "Right," he said at last. "There's no time to waste. Send everyone available out to check passports at all the hotels and pensiones. Call me as soon as you have any results." He shoved the phone into his pocket and pulled me to my feet.

"That was the *commissario*. Your instinct about Mellinton was right on. The Hong Kong money order was done through him. He's been leading a double life, but that's over. When he finds out that Enrico has disappeared and the Maestro is in our hands, he may well do a bolt."

"What about the kidnapping?"

"That too, which is why we have to get our hands on him. Back to the palazzo on the double. This is the break we needed and Liden needs to know."

CHAPTER FORTY-EIGHT

Cyrus Liden was sitting alone at the table in the big *salone*. He looked around as we came in. Richard went up to him. "The *commissaire* just called. It's confirmed, the money from Hong Kong was sent to Thomas Mellinton. That proves he's the front man for the Chinese. The *commissario*'s men are out checking hotels and pensiones."

Liden stood up. "He may be connected to the kidnappers." He stopped as Richard's phone rang. Again, the voice speaking fast.

Richard listened, then nodded. "I'll tell Mr. Liden. See what he wants to do and call you back." He looked at Liden. "The *commissario*'s men didn't have to look far. Mellinton was staying at a small pensione near the Duomo. The woman there said he left in a hurry this morning, not even waiting for his laundry."

Liden frowned. "Tell the *commissario* he must be found, no matter if he has to call in militia. He can't have gone far."

"Bad news, sir. The *commissario* has already checked the airport. Mellinton was on a flight to Heathrow. It left half an hour ago."

Liden drew himself up. The goatee quivered. "Then steps must be taken. Call the officials at Heathrow. Have him picked up as soon as he gets there."

Richard shook his head. "They'll need evidence to detain and hold him. In any case, it will take time to find the right officials and persuade them to act."

"How much time before he lands?"

"If you add flight time, customs, and security, I'd say three hours max."

"Then bring in private investigators, anyone with authority. You must have resources. Offer big money."

"It's not a question of money, sir, though being outside the states makes it more difficult. Mellinton will know his handlers will be after him. It'll be a race to find him first, and the chances of getting a resource out to Heathrow at such short notice are minimal."

Liden hit the table with his fist. "No excuses, Redson. You're the expert. I expect results from you, and I want that man in our hands."

The two men stood looking at each other. I clenched my fists. An impasse. Liden was asking for the impossible, but if Mellinton disappeared, Richard would be blamed.

This was not a moment for face saving—or for letting the past get in the way of the future. I stepped forward. "Maybe I can help," I said. "I happen to know someone in London who has clout and can act quickly."

Liden stared. "Who?"

"His name is Andrew Rodale. He works undercover for the British Secret Service. He can push levers. What's more, he has contacts in Hong Kong, but he's a very busy man. There's only one reason for him to do this."

"Which is?"

"He's deep into tracking down global cybercrime. Finding a man who's connected to Chinese handlers might interest him. That is, if he's in London."

"Call him."

"Actually, it would be better if Richard—that is, Mr. Redson—makes the call." I gave Rodale's number to Richard. This was against my vow to cut the cord with Rodale, but with luck we wouldn't have to speak.

Rodale was in London. The talk lasted for several minutes. "Done," Richard said as it ended. "Mrs. Streat was right. The thought of cybercriminals with a new program did the trick. He's sending one of his people to Heathrow. It may be difficult to take the man into custody, but at least he can be followed. Rodale will call when he knows more."

Liden pulled at the little goatee and looked at me. "That was helpful, Mrs. Streat. Tell us about this Andrew Rodale."

I hesitated. "He—well, he has a compulsion to hunt down bad actors. If anyone can find Mellinton, he will."

Richard cleared his throat. "There's another possibility. If Mellinton was connected to the kidnappers, his leaving could trigger a ransom offer. Boysie should be alerted."

Mr. Liden nodded and turned toward the small door. I looked at Richard. "I'd better go back to my room," I said.

"I'll take you there."

Once again, we walked down the endless parquet floor. Oxygen tanks lined the wall by the door, along with large plastic bags. Without staff coming in, the refuse was piling up.

Al was standing there, arms crossed. "Back in a minute," Richard said. As the door closed, he took my hand. "Brace yourself for action. By now the kidnappers know they're in big trouble. Mellinton has bailed out, and if Anna is deteriorating, they'll need to get their hands on some money before it's too late." He paused. "Thank you for producing this Rodale fellow. Why didn't you want to talk to him yourself?"

"There were reasons," I said. "Nothing that matters—"

"Mr. Redson. Wait."

We turned. Al was thumping down the hall, breathing hard. "The call just came. You're wanted."

I let go of Richard's hand. "Let me know—"

"Don't argue. You're part of the team. Come."

CHAPTER FORTY-NINE

The small door in the *salone* led to a long hall. As we went in, a white uniformed nurse carrying a covered bowl hurried by. Richard pushed a door open.

I stepped inside a large room. The walls were lined with tapestries. A long table against the wall was covered with a map and electronic equipment. A smaller table held empty coffee cups and dirty plates. A cot stood in a corner. A fan whirred loudly.

Boysie was bending over a machine. Liden was standing next to him. He spoke to Richard. "They're asking for a ransom. The *commissario* was in the palazzo checking IDs. He's on his way."

"Good. We'll need his help." A moment later, the door opened. The *commissario* came in, followed by a handsome young man in uniform.

Boysie turned to him, hands on his hips. I could see he was excited. "Yep. It finally came. He spoke bad English, thick Italian accent. Wants three million euros in cash left under a certain chair in the Duomo before ten tonight. If not, the woman will be killed and pieces of her sent through the mail. It's all recorded." He tapped a small machine.

"I would like to hear the voices."

"Yep." Boysie pushed a button. A voice reverberated through the room, shouting in Italian.

The *commissario* nodded. "As I suspected. That one is from the south, not Florence. You were able to get the location?"

"Yep." Boysie leaned down and pointed to a screen.

The *commissario* studied the screen. "*Ecco*, I know the place. It is near the villa of the old man who pretends to be Galileo. There is another road beyond. At the end, a villa. It is owned by an Englishman, but he comes only in summer. It is rented for much of the year."

Richard frowned. "So it could have been vacant. Taken over by these people."

"That is possible. If the money is ready, the drop in the Duomo can be made. I myself will be there—"

"No." The word exploded out of Liden's mouth. "That will take too long. Your men must go to that villa and free her. Now."

The *commissario*'s head jerked around. "Now? A raid on the villa? It cannot be done. Taking a place by force requires preparation. One mistake and the victim is killed. I have seen this happen. It is safer to leave the money as directed."

"No, I say. You are to bring her from that place immediately, no matter how many men it takes."

The *commissario* gave Richard an anguished look. "Signor, you must know this is asking too much. We have what you call SWAT teams. Men with experience, but they must be prepared. All must be well planned." His voice was rising.

Richard straightened. "I agree," he said calmly, "but in this case waiting is not an option. Signora Deglos is very ill. By now she is in great pain. She must receive medication as soon as possible."

The *commissario* raised his hands. "I regret very much the pain, but we do not know how many are in the house. If they see men approaching, they will shoot. I will not put my men in danger without preparation. That is my last word." He drew himself up and put his hands behind his back.

The room was silent. I watched, holding my breath. The *commissario* was standing firm, and nothing could be done without his help.

Finally, Richard nodded. "I agree," he repeated. "Your men must not arrive in plain sight, but there are other ways."

"Other ways?"

"One is the use of surprise. My company has conducted a number of rescue operations. A few years ago, we ran a hostage rescue in Germany. Men were brought to the scene hidden in a furniture van. The rescue was made without loss of life. I suggest we try to do that here."

The *commissario* stared. "Hide my men in a van which is used for furniture?"

"The owner of the villa has ordered a large new sofa to be delivered to the villa. It requires a van with a driver and a helper. The van stops in front of the house. The sofa is lifted out and carried to the door. The people inside are not likely to shoot workmen. Paperwork is shown, creating a moment of distraction. Your men waiting in the back of the van then use that moment to rush the door."

Again, I held my breath. Would the *commissario* accept this compromise?

He shook his head. "No. I regret, but this is not possible."

"Not even for your well-trained men? It would be a notable success for you and the Florence *polizia*."

He considered, smoothing his receding hair. Then he looked at his lieutenant. "Raffaele, there is a man on Via Palchetti who restores fine furniture. Go to him at once. Tell him he will be paid well for the use of his van for the afternoon and evening."

"*Prego*." The lieutenant saluted smartly and disappeared.

Richard looked at his watch. "It's now nearly noon. Six o'clock would be a reasonable time for such a delivery."

Again, the *commissario* shook his head. "To find the right men will be difficult. However, I do what I can—and my lieutenant will be in command of the operation. Is that understood?"

"Understood. I'll follow in a car," Richard said. "I should be there when Mrs. Deglos is found. She must be treated with great care."

"Very great care," I said, speaking for the first time. "There should be a soft mattress or cushions in the back of the van. Something for Mrs. Deglos to lie on."

"*Capisco.*" The *commissario* made a note. He turned to Richard. "I go now. I will keep you informed."

Overhead, the fan whirred. The smell of discarded food was pungent. Liden looked at Richard. "What do you know about Italian SWAT teams?"

"Capable, from all I've heard."

"It seems we have no alternative. I will go with you in the car, bringing her pills."

"No, sir. Not possible. I understand your feelings, but that would only add to the risk. Aside from the chance of your being taken hostage, you're needed here. If Mellinton has been detained at Heathrow, Rodale will want instructions. Or there could be another call from the villa."

"All the same, I must go."

Another impasse. I pushed back my hair. "I'm not a nurse," I said, "but I've looked after sick people. She knows me. I can give her the pills and ride back with her in the van."

"Very well. Do your best." His lips tightened. He left the room abruptly.

I looked at Richard. "I hope it was right to step in."

"It saved an argument with Liden. Boysie, you had two tours in Iraq. You'd better come. Liden will have to take any calls."

"Yep."

"What time should I be ready?" I asked.

"You'll get a heads-up. Wear warm clothes. No heels. With any luck, the thugs won't expect action so soon after the call. Al will take you back to your room."

I nodded and started toward the door. There was no way to know what we would find, but going was one small way to ease the guilt of not saving Anna from those men.

CHAPTER FIFTY

By four o'clock I was pacing the room, wearing my black trouser suit, running shoes, and a scarf around my head. By now I had a history of plunging into crisis situations. Most recently, I had persuaded Agent Howard to take me with him into the school. The adrenaline was running.

It was almost six when the green Fiat left the back courtyard and was on the road with Richard at the wheel. Boysie sat in the back seat. Both were wearing dark fleece jackets.

The traffic at this hour was heavy as we passed through the city and out into the countryside. I recognized the roadside shrine and the view of the vineyards, shadowy in the evening sun.

When we came into the village, Richard stopped in front of the Jolly Caffe. "What happens now?" I asked, breaking the silence.

"We wait for the van, then follow at a distance. Stay out of sight until the SWAT team is inside. They have orders to take the thugs alive for questioning." His voice was tense. He flexed his fingers. I wanted to lean over and take his hand, but Boysie mustn't see that we had more than a working relationship.

"Hey." Boysie spoke from the back seat. "While we're waiting, I'll go in and get us some food in case of delays. Always keep the supply lines open."

In a moment he was back. He handed me a hunk of loosely wrapped bread and cheese, but my mouth was too dry to swallow.

Reality was taking hold. Would Anna still be alive? If she was in terrible pain, what would I do?

I put what passed for a sandwich on the floor. Inside the café, the woman behind a counter was talking to a customer who was holding a child by the hand, a little girl in white stockings and black shoes with a kerchief tied under her chin. A man in a brown sweater was pouring wine from a barrel into bottles.

Richard looked at his watch. "Nearly seven. The *commissario*'s men should have contacted me by now."

"They're here," Boysie said.

I turned my head. A van was coming down the street. A brown van with Mobilia Fusco painted in gold on the side. As the driver came closer, he raised two fingers. Richard returned the signal. The van moved on.

As we passed the turn to the steep hill that led to Bruno's villa, I closed my eyes. *Oh God, let the commissario's men do this well. Let it be over quickly with no one hurt.*

The car slowed. I opened my eyes. Richard shifted gears as we turned and followed the van up another road. In the distance I could see a house tucked into the side of a hill. It was yellow like Bruno's, with green shutters, but this place showed no signs of neglect. There was a large swimming pool off to the right. White chairs and tables stood near a small building for changing.

Richard slowed again. "Those trees will give us cover," he said, and pulled off the verge to a row of cypress trees.

We got out and stood where we could see over the top of the car. All was quiet and serene at this upscale place. Grass cut, no broken tiles on the roof, no peeling paint on the shutters. The absentee owners would be appalled when they heard how their home had been used.

The van had stopped at the big front door flanked by lemon trees in large pots. Two men wearing blue coveralls got out and went to open the rear door. Moving slowly, they attached a slider and eased a large yellow-and-brown patterned sofa to the ground. Stood there for a moment, then one of them went to the door and knocked. Waited. No one came.

"Jeez, what are they waiting for? I wish this was our operation," Boysie muttered.

Richard's face was rigid. "They're not sure what to do."

The man knocked again. "Move your asses," Boysie growled. "Don't botch it now." But as he spoke, men in battle gear poured out of the van and jumped over the sofa, assault weapons at the ready. One was carrying a heavy tool. In seconds the door gave way. They disappeared into the villa.

We stood like statues, straining to hear shouts, shots, but the only sound came from birds in the trees, exchanging the evening news.

In silence, moments passed. Tension mounted, as tangible as the grass under our feet. At last Richard's phone rang. He pulled it out, listened, then put it back in his pocket. "That was the lieutenant. They've been through the house. No one there except a woman on a bed. They're going to search the grounds and outbuildings, but he says it's safe to go in."

Boysie ran a hand through his red hair. "About time," he said and pulled out a pistol.

Richard touched his shoulder. "I go first. Emma stays until she gets the all clear. Here." He handed me a bottle of pills and a small flask. "Water for the pills."

I watched, clenching my fists as they walked up to the battered front door. The lieutenant hadn't said whether Anna was alive or dead. When Richard appeared in the door and motioned for me to come, I ran.

"She's alive," he said, "but be prepared for a shock." Taking my arm, he hurried me through a big room. I had a glimpse of overstuffed sofas and chairs. A table covered with dirty plates and glasses. Ashtrays overflowing with cigarette butts.

A young man in battle camouflage was standing in a narrow hall. "Hold your breath," Richard said. He opened a door and we went in. I gasped and put my hand over my mouth to hold back nausea. The smell of body waste was overwhelming.

Anna was lying on a carved wood bed, eyes closed. Her hair was tied back with a dirty string.

Richard leaned over and raised an eyelid. "Drugged, but that may be a good thing. Don't try to give her those pills, she may not be able to swallow." He straightened. "Boysie and I will carry her to the van, but we need cover from the lieutenant. Back in a few minutes." He touched my hair. "All right?"

"All right," I whispered.

"She's alive. Think ahead. Think Paris." He touched my hair again and was gone.

The smell was horrible. I ran across the room and opened a window. Fresh air began to flow into the room, enough to lessen the stench. Somehow, I must control my outraged stomach and try to clean her up.

There was an adjoining bathroom, but it had been trashed. Mud on the floor. Black hairs in the scummy basin. I pulled towels from a shelf—expensive thick white towels—and wet them with warm water.

"Anna, it's Emma," I said and leaned over her. "You're safe. You're safe now. No one's going to hurt you. I'm going to wash your face."

Her expression didn't change, no flicker of eyelids, but at a deep level of unconsciousness I hoped she could hear. She was still in the silk shirt and trousers she had worn to go shopping. Doing my best to be gentle, I pulled off the saturated clothes and threw them into a corner. She had lost weight. Her body was thinner. It was like cleaning off a sick baby. I cleaned her as well as I could and patted her dry.

"Animals," I muttered, fighting tears. There was no way I could remove the soiled sheets and she must be kept warm. I opened a closet door and found extra blankets. Tucked one around her and sat down to wait.

Years ago, while Jake was being born, the labor nurse had held my hand and I never forgot the sense of support. I took Anna's hand. "Anna, you're safe. You're fine. You're safe." The same words, over and over. She didn't respond.

Moments passed. Her breathing was becoming shallow, not a good sign. I sat there, feeling helpless. Dear God, we had come to save Anna's life—where was Richard? By now we should be in the van and on the way to Florence.

Muffled shouts sounded in the distance, then an ominous silence. I got up and went to the door. The young soldier had disappeared.

Anna moaned. I sat down again and went on with the litany—"Anna, you're safe"—but by now I was feeling desperate. What could be keeping the rescuers? Where were the kidnappers? What would I do if one of them came running through the door?

At last, voices in the hall. Boysie came in, followed by the young soldier. He was carrying a mattress.

I laid Anna's hand down on the bed. "For God's sake. What took you so long? Where's Richard?"

Boysie wiped his eyes. Muscles twitched in his craggy face. "It shouldn't have happened. He's gone."

"What do mean, he's gone? Gone where?"

"A bastard shot him. He's dead."

I stood up. I shook my head. "Dead? He's dead? I don't believe you. I didn't hear any shots. He just went out to get the lieutenant."

Boysie wiped his face again. "Silencer on the pistol. Shot the lieutenant, then him. I tell you, he's dead. We're leaving."

I doubled over as if he had hit me in the gut, then reached out and grabbed his shirt. "I'm not leaving until I see for myself."

"For Chrissake, woman, pull yourself together. He's gone. We have to finish the job." He pushed me aside. "Give me the mattress, then you take this end," he said to the soldier.

He might as well have slapped my face. I swallowed convulsively, picked up more towels, and followed the improvised stretcher. Several of the soldiers were standing outside the front door, staring at the ground. The sofa had been moved onto the grass. There was no sign of Richard. Where had they taken him?

Boysie and his helper lifted Anna into the rear of the van. I climbed in and lay down beside her on the dusty floor. The door closed.

It was dark in the van as it bumped its way down the hill. My head seemed detached from my body. This couldn't have happened, not to Richard. A few moments ago, he had been with me, standing beside Anna, asking me if I was all right.

Anna stirred and moaned. I put an arm under her shoulders and tried to ease the jolts. They lessened as we reached the long smooth road that led into Florence, but Anna's breath was slowing.

Richard had died in the effort to save her life. I tightened my hold and began to talk into her ear. "Anna, Anna, we're on the way to Florence. You're safe. Please, please don't die on me now."

The vibrations under the wheels changed as we came into the city. Turns and more turns as the driver navigated the narrow streets. One last turn and the van stopped.

Voices sounded at the door. No way could I face people. I let go of Anna and folded myself into a dark corner. Hands reached in and pulled the mattress out. Exclamations of horror in Italian. Consultations, then a man spoke: "The signora has been drugged, that is evident, but she can receive care in the palazzo. There is no need to take her to a clinic."

Footsteps receded. Boysie's face appeared in the door. "Come out or you'll be trapped in there."

I climbed stiffly down, blinking in the light, and leaned against the van. "I have to know. How did it happen?"

Boysie ran a hand through his hair. "When they saw the van, they ran out the back. Weren't going to take any chances. The lieutenant and his men checked the pool house. Found four of them. Brought them out and body-searched them for weapons. Redson turned to tell the lieutenant about taking Mrs. Deglos. That's when—" Boysie stopped. He hit the side of the van with his fist.

"Go on."

"One of the bastards pulled a Walther out of his sock. It had a silencer. He shot the lieutenant in the leg—he'll live—then Redson. It was over in a few seconds. Nothing I could do. Nothing anyone could do. Hell of a thing."

"Yes." A strangled whisper.

Boysie straightened. He put a hand on my shoulder. "I didn't think she'd make it, but she did, and you helped. I see the manager coming. He'll take you to your room. You okay? You want to see the doctor?"

"No."

The manager was full of apologies as he led me past the private part of the palazzo and into the maze of halls. "They are a disgrace, the scum who come to our city. They must be punished. The *dottore* who was here comes often for the sick man. He will do his best for the signora. Thanks be to God the trouble has ended—and ended well."

CHAPTER FIFTY-ONE

September 19

I had known loss, but until now the pain had been shared by family and friends. I spent the night reliving the few times that Richard and I had been together. Richard touching my face. Smoothing my hair. Giving me the ring. What had been done with his body? I needed, desperately, to be in my own place, surrounded by my own things.

By morning, I was forced to leave memories and face reality. The affair had been tentative—there was only a glimpse of a possible future—and no one knew that Richard and I had made plans to go off together.

The room service waiter brought tea, the only thing my stomach could tolerate. I was starting to drink it when the phone rang. It was Boysie.

"Hey. Sorry if I woke you."

"I'm awake. Actually, I was about to call the concierge. See how soon he can get me on a flight to Boston. Now that Anna's back, I can leave. How is she today?"

"Stable. Detoxing from the drug." A pause. "Liden wants to see you."

I put down the cup with a thump. "I'm not on his payroll. I really don't want to see him again."

Boysie cleared his throat. "I think you should. Losing Redson has hit him hard—and he knows that the two of you were an item."

"He knows?"

"Redson told him he had plans to go off with you when this job was finished. It's far from finished, and he's missing Redson."

"Well, all right, but only for a few minutes. What about Bruno?"

"Touch and go. Doesn't look good."

Moving mechanically, I dressed and rubbed concealer over the blotches around my eyes. No matter how difficult, I must hide my feelings.

Liden and Boysie were sitting at the big table. In the past, Richard always came forward to meet me. I bit my lip and kept walking.

Liden motioned me to a chair. "Thank you for coming after such a distressing night. First, let me say how much I appreciate your care of Mrs. Deglos. She remembers very little, but she was conscious that someone was helping her, holding her."

He paused. "I needn't tell you that losing Redson is a sad blow. He was a friend and colleague, close to irreplaceable." His voice wavered. He took a deep breath and went on. "I understand that the two of you had come to some kind of—shall we say—understanding. That you had met before."

I sat still, surprised by Liden's emotion. "That's true," I said. "We met in Maine one summer. I never expected to see him again, but when we began to work together, we found—we felt—" I stopped.

"I understand." A concerned look in the pale blue eyes that could be so cold. "I want you to know that I plan to use every resource at my disposal to bring down those responsible for his death. To do this, we must locate Thomas Mellinton and extract information from him." He paused. "Redson told me that you've had experience in tracking down criminals. I'm impressed by the way you handled a number of difficult situations. I hesitate to ask more of you, but would you consider staying on as a member of the team?"

I shifted in the chair. This was not what I wanted to hear, not when I needed, desperately, to distance myself from what had happened last night.

"I'm not sure how much I could help," I began. "You must have many experts on call."

"It would take time to bring them here. You were the one who first suspected Mellinton. You know him. No one can replace Richard, but we must move fast. The situation is critical."

The two men were looking at me. My mind raced wildly. I could say I was too tired. I could say I was needed for the trial—but that was several weeks away. Being on Liden's team would give me professional status—and it was the last thing I could do for Richard.

I touched his ring. "I can stay for a few days, but then I have to get back for a trial."

"We must make good use of that time, starting with the *commissario*'s report. He's on his way." Now that Anna was back, Liden was in full control.

A few moments later, the *commissario* was seated at the table. He clasped his fingers and coughed nervously. "Allow me to say that I regret very much the loss of Signor Redson."

"Regrets after the fact cannot undo the loss. A serious mistake was made by your men. Continue." Liden remained calm, but an undercurrent of anger was visible.

The *commissario* cleared his throat. "The four abductors were taken to headquarters and interrogated. The leader, one Guido Santore, is from Valentia, a town in Calabria in the south, a center for mafia."

Liden raised his eyebrows. "I was told that the mafia never talks. 'Omertà,' I believe they call it."

"This one talked. He stated that Signor Mellinton contacted him two weeks before the arrival of the art group. The signor asked him to organize a team to take part in an operation. He would be paid thirty thousand euros up front. Fifty if the operation was successful." A pause. "Santore came to Florence with four trusted men and a woman. He bribed two among the palazzo staff. The room service waiter was ordered to contaminate the Liden suite with electronic devices. The attempt failed. Santore admits to meeting the waiter in the alley and refusing to pay. The argument ended when Santore stabbed the waiter in the back to insure his silence."

"The other?"

"A young porter in the palazzo who passed the information that Signora Deglos was about to go out on the streets. He calls Santore who moves quickly. The signora is taken to the empty villa. The man in charge, Mellinton, insists that calls for a ransom must wait. But now the signora becomes ill. She may die. The signora's friend has many millions, enough to make Santore a rich man. When Mellinton disappears, he makes the call to Signor Liden. A raid is organized, the signora is rescued, and the abductors will be punished. Punished to the fullest extent of the law."

Liden raised his hand. "What steps have been taken to keep the press from hearing about this story?"

The *commissario* rolled his eyes. "*Dio*, a man is murdered at the palazzo. A guest is abducted. An American is killed in a raid. To maintain silence may not be possible."

"Do what you can. Continue to interrogate these men and keep me informed." He stood up, ending the talk. The *commissario* picked up his papers and left.

Liden sat down and shook his head. "I doubt if we'll be needing the *commissario* much longer." He turned to me. "Back to Mellinton. Your contact, Andrew Rodale, called during the raid. He told me that Mellinton was spotted as he went through customs, but there was no way to apprehend him. He went to another terminal and left on the next flight to Shannon Airport in Ireland. Unfortunately, surveillance was unable to follow. From what you know of Mellinton, do you have any idea if he would be likely to stay in Ireland or go on to another part of the world?"

"Actually, I do," I said as my mind flipped back to dinner at the Palazzo Bracciolini. "At our first dinner, Mellinton told me he went to Ireland before coming here. He said he has a cousin in the west part of the country. He didn't give a name, but if he knows the area, he might go into hiding there."

Liden nodded. "Worth a try. Boysie, put in a call to Mr. Rodale. He's waiting for further instructions."

Boysie left. This was the first time I had been alone with Cyrus Liden. My status had changed from suspect to part of his team, but it was hard to know what to say. I took a deep breath. "Boysie told me Mrs. Deglos is stable and improving. I'm so glad."

It was the right note. "The drug is wearing off, but she's very weak. Unfortunately, it may be some time before she can fly. As for the Maestro, his organs are failing. A brilliant man who should never have left California." He paused. "I've talked to Redson's sister in Sacramento. She asked to have him cremated. His ashes will go back with us."

Ashes. The surprisingly heavy particles of bone and powder. I stared at the floor, willing myself not to break down, and was relieved to see Boysie coming back with a phone. "Mr. Rodale's on the line," he said, and placed it on the table.

Liden wasted no time. He gave a brief summary of the *commissario*'s report, ending with the fact that Mellinton told Mrs. Streat that he had a cousin in the west of Ireland.

For the first time, Rodale spoke. "Ireland. We did a background check. Mellinton grew up near London. Was married and divorced early on. No children. An uncle, a judge in Hong Kong, gave him a start in the Civil Service. After the People's Republic of China took over in 1997, he stayed on. He spent time at his clubs. He was well-liked."

"How do you know that?"

"Through my sources out there. It seems he was an obsessive collector of white jade. A very expensive interest. He gambled heavily at the races and lost a great deal of money. My guess is that an astute Chinese individual—or group—saw him as a way to collect information at his club and at dinners. In any case, his debts were paid. It happens. One mistake, and a formerly honest man goes down a slippery slope."

"But why send him to Florence?"

"I'd say when his handlers heard about Maestro Bruno's code and needed a front man, he was the best they could do, a respectable Brit who could fit into this art collector group."

"We know the outcome. What now?"

"Ireland is a small country. Mellinton is an unusual name and we have a database. Local gardai can be notified, also banks where he might go for cash. Garages where he might rent a car. Airports and train stations alerted."

"If he's found, on what grounds can you hold him?"

"Assuming that he's a British citizen with a valid passport—that could be a problem."

"No doubt there are ways. You will have whatever resources and funds you need, with one caveat. You yourself stay in charge. No handing off to a subordinate."

My neck tensed. Both men had big egos. Both knew how to use power. Both were used to making quick decisions. There would be no lengthy discussions, no petty haggling. Rodale was no mid-level employee.

His reaction came quickly. "No caveats. If I am to continue with the case, I do whatever is necessary, including the use of subordinates."The clipped Brit accent resonated from the phone.

Liden sat back. His fingers drummed on the table. I could

understand his dilemma. Giving up control went against the grain. On the other hand, to lose Rodale now would be counterproductive.

"Very well. Will this search for a cousin take long?"

"Several hours, possibly more. To whom do I give the results?"

"To me. My colleague Redson was killed last night in the raid."

"Redson was killed last night? I'm extremely sorry to hear that."

"Another reason why I am determined to lay hands on Mellinton."

"I'll start the process at once. With our data, it won't take long," Rodale said and clicked off.

Boysie picked up the phone. "That one acts like he's lord of the manor, talking in that fancy accent."

I shifted again in my chair. Little as I wanted to, it was important to smooth ruffled feathers. "He is," I said. "He *is* a lord. Sitting in the House of Lords is good cover for his undercover work."

Liden's lips thinned. "Indeed. I was once a farm boy. I don't get on well with British elites, the old boy network."

I bit my lip. Liden was no longer a farm boy. Rodale did *not* depend on the old boy network. "He can be high-handed," I said, "but as I said before, he's very good at what he does."

Liden frowned. "Then I will reserve judgment." He stood up. "Mrs. Streat, once again you have been most helpful. I must go to Mrs. Deglos. I'll let you know as soon as Mr. Rodale calls."

CHAPTER FIFTY-TWO

I returned to Caroline's opulent suite with mounting dismay. Liden's unexpected sympathy about Richard had lured me into taking on work above my pay grade. I should have made an excuse and followed my first instinct to leave.

I was pacing the room when the phone rang. It was Boysie. "Hey, put on your running shoes. The lord is on the phone."

I ran. As I reached the table in the *salone*, Rodale was speaking to Liden.

"My sources have located a Margery Crale. Maiden name Mellinton. Married to Hugh Crale and lives at Crale House in County Galway. They do some farming, take in a few paying guests. The next step is to find out if she's the cousin Mellinton visited on his way to Florence and if they've been in touch."

"How can that be done?"

"I can send a team to ask questions in the area, but if Mellinton is there and gets wind of it, he might do another bolt. Another way would be to book an operative into Crale House. Someone who could fit into the role of a paying guest. Look around without arousing suspicion. Is Mrs. Streat still there?"

"She is, and she has agreed to stay on for a few days."

"Then I suggest you ask her to go to Crale House. She's met Mellinton, she could see through a disguise, and no one would suspect her of being an investigator."

I must have looked as startled as I felt. Liden hesitated. "I agree that Mrs. Streat is a good choice, but Mellinton's handlers are ruthless people. If she's suspected, how would you protect her?"

"I would provide backup, someone who knows the area. He would liaise with me on a secure line. As well, the local gardai could be alerted."

"One moment." Liden put his hand over the telephone and looked at me, eyebrows raised.

Again, my mind raced. I would lose my security, but being away from Florence changed the situation. And—if I started worrying about security now, I might as well go home.

"A lot of Americans go to Ireland to trace their ancestors, a valid reason to drive around asking questions. I can manage a few more days," I said to Liden.

He lifted his hand from the phone. "She'll go for a few days," he said. "As soon as arrangements are made, she'll have the use of one of my planes. That plane and crew will be on standby at Shannon Airport to take her home—or in case she runs into trouble."

"We might as well act quickly. I'll contact Crale House and make a reservation, starting tonight. If they can't take her, we'll have to rethink. I'll be in touch." He disconnected.

Liden looked at me. "I'm still concerned about your safety. Do you know Ireland?" he asked.

"I've been there once." No need to tell him I had flown over with Cathy Riordan's ashes under the seat, then nearly lost my life in County Waterford.

"Well, I have every confidence in you. I'll let you know as soon as Rodale confirms."

Back in Caroline's suite, I pulled out my clothes and made a pile on the bed. Most of what I'd brought for the unveiling wouldn't be much use in Ireland, but I might be able to pick up a few warm sweaters at Shannon Airport.

As I worked, I thought about Rodale. Five months ago, we had slept together in France. I had shared other beds with him. In a Venetian palazzo on the Grand Canal. A Jacobean four-poster in England. High octane moments, but we always parted in anger. It made sense that he had suggested me for this job, but he had made it clear that we wouldn't meet.

At two o'clock, for the last time, I walked down the hall to the *salone* under the eyes of the fat cupids on the ceiling. Liden was waiting for me.

"A few details before you leave. A car is waiting in the back court. I'm keeping the G650 here, so you'll be on a smaller plane. By the way, your bill here has been paid."

"That's really not necessary."

"It's done." He pulled out a card. "If you need to reach me, call this number. Not many people have it."

"Thank you. I'll try not to use it," I said. To give me his private number showed how much our relationship had changed.

"Remember, any sign of bad actors and you fly out." He hesitated. "This has been a difficult time for you, for us all. I find it hard to put my feelings into words, but you have my warmest sympathy. I have great confidence in your ability. I will be waiting to hear what you find—and be careful." He gave my hand a quick shake and left.

Boysie appeared. He gave me a hug. "Find the bastard. Stay cool." I hugged him back, a boy from the hills who was making the most of his smarts.

At the door, Al shook my hand. "Good luck, Mrs. Streat."

"You too, Al."

The manager was there to take me to the car, a limousine with dark tinted windows. "*Buon giorno*, Signora. I regret the unpleasantness. I hope you will one day return to the palazzo. You will be most welcome."

In the wider streets, throngs of tourists were out in full force, immersing themselves in beauty and history, a world far removed from sudden death and cybercriminals.

We crossed the river and headed for the airport. Four days ago, Caroline and I stood on the tarmac watching as Liden and Anna disembarked at the start of an ill-starred event. Was taking on another risk fair to my lawyers who had never wanted me to make this trip? I was still a target, the Mrs. Streat who asked too many questions. In Florence I had been with people every time I left the palazzo. In Ireland I would be far more vulnerable.

Was it fair to my boys? They needed a mother who would build a new home for them. Do volunteer work. Play paddle tennis. But now the train was gathering speed—and there was no way I could pull the cord and get off.

CHAPTER FIFTY-THREE

The sun was still shining when the big Gulfstream drifted down over the patchwork quilt of small fields, each a different shade of green. But instead of arriving at the busy terminal, we taxied to another part of the airport.

A small red Ford Escort was waiting on the tarmac. I thanked the pilot and turned to meet a man with a round face and a curly white forelock. He was wearing a battered deerstalker hat and a worn tweed jacket with patches at the elbows.

"Mrs. Streat, is it? I'm Michael. Ye're very welcome."

"I'm glad to be here. There's just this duffel."

"It can go in the boot, so. Holy Mother, when I saw the plane, I was thinking a head of state was coming in." He opened the door with a flourish, and I got in beside him, folding my legs into the small space.

Once we were away from airport congestion and into open country, the air felt cool and moist, as soothing as skin lotion after the heat of Florence. No crowds of pushing tourists, no high walls, no struggle to understand the language. It would be all too easy to relax, but there was no time to waste.

As we reached a wide dual highway, I glanced at Michael. Rodale hadn't had much time to vet him. "To be honest," I began, "I don't know how much information you've been given. Or what you've been asked to do."

"I was told to watch yer back. Report to a fella called Mr.

Andrew. Ye're to let me know whenever ye leave Crale House. I'll follow in my van with a sharp eye for strangers."

"Do you know the area?"

"Like the back of me hand. I was sixteen years with the gardai, what ye call police."

"Well, here's the thing," I said. "I've been sent to look for a criminal on the run. His name is Thomas Mellinton and there's a bunch of very nasty people who want to find him first. They're the ones we have to watch for, but I don't have any descriptions of them."

"I'll be keeping an eye out, never fear."

"Crale House. How far is it from here?"

"A little over an hour, give or take. D'ye know Ireland?"

"Not really. I've been here once, and I always wanted to come back. My story is that I'm an American widow who's come to find her Irish roots. It's a good excuse to go around asking questions. Mention the name Mellinton without people getting suspicious. But I'll have to be quick in case he hears and runs away—or those other people hear too."

"Mr. Andrew said the same. He sent over a picture if ye feel the need to show it." He reached into the glove compartment and handed me an envelope. I opened the flap. The small black-and-white picture of Thomas had the fixed stare of a passport photo, but it was recognizable.

"Not bad. I can say he's a lost relative—no, there needs to be more, like a death in the family. Or maybe he's come into money."

"Ah, money would catch the ear entirely. Offer a reward and there'll be sightings at every crossroads."

"No reward, and I don't want word of what I'm doing to get back to Mrs. Crale. He's her cousin. Is there a town near Crale House? I mean, where would I start asking about him?"

"In Rathgally. Ye'd go down the street asking at the shops. I'll follow at a distance."

"Sounds like a plan." I put the envelope in my carryall. So far so good, but the Irish were apt to tell you what you wanted to hear. It was part of their great charm—that and their gift of telling stories. How quickly would Michael act in a crisis? Anna had been snatched away in seconds.

The traffic lessened as we reached open fields. Moments later Michael turned onto a secondary road lined with hedgerows. At home, the leaves would soon be reaching their peak brilliance. Here the autumn colors were far more muted; the sky was low, almost touching the ground like a gray protective blanket.

We passed a middle-aged woman in a brown felt hat, pedaling fast on a bicycle. "About the Crale family," I said. "Tell me about them."

"Ah, she's an O'Brien on her mother's side."

"Why does that give her roots?"

"The O'Briens once ruled here. Kings, they were. Held meetings on the mounds. Rounded up vassals. The Crales, now, they came over from England and took away the land. I'm told he's a deep one for history. It's said he'd talk the ear off a donkey given half the chance."

"Are there children?"

"Grown and living in England. They'll come over for the fishing and the races," he said and swung the car onto a narrower road. We passed several small stone cottages. Further on, there was a row of half-finished concrete houses, abandoned when the financial crisis hit years ago.

As we reached a crossroads with signs in English and Gaelic, Michael slowed. "Ye wouldna want me driving up to the front door. I left me van at a friend's place, then ye'll have the car. I'll make sure ye have the hang of it."

"I'm glad it's automatic. I haven't shifted gears for ages."

The friend lived in a neat white cottage with a few flowers in the front. Michael turned into the yard and pulled up beside a battered green van. A large black-and-white dog barked and hurled himself to the end of a chain. The smell of pigs was powerful.

A boy of about six came running from the house. He was neatly dressed in dark shorts and a white shirt.

"Home from school are ye, Timmy?" Michael called. "I'm come for the van."

The boy grinned and disappeared. We got out. Michael scratched his bristly neck. "Here's the keys. Crale House is a mile or two down the road, give or take. Go straight till ye come to the stone pillars and mind ye keep to the left."

"I'll try. How do I get in touch with you?"

He rummaged in the pocket of the frayed tweed jacket and handed me a grimy card. "This will find me day and night. I'll let Mr. Andrew know ye've arrived safe and sound. Until tomorrow, then," he said and got into the van. It started with a wheeze, sputtered off, and I was on my own.

I adjusted the seat for my long legs and left the yard. The sun was going down, casting long shadows on the grass. A man was coming down the road leading a donkey. He gave a little salute and I waved back.

It was easy to see the two stone pillars and make the turn. In novels, big Irish houses were often described as decaying, with avenues overgrown with weeds. This was bordered by rhododendron bushes, higher than the car, and there were only a few weeds. It ended in a graveled circle with a tree in the middle. The big house was a fine classic Georgian made of warm stone, with a fan light over the front door.

There were no other cars in sight. I parked in front of a wall covered with ivy and braced myself for the first meeting. From now on I was a widow on my way home from Italy. My great-grandmother, Mary Ross, sailed off to Boston during the famine. She came from around here and I would like to find a grave. Pay my respects. Not difficult, but being a paying guest in someone's home could be tricky, a mix between staying in a hotel or with friends.

I got out, retrieved the duffel, and walked to the big front door. It was open. Inside, a dog began to bark. As I hesitated, a woman came around the corner. She was tall, with a thin, lined face. She was wearing brown corduroy trousers and carried a gardening spade.

"Mrs. Streat? I'm Margery Crale. I hope you haven't been standing here long." She had a low voice, not clipped British or Irish brogue.

"Only a moment. I wasn't sure where to put the car. Shall I move it?"

"No need. It's not in the way."

The front hall was large and long; glass doors at the end led to a rough lawn. The table in the center was covered with gloves and papers. Tattered military flags hung from the walls. A black-and-white terrier came toward us, barking shrilly.

"Quiet, Jasper. That's enough." He gave a final yap and sniffed my ankles. A greyhound with a white muzzle rose stiffly from a basket under the table.

"Daffy and Jasper," Mrs. Crale said. "I hope you like dogs."

"I do. I used to have a Jack Russell who ruled the roost."

"Jasper is Jack Russell mixed with fox terrier. I'll take you up to your room."

Wide stairs led to a landing under the central window, the landing then branched off in two directions. At the end of a hall on the right, Mrs. Crale opened a door.

"I hope you'll be comfortable here. Drinks are at seven in the drawing room. We dine at seven thirty. I'm afraid there's no bell or telephone, so if there's anything you need, you'll have to come down and call."

"Thank you. I will," The door closed behind her. I put the duffel on a rack and looked around. Instead of frescoes, there were hunting prints on faded papered walls. A biscuit tin and carafe of water. Flowers on the dressing table. An old-fashioned bedroom, much like my Boston grandmother's house, a grandmother who would accuse me of practicing deception.

The wood floor creaked as I crossed the room to the open window. Instead of a courtyard, I saw a lake in the distance. Instead of the clanging bells of Florence, rooks were calling from the trees, settling themselves for the night.

It was now half past six. I went into the large adjoining bathroom. There was a slightly worn blue carpet and a small comfortable chair. A long bathtub with a handheld shower and a tray for soap.

I lay and soaked and pondered. Granny was right. I was not brought up to be deceptive. How long could I keep up the pretense? My best hope was that Mellinton was still alive and hiding nearby, that tomorrow someone would say, "Ah, that one came in yesterday for his bread and bacon." Beneath Mrs. Crale's conventional manners, I sensed shyness and reserve. At some point I might have to tell her that her cousin was a man on the run, a criminal in danger of being killed by other criminals. There would be dismay and questions—questions that would be next to impossible to answer.

CHAPTER FIFTY-FOUR

At exactly seven, I left the room. It was hard to know what to wear, but I finally settled for the old black sheath, a utilitarian black cardigan, and the Prada sandals.

Evening light was slanting through the window on the landing as I made my way down the stairs and into the front hall. Voices wafted out from behind a door. I opened it and made a quick survey.

The room was long and large. Maroon curtains hung from elaborate pelmets. There were a number of small tables holding military medals and miniatures. Big chairs and sofas. Lamps with fringed shades.

A tall man wearing a green velvet smoking jacket came forward.

"Mrs. Streat? I'm Hugh Crale. Welcome to Crale House."

"Thank you. I'm glad to be here."

"Let me introduce you to my aunt who lives with us," he said and led me to an elderly lady sitting by the fire. She was wearing a shapeless black dress and a rope of pearls.

"How do you do?" I said politely.

"I do very well," she snapped. No lorgnette, but she reminded me of the Dowager Countess of Grantham in *Downton Abbey*.

A young couple stood nearby holding drinks. The woman had a mass of crimpy black curls and was wearing a black tank top.

"And these are your fellow guests, Mr. and Mrs. Keegan, who

arrived this afternoon from Boston. What will you drink? Sherry? Gin and tonic?"

"Gin and tonic, please."

Mrs. Crale came in carrying a plate of cheese biscuits. She had changed from the brown corduroys into black trousers and a wrinkled Chinese tunic. She handed the biscuits around and disappeared. Mr. Crale handed me the drink, then took up his stance in front of the marble fireplace.

The Keegans looked uncomfortable. "Actually, I'm from Boston, too," I said, smiling. "Are you here for a holiday, Mrs. Keegan?"

"It's Tessa. His dad wanted to find the old place. He's got heart problems, so he paid John and me to come for him. Seems there was a Keegan farm around here. We'll check out the graves. If that doesn't work, we'll try church records."

Old Mrs. Crale sniffed. Had she given an O'Brien a hard time when she married into the Crale family? I was relieved when Mrs. Crale opened the door and announced dinner.

The family portraits in the dining room were badly painted and dark. The table was set with tall silver candles and Waterford glass. We sat down to smoked salmon and squares of brown bread. The plates were removed by a young maid in a dark green dress and white apron, breathing heavily.

Tessa put down her fork and turned to Mr. Crale. "I just don't get it. You live in Ireland, but you don't have an Irish accent."

The old lady frowned. "He speaks as he does because the Crale family is English. My sons went to Eton and Sandhurst." Her voice could have cut stone, but Tessa wasn't giving up.

"Sure, but if a person lives here—"

"Irish history is complicated," I said quickly. "Very hard for Americans like us to get it all straight."

It was the right button to push. Hugh Crale wiped his mouth with his napkin.

"In the earlier centuries, the country was ruled by the native kings and the churches, with invasions by the Vikings and then the Normans. In 1177 King Henry the second gave the title Lord of Ireland to his youngest son, Prince John. Mind you, since then there isn't a field that hasn't been pulled back and forth between opposing forces. In many quarters resentments still run deep."

The maid passed around a bowl of berries lined with ladyfingers. I cleared my throat. "Talking about the past, my Irish nurse used to tell me stories about little people. Leprechauns. Was she making them up?"

"Perhaps not." Mrs. Crale picked up on my effort to start a new conversation. "There's a fairy shoe that belongs to the Somervilles at Drishane House. Found many years ago in the mountains. Two inches long, made of leather, with tiny stitches, and there were signs of wear." She stood up. "Coffee in the drawing room. Hugh, would you show Mrs. Streat the library and the other rooms? There wasn't time earlier."

"Delighted. Come along, Mrs. Streat."

I followed as we made a quick tour of morning room, library, gun room, cloakroom. Everything was orderly, but there were small signs of decay. Bits of plaster missing. Wallpaper peeling from a wall.

When we returned to the drawing room, Margery Crale was putting turf on the fire. "The Keegans have gone to the library to watch television and Hugh's aunt goes to bed early. How do you take your coffee, Mrs. Streat?"

"Black, please."

"About tomorrow. Breakfast is from eight to nine in the dining room. We don't serve lunch, but I can pack you some sandwiches." In other words, guests were expected to take themselves off for the day.

"Couldn't I get something in a pub?"

"If you're not too fussy. It's mostly what we call ploughman's lunch."

"I'm not fussy." I finished the coffee and put my cup on the tray. "Delicious dinner. Actually, it's been a long day. I think I'll go up now."

"Nights can get quite chilly. There are extra blankets in the bathroom cupboard. I hope you sleep well."

"I'm sure I will. I'll see you in the morning." I left, remembering to close the door behind me.

It was still light when I reached my room, too early to think of sleep. I sat down on the bed. After an evening of observation, I had reached a few conclusions: The Keegans would be out of here by tomorrow. The aunt was a severe trial. The husband wanted to turn back the clock and live in the past. His wife did most of the work, doing her best to keep up the old standards with very little help. And my first assessment was right—this was a deeply reserved woman. It would be hard, very hard, to break through the barrier of impersonal politeness.

Before asking questions, I must establish myself as a reliable person. Few people wanted to hear that a relative was in trouble. In fact, if Mellinton *was* a relation, she might want to protect him. Do everything she could to throw roadblocks in my way.

CHAPTER FIFTY-FIVE

September 20

> *'Twas a misty, moisty morning, and stormy was the weather,*
> *When I chanced to meet a small man, dressed all in leather*

I woke to a misty, moisty morning—my old nurse, sweet Biddy McGee used to croon me to sleep with this poem. It was the Ireland I longed to explore in my little red car.

At eight thirty, wearing the all-service black trouser suit, I went down to the big dining room. No one was there, but carafes of coffee and hot water stood on the sideboard along with soda bread, butter, and jam.

"Good morning." Mrs. Crale came through the door carrying a teapot. She was wearing the brown corduroy trousers. "I hope you slept well."

"I did. Not a sound except birds. I hope I'm not late."

"No, the Keegans left early." She put down the teapot and went to check the sideboard.

"There's a heavy mist in the field," I said. "Will the sun be out later?"

"Hard to say. Is there anything you need before I go to the garden? Sandwiches? A thermos of coffee?"

"Not a thing. Do you have a big garden?" I asked, wanting to get beyond bare civilities.

"Rather small. Tea is at four thirty if you're back by then. Have a pleasant day," she said and left.

I helped myself to a second piece of soda bread and called Michael on a new disposable phone.

At ten o'clock the green van was waiting in the farmyard. Michael was leaning against the side, smoking a pipe. He knocked it out as I arrived, holding my breath against the smell of pigs scratching their backs on a fence nearby.

"Good day to ye. Are we off to Rathgally?"

"We are, but first let's go over the plan. I follow you, then go down the street showing the picture. I'm a friend and I'm trying to find this person. A death in the family and he's needed."

"That's the right of it. Park yerself in the square and start with Casey Quality Meats."

"How far away is this town?"

"A few miles, give or take."

The road to Rathgally was winding, with a splashing brook on one side. In the distance, a crumbling tower stood on a mound. My hands tightened on the wheel. Mellinton could be in Belfast. He could have flown out of the country. Or—he was dead, taken down before he could give us names.

The shops in Rathgally were gray stone with faded signs above the doors. Turf Accountant. Wines and Spirits. A police station with a blue light over the door.

The square in the center was small, but I found a place between a truck and a motorcycle. Picked up the carryall with the photo and got out. Women with shopping baskets were chatting on the narrow pavement. At this hour the children would be in school.

Casey Quality Meats was at the end of the street, next to a green-and-yellow telephone booth. Pieces of beef and a few scrawny chickens were on display in the window. I raised my chin and walked through the open door. A large man in a stained white apron stood behind the counter, talking to a gray-haired woman. I waited until she paid for her lamb chops and left.

"Good morning," I said with my friendliest smile.

"Coming on fine. American, are ye?"

"I am."

"Most drive through, they've no need for meat. What may I do for ye?"

"Sorry, but I'm afraid I'm not here to buy. I have a question. It's about this man." I pulled out the picture. "I have to find him because his mother died. She's my aunt, and there's money involved. We heard he was staying around here, so maybe he comes into town to shop."

The butcher studied the picture, holding it to the light. After a few seconds he shook his head. "I've not seen *him*, but there's two fellas came in yesterday and showed me a picture of this same man. The snap was in color but 'tis the same face. They were saying he's wanted for writing bad checks."

"Bad checks," I repeated, trying to keep my voice steady. "What did they look like? I mean, were they young? Did they speak with an accent?"

"One showed a badge, the other stood by the door. Nothing about them that ye'd notice." He gave me a quick look. I could see he was wondering who I was and what to believe.

"I didn't know there was that kind of trouble." I put the picture back in the carryall. "I'm sorry to have bothered you."

"No bother. The gardai down the street, they'd be the ones to know about this fella, unless he has reason to hide himself. What will it be today, Mrs. McGrath?" he said as a stooped old lady came in. "I've a nice bit of pork loin and some fresh-killed chickens."

I went out and stood on the pavement, telling myself not to panic. The garda station with the blue light over the door was only a step away, but this was not a matter for the police. Not yet, anyhow. I should try one more shop.

The last on the block was McMahon's Fine Groceries. I waited until customers left, then showed the picture to the freckled woman behind the counter. "I'm sorry to bother you, but did this man ever come into the shop?"

She put on her glasses and looked. "I can tell ye this. That one never darkened the door, but a fella came looking for him."

"When?"

"Yesterday. It was just as the children were in for their after-school sweets. He said the fella was wanted for something."

"Did he have an accent? Do you think he came from around here?"

"Well enough dressed, he was, but I didn't pay him much mind. A boy was sneaking a box of choccy bars."

"Thank you for your time," I said and went out. I mustn't look around for Michael or run to my car.

A feeble sun was showing a reluctant face. I made a show of looking at my watch. It was nearly noon, a reasonable time to eat. There was a pub on the other side of the square. I walked over and went in.

The man behind the bar motioned me to an empty booth. The air was warm, smelling of wet wool. A fire burned in the grate. I sat down on the hard bench and loosened my jacket.

"What will ye have?" A young woman with frizzy hair and deep cleavage was standing by the booth. I picked up the worn menu.

"A sandwich. Ham and tomato. And tea, please." My mouth was very dry.

The room grew noisier. The bartender pulled the Harp lever and filled glasses. Men in tweed caps, most of them smoking, were lined up at the bar. I heard snatches of talk about a favorite at the races next Saturday.

The bread was as dry as my mouth. I swallowed it down with a few sips of tea. Suddenly the situation had changed. Michael must contact Rodale. I must talk to Mrs. Crale.

The noise was getting louder. I paid the bill, aware of curious stares, went into the square, and walked toward my car. Michael's van was parked nearby. He saw me and started to open the door. I walked by.

"They've been here," I said under my breath. "I'm going back to Crale House. Watch for followers."

I drove fast. When we reached the farm, a woman was hanging sheets on a line. She waved and disappeared. Michael pulled in and got out of the van. "Holy Mother, it's a good thing the gardai weren't on the road."

"Listen. Yesterday two men went into the shops and showed pictures of Mellinton. Were you watching me?"

"I was, so. Not a soul on the street but the mothers and the old people. No one followed ye here."

"All the same, this is bad. I'll talk to Mrs. Crale, try to find out if Mellinton has been in touch, but first you have to call Mr. Andrew," I said and got into the van. It was littered with discarded candy wrappers and smelled of unwashed clothes.

Rodale must have been keeping himself available. A moment later he was on the line. "It's O'Shaughnessy from Gents Outfitters," Michael said to him. "Yesterday there was two fellas in the shops looking for another fella, saying he wrote bad checks. I have a lady here, she's going back to where she's staying, see if there's any news of him there. Is it time to bring in the gardai, so?"

"First see what the lady can do," Rodale replied. "Let me know." The call ended.

Michael frowned. "It may be they've given up and gone to hunt for the fella in Limerick. Maybe Dublin."

"Or maybe they haven't. You'd better follow me to Crale House."

CHAPTER FIFTY-SIX

It was after one when I parked the red car at the far side of the house. As I went in, the old greyhound raised his head from the basket. No sign of Jasper the terrier.

"Mrs. Crale?" I called.

No answer. I opened the door to the dining room and went into the kitchen. It was large, with a scrubbed table in the center and two stone sinks. The little maid was cutting bread into thick slices. She jumped when she saw me.

"I'm looking for Mrs. Crale," I said. "Is she around?"

"She'll be down in the kitchen garden, so."

"How do I get there?"

"Go around the house and ye'll see the walls."

I passed an empty greenhouse with broken windows and came to high walls built of weathered brick with a rusty door.

Long rows of vegetables grew between gravel paths. Mrs. Crale was at the end of a row, pulling weeds. I squared my shoulders and went toward her. Giving her a hand might be a way to start what was sure to be a painful conversation.

"Mrs. Crale?"

She straightened. "You're back early." A hint of annoyance.

"Don't stop on account of me. Can I help?"

"That's very kind, but—"

"Please. I love to dig and there must be something that needs tying back or weeding. I've tried to copy herbaceous borders, but I never got it right."

"If you're sure, you could stake the dahlias. There are stakes and string in the basket."

For a few moments we worked in silence. I tied up a dark red dahlia and decided to make the leap.

"Mrs. Crale, I'm afraid I haven't been open with you, why I came back early. The truth is, I'm not looking for an ancestor. I came to Ireland to find a man named Mellinton. Thomas Mellinton."

"Thomas?" She put down her trowel and turned. "Thomas is a distant cousin. Our grandmothers were sisters. Why do you want to find him?"

"Because Mellinton—Thomas—and I met in Florence last week. We were with a group of art collectors. He told me he stayed in Ireland with a cousin between leaving Hong Kong and arriving in Florence."

"Several weeks ago. He said he was going to Florence, but I had no idea that he collected art."

"Have you heard from him in the last few days?"

"No, and I wouldn't expect to. We lost touch long before he went to Hong Kong. In fact, we were quite surprised to see him again after so many years." She hesitated. "May I ask why you are looking for him?"

"Yes." I put the bundle of stakes on the ground. "The thing is, I'm afraid Thomas is in a lot of trouble."

"Trouble? What kind of trouble?"

"It's bad. Very bad. He's on the run. He may have come back to Ireland to hide in a place he knows well."

She frowned and wiped her hands on her trousers. "This is hard to believe. What makes you think he's here?"

"Because he flew to Shannon yesterday. This morning I went into Rathgally. I showed his picture in two shops. Asked if anyone had seen him. No one had, but two men were there yesterday, asking the same question. If they find him, they most certainly will kill him."

"*Kill* him?"

"Yes. It's as bad as that."

She glanced at me, then picked up the basket. "We must talk. Jasper, come," she called, and the terrier came scampering from the corner where he'd been digging.

A small yard at the back of the house held a number of box stalls filled with empty bottles and farm clobber. A stone passage led to the kitchen.

The maid was lifting a kettle from the Aga stove. "The old lady is wanting her tea early," she mumbled and disappeared with a tray.

Mrs. Crale refilled the kettle, pulled a sponge cake from a tin, and set another tray with Spode china and linen napkins. No matter what the crisis, the English remedy was a proper tea. "We'll go to the morning room," she said. "You can take the cake."

In the hall, the old greyhound rose from the basket and followed. Jasper capered beside me, eyes on the cake.

The morning room looked out on the rough field. There were chairs covered with faded chintz and a large desk stacked with papers. As we sat down, she placed the tray on a table. "How do you like your tea?"

"A little milk, no sugar."

She poured, added milk, and handed me a cup. "We'd better start over. You say that Thomas is in trouble. You want to find him, and you are here under false pretenses. What is your part in this? Are you connected with the police?"

"Not with the police."

"Who, then?"

"It's hard to explain, but for years I was a stay-at-home mother, bringing up two boys. My husband was killed by a hit-and-run driver outside our home. I decided it wasn't an accident and I looked for answers. That's how I became involved with intelligence agencies at home and in England."

"You're a detective?"

"More of a consultant."

"For whom are you consulting now?"

"I can't give names, but here's what we know about Thomas. He gambled heavily in Hong Kong and was bailed out by a group of Chinese cybercriminals. They made him go to Florence to get them a valuable program. He failed and left Florence in a hurry. We traced him to Heathrow and onto a flight to Shannon. What happened in Rathgally shows these people are still after him. He knows too much, so he has to be silenced. We need to find him first."

She shook her head. "This is distressing, to say the least. Poor Thomas, so staid and proper. We used to tease him for being such a stick-in-the-mud. To be running for his life—tell me this. What happens if *you* find him?"

"He was forced into crime. People were hurt, but he'll get official protection. All we want is the names of the blackmailers." I ran my hand over the worn chintz. "If he's in Ireland, do you have any idea, any idea at all, where he might be hiding?"

The old greyhound leaned against Mrs. Crale's knee. There was no expression on her thin, worn face. I waited, holding my breath. She stroked the greyhound's smooth head, then gave me a searching look.

"I hope I'm doing the right thing for Thomas, but I feel that I can trust you. If he's in Ireland, he'd have gone to Rossmartin. That's where his grandmother lived. When he was a boy, he spent time with her."

I put down my cup. A place, a thread to follow. This was more than I had hoped for.

"Rossmartin," I said, keeping my voice calm. "Is that far from here?"

"Not far. His parents were only too happy to ship him there for his holidays. Old Mrs. Brandon was much loved, everyone in the village called her Lady. She died years ago, but as I remember, one of the maids acted as his nanny when he was there. He might have gone to her."

"Is she alive? Do you know her name?"

"Let me think. Bridey, Annie—no, it's Julia. Julia O'Reilly. By now she must be in her late eighties. Lady took her out of the bog and trained her. For Lady's sake, she'd take him in, no matter what. Anyone can tell you how to find her cottage, but you're a stranger. She'd never tell you if he's there, not even if I gave you a note."

"All the same, I think I should go to Rossmartin and try to talk to her. The sooner the better." I stood up. "I'm sorry, truly sorry to have troubled you with this."

My carryall and phone were still in the car. I hurried through the hall and out to the graveled drive. A ginger cat was lying on the hood of the car. It gave me an angry look and leaped toward the bushes. I punched in Michael's number.

"I've just talked to Mrs. Crale," I said. "She says Mellinton used to visit his grandmother in Rossmartin. A woman named Julia O'Reilly looked after him. Do you know her? Where she lives?"

"Ah, yes. She's grand in herself. Will ye be wanting to go there?"

"Yes. Now, but in your van. If those men are around, they may have seen me in my car. Go to the farm and I'll meet you there." It was important to keep a cool head.

Michael was waiting in the yard when I arrived. I parked the red car on the other side of the shed. He cleared a newspaper off the seat in the van. I jumped in and we started down the road.

"It may be a wild goose chase," I said. "I'm a stranger to Mrs. O'Reilly. How well do you know her?"

"Ah. One of her sons and I were friends."

We came up to a crossroads and turned onto a straight road with bare stretches of limestone. A black-and-white magpie flew up from a field.

"Bad luck when a magpie flies over ye," Michael muttered.

This was not what I needed to hear. "Tell me about Julia O'Reilly," I said.

"Ah, she's one of the few who keep to the old ways. A bit lonely since the young ones left for the States. She'll be wanting to give ye a cup of tea, make the visit last."

"When we go in, you could say that I'm a friend of Mrs. Crale's and that I'm staying at the house. How much longer?"

"Five minutes, give or take."

There were more open fields. At last Michael turned. The van squeaked and bumped down a dirt lane to a small whitewashed cottage, the traditional two-up two-down. The garden in front was planted with a mix of root vegetables and fall flowers.

No one was in sight. We walked down the weedy path to the open door. "Mrs. O'Reilly," Michael called. "Are ye there? 'Tis Michael Fogarty and I've brought ye a visitor."

A small woman appeared, wiping her hands on her apron. Her teeth were bad, her hair was white, and her eyes were as blue as mine.

"If it isn't young Michael. Ye've been a long time coming."

"Too long. How are ye keeping?"

"Old bones, but they've not let me down yet. And who might ye be?"

"I'm Emma Streat. I live in Boston and I'm staying at Crale House."

"From Crale House, is it? Ye're heartily welcome. Come in, come in. I'm just baking a bit of bread."

In the small front room, a turf fire burned on the hearth and a radio was blaring out a song in Gaelic. She turned it off, pulled a few straight chairs up to the table, and covered a mound of dough with a checked towel.

"The kettle's on. And how is Mrs. Crale? We've not met in donkey's years. Will ye give her my kind regards?"

"I will. In fact, I've come because she thought you might be able to help me."

"Now how can that be?"

"It's a long story, but I'm looking for her cousin Thomas Mellinton. I need to talk to him and it's very important. She knew you took care of him when he came to stay with his grandmother."

Mrs. O'Reilly raised her gnarled hands. "Holy Mother, she remembered that?"

"What's more, she said if he's here, you must tell me. It's important."

"Then I will, so. I could hardly believe me eyes when I saw him walk down the path after all these years. He told me bad people were after him and he needed to hide himself for a few days. I gave him the bed upstairs. Lady's grandson and such a nice quiet little boy."

"Is he—where is he now?"

She shook her head. "Pity, ye should have come a wee bit earlier. He's gone these past few hours. He hired McMahon's car. He's on his way to the big airport."

It took a few seconds for this news to sink in. "Mrs. O'Reilly, tell me this," I said, trying not to show dismay. "Did something happen to make him leave?"

"It did, so. This morning I went by the bus to Rathgally. Casey the butcher was telling Mrs. McCarthy about two men looking for a man named Mellinton who wrote bad checks. When I came back and told him, Thomas went white as the flour on that board. In no time he was packed and gone. Left me fifty punts, he did."

"Did he say where he was going? I mean, from the airport?"

"He did not, but if anyone came to ask, I was to say he was going to New York. To a jade auction, whatever that may be."

"What time did he leave?"

"It must have been going on for three. I'd fed the hens and started the loaf." She gave me a worried look. "I'd have said nothing except ye came from Mrs. Crale—and Michael here is a good lad."

"You did the right thing." I looked at Michael and stood up. "I'm so sorry, I wish we could stay for tea, but I'm afraid we have to leave."

"Is it to do with Thomas?" A gnarled hand went to her throat. The blue eyes were bewildered. "Is he in bad trouble?"

"Ye're not to worry," Michael said quickly. "If anyone else comes, tell them about the jade in New York and say a rosary for him."

"What do we do now?" he asked as we hurried down the path to the van.

"I'm not sure. You'd better put in a call for Mr. Andrew."

Calls from O'Shaughnessy in Ireland must have had a high priority. In a moment Michael was talking to Rodale.

"The lady here just had word that the fella is on his way to the airport in a hired car and the others may be after him."

"Right. I'll get onto it. Tell the lady to go back to where she's staying and wait for instructions."

"I will, so." Michael started the engine and we bumped back down the lane.

"I don't *believe* this," I said, biting my lip. "We almost had him."

"We did, so. Holy Mother, it'll take a blessed miracle to find him now."

CHAPTER FIFTY-SEVEN

It was after five when I got back to Crale House. The little maid said that Mrs. Crale had gone out and wouldn't be back until dinner. I did my best to stay calm, but even Rodale couldn't work miracles. It would take time to organize support in the area. By now Mellinton could be in the air—or he could be tied hand and foot in the trunk of a car on the way to his death.

Promptly at seven, I was in the drawing room, wearing my green jacket. Too sporty for evening, but it had a pocket for my phone in case Rodale called.

The older Mrs. Crale was sitting by the fire, wearing the same shapeless black dress and pearls. A middle-aged couple stood nearby holding drinks.

Mr. Crale greeted me with a smile. "I trust you had a pleasant day. Gin and tonic, if I remember. May I introduce Mr. and Mrs. Sedway from London, here for a Friends of Yeats gathering tomorrow."

We nodded and murmured greetings.

Mrs. Crale came in with the cheese biscuits. She passed them to the others, then stopped in front of me. "Was Julia O'Reilly any help?" she asked in a low voice.

"He'd been there, but we just missed him."

"Does that mean—" She turned away as Mr. Crale handed me a glass.

Drinks over, we moved into the dining room for soup and shepherd's pie. Mr. Crale turned to me. "Tell me. How did you spend your day?"

"Oh, I just drove around. I had lunch at a pub in Rathgally. A bit noisy but fun."

"Perhaps I should have warned you—" He stopped as a bell jangled faintly in the distance. Jasper began to bark.

"I'll go," Mr. Crale said. In a minute he was back, looking distinctly annoyed. "It's two gardai from Rathgally. They want to speak to you, Mrs. Streat. I told them you were at dinner, but they said it was urgent."

"Excuse me," I said and stood up. The Sedways stared. Old Mrs. Crale nodded as if visits from gardai could be expected with strangers in the house.

An official-looking car was parked in the drive. Two men in uniform were standing just inside the door, holding their caps. The older one stepped forward. Jasper was barking hysterically.

"Mrs. Streat? Sergeant Malloy here. I'm sorry to bring you from your dinner, ma'am, but we've had instructions to take you to Shannon Airport straightaway."

"*Quiet*, Jasper. Did the instructions say why?"

"No, ma'am. Orders were to take you and be on the watch for trouble."

I hesitated, but only for a second. Rodale and I had always been able to act quickly in a crisis. No explanations required.

"I'll come," I said, "but it'll take me a few moments to pack."

"We're vexing the little dog. We'll wait in the car."

As I turned, Mrs. Crale appeared. "What's happened? Is this to do with Thomas?"

"Mrs. O'Reilly said he left for the airport just ahead of us. The gardai have instructions to take me there. That's all they know, but I'm off. Please, could I have the bill?"

It didn't take long to throw my things into the duffel. As I ran down the stairs, Mrs. Crale was waiting by the center table. She handed me the bill. "I've told the others you've had bad news and had to go home. My husband dislikes a fuss, but please let me know the outcome. That is, if you can."

"I'll try," I said, scribbling a check for a larger sum. "I wish I'd been here under different circumstances, it's such a lovely place. Goodbye, Mrs. Crale."

The engine was running. I got into the back seat and saw my little red car by the far wall.

"Wait. That's a rental car," I said. "Michael Fogarty made the arrangements."

"Have ye the keys?"

"Under the mat."

"It will be returned, not to worry."

It was still light as we drove down the avenue and out onto the road. No chance to say goodbye to Michael, a small man who smoked a pipe and wore worn clothes. No doubt he'd been paid a big whack for this job. His part was ending, mine wasn't, but maybe someday I could come back. Go to see Yeats's Tower. Visit ancient ruins.

The younger garda drove fast. There was very little traffic on the road. A spatter of rain hit the windshield as we reached the first group of airport buildings. Sergeant Malloy talked on his phone, then turned. "We're to go to the back entrance near Duty Free. Security will meet you there."

The back entrance had a ramp. Vans were parked nearby. As we pulled up, a man emerged with an umbrella and opened the door.

"This way, ma'am," he said, and hurried me into a brightly lit corridor. We passed the Duty Free shopping area with its counters of china, hand-knitted sweaters, and Waterford glass. Another corridor was lined with closed doors. "In here, ma'am," he said.

The room was small, with a wildly figured brown-and-orange carpet. A stocky man in a business suit came forward. His brown eyes and hair matched his suit.

"Connor White, head of airport security. No trouble on the road, I hope."

"No, but to be honest, I'm not sure why I'm here."

"Which I can understand." He motioned me to a brown upholstered chair and seated himself behind the desk. "I'll get straight to the point. At four thirty we had a call asking us to detain a Thomas Mellinton."

I leaned forward. "Did you?"

"We did. He was booking a flight to Montreal. He was taken to an interrogation room where he is now. We've been dealing with an intelligence official in London. He's waiting for your call." He picked up his phone, punched in a number, and handed it to me.

In seconds Rodale was on the line. "You made good time. Mellinton was picked up, but now there's a problem. He's a British citizen, his passport is in order. He's making a hell of a fuss, says he's being unlawfully detained. Threatening repercussions and giving airport security a hard time."

"I'm not surprised, but what do you want me to do?"

"Talk to him. The aim is to get him on Liden's plane, the one that's standing by for you. Fly him to London for questioning."

I clutched the phone. "Hold on. You're asking for the impossible. He's not going to change his plans because of me."

"Perhaps not, but you're the only boots on the ground. Try to persuade him that being with us in a safe house is better than years of running for his life. Or losing it."

I swallowed. "I'll try," I said, "but he'll dig in his heels. There might be more of a chance if we're alone, no security standing there."

"Understood. Just do your best."

I handed the phone to White. They talked. As the call ended, he looked at me and stood up. "I'll take you there. The garda will leave the room, but he'll stay outside the door. Any sign of trouble, any raised voices and he goes in."

CHAPTER FIFTY-EIGHT

The windowless room was small and smelled of stale cigarette smoke. Mellinton was sitting on one side of a steel table, rapping the top with his fingers. He glanced around, looked again, and got to his feet. There was no outward sign of the shock he must be feeling.

"Mrs. Streat. This is quite a surprise. I thought you left Florence with your godmother."

I put my carryall on the floor and sat down on the other side of the table. This man had fooled me once. I mustn't underestimate him again.

"Actually, I didn't go back with her. In fact, I've been in Ireland. At Crale House."

His eyebrows went up. "Crale House? I know it well. Margery Crale is a distant cousin." A pause. "I knew they took in paying guests, but how did you hear about the place?"

"From you, actually. Mellinton's an unusual name. You told me you stopped off in Ireland to visit a cousin."

"Did I? You have a good memory. But that doesn't explain why you are here. Are you flying out of Shannon?"

"Not exactly." I hesitated, then decided to go for the jugular. "You may not have heard, but after you left Florence, Anna Deglos was rescued from the villa where she was being held. One of the kidnappers, Guido Santore, told the police that *you* gave him orders to kill Mario the waiter and that *you* ordered the kidnapping."

Mellinton didn't blink. "My dear Mrs. Streat, what a lot of malarkey, as they say in Ireland. I've never heard of—what's his name?"

"Guido Santore."

"If I understand you correctly, this man is telling lies about me, but there is no reason to believe him. Again, what odd circumstance brings you here?"

I pushed away a dented ashtray filled with cigarette stubs. "Not odd. I think you know I became involved with the waiter's murder. I was with Anna Deglos when she was kidnapped. I stayed on in Florence to help identify the woman who was part of the mafia group you hired. I've had experience with other investigations, which is why Cyrus Liden has asked me to help with this one. He's determined to get the names of whoever gives you orders."

"My dear Mrs. Streat, believe me. I had nothing to do with these unfortunate events. I resent being detained here. If necessary, I will be forced to take steps."

This was not going well. I leaned forward.

"Thomas, let's not waste time beating around the bush. You rushed away from Florence when the project with the Maestro ended in failure. You went into hiding with Julia O'Reilly. When she heard men were asking about you in Rathgally, you knew they would silence you and you ran for your life." I paused for breath.

He didn't move. "Here's the thing," I said. "I'm offering you protection in return for information about your handlers. One of Liden's planes is standing by to fly you to London. Take you to a safe house."

Mellinton's lips thinned. He shook his head. "Offer me protection? From what I know of Cyrus Liden, it's more likely he wants to see me tried and convicted for what he assumes to be my part in the kidnapping."

"That's not—"

"For some reason I am being detained here. That happens. Many names are blacklisted, and it often turns out the authorities are holding the wrong person. There's an important auction of white jade in New York tomorrow. I plan to be there."

Out on the runway a plane left the ground with a roar, the smell of fuel penetrating the room. I stared at the neatly dressed man with his impeccable Brit manners. A lawyer who was sticking to his denial of guilt.

I put my hands on the table. "Mr. Mellinton—Thomas—let's go over this again. Your Chinese handlers sent you to get the Maestro's program. You failed, and now they have to make sure you can't talk. Two men were looking for you in Rathgally. If you made any phone calls like the one to call a taxi, that's all they need to find you. They may be here in the airport, looking for you, and they sure as hell aren't going to let you get away."

Another plane roared overhead. As the noise lessened, Mellinton cleared his throat. "This is quite a story, worthy of a writer, but I have a plane to catch. The head of security wants to avoid trouble. He'll see that I leave safely."

I dug my nails into the palms of my hands. In his mind, the chance that he might be killed as he crossed the airport seemed less threatening than an uncertain future in Liden's hands.

"Wait," I said. "Even if you manage to get on that plane, they won't be far behind. You'll never stop running. Besides, you could have a dozen gardai with you and still be killed here. A quick stab. The prick of a needle. Margery Crale seemed fond of you. Maybe she'll arrange for your funeral. Have you buried next to your grandmother, Lady."

"That will do." His expression didn't change. He stood up and reached for his bag.

Desperation was setting in. "Listen to me," I said, lowering my voice. "We *know* you got into debt in Hong Kong and were blackmailed by vicious cybercriminals. We *know* they forced you to go to Florence to get them that project. Forced you to hire thugs from Calabria. Forced you to do things that were totally against your nature. We *know* you would never willingly hurt anyone." I paused for breath. "About Cyrus Liden, you're wrong. Absolutely wrong. Give him information and he'll protect you. If you're killed, it will be harder to catch them—but he will catch them with your help, and you'll be free of them. It's as simple as that. Your choice."

Footsteps were coming down the hall. For a moment, he stood there, not moving, staring at the floor. A muscle in his jaw twitched. "Those people," he muttered. "They ruined me. Those people ruined me." He collapsed onto the chair and put his head in his hands.

CHAPTER FIFTY-NINE

My throat constricted. I got to my feet. Replacing threats with compassion had worked, but my job wasn't finished until he was on the plane.

"Thomas." I reached out and touched his shoulder. "This has been a terrible ordeal. You must be very tired. Wait here. I'll be back in a moment," I said. Opened the door and went out.

Connor White was speaking to the garda. He turned when he saw me. "I was coming to check. Have you made any progress?"

"He'll fly to London. Cyrus Liden's pilot needs to be alerted."

"Problem solved. He'll need to file a flight plan, but that won't take long."

"Mellinton is upset. I think the garda should be with him. May I go back to your office and make another call?"

Rodale answered on the secure line. "He broke down," I said. "He'll be on the plane."

"Well done. Did he give you a hard time?"

"He held out, but he's afraid Liden wants revenge and will send him to prison, not give him protection. He was about to head off when I told him we thought of him as a victim. It was my last shot, but it worked. He's very tired. He'll need careful handling."

"I'll meet the plane myself. What about you?"

"Wait here, I guess, until the plane comes back. Or get myself to Boston another way."

"Stay where you are while I ring Liden with the results. Shouldn't take long."

I handed the phone back to Connor White. "I'm afraid you'll have to put up with me until there's another call."

"No trouble. I'm glad the situation is resolved. Would you like a cup of tea?"

"Not right now, but thanks."

The brown-and-orange swirls in the carpet were dizzying. I sat back and closed my eyes. A near failure, saved in the last few seconds. Once Mellinton was on board, I would try to find a hotel.

More planes took off. Connor White sat at his desk and made several calls. There was a knock on the door and the garda who had been with Mellinton came in.

"You need to hear this," he began, looking at Connor, then at me. "The fella says he won't leave unless the lady goes to London with him."

Connor stood up. "Does he give a reason?"

"He says he doesn't trust the London people and he wants to make sure he'll get what was promised him. He's very set in that. Ye'd have to use force to get him on that plane without this lady."

I stared. "What?"

The garda shuffled his feet. "I'm telling you, if we force him he'll call it a kidnapping."

I closed my eyes. For endless hours I'd been forced to make snap decisions. I'd done everything that was asked of me and reached the limits of my strength. I needed to get home and sleep in my own bed. It was unfair to make more demands on me, but by now I should know that life wasn't fair.

Connor White leaned forward. "Mrs. Streat?"

I stared down at the convoluted carpet, trying to put myself in Mellinton's mind. I was still his adversary, but I was his only link to Liden. I had made a promise and I must be there to make sure Liden kept his word. I had no choice. As a substitute for Richard,

I must dig deep for the endurance to push on and deliver Mellinton to Rodale.

I raised my head. "It's the last thing in the world I want to do, but I'll go," I said. "You'd better alert London that I'm coming." No doubt he'd be relieved to see an end to this time-consuming, unusual incident.

Liden's clout worked fast. In less than an hour, Mellinton and I and two security guards walked onto the plane. Mellinton's shoulders were hunched. He seemed to have retreated into silence and didn't look at me. I sat as far away from him as I could. Minutes later we were in the air.

Slowly, the adrenaline rush that had sustained me subsided. My head was beginning to ache, a heavy weight over my eyes. I lay back and tried to concentrate on the drone of the engines.

It was a short flight. We landed in a gust of wind and rain. Two cars waited on the tarmac. One was a small black sedan, the other a big maroon Bentley. As Mellinton preceded me down the steps, Rodale walked forward with an umbrella.

"Mr. Mellinton? My name is Rodale. I'll be taking you to a safe house where you can rest."

A young man was standing nearby. Rodale turned and spoke to me under his breath. "Liden has put his flat here at your disposal. This is Frank Tisdale from Liden UK. All communications will be through him. I'll see you in the morning." Turning back, he took Mellinton's arm and led him to the small car. Two men were sitting in the front seat. No one was taking any chances.

The young man had a round face that looked tanned even in the rain. "A pleasure, Mrs. Streat. Any luggage?"

"Just this duffel."

"Then we'll be off." He handed me carefully into the big car. "The head of Liden UK would have met you, but he's in Wales. I'm from the California office, learning the ropes and looking after Liden executives coming through."

"Thanks for meeting me," I said, "but I'm very tired. Do you mind if we don't talk?"

"I sure don't. You just lie back and relax."

A veil seemed to have dropped between me and the rest of the world. Through blurred eyes, I was aware of familiar landmarks. Apsley House. Hyde Park. Park Lane, and finally a tall tower. We got out. Frank waved off a porter, picked up the duffel, and steered me to an elevator. "Half the tenants are Russian or Chinese billionaires. I'll just see you settled." He pushed a few buttons and opened a door. Lights went on and I stepped into an expanse of gleaming chrome, glass, marble.

"I'll put your bag in the bedroom," Frank said. "Mr. Liden likes his privacy, so no staff will be hovering. Anything you want, use the intercom and someone will come running. Anything else I can do?"

"Not a thing. Thanks so much for your help."

He left. Moving like a robot, I pulled out my T-shirt, brushed my teeth, and climbed into a bed the size of a squash court. No point trying to think ahead. I might as well resign myself to being moved around like a piece on a chess board, with no sense of when the game would end—or how.

CHAPTER SIXTY

September 21

The ringing bedside phone woke me. I fought my way to consciousness and croaked a muffled, "Yes?"

"Frank Tisdale here. Sorry if I woke you, but a plan is underway. Someone else is coming to pick you up."

I glanced at the clock. It was a little after nine. "When?"

"You're to be at the front door at ten sharp. Is that okay?"

"Uh—yes. I'll be there."

"By the way, the flat is yours for as long as you want it. Orders from Mr. Liden himself. I left my card on the table by the door. Anything you need, just call."

"Thanks, I will," I said, and gave my head a tentative shake. It felt heavy, but nothing that a hot shower and coffee couldn't cure.

Promptly at ten, I was standing at the front door of the black glass lobby. A long limo pulled away and a small sedan took its place. A man got out. It was Jenkins, Rodale's wiry personal driver and jack-of-all-trades.

"Jenkins. It's been a while," I said. "How are you?"

"Very well, thank you, madam. His lordship thought it safest to send me." A discreet little man. I could only guess how many ladies he had driven in this car. So far Rodale had treated me like a professional—and that's the way it would stay.

On this fine autumn morning, the sidewalks in Oxford Street

were crowded with people of every color and nationality. "London is changing," I said.

"It is, madam, and not for the best in my opinion."

We passed through the heart of the city and into an area of small shops and working-class houses. The ones on this street were identical; each had a bay window and a tiny patch of garden in front. Jenkins slowed, pulled to the curb, and turned. The engine was still running.

"You're to walk back to No. 245, madam. The one with the brown painted door."

"Thanks, Jenkins," I said and got out. It was clear that Rodale did not want to attract attention to this house.

I walked slowly up the steps of 245 and pressed the bell. Reminded myself that Rodale had the training and the experience. I must sit back and let him take the initiative.

Rodale opened the door a few inches and I slid in. He looked tall and formidable in the small dark hall. "I hope you had a good night," he said. "Mellinton doesn't seem cooperative, but with you here, he's less likely to give us misinformation. It'll all be recorded."

The front room was nearly as dark as the hall and smelled just as musty. Heavy curtains were drawn over the bay window. A few large chairs were placed around a table covered with newspapers and magazines.

Mellinton was sitting in one of the shabby chairs. He had shaved, but his clothes were rumpled. He gave me a quick look, then stared at the floor as if regretting his decision to be here.

Rodale and I sat down. "Mr. Mellinton, before we start, I want to make this clear. We're not here to judge you. We only want to identify the people who gave you orders and find them," Rodale began.

No answer. I could see that Mellinton was going to be difficult—and so did Rodale. He put his hands on the table.

"Very well." A pause. "To sum up, you were given a good deal of responsibility when you were sent from Hong Kong to Florence. You hired kidnappers. You ordered the palazzo staff to carry out orders that included placing a threatening note in Mrs. Streat's room. You bribed Maestro Bruno's assistant to give you a breakthrough program. All criminal offenses. If you had been able to get that program, what were your instructions?"

"To go to the Excelsior Hotel in Rome where I'd be contacted. I wasn't given a name. These people have thick firewalls. They're extremely careful."

"But mistakes are made. You were traced to a bank in Hong Kong. You must be aware of other mistakes, ones that can lead us to these people."

A long pause. Mellinton cleared his throat and looked at Rodale. "As you know, I was a lawyer, rather a successful one. I believe in quid pro quo. You want information. In return, I want a guarantee, in writing, that I will be protected until these people are found. I have no intention of giving you names and finding myself out on the street."

Rodale's eyes narrowed. "I understand, but giving us information takes priority. Then we can talk about your safety."

I held my breath. This was becoming a duel of wills fought with words. Mellinton cleared his throat again. "Very well. When I was in Florence, I received an encrypted email meant for one of my handlers. It contained the name of a bank and a name."

Rodale leaned forward. "What bank?"

"Rousseau. The Bank Rousseau."

"What name?"

"Atlas. I don't know if there's a connection."

I sat straight up and looked at Rodale. "We have to talk," I said.

Rodale didn't hesitate. He got to his feet and led the way into the dark hall. "What?"

"He may be lying about the bank, but Atlas exists. It handled the two guys at the New Jersey school. Blackmailed a money manager who committed suicide."

"Which indicates an outfit with a long reach. At this point I think you should take over. See if you can winkle out more about Atlas."

We went back to the musty room. Mellinton was slumped in his chair, his hand over his eyes as if, after one demand, he had retreated from reality. I sat down beside him.

"I happen to know about Atlas," I said softly. "They blackmail and they're ruthless, they hire killers to do their dirty work. They must be stopped before they can do more harm. Isn't there anything else, anything at all, that you can tell us about them?"

"Nothing."

"Are you sure?"

"Nothing, I tell you. *Nothing.*" The voice of a man who had reached the end of his endurance.

Rodale stood up. "Thank you, Mr. Mellinton. That's all for now. Marston will take you back to your room."

Marston was a muscular young man with a cockney accent. "Come along, sir. I've a tasty bit of chicken for your lunch. Then you can have a nice laydown." He led Mellinton away.

As the door closed, Rodale took out his phone. "I think he was telling the truth. I was hoping for more names, but it's a start. I'll ring Liden. He may know something about that bank."

I got up and went to the fireplace. There was a dusty bowl of plastic fruit on the mantel. I studied it while they talked. "I'll have to ring you back," Rodale said at last. He clicked off and turned. "Liden doesn't waste time. The London plane will take Mellinton to Liden's ranch in Texas. It's remote, with a reliable manager."

"That should work. What about the bank?"

"It's in Geneva, Switzerland. Privately owned. There's a problem.

By now Mellinton's handlers must know that he's been picked up and can give us information. They may close any accounts."

"So what happens now?"

"I'm getting to that. Swiss banks are notorious for throwing up roadblocks. The directors will demand evidence before giving names. Liden wants to move fast and send us there this afternoon."

"Send us, you and me to Geneva? Why?"

"Because we're familiar with the situation. We can back each other up in case of trouble. I said I'd talk to you."

I picked up a piece of fruit and put it down. Once again, I was being asked to step into uncharted waters, but by now I should be used to surprises.

"Is this a good idea?" I asked.

"Frankly, I have other commitments, but this case has priority. It shouldn't take long. His plane can take us there this afternoon, but he needs an answer now."

I hesitated. To go off with Rodale was another challenge, one that might not end well. On the other hand, Rodale and I had a history of working well together. I discovered unlikely connections. He provided sharp intelligence and resources. In crisis situations, we had learned to trust each other—and so far, he had kept his distance and treated me like a fellow professional.

"Liden's waiting. What's your answer?"

"I think we should do it," I said.

CHAPTER SIXTY-ONE

At six o'clock, Jenkins came to drive me to the airport. Rodale had already boarded the Gulfstream G650ER, the flagship of the Liden fleet, and was sitting by a window. He was wearing one of his bespoke dark pinstripe suits. By now my black trousers and jacket felt almost like skin.

He smiled as I walked down the aisle and sat down. "Not a bad little craft."

"Not bad at all."

A voice spoke over the intercom. "Captain Rawson here. Welcome aboard," he said. "We have a tailwind and flight time is approximately an hour. Once we're in the air, feel free to walk around. The steward will serve drinks and dinner at your convenience."

Moments later, the flying palace roared down the runway, lifted into the air, and leveled. As the seat belt signs went off, a steward, dressed like a navy admiral, appeared.

"What may I serve you, madam?"

"A gin and tonic, please."

"And for you, sir?"

"Scotch, please. Single malt, if you have it. No water, no ice."

It was time to find out more about arrangements. I got up and went to the large leather chairs in the rear. Rodale followed. He leaned down and rubbed his right leg, injured years ago in an IRA ambush. This morning he had been limping.

The steward brought the drinks on a silver tray. "Cheers," Rodale said as we lifted the glasses.

"Cheers. What happens when we land?"

"We're booked into different hotels. We mustn't be seen together. For security, you'll be assigned a man my outfit has used for operations in that area. He'll be your shadow whenever you go out."

"What's his name?"

"Philippe. He's local, a Genevois. Something else." He reached into a pocket and handed me a small black phone. "Encrypted for use if and when we communicate." He paused. "How well do you know Geneva?"

"Not well. My husband and I came twice on business. About tomorrow. What should I do?"

"Hard to say. I'll go to the bank. Liden gave me a million euros to open an account."

"A million euros. He really trusts you."

"Small change for him. He knows I won't go scarpering off. I'll go first thing in the morning and contact you with any results."

I nodded. "Actually, I happen to have a connection in Geneva. A Madame Lucrezia. A diva from my singing past, a kind of mentor. She's Russian, never uses her last name, and she retired to Geneva a few years ago. We haven't met for years, but I send her Christmas cards."

"Would she be any help?"

"Well, she's the kind of person who meets everyone. She'd know the bigwigs at the Bank Rousseau plus any gossip about them. She might even give you introductions."

"But she'd be no help in finding Atlas."

"Probably not, but think of all those expats who run off to Switzerland to escape taxes or worse. I could ask Madame if she knows about any shady group or somebody with a bad reputation."

"Nothing to lose, but these people could be anywhere.

Running networks from thousands of miles away. By the way, Liden told me that Maestro Bruno died this afternoon. He never regained consciousness. Never produced that program."

"Which may be a blessing—but it was so sad, the way his life ended."

The steward appeared with a menu. I chose a soup and chicken salad. Rodale had Mexican tamales and an arugula salad. A table set with crystal, silver, and starched linen was wheeled out. As we moved, Rodale rubbed his right leg again.

"More trouble with your leg?" I asked.

"Better now, but two months ago the pain flared up. Put me in the hospital for two weeks while they did repairs."

"Two weeks is a long time."

"The truth is, I damn near lost that leg." He hesitated. "I lay there with nothing to do but think about what had gone well and not so well. I began to realize that the job was taking its toll."

"I'm sorry," I said. Had something other than his leg changed him? There were new lines in his face.

The steward brought coffee. "The captain is starting his descent sooner than planned," he said. "I'll have to ask you to return to your seats."

I fastened myself in and sat back, feeling confused. I hadn't expected that we could still talk so easily—and it was impossible not to face the fact that we were more than just colleagues. I knew that he had a jagged scar on his shoulder. Hated tea and took his coffee black. Loved his dogs and his horses and good-looking women with low voices. He was also demanding and arrogant and his work had always come first.

I stared at his neck, the way it fitted his shoulders, and memories I wanted to forget came creeping back. He was leaning on a balcony in Venice, blue shirt rolled to the elbows. I was waking up in his big bed in Wiltshire and he was bringing me oatmeal, warning me not to throw it down the drain. He had helped me get over my guilt at the loss of Cathy Riordan. He had been an important part of my search for Lewis's killer. It was a unique relationship.

The lights of the city showed beneath us. I crossed my legs and grappled with unwelcome truths. I had no man in my life, but Rodale would never be without a woman for long. By now he was sure to be in a new relationship—and I was a backup colleague on a temporary mission. Nothing more.

CHAPTER SIXTY-TWO

September 22

On my last visit, the weather in Geneva had been typically gray and sunless, but this morning Lac Leman was reflected in the blue sky. Mont Blanc, an elusive sight, was a faint pink outline in the distance, but dull brown was the dominant color in my five-star hotel suite. The curtains were brown, the highly polished furniture was brown, the figured carpet was utilitarian brown.

Last time, while Lewis was in meetings, I had passed the day walking along the lake, looking at the austere line of buildings in the old city. Playing hostess at stiff business dinners in expensive restaurants. This time I had work to do.

By nine I was showered, dressed, and had finished the coffee and rolls. The Swiss telephone system was a model of efficiency; I picked up the functional phone and called the operator.

"It's Mrs. Streat in suite 37. I need a number for a Madame Lucrezia. She may have a Russian last name and live at 41 Quai Wilson." It was the address I used for Christmas cards.

"One moment, madame."

I waited, tamping down thoughts of worst-case scenarios. By now Madame was in her late eighties, and at her age anything could happen. She might be dead, or like Caroline, she might be losing her mind.

In a moment the operator was back. "I have a number for a Madame Lucrezia."

"Thank you." I grabbed a piece of hotel stationery and wrote it down.

In the long-gone days, Madame was a large woman with a beehive mass of black hair. A diva of the old school who demanded constant attention from the manager and his underlings. Flowers, limousines, special food. On the other hand, she was generous to young singers like me. "Do not worry if a note is lost. I will cover for you."

At nine thirty Rodale called. "I'm off to the bank. It's on the Rue de la Confederation. I've alerted Philippe, your security. He'll be waiting nearby. Ring this number when you want to go out."

"Got it."

"What about your diva?"

"I have her number, but I'll wait a little longer to call. Retired divas may sleep late."

"Let me know if you get anything of value."

At ten thirty I braced myself and dialed. Four rings. Five. At last, a plummy voice. "Yes?"

"Madame Lucrezia, it's Emma Streat—I mean, Emma Metcalf. We did a *Rosenkavalier* at Covent Garden. I was Sophie. Then we did a *Marriage of Figaro*. It's been years. I hope you are well."

A long pause. Then—"Emma Metcalf. Emma with the beautiful red hair. The beautiful voice. We were all saddened about the operation. Such a loss."

"It was hard. Very hard."

"So kind, to send me cards—and now you call. To what do I owe this pleasure?"

"I would like very much to see you again, but I'm only in Geneva for a short time. In fact, I may have to leave later today."

"Then we must be quick. I am occupied this afternoon, but will you come for coffee? I have it every morning at eleven thirty."

"Coffee would be lovely."

"You have my address. We will talk of the old days, yes? And you will tell me about your life."

"Eleven thirty. I look forward to it," I said and clicked off. The first step was taken. She remembered me, she had invited me for coffee, but that was all. She might have a bad heart and never go out or see people.

Next, Philippe. "It's Mrs. Streat," I said. "I have to be at 41 Quai Wilson at eleven thirty. If it's not too far, I'd like to walk. How long would that take?"

"You wish to walk? Fifteen minutes, perhaps." Philippe's voice sounded high and reedy; the accent was French.

"I'll be out at a quarter past eleven, then. I'll be wearing a black suit and a white shirt."

"I wear a gray coat and I carry a black case. I follow, we have no need to speak. Turn left at the front entrance. Go one block and you will be on the Quai du Mont Blanc. Another block and this becomes Quai Wilson."

Later, as I crossed the lobby, I saw a florist shop down the hall. It wouldn't hurt to arrive with a large floral offering, so I emerged into the sunlight holding flowers wrapped in cellophane and tied with a pink satin bow.

A small man with a black case was standing nearby. His hair was as gray as his suit and his complexion was pallid. No one would look at him twice.

The wide Quai du Mont Blanc was lined with sculptured plane trees and formal circles of stiff flowers. Quai Wilson was fashionable. A Rolls-Royce and a Jaguar were parked by the curb.

At number 41, a paved courtyard led to a small lobby. I gave my name to the concierge and stepped into a grilled elevator. As it reached the fifth floor, a door opened, and Madame stood there. She was carrying a little Yorkshire terrier with a jeweled collar.

"*Chere* Emma." She opened her arms wide with a dramatic gesture, almost dropping the dog.

"Dear Madame, this is so kind of you." I handed her the flowers.

"Roses. My favorite. Come," she said and motioned me inside. "You have aged well. I should know you anywhere. Hilde," she called in a voice that was still commanding.

An elderly maid wearing a white apron appeared. "Hilde, put these in a vase. Then we have our coffee."

I followed her into a room overflowing with gilt chairs, inlaid tables, Boulle chests. The top of the concert piano was covered with signed photographs in silver frames. The perfect setting for a celebrated diva in retirement.

As we sat down, I was able to study Madame. She was heavier, but the hair piled on top of her head was kept an inky black. There were ropes of pearls on the substantial bosom.

"I give you coffee, then we talk," she said as Hilde placed a tray on the low table between us. "Cream? Sugar? And one of Hilde's little pastries?" She handed me a small plate and a lacy napkin. "Now we talk. Tell me more than can be written on a card."

"I'll try," I said and told her about marrying Lewis, my two boys, my life as a hands-on mother and corporate wife. How Lewis had died less than two years ago.

"Ah, a sad loss. Another little pastry? *Non*? And none for you, Bijou," she said to the fat little dog on her lap.

"That's my story," I said, smiling. "Please tell me about yourself, Madame. You were always such a presence. So generous. How do you spend your time?"

"It is never finished, the music." She went on to say that she gave lessons at the Conservatoire, that she found Switzerland an orderly country, free from revolutions and terrorists. "The Swiss, they have a sensible way of managing their affairs."

"Which is rare these days." I put the little plate back on the table. We had come to the end of polite discourse. Now I must be open about the reason for my visit.

"Madame, you were very kind to me in the old days," I began. "That's why I have come to ask for your help."

"You want my help?" A wary glance.

"I mean, help like advice."

"Ah, that is not so difficult. In what way may I assist?"

"I'm afraid it involves some very unpleasant people."

"So? I have lived a long life. There is little that can surprise me."

She listened, plucking at the pearls, as I gave her a pared-down version of my involvement with intelligence agencies. The search for cybercriminals.

"*Tiens*. You do not have the appearance of a detective."

"Maybe not, but I'm here because one or more of these criminals may be living in Geneva."

"*Ma chere* Emma, you ask too much. I am not, like you, a detective."

"No, but you know the city. You meet a great many people."

"That is true, but to find such people would be like the needle in a stack of straw."

"No doubt, but their money has been traced to the Bank Rousseau. A great deal of money. They could be showing it off or they could be staying in the shadows. And—they may be here illegally. Is that possible?"

Madame rolled her eyes. "Ah, to live here, one must have a *permis de sejour*, present a passport and a birth certificate. The Swiss, they love documents. After that, few questions are asked, unless there is trouble with the police."

"Who holds these *permis*?"

"The commune in which the person lives."

"But what if the papers are forged? There must be some way to investigate."

"For that, it would mean much, how you say, red tape. Many difficulties. I regret, but I fear I cannot help you with this." She began to adjust the collar on the little dog.

I must try once more. I leaned forward. "Madame, I've already taken too much of your time, but these people are dangerous. They kill. They've even tried to kill me."

"Is this true?"

"True, and others will die. Madame, you have great perception, you know many people, and this is not a large city. Have you ever wondered how someone became so rich?"

Madame shook her head. "There are several what you call playboys with expensive women and custom-built cars. Only the blessed Lord in heaven knows from where comes the money, but let me consider." She closed her eyes and stroked the little dog's ears. "Too old," she muttered. "Not enough money." A pause. "*Dommage*, but I can think of no one."

Madame was losing interest. I put the little cup back on the tray. "One last thought. These people must communicate with networks all over the world. For that they would need fancy equipment, one of those big dishes or a tower that no one else could see. Privacy. No close neighbors."

"Ah. Privacy. No close neighbors. I will think again."

I waited. Madame's balcony had a view of the lake. In the old town, the cathedral spire rose high. Spray rose from the famous Jet d'Eau, twisting in the wind. From below on the street, a siren sounded.

"*Tiens.*" Madame raised a hand.

"What?"

"There is one who bought a villa on the lake several years ago. It is very secluded, next to a vineyard. He put up—how do you call it—a tower that was seen from the lake. There were complaints. He was forced to take it down."

"Do you know his name?"

"I do not."

"Is this place far from the city?"

"Only a few kilometers."

"Is there any way I can find out who he is?"

"Ah." She hesitated. "This is of great importance to you?"

"Great importance. To me and many others."

"Then for you I ask a favor. I have an acquaintance with whom I play bridge. He is retired from banking, but he has many contacts. He would know who owns this villa. He might even know if this person is a client of the Bank Rousseau."

"How soon can you speak to him?"

"I am expected later for a master class at the Conservatoire. I will call him this afternoon, but I make no promises."

She got up, clutching the little dog, went to a table, and picked up pen and paper. "A number where I can reach you?"

"This." I wrote down the number of the new encrypted phone. "This will always reach me." I stood up. "What can I say, Madame, except thank you. Thank you so very much."

"It gave me much pleasure to see you again, my child. I hope this matter that so concerns you will be resolved."

"I hope so, too," I said and kissed her cheek. "I hope so, too."

The open grill elevator moved slowly down to the ground floor. I moved to one side of the lobby and put in a call to Rodale.

"I'm leaving Madame Lucrezia's apartment at 41 Quai Wilson," I told him. "It took a little doing, but she told me about a man who owns a villa on the lake. He put up a big tower, but there were complaints and he had to take it down."

"Did you get a name?"

"She doesn't have one, but she's going to call a retired banker who might."

"When?"

"Sometime this afternoon, the best I could do. She has my new number. I'll go back to the hotel and wait to hear from her. What about you?"

"I talked to several people at the bank who are not about to give me information. I'll contact a few sources, try to find out more about the bank's directors. Let me know as soon as you have that name and I'll check it out."

The call ended. I walked across the court and out to the street. Looked around, but there was no sign of Philippe. Two police cars were parked several yards away. The officers stood on the curb, talking.

I waited for a moment. Still no Philippe, the man who was supposed to be my shadow. I went back to the lobby and spoke to the elderly concierge. "Did a small man carrying a black briefcase come in while I was visiting upstairs?"

"No, madame. No one of that description has come in, but a man fell in the street. He was hit by a passing van."

"I heard a siren. Was he badly hurt?"

"The police came. He was removed in an ambulance. That is all I know."

"Thank you." I went outside again. The police had disappeared, so no chance of asking about the accident. In any case, I mustn't risk walking alone. The concierge would have to call me a taxi. I'd call Rodale as soon as I got back to the hotel.

The taxi came. We went back along the quai, passing the little island at the mouth of the Rhone River. On my last visit, I had crossed on a footbridge and fed the ducks.

As we drew up to the hotel, I opened my wallet, dug out the fare and what I hoped was the right amount for a tip. I had wanted to find a little bistro, have a glass of wine and a sandwich, and watch people. Now I'd have to order lunch from room service or face the formal hotel restaurant.

Two well-dressed ladies were walking just ahead of me. The doorman pushed the revolving door for them.

A man came down the steps. He saw me and stopped. "Mrs. Streat. It's good to see you in Geneva again." A pleasant-looking man wearing a navy blazer. He must have been at one of those boring dinners hosted by Lewis.

"It's good to be back," I said. "I'm sorry, but I'm afraid I've forgotten your name."

"Paul. Paul Reynolds." He took my arm. "Be quiet," he said in my ear. "There's a needle in my other hand. Make one sound and you'll be dead before the doorman turns around."

CHAPTER SIXTY-THREE

The impulse to scream froze in my throat. The hand tightened on my arm. The pleasant voice spoke softly in my ear. "Walk slowly to the corner. Turn, and get into the green car."

A small Renault was parked in front of a patisserie. He opened the door and handed me in. Took a set of handcuffs from under the seat and snapped them around my wrists.

I sat there, stunned. This couldn't be happening, not in front of the hotel. Not in bright daylight with people around us.

Moving quickly, he got in and turned on the engine. Pulled out into the heavy traffic on the bridge. At first, my vision was blurred, but as adrenaline kicked in, my eyes began to focus. There were cars in the lane beside us, but my window was closed. Impossible to open the door or grab the wheel. Without the use of my hands, I was helpless.

We reached the end of the bridge. Instead of continuing straight into the city, he turned left. I moved my wrists to ease the pain where sharp metal was cutting into my skin. "Whoever you are, you're making a big mistake," I said. "I'm just a tourist here. I can't pay a big ransom, so please turn around and let me out."

He smiled. "Emma. Emma Streat, I know who you are, and I know what you want. Coming to find me in Geneva was a mistake. A very big mistake."

It took a few seconds for my dazed brain to understand what he had just said. Not a kidnapper after a ransom. He was part of the Atlas network. He must have followed me to Madame Lucrezia's, disposed of Philippe, and gone back to the hotel. Seen his chance and pounced. Where was he taking me? I had always known there was a risk, but never that it would happen this way.

The road wound around the curve of the lake. A white excursion boat steamed by. Except for the handcuffs, we could be out for an afternoon drive. The sandy hair, those forgettable features—he could be a car dealer, a salesman, a member of the local Rotary Club.

The sun was giving way to Geneva's habitual gloom. We passed a number of large villas set behind high walls. He could be taking me over the border to France or up into the mountains, but a moment later he slowed, turned, and we started down a short straight drive lined with poplar trees. The house at the end had the look of a small French chateau. It was built of yellow stone and had long windows with green shutters.

He stopped at the front door and turned off the engine. Came around and motioned me to get out. It was hard to keep my balance with my hands cuffed. I got out, took a step forward, and nearly fell. He removed the cuffs and picked up my bag.

"The grounds are wired. No one gets away," he said, opening the door with an electronic device. Took my arm and led me down a wide hall. At the far end, glass doors led to lawns sloping down to the lake. There were rooms on each side. Formal, with chandeliers and period furniture, as if the house had been rented fully furnished.

"This way." He opened the door to a large kitchen, a model of sleek white cabinets and stainless steel appliances. "Sit down," he said, pointing to a black glass table and armless chairs in front of a bay window.

I sat down, every nerve alert. He had delivered the goods, and at some point, a higher-up would appear, maybe more than one.

I would be grilled for information and then—I mustn't think ahead.

A gray-and-white striped cat came slinking from behind a door. It looked at me with disdainful eyes, then rubbed against my ankles. I moved my feet under the table. Its ears went back. It hissed, tail switching.

"I see you don't like cats." He picked it up and tickled its stomach. "Be nice to our guest, Miranda," he said, then went to the marble counter and took a wine bottle from the shelf above. Added two glasses and began to arrange cheese and crackers on a plate. "The brie is starting to run. Nothing worse than unripe brie."

My mouth was too dry to speak. The sudden change in his manner was almost more frightening than threats. He poured the wine, brought the glasses and plate to the table, and sat down.

"To your good health, Mrs. Streat." He took a sip of wine, rolled it around in his mouth, put the glass down, and looked at me. "When mistakes are made, they must be corrected. Weak links eliminated. What brought your attention to Mellinton?"

I hesitated. He was testing me, but now nothing could be lost by being open. "His name was on a check sent from a bank in Hong Kong."

"Where is he now?"

"In a safe house. I don't know exactly where."

"When you talked to Mellinton in London, did he give you names?"

"No. He didn't have any."

"Why did you come to Geneva?"

"I came to see an old friend. I certainly didn't expect to be pushed into a car and taken here." I leaned forward. "As far as I'm concerned, this never happened. It's not too late to take me back. When I'm missed, there'll be a search. A big one. You and whoever gives you orders won't get away with this. You'll be found and—"

"Stop." He hit the table with his fist. "*I* give the orders. *I* control my people and my plans always succeed. Always."

Fear rose in icy waves from the base of my spine as reality struck. This was no underling. In mythology, the omnipotent Atlas held up the earth. This ordinary-looking man had taken on the persona of Atlas. He was the mastermind of multiple networks—and I had penetrated his firewall.

He shrugged, sat back, and took a sip of wine. "You were followed by my cutting-edge trackers. You gave me trouble with Langer, then at the school in New Jersey. Attempts to kill you failed. I could tolerate your joining forces with Liden to find Mellinton because it helped me identify my adversaries, but to come here—you have tried my patience too far. This interference with my operations has to end. Miranda and I dislike interruptions."

I stared at his polished loafers. I had been close to death before, but never at the hands of a brilliant psychopath. By now Rodale might realize I was missing, but he could never find me. I jumped as the phone in my bag, lying on the counter, began to ring. My captor reached into the bag and handed it to me.

"Answer it."

Rodale was on the line. "I've talked to my sources about the Bank Rousseau," he said. "Have you heard yet from Madame Lucrezia?"

My hand tightened on the phone. The ability to understand each other in a crisis had worked in the past. Would he sense that this was a call for help?

"No, Colonel, and since you ask, it was exactly like the situation with Robina Fyfe. It was extremely hard to get away."

A short pause. "So, not what you expected."

"No. I'm afraid it wasn't." I let my voice trail off. Colonel was the cover name for a man in the British Secret Service. Robina Fyfe had organized my husband's murder.

"Right," he said. "Too bad about Madame. No matter. I'll have lunch and talk to you later." The call ended.

My captor took the phone. "Why did you call Rodale 'Colonel'?"

"Because he is one. In the Royal Welch Fusiliers."

"Who is Robina Fyfe?"

"An Englishwoman we both know. She talks a lot."

"Why is Rodale here?" He was talking faster, a sign that he hadn't liked the call.

"He came to open a Swiss bank account for Cyrus Liden. You know so much about me, you must have heard that Rodale and I have a . . . a relationship. We were planning to go to Lausanne and take a train up into the mountains. If I don't show up at the hotel soon, there'll be questions."

The cat jumped onto his lap. He cracked his knuckles and set his wineglass down with a thump. "Rodale came to find me through the Bank Rousseau. Enough of your lies. Miranda says it's time for a little ride in the boat." He went to the counter and opened a drawer. Pulled out a piece of rope. Walked to a closet and brought out four heavy weights.

I watched, my hand at my throat. So this was how it would happen. We would go down to the lake where he had a boat. He'd row far out, knock me on the head, then push me overboard. The weights would drag me to the bottom. No blood would stain his clothes. Until now he had always hired killers to do his dirty work—but he lived alone with his cat.

I took a deep breath and sat up straight. By now I knew the rules for survival. Keep your head. Try to get inside the other person's mind. Play for time. Somehow, I must try to find a way of saving myself. Make inroads into that twisted mind.

A distant boat sounded a horn. There was still activity on the water, a small window of time.

"You should think twice about this," I said, keeping my voice steady. "You're an incredibly brilliant man, it takes real genius to juggle all those networks. By now you must be a very rich man, but what drives you to lead this kind of life? What more do you want to do?"

He frowned, but the lure of talking about himself was too strong. "I have a score to settle. Money means power. With enough money I will destroy my enemies. Make them regret their actions—"

The phone was ringing. Once again he picked it up and handed it to me.

"Yes?" I said.

"Emma, *ma chere*." Madame's fruity voice filled the room. "I have talked to my banker friend. I told him you were looking for a person who once had a tower on the lake. The name of the man who owns the villa is John Loros. My friend confirms that Monsieur Loros has an interest in the Bank Rousseau. I hope this is the information you require. Now I must leave for a concert. Is there anything more I can do for you?"

"No, Madame. Nothing. Nothing at all."

CHAPTER SIXTY-FOUR

He came around the table and hit me in the face, a stinging slap. His face resonated with fury, eyes half-shut, mouth twisted into a crooked line. The cat jumped onto the table. He threw it across the room. It landed on four feet, yowled, and disappeared. I waited for fingers to close around my throat, but he pulled the handcuffs from the pocket of his blazer. Snapped them over my wrists and picked up the rope.

"Walk." With one hand gripping my shoulder, he pushed me toward a large refrigerator and opened the door. There was no food inside, just a steel door at the back. He unlocked it and switched on a light.

"Move." Tightening the grip on my shoulder, he shoved me down a flight of cement stairs and into a large windowless room. It was bare except for a swivel chair, a long table, and a line of computers. He propped me against a post, wound the rope around my chest, and went to the table.

Blood was running down my chin. I was still alive, Rodale might have understood my message, but unless he communicated with Madame he wouldn't know where I was. It would take time to cut through red tape and organize a rescue operation. Worse, the driveway was wired to kill intruders.

Loros—he now had a name—was working at a computer, transferring data onto a large iPad. I watched, counting every agonizing minute. So this was how a giant spider, working alone, was able to run his various networks, making millions for himself off human frailties. His empire had evolved from technology conceived in this hidden underground room.

More time passed. More data was transferred. He moved the swivel chair to another computer and shucked off his blazer. There were dark patches on his white shirt. When he finished, it would be dark enough to go out on the lake.

By now my legs ached from standing. The bleeding had stopped, but my cheek was beginning to swell. I bit my lip against the pain. My boys—I would never dance at their weddings, hold my grandchildren. But they were grown and starting to make their own lives. They would be surrounded by family and friends. Caroline needed me most as she slipped into the shadows.

Wood scraped on cement as Loros pushed back his chair. "Done," he muttered, and turned off the computers. The iPad went into a small bag. He slung it over his shoulder, then prodded me back up the stairs, through the steel door, and into the kitchen.

"Sit." He shoved me into the chair by the window and began to open drawers. Brought out papers and stuffed them into a briefcase. Yanked a box from under a counter and began to fill it with food, muttering under his breath. "Pack of fools . . . should have killed her in New York . . . should have killed her in Ireland . . ."

Fear was driving him into a manic rage. I watched, trying to shrink into the chair as he filled several boxes, then ran to another door and pulled out a fleece coat, a pair of boots, a wool cap. Breathing hard, he threw them into a plastic bag and carried everything into the hall. Came back, picked up a rope, and stood in front of me.

"I've changed my mind. Drowning's too good for you. I have a place in the mountains above Gstaad. You'll be tied to a tree with this rope. No water. No food. You'll never be found."

"No." Bile rose in my throat. I tried to twist away.

He reached out and pulled me to my feet. "It'll take you days to die and I'll be watching. Move." He gripped my arm, then looked up. "Christ," he said under his breath. The light fixtures in the ceiling were dimming. They flickered wildly for a moment and went out.

Instinctively, I flung myself away. Not fast enough. He grabbed my foot. I pivoted and struck at him with all my strength. The steel handcuffs hit his face, cutting into soft tissue. He screamed and let me go.

There was still a glimmer of light outside, enough to find my way to the hall. The glass doors at the far end were locked. I raised the handcuffs and broke the glass. Found the lock, kicked the doors open, and stumbled out onto the lawn.

A grassy slope led down to the water. I ran halfway down to the first clump of bushes and fell onto the wet grass. Lay still, fighting for breath, then made a quick assessment. Blood was trickling down my hand, a cut from the broken glass, but it wasn't spurting from an artery. The whole place could be wired, but when my legs stopped shaking, I would crawl down to the water. The lights going out had saved me, but it could just have been a power failure.

Little curls of mist were rising from the lake. All I could hear were waves meeting the shore. I lay there, shivering, watching the dark house. Even hurt, he might chase after me, maybe with a gun.

A light gleamed in the kitchen. Loros must have found a flashlight and was moving about. I struggled to my knees, ready to run.

Voices sounded through the open door. Feet crunched on broken glass. A dark figure stepped out onto the grass. A beam of light circled the area.

"No sign of anyone out here," a man said.

"She can't have gone far. We'll have a look around." Rodale's voice.

I scrambled out from under the bushes and stood up. The

light circled again. "There's someone down by those bushes," the man said.

"Give me that light." A figure ran down the slope. In seconds Rodale was beside me. "God, Emma." He dropped the light and put his arms around me. "God. Emma, when I thought I'd lost you . . ." His voice broke. "You're here. You've alive." His arms tightened, then he let me go and stood back. "You're bleeding, Your face. Your arm. Max, hold the light." He snapped off the handcuffs. Took out a handkerchief, wrapped my wrist, then put his arms around me again, holding me against his shoulder. "It's over. He can't hurt you now."

A spasm of violent shivering shook my body. He turned to the other man. "She's in shock. Find blankets, then drive her to Dr. Gerard's clinic. Emma, can you walk?"

"Yes." He put an arm around my shoulders, and we moved forward step by step. I took a deep breath. There were things he had to know. "The driveway. It's wired. You could have been blown up."

"We cut the line on the main road. Didn't know what we'd find."

"He's . . . he's—where is he?" My voice seemed to come from a distance.

"Tied up. His face will need treatment, then we'll interrogate him. What happened?"

"He was at the hotel . . . he threatened me with a needle . . . he brought me here. When Madame called and gave me his name, he went mad. He was going to tie me to a tree and leave me to die in the mountains."

"Good God."

"There's an underground control center. A door behind a fake refrigerator. He put everything from the computers on an iPad." I stumbled. He moved his arm to my waist for a better grip.

"We'll find it."

"I tried to tell you—I wasn't sure if you understood—"

"It was calling me Colonel that did it. I rang Madame Lucrezia. She told me about Loros and gave me the location. Then I got hold of Max. He's Swiss, he's trained, and he knows the area."

A minivan was parked beside the green Renault, motor running. Max, a bearded young man wearing blue jeans opened the door.

"Steady." Rodale eased me onto the back seat and wrapped a blanket around my legs. "I'll alert the clinic, they'll take good care of you. I'll be in touch when I can."

Once again I was on the secondary road that bordered the lake. Blood was seeping through Rodale's handkerchief. I took a deep breath and tried to float above the pain in my face and wrist. I was too stressed out to think clearly, but a number of pictures were surfacing. For months I had struggled blindly to make connections. The enemy had turned out to be a ruthless psychopath. I had suffered but I had survived. No more fear of being followed. Instead of being tied to a tree, starving to death, I could think about starting a new life. Build a house with a red door. Spend more time with Caroline and my boys.

We were nearing the city. Max glanced at me. "You will soon be in good hands," he said in careful English. "Are you all right?"

It was the expression Richard and I had used. Richard—I touched his ring and looked out. At this hour, no Jet d'Eau rose from the dark water, but the lake around Geneva was ringed with light.

CHAPTER SIXTY-FIVE

September 24

Two days later I stood on tiny Ile Rousseau, situated between the hotel on one side and Old Town on the other. An urgent request to meet had come from Rodale; after I met with him, Liden's plane would take me home. My wrists and face still hurt, but thanks to the efficient Swiss clinic, I was back on my feet and functioning.

An old lady wearing a head scarf was throwing bread to the hungry waterfowl. I watched, aware of the bright plumage on a bird's throat, the warmth of the sun on my neck. There had been real anguish in Rodale's voice when he'd raised me from the wet grass and held me as if he never wanted to let me go. It meant little. He hadn't come to the clinic. By now he must be deep into handling the Loros investigation.

He was late. As he walked over the bridge and came toward me, I saw that he was limping badly.

"Sorry to keep you waiting," he said. "I chose this place figuring we both could use some sun and fresh air."

There was an empty bench near the statue of Rousseau, the Swiss philosopher. We sat down. Rodale looked at me. "Your face is still pretty battered. How are you feeling?"

"Not too bad. By the way, what happened to my poor little shadow?"

"A bad concussion, broken ribs, enough to put him out of action."

"What about Loros?"

"We grilled him most of the night, then handed him over to the Swiss. They don't like cybercriminals using their banks, or fugitives running from the law and breaking theirs. He won't get off lightly—and he may be extradited. Liden had a lot to say about him. Turns out he worked for one of Liden's companies in Silicon Valley. Brilliant, innovative, but he was caught stealing breakthrough code. He'd have gone to prison if he hadn't skipped the country. Set himself up to find victims and extort money."

"Better than breaking into grids and national security systems, but I'll never understand how one man could juggle so many networks. He said he did it for revenge, to bring down his enemies."

"Sooner or later it had to end. You helped by outing Mellinton."

"It was a joint effort."

"One that finally paid off." He looked at me. "What are your plans when you get home?"

"I'll work with my lawyers, get ready for this trial. My godmother's still in a bad way. She'll need care, so will Agent Howard." I looked at him. "What about you? When will you go back to London?"

"Tomorrow." He cleared his throat. Hesitated, then cleared it again. "This will surprise you, but I've decided to give up my undercover work."

I swiveled around. "Give up your work? That's hard to believe. Really hard. Is it because of your leg?"

"No, though I wouldn't want to climb out any more windows."

"What then? I mean, what will you do with yourself? Be a landed squire? Farm? Race more horses?"

"None of those." He frowned. "I'll try to explain. We know cyberattacks are coming, big ones, and we have to be better prepared. Liden and I are forming a consulting company. He'll provide the latest technology and some start-up funds.

"A new company. That's impressive."

"It will fill a pressing need. A global mission, and failure is not an option." He hesitated. "I realize you've been through the wringer, but before you leave, there's something I need to ask you. It's this. Liden and I want you on the team. Wait." He held up his hand. "Don't say you're not qualified because you are. You have a track record for connecting remote possibilities. A feel for human intelligence. As a partner, you can decide which cases you want to take on, how they would fit into your life. You wouldn't have to live in England."

The old woman was now muttering to herself in French. I sat still, trying not to show shock. A new company backed by Liden. A chance to work with pros and still make a life for my boys—it was a compelling offer, but Rodale was right. I wasn't ready to take on a life-changing commitment. And there was another obstacle.

"I appreciate the invitation," I said slowly. "Of course I do, it's a great compliment, but there's a problem. You and I, we have a lot of baggage to sort out. Our relationship has been too much like a roller coaster. Up and down. On and off."

"True." He hesitated, then put his hands on his knees. "You had some hard words for me at the mill about being high-handed. Not respecting your needs. It took a while to accept that, but I have." A pause. "I'll be frank. I didn't expect to see you again, let alone work with you. Flying here, talking and having dinner, it brought back some of the old feelings."

"You managed to hide them pretty well."

"Until two days ago when I thought I'd lost you." Another pause. "You made it very clear that you never wanted to see me again. I tried to respect that wish. We did well together with Loros, but if you can't see us working together in the future you should tell me now."

I swallowed. This was a turning point. If I wanted to keep him in my life, I would have to be open about my feelings.

"It's hard to explain, but I've had time to think about the way I behaved at the mill. It was wrong to resent the fact that your work always comes first and I'm sorry."

"No need to be sorry. The fact is, we've both changed since we first met."

I smiled. "You're right about that. I'll never forget our first meeting at the House of Lords. You walked toward me wearing a pinstripe suit, the very picture of an arrogant Brit. I wanted to stick a pin in you."

"You didn't come across as all that clever, but you outed Robina, then got your niece out of trouble. I've come to appreciate your uniqueness. You're needed on the team. It's still a question of whether you think we can put the past behind us and move on."

The old woman was emptying her basket and leaving. I got up and took her place at the balustrade. Cars were moving along the bridge. Two days ago I had crossed that bridge, and was facing death at the hands of John Loros. Rodale had saved me. Today he was offering me a new way of life—and he deserved an honest answer.

I leaned on the warm stone and stared at the Jet d'Eau. In the Old City, a church bell rang the hour. Boats were out on the lake, white sails moving in the wind.

He got up and stood beside me. "You're still shaken. I shouldn't have brought this up." His expression didn't change, but I could sense the disappointment.

"Wait." I took a deep breath. Here's the thing. "I once heard that a life nearly lost must be lived fully and well. I'm alive, and now I have to figure out how to spend the rest of my life. I was passionate about my singing. I was passionate about bringing up my boys. I was never into technology, let alone cybercrime."

"So your answer is thanks, but no."

I turned. A covey of teenagers was passing by, talking and texting, unaware of cyberattacks that could destroy their world. I watched them, then placed my hand on his.

"This is my answer: We made mistakes in the past, but you're right. We've changed. We have a chance to set new parameters. As for living fully and well, I'm beginning to understand what it means."

"What, then?"

"When your life is saved, you have an obligation. You must pick up the pieces and go on your way with gratitude, kindness—and with joy."

The End

About the Author

Photo credit: Shealah Craighead

Eugenia Lovett West (known to her friends as Jeannie) was born in Boston, Massachusetts. Her father was Reverend Sidney Lovett, the widely known and loved former chaplain at Yale. She attended Sarah Lawrence College and worked for *Harper's Bazaar* and the American Red Cross. Then came marriage, four children, volunteer work, and freelancing for local papers. Her first novel, *The Ancestors Cry Out*, was published by Doubleday; it was followed by two mysteries, *Without Warning* and *Overkill*, published by St. Martin's Press. West divides her time between Essex, Connecticut, and Holderness, New Hampshire, where she summers with her large extended family. Visit her at www.eugenialovettwest.com.

SELECTED TITLES FROM SPARKPRESS

SparkPress is an independent boutique publisher delivering high-quality, entertaining, and engaging content that enhances readers' lives, with a special focus on female-driven work.
www.gosparkpress.com

And Now There's You: A Novel, Susan S. Etkin. $16.95, 978-1-68463-000-4. Though five years have passed since beautiful design consultant Leila Brandt's husband passed away, she's still grieving his loss. When she meets a terribly sexy and talented—if arrogant—architect, however, sparks fly, and neither of them can deny the chemistry between them.

Peccadillo at the Palace: An Annie Oakley Mystery, Kari Bovée. $16.95, 978-1-943006-90-8. In this second book in the Annie Oakley Mystery series, Annie and Buffalo Bill's Wild West Show are invited to Queen Victoria's Jubilee celebration in England, but when a murder and a suspicious illness lead Annie to suspect an assassination attempt on the queen, she sets out to discover the truth.

Sarah's War, Eugenia Lovett West. $16.95, 978-1-943006-92-2. Sarah, a parson's young daughter and dedicated patriot, is sent to live with a rich Loyalist aunt in Philadelphia, where she is plunged into a world of intrigue and spies, her beauty attracts men, and she learns that love comes in many shapes and sizes.

Found: A Novel, Emily Brett. $16.95, 978-1-40716-80-0. Immerse yourself in life-changing adventures from a nurse's perspective while experiencing the local color of countries around the world. *Found* will appeal to not only medical professionals but those who are drawn to suspense, romance, adventure, and self-discovery.

The Absence of Evelyn: A Novel, Jackie Townsend. $16.95, 978-1-943006-21-2. Nineteen-year-old Olivia's life takes a turn when she receives an overseas call from a man she doesn't know is her father; her mother, Rhonda, meanwhile, haunted by her sister's ghost, must face long-buried truths. Four lives in all, spanning three continents, are now bound together and tell a powerful story about love in all its incarnations, filial and amorous, healing and destructive.

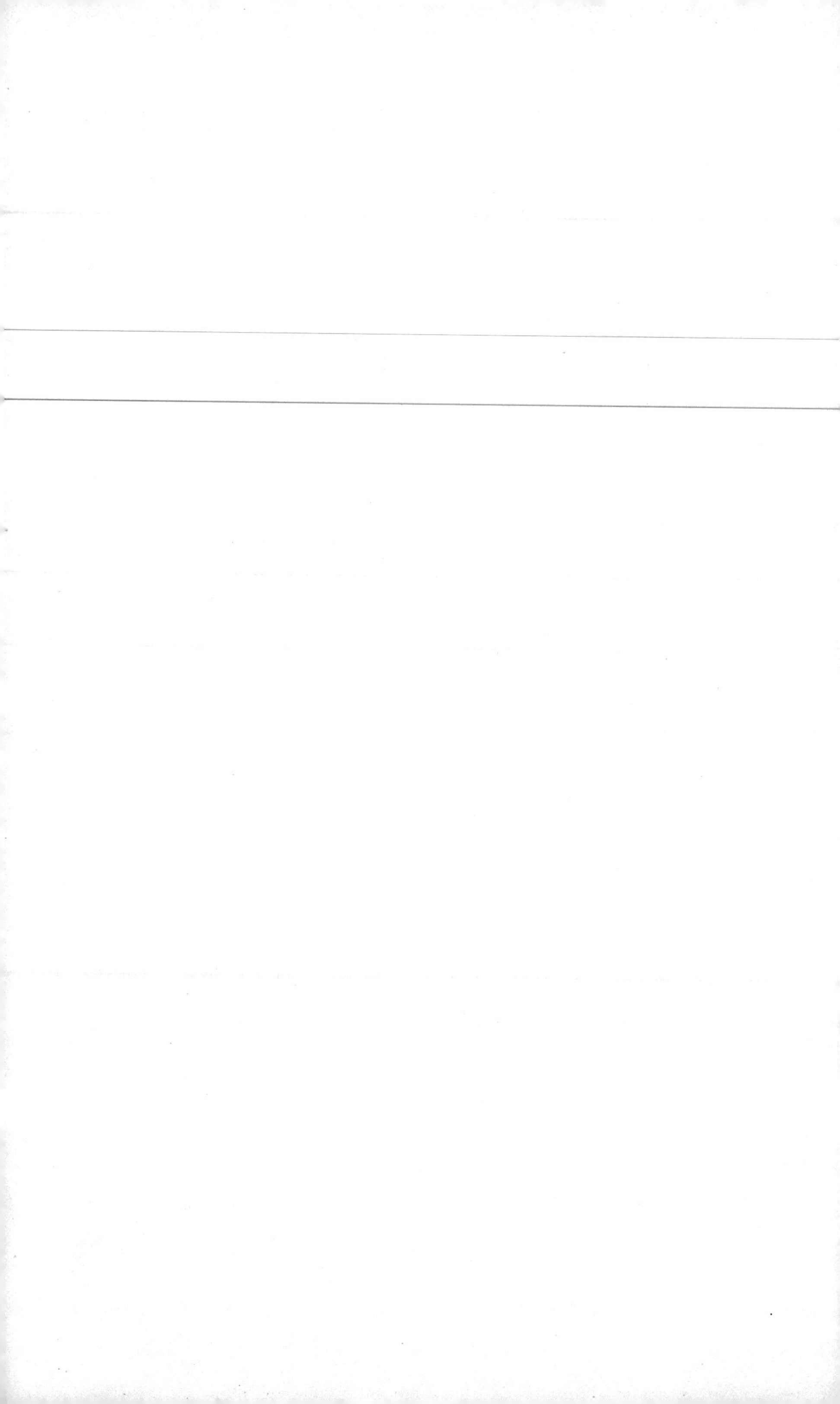